THE

Devil's Band

the devilstone chronicles
volume 1

RICHARD ANDERTON

First Published in 2015 by JBA Books

An imprint of Jenny Brown Associates

Copyright © Richard Anderton

ISBN-13: 978-0-9933730-1-5

1

LONDON, SPRING 1524

Thomas Devilstone stood in the doorway of the tavern and sniffed in disgust. The air was foul with smoke from cheap, mutton fat candles and from the other odours assaulting his nostrils, he guessed that the soiled rushes on the floor hadn't been changed all winter. In spite of the stench, the inn was crowded with drunken revellers celebrating the last days before Lent but there was no sign of the man he'd come to meet.

"Here lad," said Thomas, catching a scruffy pot-boy by his collar, "I'm looking for Master Pynch."

"What would he want with a flea bitten beggar like you?" said the boy insolently.

"Watch your lip, spawn of a whore and take me to the shylock if you know what's good for you," snapped Thomas and he raised his hand to cuff the boy about the ear. As the urchin flinched, he caught the hunted look of the outlaw in the stranger's grey eyes but he still refused to reveal the whereabouts of the moneylender Samuel Pynch.

"My master only deals with gentleman of quality but you look like something a dog wouldn't piss over," the pot boy taunted and Thomas could hardly disagree. Though he was tall and blessed with the well-formed features, athletic build and refined speech of a young nobleman, his thick black hair and short beard were matted with dirt whilst his grubby doublet, torn hose and threadbare cloak only added to his look of shameless poverty. His gold chain and jewelled rings had been sold months ago, for a fraction of their true worth, but he still possessed one item of value.

"He'll see me and this is my letter of introduction," hissed Thomas and he turned back his tattered cloak to reveal an unsheathed falchion hanging from his broad leather belt. Thomas' face may have been be encrusted with dirt, and his once expensive clothes now reduced to rags, but his heavy, cleaver-like sword shone bright and keen in the candlelight.

The boy knew that this bone-crushing blade was a weapon much favoured by the lawless bandits of the north and its sight finally persuaded him to take the stranger to his master. The inn's drunks were too busy filling their bellies with everything forbidden during Lent to pay any attention to a pauper and even the tavern whores ignored Thomas as he followed the boy through the throng. In spite of his dark and brooding good looks, a single glance at his filthy tatters was enough to convince any harlot that this man's purse was as empty as a king's promise.

A moment later Thomas was standing in a curtained booth at the back of the inn where Pynch was seated behind a large oak table. A pair of burly, stone-jawed twins stood behind their master's chair and Thomas recognised them as Nat and Ned, two bareknuckle fighters with reputations for unimaginative but effective violence. By contrast, their master was a corpulent, slug of man with a head utterly devoid of hair and piggish eyes that seemed to be sinking slowly into the glistening fat of his jowls. The pot boy mumbled an introduction but the moneylender said nothing and carried on counting the piles of pennies arranged on the chequered cloth spread out in front of him. It was left to Thomas to break the uneasy silence.

"Good evening sir, do I have the honour of addressing Master Samuel Pynch?" Thomas said politely.

"You do and I'm a busy man so state your business or piss off," grunted Pynch.

"Very well," said Thomas, fighting the desire to teach the surly usurer some manners, "You see before you a well-born gentleman of The North who finds himself temporarily short of funds..."

"Cut the crap," snapped Pynch, who at last deigned to look at his visitor. "The interest is a shilling in the pound with the debt repayable, in full, by Michaelmas. Now how much do you want and what security can you offer?"

"I can offer you my word as a gentlemen..."

"You a gentleman?" sneered Pynch, eyeing Thomas' ragged clothes. "You look like you haven't got a pot to piss in, so if you've nothing to offer me but your word, sod off and stop wasting my time."

"Here me out Pynch, I intend to file suit in the Court of Chancery to have certain property restored to me. I need a paltry fifty pounds to engage advocates to plead my case and on the successful conclusion of my suit I will repay the loan tenfold. I tell no lie when I say the lands stolen from me are worth over a thousand a year," Thomas declared angrily and he almost spoke the truth. His family's once extensive estates had indeed been lost but he did not want the money to hire lawyers.

"Do you take me for a fool?" snapped Pynch. "I know who you are. You're Thomas Devilstone, the king's disgraced astrologer, and as we speak Cardinal Wolsey's men are searching every Cheapside slum and rat hole for the incompetent warlock who couldn't foresee his own downfall."

"Is that so and what's this man Devilstone supposed to have done?" said Thomas, desperately trying to maintain the fiction he was a landless knight in search of justice.

"Truly you're a poor excuse for a witch if you haven't heard," said Pynch with a wicked smile, "even the lowliest fishwife knows that Thomas Devilstone stands accused of using foul witchcraft to worm his way into the king's favour and once he'd bewitched our Sovereign Lord Henry Octavius, he took French gold to curse good Queen Catherine of Aragon so she became barren before her time."

"Barren before her time? Henry's Spanish Queen is in her fortieth year and she can no more bear a child than you, though you look like you're about to give birth to an elephant!" Thomas cried.

"Let me guess," said Pynch, ignoring the insult. "You want me to lend you money to buy passage to France but you've come to the wrong place my disgraced, diabolical friend. I have Cardinal Wolsey's personal warrant to seize all those who would flee from King Henry's justice, so surrender peaceably or Nat and Ned will turn your nutmegs into mincemeat!"

Pynch snapped his fingers and the twins lumbered forward to arrest the fugitive but Thomas was ready for them.

"Me surrender to Wolsey's arse-wipe? Never!" he cried and before Pynch's men could stop him, Thomas had seized the edge of the counting table and tipped it over. The moneylender's coins went clattering in all directions and the sound echoed around the tavern like St Peter's last trumpet. The inn's sots and harlots gave a great whoop of delight and surged towards the back of the inn to gather up the fallen coins. In instant, the filthy floor was filled with a seething mass of men and women fighting, biting and scratching for the spilled pennies. Caught off their guard, Nat and Ned were trapped by the crowd, but Thomas managed to push his way towards the tavern's door.

"Seize that filthy wretch, he's a fugitive from the king's justice!" Pynch yelled to the landlord. The startled innkeeper dutifully slammed the door shut and stood guard brandishing a cudgel. In reply, Thomas drew his sword and roared at the terrified innkeeper to let him pass but the man owed Pynch too much money to step aside.

The barkeep's club was hardly the equal of a sword but Thomas couldn't cut the man down and escape before Nat and Ned reached him so he glanced around for another way out and saw a twisting flight of wooden stairs that led to the inn's upper storeys. Bellowing threats and curses, he kicked his way through the crowd scrabbling in the stinking rushes but as he reached the foot of the staircase, a steel-tipped crossbow bolt thudded into an oak pillar a hair's breadth from Thomas' head. He turned to see Pynch holding a small assassin's bow in his outstretched hand.

"A coward's weapon? You disappoint me Gore-Belly!" Thomas cried and he leapt up the stairs.

"Nat, Ned, don't just stand there, get after the bastard!" Pynch roared, as he clumsily tried to re-span his crossbow.

"But My Lord, you said he's a witch, he'll turn us into frogs or something," protested Ned.

"I'll turn your face into a porcupine's arse if you don't get up those stairs!" Pynch bellowed and he levelled the re-loaded crossbow at Ned's forehead. The slow-witted brute opened his mouth to ask what a porcupine was but, before he could speak, Nat had dragged his twin to the foot of the staircase. The brothers crossed themselves, muttered a short prayer to ward of the evil eye, and reluctantly began to climb the stairs. They were followed by the sweating moneylender who tried to instil a sense of urgency in his henchmen but Nat and Ned were not men who could be rushed.

Before the twins had reached the first landing, Thomas had reached the top of the stairs and kicked open the rat-gnawed door that led to an attic. Inside, he'd expected to find a skylight or some other way on to the roof but there was nothing except years of dust and cobwebs. Spitting foul oaths, he turned to go back to a lower floor and try another door but stopped when he heard the sound of Pynch and his ruffians lumbering up the staircase.

Growing up in the lawless northern border country, Thomas had bested better men than Nat and Ned but trapped in this small garret his sword would be no match for Pynch's assassin's bow. It seemed as if he could do nothing except wait to be dug out of his earth like a hunted fox but as his pursuers' footsteps became louder he realised there was a way out. Quickly he sheathed his sword, took a deep breath and ran as fast as he could towards the wall at the far end of the room.

Like many East Cheap tenements, the thin walls that divided each property from its neighbour were made of nothing stronger than wattle and daub. The slender strips of worm-eaten wood, with their covering of lime and horsehair plaster, were no barrier to Thomas' sturdy frame and he smashed through the wall as easily as Nat and Ned smashed those who owed their master money. With a noise that sounded like the Crack of Doom, Thomas crashed into another garret but this room was far from empty. A bedridden old woman screamed in terror as his ghostly figure emerged from the clouds of powdered plaster and splintered wood.

"Sweet Heavenly Jesus spare me! I'm not ready for death!" squealed the crone. Thomas ignored her, wiped the dust from his eyes and saw that one of the bovine twins was already following him through the attic's new doorway.

"Stand off or it'll be the worse for you!" yelled Thomas drawing his sword.

"Surrender or I'll crack your skull like a rotten goose egg," countered Nat as he tried to squeeze his hulking frame through the ragged hole.

"I warned you, stand off!" Thomas cried and he swung the falchion with all his might. Nat ducked but though the blade missed his head, it struck his hand, which was grasping one of the timbers supporting the attic's roof. There was a sickening smack as the sword's keen edge cut through flesh and bone and Nat shrieked as his severed fingers fell to the floor. The old woman screeched even louder but her scream died abruptly in her throat.

Puzzled, Thomas peered past the groaning Nat, who'd slumped to the floor clutching his mangled limb, to see Pynch holding his crossbow. Once again the moneylender's bolt had missed its intended target but it had found a mark in the old woman's neck. With a last gurgle, the crone rolled out of her bed and fell across a trapdoor in the floor that seemed to be the only way out of the room. Thomas looked at the lifeless corpse and swore. If he tried to escape through the trapdoor, Pynch would plant a bolt between his shoulders before he could heave the dead woman out of the way.

"Have a care," said Thomas brandishing his sword at Pynch. "Don't you know I'm a powerful necromancer? Loose another bolt at me and I'll summon a demon who'll rip off your head and shove it up Cardinal Wolsey's arse!"

"Save your threats for the simple minded kitchen maids and pot boys who believe them, I have the lawful authority and protection of Cardinal Wolsey, a prince of Holy Mother Church and the king's Lord Chancellor, so surrender or be damned," sneered Pynch, bracing the crossbow against his mountainous stomach.

The sweat began to bead on Thomas' forehead, in another moment he'd feel the searing pain of a crossbow bolt smashing into body but as his pursuer laboured to pull back his weapon's bowstring for a third shot, his quarry noticed a low doorway in the shadow of the attic's eaves. The door had to be there to allow goods to be hauled up from the street and Thomas prayed there would be something to support a block and tackle on the other side.

Before Pynch could reload, Thomas had kicked open the door and found the thick beam set into the wall above the opening. Without pausing for breath he grabbed the wooden spar and swung himself out into the frosty night. For a moment he hung in mid-air, his feet kicking like a hanged man below a gallows, but the sound of Ned breaking down more of the attic's plaster wall to continue the chase spurred him into action. Ignoring the pain in his muscles, Thomas managed to haul himself onto the top of the beam and clamber up the tenement's steeply pitched roof before Pynch or Ned appeared.

"Come back her, you foul servant of Satan, and face the justice of good Christians!" Pynch roared.

"You'll pay for what you did to my brother, I'll hang you with your own putrid entrails!" Ned added which did little to encourage Thomas to surrender.

"I'll see you in hell first!" he yelled and the money-lender's crossbow twanged in angry reply but the bolt was lost in the dark forest of chimneys. The pillars of blackened bricks and clouds of reeking smoke now hid Thomas from view but he wouldn't be safe for long. Pynch would soon have the building surrounded and he'd be trapped so, with his eyes and throat smarting from the putrid fumes, he began to crawl along the roof. The ridge tiles were damp and slippery with tar but Thomas made steady progress away from the tavern until the blast of a hunting horn and the sound of shouting from the street stopped him in his tracks.

"Murder... foul murder! Bring torches! Don't let the villain get away!" There was no mistaking Pynch's voice and Thomas guessed the moneylender had made his way to the street to summon help from the nightwatch and the residents of East Cheap. Pynch's pitiful pleas were quickly replaced by the angry cries of rudely awakened citizens and the street began to glow as men gathered and torches were lit.

The pools of light from these flaming brands danced like fireflies as the hue and cry spread through the alleys and Thomas realised the crowd was slowly surrounding the tenement. Cursing his luck, he began to pick his way more urgently through the maze of chimneys but his journey came to an abrupt halt at the end of the building. An alleyway between two tenements had created a chasm ten feet wide but Thomas didn't hesitate. He took a deep breath, tensed his muscles and leapt into the void. His tattered cloak streamed behind him like the wings of a giant bat and the crowd gasped at the sight of this shadowy figure that flew through the air like a demon released from hell.

"He flies! 'tis witchcraft and wizardry!" screamed a woman in the crowd as Thomas landed heavily on the opposite roof and sent a shower of broken tiles spinning into the street below.

"No... Look he's falling!" shouted another.

The spectators gasped as they watched Thomas' flailing hands and feet try to grip the roof where he'd landed but his leather shoes, worn smooth by poverty, found no purchase on the damp tiles. Slowly, inexorably, the weight of his own body dragged Thomas towards the edge of the roof and oblivion. In a frantic attempt to save himself, he snatched the falchion from his belt and smashed its point into the roof. The tiles splintered as if they'd been hit by a culverin ball but the blade bit into a wooden rafter and his descent stopped. Pausing only to thumb his nose at the crowd, Thomas scrambled to his feet and disappeared into the darkness.

"He's up, after him!" Pynch cried and to encourage the pursuers to greater efforts he declared that if the king's disgraced alchemist was caught Cardinal Wolsey would sentence the wretch to be hanged, drawn and quartered in public as a reward. The promise of this grisly spectacle had exactly the effect Pynch desired, the mob roared with delight and the chase began again.

The thought of having his privy parts sliced from his half strangled, still living body and thrown onto a bonfire of his own guts drove Thomas on but it had been days since he'd eaten anything more solid than gruel and lack of food was slowly robbing him of his strength. He forced his legs to carry him forward but his growing weariness and difficult path slowed his progress. Meanwhile, the pursuing crowd's easier route through the streets meant they soon overtook him and as he reached another group of chimneys, Thomas' instincts told him to hide. He ducked behind a particularly ornate stack of twisted brickwork just as two figures emerged from a skylight twenty yards ahead.

Even in the darkness he recognised these vengeful furies as Ned, the uninjured twin, whilst the other man's grotesque profile could only belong to Pynch. For all his fat, the avaricious usurer could run like a greyhound if there was a promise of gold and Cardinal Wolsey always paid handsomely for the head of a rival.

"Surrender you cur!" cried Pynch.

"Never, if you want me, come and face me like a man, you turd from the arse of a whore!" Thomas yelled back.

"Is that the language of a high born gentleman?" taunted Pynch as he signalled for Ned to end the game and arrest the fugitive. Behind the chimneystack, Thomas pressed his sweating fingers around the falchion's hilt and watched Ned, who was now armed with an ancient but serviceable halberd, begin his nervous advance along the slippery rooftop. The moonlight caught the combined axe blade, spear point and billhook of Ned's lethal weapon and Thomas felt the hot humours of battle course through his veins.

"You won't get me with that pig sticker!" Thomas cried but Ned was not to be put off.

"Come out from behind those pots and you'll see what I can do, I'll cut off your pox-ridden cock you pigeon livered, lack gall, northern bastard!" Ned growled.

For some reason the final taunt was too much, something snapped in Thomas' brain and he emerged from his hiding place to launch an attack but his first stroke was premature. Ned was still ten feet away and though his wits were as slow as treacle the extra reach of his halberd gave him an advantage. The instant Thomas revealed himself, Ned thrust his poleaxe towards his enemy and had he been an inch closer, the halberd's spike would have ripped open his opponent's belly. Even so, the weapon's point tore through Thomas' clothes and scraped a shallow gash across his stomach but he ignored the scratch and used the pain to fuel his anger.

With a great cry of rage Thomas rolled around the opposite face of the chimney to attack Ned from behind and as soon as he could see his target's unprotected flank, he swung his sword with all his strength. Ned saw the falchion flash through its arc but now the length of his halberd and the chimneystack conspired against him. The brickwork blocked any attempt to parry Thomas' counterattack and Ned screamed in agony as the heavy sword bit into the bones of his thigh. The brute collapsed like a felled tree and great red rivers of his blood began to stream down the roof.

"You bastard, my leg!" Ned shrieked as he tried to staunch the gore that was pouring from his partially severed limb but it was too late, in the space of a heartbeat his screams had become a death rattle. Ignored the dying henchman, Thomas turned his attention to Pynch who'd somehow squeezed his bulk through the skylight and was now standing at the end of the roof.

"Son of a Spanish bitch wolf!" Thomas yelled and he charged towards his remaining tormentor just as Pynch loosed his last shot. Panic had failed to improve the moneylender's aim and the bolt vanished into the darkness like the others. Pynch was now defenceless but the last of the once noble Devilstone family showed him no mercy.

With a chilling cry of victory, Thomas plunged his sword into Pynch's chest and gore spurted in crimson fountains as the moneylender's last heartbeats pumped blood through severed arteries. In a final act of savagery, Thomas forced the blade upwards and ripped through Pynch's ribs before withdrawing the blood stained blade. The dead man's mouth fell open in silent protest as he fell onto his face and lay still. Uttering a curse on the man's soul Thomas kicked the moneylender's lifeless body and watched with satisfaction as the mound of blubber slithered slowly off the roof. A moment later a heavy, wet thump indicated Pynch's mangled corpse had landed in the street below.

Ned and Pynch were not the first men Thomas had killed. As a boy of twelve he'd ridden with his father's band of reivers as they'd searched for Scotsmen raiding the Border Marches. They'd caught their enemies driving stolen cattle across the Rede, a small river in the hills that marked the border, and in the melee that followed he'd sliced open his first gizzard. Since that day a dozen years ago, Thomas had drawn his sword in countless Border skirmishes, and had even fought at Flodden Field, but whilst slaughtering Scotsmen in the wilds of Northumberland was one thing, butchering Englishmen in the middle of London was quite another. Killing Wolsey's hirelings meant he'd be declared outlaw and if any man or woman gave him sanctuary they too would suffer death.

The cries of horror from the crowd that had gathered around Pynch's broken body roused Thomas from his thoughts and he realised his last opportunity to escape was slipping away. Once again he ignored the ache of his tired muscles and for the next hour he weaved a tortuous path across the rooftops of East Cheap. When his pursuers began to tighten their net, he hid amongst the chimney pots and when the furore passed, he doubled back. After a while the glimmer of torches had moved further towards the great cathedral of St Paul whilst he'd moved in the opposite direction, towards the grim fortress of The Tower of London.

Despite travelling towards England's most feared prison, with each passing minute of freedom Thomas' belief that he might escape his enemies grew stronger and when he could no longer hear the shouts of the hue and cry he decided it was time to make for the river. His plan was simple. There were many Englishmen living in exile with as much reason to fear the wrath of King Henry and his cardinal as Thomas. These exiles waited patiently for the Tudors to be deposed and they'd pay handsomely for the knowledge and secrets he possessed ... if only he could reach them.

2

TOWER HILL

From his crow's nest in the rooftops, Thomas could see the masts of a hundred kogges and carracks moored against London's numerous wharfs. The ships that could carry him to the safety of Bruges or Dunkirk were tantalisingly close but Thomas reckoned that large vessels bound for France or Flanders would be the first place the cardinal's men would look. He therefore decided to make his way to the mouth of the Thames in one of the small wherries that plied the river trade and look for a bigger ship in the harbours of Tilbury or Gravesend.

As yet, Thomas' had no money to pay for his passage but that could be remedied with a little judicious burglary. His roof top journey had taken him to Tower Hill, where the grand houses of London's richest merchants and noblemen lay in the shadow of King Henry's largest, and strongest, castle. To avoid The Tower of London's disease ridden dungeons and blood stained scaffold, all he had to do was climb down to one of the luxurious bedchambers beneath his feet and find some items of silver plate or jewellery he could use to bribe a ship's captain.

He would have to be quick as the first light of dawn was in the sky, and the household below would soon be waking, but the roof on which he stood had no skylight or trapdoor. With a growing sense of urgency Thomas searched for a way down and it was with a huge sense of relief that he found tendrils of ivy clawing their way over the eaves at the back of the house. If these shoots were the crown of a sturdy plant, he could use them to clamber down to a window so he crawled to the edge of the roof and tugged on the nearest shoot. The ivy was wet with morning dew but it seemed to have a firm hold of the wall so he lowered himself into the foliage.

The ivy's musty smell filled his nostrils, and made him feel slightly nauseous, but ten feet below the roof he found what he was looking for; an arm's length to the right of his herbaceous ladder was a window with its casement slightly open. The great oak beams supporting the house's upper storey had been carved into decorative moulding that stood a few inches proud of the white plastered wall so grasping the ivy with one hand, and the window frame with the other, he eased himself along this convenient ledge until he could peer through the leaded glass. When he was sure all was quiet, he eased the window open and clambered over the sill.

As silently as a jealous thought, Thomas dropped onto the soft rug that covered the polished wooden floor and peered around the richly furnished room. There were tapestries on the wall and an ornate four-poster bed stood in the centre of the room. The bed's curtains were closed against drafts and the delicate scent of rosewater filled the air. The gentle fragrance was so different from the filthy stench of East Cheap's alleys, Thomas immediately felt as intoxicated as Odysseus in the Isle of the Lotus Eaters but he knew he couldn't stay for more than a few seconds. He forced himself to ignore the heady aroma and glanced around the room for something he could steal.

The room's occupant was clearly rich enough to be careless of her jewellery as several thin gold chains had been left on a small table at the side of her bed, where even a blind jackdaw could find them. Smiling at his good fortune, Thomas tiptoed across the room, scooped up the necklaces and put them in the battered leather purse that hung from his belt. All that remained was to leave the house as quickly and as quietly as he could but as he turned to go back to the window, he heard footsteps in the corridor outside the chamber. A moment later a sharp rap on the room's door and the shrill voice of a servant woman, turned Thomas' muscles to stone.

"My Lady, the sun is up, do you wish your fire to be lit? It's mightily cold this morning," called the servant and there was a soft murmur from the bed as the sleeper began to wake.

"No, leave me a while longer," replied the occupant of the bed sleepily.

"Very good My Lady," the servant answered and Thomas heard her faint footsteps pad away down the corridor. He began to sigh with relief but before he could make his escape the bed's silk curtains were thrown open to reveal an astonished young girl.

She was aged about twenty and should have been married but no husband seemed to share her bed. Her heart shaped face was framed by long auburn hair and she had a thin yet sensual mouth. Her skin was pale, almost translucent, but her dark eyes were almost coal black. By themselves none of her features were beautiful yet together her eyes, lips and hair wove a spell strong enough to ensnare any man. In spite of his peril, Thomas was seized with lust, it had been many months since he had lain with a woman and he wanted her. He wanted her so badly it hurt just to look at her but it was the girl who opened her mouth to scream.

Without thinking Thomas sprang onto the bed, knocking the girl backwards into the pillows, and before she could utter a sound, he'd seized her wrists and clamped his mouth over hers. The girl writhed beneath him but the weight of his body pinned her to the bed and the passion of his kiss robbed her of any will to resist. Slowly the girl surrendered and as a sign of her submission she began to explore Thomas' mouth with her tongue. No innocent virgin kissed like this so Thomas relaxed and let the girl caress his bristled chin with her eager lips.

"Are you a thief come to rob me of my maidenhood?" she whispered and when Thomas said he was the little trollop gave a sigh of delight.

"Where did you learn to kiss like that?" Thomas asked, his curiosity as aroused as his manhood and he let his hand stray to the girl's firm, rounded breast. He felt her nipple harden against the palm of his hand as the girl admitted that she'd spent time at the French court but her words became short, rapid gasps as Thomas began to explore the rest of her body.

"My Lord such haste, I beg you, cool your ardour, for if you don't I shall surely scream with passion and my maid will hasten to my rescue," the girl croaked but Thomas ignored her pleas and moved his hand to the soft smooth skin of her thigh. The girl swooned with delight as Thomas eased the hem of her linen shift up to her waist but as he prepared for the final conquest of her body the girl suddenly twisted free of his embrace.

"Are you a high born? You speak like a gentleman but you look and smell like the man who takes away the night soil," said the girl pointing accusingly at Thomas' rags. With his mind in a turmoil of frustrated lust he could do nothing but tell the truth.

"I'm of noble birth and I was a great favourite of the king until my enemies turned him against me. I've been forced to live as an outlaw these past four months but I have vowed to clear my name and slay those who've conspired against me," Thomas said angrily. The girl's eyes opened wide with excitement as she realised she was in the presence of a dangerous fugitive and she sighed with longing as she stroked his sweat-streaked face. Her touch felt strange and for the first time Thomas realised the girl was wearing long silk gloves that reached above her elbow but before he could ask why she went to bed with her hands covered, the girl kissed him gently on the cheek.

"I can see you're a man who's been greatly wronged but I can't lie with you for it's my destiny to be King Henry's queen so I must save myself for the royal bed," she whispered in apology. Now it was Thomas' turn to be surprised.

"A queen!" he said.

"Yes, a wise woman told me I shall wear the crown of England and bear Henry a strong and healthy heir," the girl said proudly.

"But Henry's already married," spluttered Thomas.

"Spanish Catherine is old and will soon die, besides, if my sister can be King Henry's whore why can't I be his queen?" said the girl and she spoke with all the malevolence of a greedy child.

"I hate to disappoint you but your wise woman was mistaken. I was the king's astrologer and I saw nothing in the charts that foretold of the queen's death or the king's remarriage," said Thomas but before the girl could reply, there was another knock at the door.

"My Lady, your father is asking for you," said the servant but the girl called out that she was passing water and ordered the woman to wait outside the door.

"You must go, if my father finds you here he'll have you flayed alive," the girl whispered to Thomas and she told him that there was a servants' stairway at the far end of the passage outside her chamber which led to a walled courtyard.

"There's a gate to the street, it's unlocked at daybreak but watch for the kitchen boys bringing water from the well. If they ask, say you have come to ask my father a favour and they won't trouble you. Now wait here while I deal with Bessie," the girl added and before Thomas could stop her, she'd climbed off the bed and closed the curtains.

Thomas groaned and fell back onto the feather mattress. His loins ached with unfulfilled lust and he prayed to Ishtar, Aphrodite and Venus not to deny him the greatest prize but all three goddesses were deaf to his pleas. From behind the bed curtains, he heard the door open and the girl tell her maid to fetch a pair of clean stockings from the press outside her mother's chamber. A moment later the curtains opened to reveal the girl's concerned face.

"Bessie will only be gone for a minute so you must go now," she said urgently.

"But at least tell me your name before I take my leave," Thomas begged.

"You'll know my name when you are worthy to hear it, besides, if you truly have the gift of foresight you'll be able to find me quite easily. Now go, before Bessie comes back," she insisted. Reluctantly Thomas climbed off the bed and slipped out of the room, leaving the girl staring into a looking glass and brushing her hair. Cursing the goddesses for their cruelty, Thomas found the stairs that led to the courtyard and, just as girl had promised, the door to the street was unlocked. As he stepped into the cold, spring sunshine, a boy carrying a wooden bucket eyed him suspiciously but said nothing.

A minute later Thomas was in the street, gazing at The Tower of London. The sight drove all thoughts of the girl out of his head and reminded him that unless he could escape from the city he would suffer far worse pain than thwarted passion. Turning away from The Tower's broad moat and high walls, he started to push his way through the crowds of merchants and apprentices on their way to London's markets. Fearful of being recognised, he took a crumpled black bonnet from beneath his doublet, crammed it on his head and pulled the brim over his eyes but he needn't have worried. Most of London knew nothing of court intrigue and had yet to hear about the previous night's gruesome killings so Thomas excited no more interest than a dead cat in a gutter.

Nevertheless, as soon as the taverns opened, the news of the two debt collectors' deaths would be the talk of the city and Thomas knew he must be on a ship bound for the continent before Cardinal Wolsey's men thought of searching the river for the assassin. He therefore hurried to Billingsgate wharf in the hope that one of the fishermen arriving on the morning tide would take him to Tilbury in exchange for a few hours' work. He was in luck. An old man with a face the colour of a walnut, and a son confined to bed with ague, agreed to take him down river if he helped unload his catch and took a turn at the oars. Thomas dutifully hauled barrels of sprats onto the quay until the tide turned then he joined the fisherman in the wherry and helped him push the boat away from the wharf.

Though Thomas had never rowed before, he'd seen enough bargemen at work to understand the principles and he found the practice easy enough once he had the rhythm. The fisherman was too busy steering the little boat through the dense river traffic to be concerned by his new crewman's lack of skill and the ebb tide helped sweep them downstream. The wherry soon passed King Henry's new Palace of Placentia and beyond Greenwich the river's muddy banks became lined with willows and alders instead of warehouses and wharfs. With the sun on his back and a fresh breeze in his face, Thomas began to feel happy until his gnarled travelling companion broke the spell.

"Did ye hear about the murders last night?" said the fisherman darkly.

"Something about them yes," mumbled Thomas as he dug the oars into the swirling brown water.

"Two of the cardinal's men done to death and a third likely to lose his hand," said the fisherman.

"Have they caught anyone?" Thomas asked casually.

"No one to catch," said the fisherman. "The murderer was a demon that flew through the air like an Irish banshee. They found one of its victims in the street with his chest ripped open by the fiend's huge claws whilst the other man had his leg bitten almost clean off and bled to death."

"I don't believe in spooks and phantoms," Thomas said firmly and there was more than a hint of bitterness in his voice. Though he'd spent the last seven years studying the secret arts of necromancy and theurgy he'd never been able to conjure a single supernatural spirit or successfully perform any act of magic. His complete and continued failure had left him with the firm belief that if angels and demons did exist, they were absolutely indifferent to the affairs of men but the fisherman was utterly convinced that London was under siege from the powers of darkness.

"I speak the gospel truth, I heard it from Stinking Jack who was there! He said the demon waved a fiery sword above its head as it flew over the rooftops looking for more victims and the whole city was only saved by the prayers of the Lord Cardinal Wolsey," insisted the fisherman and he made the sign of the cross with his stubby fingers.

"Stinking Jack is either a liar, an idiot or a drunkard," sniffed Thomas, wondering how a man with such an unpleasant name could inspire such trust.

"Jack may not be in his right mind most days but demons flying over Cheapside is a sure sign that the End of Days is nigh and soon we'll all face the Last Judgement," said the fisherman sternly and he pulled out a small amulet that was hanging on a leather thong around his neck. The old man kissed the yellowing piece of bone, which had been crudely carved into the shape of a mermaid with two tails, and began to mutter a complicated incantation that he hoped would save his soul from damnation. Thomas looked at him and pitied his credulity. He knew that those who trusted in magic never had their faith rewarded, in spite of the outrageous promises made by the wise women and self-proclaimed sorcerers who made a good living from selling these worthless trinkets.

Thomas knew this better than anyone because he'd once filled his own purse by dealing in magical charms, however his customers hadn't been superstitious fishermen. Thomas' amulets had been bought by the highest in the land but though his jewels had been made from gold, set with precious stones and inscribed with powerful spells taken from rare *grimoires*, they'd been no more effective than the tawdry slivers of wood and bone sold in the markets of Cheapside. Indeed Thomas' own personal talisman, which he'd fashioned with the help of the great German alchemist and necromancer Cornelius Agrippa, had spectacularly failed to save him from his recent ill fortune.

With nothing more to say to each other, neither man spoke until the boat had rounded the last bend in the river before Tilbury and as their destination came into view, the fisherman told his rower to pull for the long wooden jetty that stood at right angles to two enormous hulks. These apparently derelict warships had been beached, broadside to the river, on the grey mudflats beyond the harbour and though they lacked masts, the two ships still dwarfed the kogges, wherries and other boats that crowded Tilbury's waterfront.

"What are those?" Thomas asked, wondering what manner of storm could wreck such mighty arks. Their blackened hulls were covered in weed and slime, which made the ships appear abandoned, but the royal standard still flew from their sterns, their gun ports were open and Thomas could see the muzzles of bronze cannon pointing out over the river. Wisps of smoke from cooking fires on the ship's decks and lines of washing hung over the rails indicated the vessels were still manned, at least by gunners and washerwomen.

"Those rotting piles of worm eaten wood are all that's left of the *Great Harry* and *Mary Rose*. Since the King of Frogs gave our Sovereign Lord his latest bloody nose, Henry's had no money to pay for a proper army or navy so he uses his great carracks as floating forts to guard the approaches to London," the fisherman said grimly.

"So if King Francis tries to sail up the Thames he can at least be sure of a proper salute," Thomas joked but it was a hollow jest. No one in England could forget Henry's humiliation the year before when the king's attempt to seize Paris had ended in utter failure. A century before, in the time of Henry V, Englishmen had found honour and glory in the mud of northern France but Henry VIII had been born under a different star. Instead of winning great victories at Harfleur and Agincourt, the Tudor king's men had deserted in their hundreds and Henry had been forced to abandon his campaign when he was just fifty miles from Paris. The last remnants of the English army had slunk back to Calais where the men had been ignominiously discharged and sent home in disgrace.

The fisherman began to mutter something about there being more people than usual waiting for him on the fish quay but Thomas, who was having to row hard to counter the tide, couldn't turn his head to see what the man was talking about. Grunting with the effort of wrestling Old Father Thames, Thomas continued to pull on the oars until the boat clunked against the jetty's mussel encrusted timbers.

"You there, what boat is this?" Cried a burly town constable who was standing at the edge of the jetty. The man was dressed in a green and white striped tunic, the livery of the Tudor kings, and Thomas' joy at being free of the city drained out of the holes in his battered shoes.

"Christopher Martin's wherry newly returned from the city after unloading a cargo of sprats and herring," shouted the fisherman.

"I know you Master Martin but I don't know your passenger, where's your lad?" said the constable suspiciously.

"Young Simon took sick the day before last so this gentleman's been giving me a hand with the oars all the way from Billingsgate," said the fisherman.

"And who are you?" asked the constable turning to the wherry's oarsman. Thomas' mind whirled like a windmill's sails in gale. He could try and escape by plunging into the river and swimming for the far shore but the constable would quickly commandeer a boat and he'd be caught before he was a hundred yards from the dock. Even if he escaped, the river at Tilbury was far too wide for anything but a seal to cross by swimming so Thomas decided to try and bluff his way to freedom.

"I'm Robert of Durham looking for passage home to the north," he said and he immediately cursed himself for choosing an alias that still contained too much information.

"From the North are ye? Well come up here and let's be looking at you," growled the constable. Thomas obediently climbed the wooden ladder tied to one of the jetty's pillars and as soon as he'd reached the top, he was surrounded by a dozen guardians of King Henry's peace. They were all dressed in the same grubby green and white smocks and armed with a variety of staves and halberds.

"You say you're returning home but can you pay your passage? By your garb I should take you for a vagabond and throw you in the stocks for a week," said the constable looking at Thomas' filthy clothes with disdain.

"I'm gentle born and I've never begged in my life! London's footpads emptied my purse and stole my clothes but

I was given these rags by a kindly abbot and I fully intend to work my passage home. Now let me pass before I lose my temper and curse you for a knave," Thomas snapped.

"Keep a civil tongue in your head," replied the constable. "We're looking for a murderer or haven't you heard?"

"The fisherman told me two men in East Cheap had been killed by a demon but surely you can see I'm flesh and blood," Thomas announced to the crowd that was gathering to watch the commotion.

"Demon be damned! The villain we seek is of this earth, though his soul is most surely destined for hell. One of his victims still lives and he told us the murder is Thomas Devilstone of The North. Wait a minute, isn't Durham in the north and what's that at your side?" cried the constable. With uncharacteristic speed, the slow-witted dogberry drew his sword and pointed it at the falchion hanging from Thomas' belt. Everyone in the crowd could see the stranger's unsheathed sword and its blade stained with dried blood was as good as a confession.

"God's Wounds, take him men!" cried the constable and before Thomas could make a fight of it the other men-at-arms had their weapons pressed against his chest.

"Raise your arms you murderous dog!" cried the constable. Outnumbered and exhausted from his flight over the rooftops, Thomas had no choice but to lift his hands high above his head. As he did so the constable stepped forward and deftly cut Thomas' belt with the point of his sword so that the falchion fell onto the jetty's wooden planks with a dull thud.

"I acted in defence of my life," Thomas shouted before a cudgel smashed the wind from his body and he doubled up in pain. Whilst his lungs fought for breath, another guardian of the king's peace struck the back of Thomas' head and the last thing he heard before his world went black was the constable's triumphant voice.

"Careful with him lads, the Lord Cardinal wants this evil bastard alive!"

3

THE FLEET PRISON

Thomas woke and soon wished he hadn't. His head felt like Beelzebub was hammering nails into his skull whilst his arms and legs seemed unusually heavy. It took a few moments before he realised that the extra weight of his limbs was due to the fetters that had been fastened around his wrists and ankles. Painfully, he hauled himself into a sitting position and peered into the gloom. A tiny, barred window, set high in one wall, let in just enough light for Thomas to see he was in a large, dungeon, about thirty feet square, and the only entrance was an iron bound, wooden door.

The dungeon was so large its vaulted roof had to be supported by a central pillar and its corners were hidden by shadows. There was no furniture and the only comfort was a thin layer of grimy rushes that covered the damp stone floor. In desperation, Thomas tested the strength of his shackles but the iron links were sound and the ends of his chains were fastened to a ring that had been firmly cemented into the wall. A fog of pain and desperation clouded his mind but he had enough wits to bawl a stream of violent threats and blasphemous curses at his unseen gaolers.

"Hear me you mother buggering servants of the tyrant Wolsey, I'm a friend of the king and I swear by God's bastard Son, if you don't free me from this stinking dungeon within the next five minutes, you'll be sorry. The Crucifixion will feel like the gentle tickle of a whore's merkin compared to what I'll do to you!" Thomas cried but his torrent of oaths was interrupted by a voice from the darkness.

"You dare mock Christ's Passion? If I weren't chained like St Peter in the Mamertine, I would teach you a lesson in scripture!" bellowed a man with a deep, guttural accent.

"Be silent preacher, some of us are trying to sleep," said another foreign voice from the shadows.

"Is it not enough I'm imprisoned in this filthy pit? Must I also be tormented by your childish squabbling?" said a third man, who spoke in strangely regal tones.

Astonished that he was not alone in the dungeon Thomas fell silent and as his eyes became accustomed to the gloom, he could see there were three other men chained to the cell's mouldering walls. All three of his fellow prisoners were just a few years older than himself and though, judging by their filthy rags and matted hair they'd been incarcerated for several months, the light of rebellion still burned bright in their eyes.

The largest of the prisoners was a muscular, pale-skinned giant whose saturnine, beetle-browed face was covered by a tangle of filthy red hair and a great bush of a beard. Two intense green eyes stared out of this forest, like those of a tiger gazing out of a bamboo jungle, but the man's shoulders were as broad as a bull's and when he talked he bellowed like an enormous brown bear. Thomas thought that the powerful build and ruddy face of this beast of a man suggested he was German or perhaps his ancestor had been a Viking berserker left behind by the Danes who'd once pillaged London.

By contrast the second man was of more normal height and build. He had soft brown eyes, set deep in a handsome face that was almost totally obscured by his jet-black hair and what had once been a neatly clipped beard. A lifetime spent disobeying orders and biting his thumb at those who imagined they could command him, had etched a look of defiance into his high cheekbones and thin mouth. It was a look that women loved, but men feared, and from his olive skin Thomas thought he might be a Spanish sailor who'd deserted his ship and committed some dreadful crime whilst drunk on strong English ale.

The third prisoner was the most exotic of the three, he was an African with skin as dark as ancient bronze. Knots of thick black hair tumbled from his head like the coiled leaves of a fern, yet his tightly curled beard was thin and covered his chin in little clumps like thorn bushes in a desert. As with the other prisoners, his marble-white eyes burned with hatred for those who sought to rule him yet there was something regal about his fine features and noble bearing. He exuded this effortless aura of superiority even though he was chained to a wall and Thomas was acutely aware he'd only ever seen such pride in the faces of the foreign princes who swaggered about King Henry's court.

Like the red bearded giant, the African was tall and well muscled. Even seated the two titans dwarfed the Spaniard but whereas the German appeared to have the brute strength of a crusader's longsword, the African had the subtle power of a Saracen's scimitar. The reason why these three men should be rotting in a London dungeon Thomas could only guess, however they all seemed to have stayed strong and healthy despite their incarceration.

"So what brings you to Hell's ante-chamber?" said the African. He spoke English with a soft, musical accent yet his words sounded like a royal command rather than a question.

"Don't you recognise him? It's King Henry's alchemist and necromancer, the man whom Cardinal Wolsey ordered arrested for witchcraft," replied the swarthy man gleefully. He too spoke good English and Thomas reckoned he was no stranger to London.

"Are you a witch? By the flaming sword of Saint Michael, if you've made a compact with The Devil I'll snap these chains and choke the life from your worthless carcase with my bare hands, for God commands good Christians not to suffer a witch to live," growled the red bearded giant. He too spoke in thickly accented English and Thomas was about to remark that God also commanded good Christians not to murder each other when the African interrupted him.

"I've never yet seen a witch that could produce anything but lies and tricks," he said bitterly. "When I was born my mother's astrologers cast my horoscope. They predicted heaven would grant me a long life, the love of my people and many victories on the battlefield, yet I find myself far from home in this stinking dungeon awaiting a peasant's death on the gallows."

"You don't believe in man's power to bind and loose Dark Forces?" said Thomas earnestly and as his question hung in the air awaiting an answer, the swarthy looking prisoner burst out laughing.

"Are you hoping to call on the powers of Hell to free you? If so the legions of the damned have been little help to you up till now. Where were your demons when Wolsey's men knocked you senseless and brought you here to The Fleet?" he taunted.

"The Fleet?" said Thomas in surprise. "God's teeth! You mean I'm back in London not Tilbury?"

"This is indeed The Fleet Prison, where those summoned before the corrupt and wicked judges of The King's Bench are incarcerated to await their trial or their death sentence," said the swarthy man.

"Yet a prison is also a place of repentance, so witch, be truly sorry for your sins, put your faith in God and He may yet be merciful," added the red bearded prisoner.

"I'm no witch and though I did study the Natural Sciences with the great magus Cornelius Agrippa all I've ever sought is knowledge and truth. Yet for this, my enemies have conspired to destroy me," Thomas declared.

"If you seek knowledge only for its own sake then you are a fool, what use is knowledge unless it brings you wealth and power?" said the swarthy man.

"If my mother was still alive she'd probably agree with you," said Thomas ruefully and with nothing else to pass the time, he found himself telling his fellow prisoners of how he'd come to follow the tortuous path that had raised him so high and brought him so low. It had been a long journey and he'd taken the first steps almost ten years ago.

A year after the English had won a crushing victory over the Scots at Flodden Field, Thomas' father, an impoverished knight in the service of the Warden of the Marches, had been killed in a minor raid on the Scottish town of Hawick. The fifteen year old Thomas, who'd seen his father die, had sworn revenge but his widowed mother had been determined to stop her only son from being killed in some futile Border feud. His mother had used the last of the once sizeable Devilstone fortune to send her son to the great school of medicine in Padua however Thomas had found more to interest him in the city's taverns and brothels and it was here he'd met the lawyer, physician and necromancer Heinrich Cornelius Agrippa von Nettlesheim.

A German of noble birth, Cornelius Agrippa had spent his youth in the service of the Holy Roman Emperor Maximilian of Hapsburg who was fighting a long and bloody war with the king of France for control of Burgundy, Flanders and Italy. Whilst campaigning with Maximilian's murderous *landsknecht* mercenaries, Agrippa had proved himself to be a loyal and courageous soldier but after being knighted by the emperor on the field of battle, he'd abandoned the martial life to resume his education. First he'd studied law and then medicine before succumbing to the lure of the occult.

Over several large flagons of wine in a Paduan tavern, Thomas had begged to become the great magician's apprentice. Eventually Agrippa had agreed and had taught the youthful Englishman the secrets of astrology, alchemy and divination. Thomas had also learned the essential skills of an imperial courtier, which included swordsmanship and dancing as well as the darker arts of using codes and poisons. Together, master and pupil had travelled across Europe in pursuit of more secret knowledge but, after being driven out of Geneva by jealous rivals, they'd quarrelled.

For reasons Thomas was only now beginning to understand, his master suddenly seemed to lose all faith in magic and the occult. One evening, without any warning, Agrippa had declared he was renouncing the truth of all he'd previously believed and was abandoning magic to renew his studies in medicine. Thomas, in his youthful ignorance, had been appalled at his master's apostasy and after a bitter row he'd left Agrippa to continue his own journey along the sacred river of hidden truth. Thomas had become convinced he could use his knowledge of the arcane to restore his family's lost lands and titles so, after a year in France hiding from his creditors, he'd returned to England.

At first he'd used what Agrippa had taught him to make magic amulets that were as beautiful as they were ineffective. Thomas' skill, wit and youthful good looks had soon attracted a long list of wealthy female patrons and his growing fame had quickly secured his appointment as King Henry's personal astrologer. The casting of the king's charts was easy enough but, in spite of all he'd learned, Thomas had failed to foresee the growing jealousy of the most powerful commoner in England: Cardinal Wolsey, the king's Lord Chancellor.

"I admit I've cast spells and fashioned amulets but only to help King Henry in his quest for a son to succeed him," said Thomas bitterly. "Yet despite my lack of success, Wolsey envied my high standing at court and started spreading the false rumour that I'd cast a spell to make the queen barren. Eventually the king began to believe the Ipswich butcher's lies and I was forced to flee for my life."

"You're not the only one to have suffered at the hands of that lying, crooked cleric," said the swarthy man when Thomas had finished his story. "I was a captain of Queen Catherine's Spanish guard with a nice safe job until I was falsely accused by Wolsey's spies of seducing her lady in waiting."

"You're a Spaniard?" said Thomas.

"Me, a Spanish Don? I should say not," spat the swarthy man. "I am Luis Quintana of Lisbon. I'm Portuguese and though you may not know me, I know you, Master Thomas Devilstone. I saw you many times in King Henry's palaces and I was there during the farce of the queen's last pregnancy."

"You saw that?" said Thomas and he swallowed hard as he recalled a night he'd much rather forget.

"I was guarding Queen Catherine's chamber during her last confinement," said Quintana tapping the side of his long, thin nose knowingly. "I was there when you cast the old sow's horoscope and predicted that she'd give birth to a healthy prince before the night's end. You made an unholy mess of that my friend. A blind sawbones couldn't mistake trapped wind for birthing pains, but you did."

The failed fortune-teller fell silent with embarrassment as he remembered the ignoble end to his career in astrology. His reputation, and Henry's last hope of his ageing queen producing a male heir, had evaporated in the cloud of foul smelling gas that had erupted from beneath Catherine of Aragon's nightdress. Worse still, Thomas' failure to reveal the truth about the queen's phantom pregnancy had been the perfect opportunity for Wolsey to turn the king against him.

The cruel irony was that Thomas had known it would've been impossible for Catherine to conceive a child naturally because, according to her maids, the queen had ceased her monthly courses more than a year ago. He'd also known that it had been five years since the queen's last true pregnancy had produced a stillborn child and a decade since she'd been delivered of the healthy Princess Mary. The conflict between the facts known to everyone at court, and the stars' confident prediction that King Henry was destined to become a parent in the fifteenth year of his reign, had finally convinced Thomas that there had to be a fatal flaw in the supposed wisdom of astrology.

"I learned that night that a man can no more see his future in the stars than in the nightsoil floating in his pisspot," Thomas declared and he was surprised at Quintana's reaction.

"But you were right all along! As you shall see when you hear my tale," he said mysteriously.

The Portugee was happy to admit he'd been an insignificant member of Catherine of Aragon's guard until an anonymous informer had accused him of seducing Mary Boleyn, the queen's maid of honour and the king's mistress. Though Mary was married to an obscure country squire, all London had known of her adulterous affair with the king and no one believed the child growing in her belly had been sired by her lawful husband. Quintana also insisted that, although he was no angel, he was not so stupid as to bed 'the king's whore' and his arrest was part of a deeper plot to discredit the queen.

"So you see my incompetent star-gazing friend, we're both victims of the same intrigue. Henry is the real father of Mary Boleyn's brat, so hers must be the child your charts predicted," said Quintana triumphantly. Thomas was about to point out that his astrological charts had definitely shown it was Catherine who was to bear Henry's son, when the Portugee began to describe his unwilling role in the second part of the king's dastardly plan to rid himself of both his wife and his mistress.

Quintana insisted that though Mary Boleyn's pregnancy had proved Henry was still strong and virile this was only the beginning of the king's problems. A royal bastard could never inherit the throne without starting a civil war so Henry had to prove he was *not* the father of Mary's child *and* find a way to put aside his barren wife so he could plant his seed in more fertile ground. Unfortunately for the queen's Portuguese captain, Henry had decided that Quintana was dispensable enough to provide the solution to his dilemma.

"I was dragged to The Tower where the king's own torturers threatened to nail my nutmegs to the rack and tear off my mainmast with red hot pincers unless I confessed that I'd ploughed the king's wife as well as his mistress," Quintana said grimly and he suddenly stopped talking as he remembered the blood-chilling horror of that night in the king's dungeons. There was an uncomfortable silence until Thomas asked the question they all wanted answered.

"Did you admit to committing adultery with Catherine of Aragon and Mary Boleyn?" he said.

"Of course I did. I lied like an abbot caught in bed with his catamite and told them anything they wanted to hear. If a fat English king wants to abandon his faithful wife and pregnant whore so he can marry some other inbred, blue-blooded, brood mare what do I care? I'll face any man in a fair fight but I'll not suffer the torments of the rack for anyone," said Quintana defiantly.

"But your lies didn't save you did they? The king has sentenced you to hang and quite right too. Whether you committed treason with the queen or not, God's commandments forbid the bearing false witness as well as adultery and the wages of sin is death," interrupted the red bearded man.

"Perhaps God's commandments should also forbid the torturing of innocent people but at least I'll suffer a quick, clean death as a good Catholic and not as a heretic

Lutheran! Me they'll hang quickly, but you they'll roast slowly like a side of good English beef," countered Quintana.

"I do not fear a martyr's death at the stake," said the red bearded man. "I've heard the true word of God from the monk Luther and I no longer wish to live in a corrupt world ruled by Satan and his servant, the anti-Christ Pope Clement."

"This prophet of doom is Bos de Vries," said Quintana to Thomas. "He's a mad Frisian from some godforsaken sandbank off the coast of Holland. He thinks he's been sent by Jesus to preach Luther's New Covenant but don't let him fool you. He's nothing but a failed priest who abandoned the pulpit for the life of a pirate and a rebel and Wolsey will have him burned at the stake once the holy days of Lent have passed."

"I am condemned for heresy not piracy or treason," complained Bos who seemed strangely proud of his crimes. "I shall burn for a few minutes and then enter paradise but you, you traitorous Portuguese liar, shall burn for all eternity for betraying your lawful queen!"

"Is me betraying my queen any worse than you betraying your God?" retorted Quintana and there followed a bitter discussion as to whether apostasy, heresy, bearing false witness or fornication was the lesser sin. Thomas listened with amusement as Bos admitted that, in his youth, he'd harboured ambitions to become a Catholic priest until his theological education had been interrupted by a rebellion against the Holy Roman Emperor Maximilian of Hapsburg.

Despite ruling an empire that stretched from the German Ocean to the Adriatic Sea, Maximilian had sought to add the tiny, independent Duchy of Friesland to his territories. Taking advantage of a local feud between claimants to the ducal coronet, the emperor had backed the pro-Hapsburg candidate, but the Frisians had refused to recognise the imperial puppet and had fought a long and bitter war, to depose him. To crush the rebellion once and for all, Maximillian had raised the infamous Black Band and these pitiless mercenaries had systematically laid waste to Friesland. Outraged by the bloody atrocities committed by the Black Band, Bos had left his seminary and joined the rebels.

"In the end God deserted us and we were defeated," he said sadly. "Most of my comrades were hanged but I escaped to England where I learned the truth about the pope and his heretical church. In my desire to save others from the errors of the Roman Rite, I preached Luther's New Gospel until that poxed, papal poltroon Cardinal Wolsey had me arrested. Yet I forgive him because after Easter I shall be with Christ and wear the golden crown of martyrdom."

"If the angels can find a diadem big enough to fit your great fat Frisian head," said Quintana prompting Bos to roar with anger and lunge at the Portugee but he came to the end of his iron tethers long before he could reach his target. Frustrated in his murderous ambition, Bos sank bank into the filthy straw and growled at Quintana like a whipped dog.

"How about you African? You're a long way from home so how did you come to be in a foul English prison?" said

Thomas, "Have your heathen gods abandoned you just as our God has abandoned us?"

"I am no heathen," said the African quietly. "My home is the desert kingdom of Nubia, which lies to the south of Mahometan Egypt, yet my God is the Christian god. Indeed my people accepted Lord Jesus into their hearts at a time when you Englishmen were still worshipping stones and trees."

"You're a Christian?" said Thomas in surprise.

"For a thousand years all Nubia honoured the Lord Jesus until our land was conquered by the infidel Funj and now our people are the oppressed slaves of the Mahometan Caliphs," replied the Nubian.

Thomas had never heard of 'The Funj' so the Nubian told him that his enemies were a pagan tribe from beyond the marshes that marked the southern border of his kingdom. Twenty years ago, The Funj had overrun Christian Nubia, however their victory had been fleeting as they in turn had been invaded by Islamic Turkish armies, who were expanding south after their conquest of Egypt. In an attempt to preserve his independence, the Funj king Amara Dunqas had converted to Islam and forced his Nubian subjects, both pagan and Christian, to renounce the faiths of their ancestors.

"This happened in my father's time," said the Nubian. "My Father was Djoel, King of Dotawo, last of the four Christian kingdoms of Nubia, and I'm his son, also called Djoel, rightful king of all the lands between the First and Sixth Cataracts of the Nile."

"He spins a good yarn but the truth is his name is Prometheus and he was a Southwark prizefighter until he was caught rigging crooked bouts," sniffed Quintana. "Royal blood or not, he'll be hanging from a gibbet by Pentecost, just like the rest of us."

"Only my poverty drove me to a life of sin," said Prometheus angrily. "When my father died, I fled into the desert with a few loyal companions and we carried on the war against The Funj but I was betrayed and captured. I refused to renounce Jesus so my captors sold me to the Barbary corsairs and I was sent to suffer a living death chained to the oars of their filthy galleys."

Prometheus told of how he'd been freed during a sea battle between the Muslim corsairs and a Christian fleet from Venice. After his liberation he'd joined the crew of a Venetian merchantman sailing for England but once his ship had arrived London his luck had turned. Whilst their captain waited for a new cargo, the sailors had passed the time playing dice and Prometheus had quickly developed a passion for the game. Unfortunately, his desire to win had become so strong he'd killed one of the sailors he'd caught cheating with a single blow. The captain had ordered the Nubian to be hanged at once but, using only his fists, Prometheus had managed to fight his way off the ship and disappear into the twilight world of Southwark's brothels, bear pits and boxing booths.

"I will not be cheated by those who are so low born they have to look up to see the bellies of snakes but I knew it was wrong to kill the man," said Prometheus. "I tried to make amends by using my gift for healing to make my way in the world but the Mark of Cain was upon me."

The Nubian explained that during his years spent fighting for his throne, the Christian hermits who lived in remote desert caves had taught him the skills of a physician so he could treat his men wounded in battle. He'd learned how mouldering grain could cure fever, how acacia thorns and goat sinew could stitch wounds and how snake venom could make thick humours flow. Prometheus had tried to use this knowledge to earn his living as an apothecary but the residents of Southwark and Bankside had not trusted the potions and physicks sold by an enormous African.

In desperation, Prometheus had turned to his other talent, knocking people senseless with one punch, and joined a boxing booth. He'd fought under the name of 'Prometheus The African Titan' but he'd soon tired of splitting the lips and blacking the eyes of drunken blacksmiths and costers. Impatient to earn enough money to buy his passage home, he'd agreed to start losing bouts in exchange for gold. After one particularly egregious fraud had resulted in a riot, Prometheus had been arrested, convicted of cheating those wagering on the bout and sentenced to hang.

"But if you can't bear to be cheated by lesser men why did you agree to lose?" Thomas asked.

"Because I wasn't losing, I was winning a fortune by betting against myself," said Prometheus with a broad grin. "Yet once again I was cheated of what was rightfully mine by the greedy lawyers who were supposed to plead my case and by the magistrates who took my bribes yet still condemned me to a pauper's death."

"What a fine quartet we make," laughed Quintana when the Nubian had finished his story. "A witch, a liar, a heretic and a cheat but at least we all have one thing in common. We've all failed most miserably in our criminal ambitions and we shall suffer death for our failure!"

"Not me, I intend to leave here as soon as possible and lead a rebellion that will drive the Tudors from England!" Thomas announced boldly. Having heard Bos and Prometheus boast of their parts in their country's rebellions, Thomas confidently expected that they'd be the first to offer him their support but he'd gravely misjudged their mood.

Bos declared that whilst it was every man's duty to resist a tyrant who threatened the ancient rights and liberties of a free people, just as the Frisians had resisted the oppression of the invading Hapsburgs, rebellions against lawful monarchs were born from the sin of pride. The ex-priest added that pride was the worst of all sins as it had led to Lucifer's army of rebel angels being cast out of Heaven and in their fall were sown the seeds of Adam and Eve's expulsion from the Garden of Eden.

Prometheus also insisted that he was no rebel and argued that his war against the Funj had been a holy war to liberate his people from foreign infidels and invaders. Even Quintana, who had plenty of reason to hate the Tudors, scoffed at the idea of a risking his neck in a foolhardy rebellion but Thomas was not to be put off.

"Henry Octavius is not my lawful king, he's a usurper and the crown of England rightfully belongs to Richard de la Pole exiled Duke of Suffolk. This prince of the Royal House of York is now in Burgundy, waiting for a chance to free his people from the Tudor tyranny, and once I'm at liberty I'll seek him out. With my knowledge of the secret arts to help him, Richard will soon drive Henry back behind the Welsh mountains where he belongs and so gentlemen, may I propose a bargain? If you aid me in this great endeavour, I'll make you all rich once the White Rose is crowned Richard IV," he cried.

If Thomas had hoped his rousing declaration of loyalty to the last Yorkist pretender to the English throne, and his offer of generous rewards, would change the other prisoner's minds he was again mistaken. Bos, Prometheus and Quintana simply looked at him as if he were a raving madman, then they roared with laughter and rattled their fetters to remind him that stone walls and iron bars made a very effective prison, even for witches and rebels.

"It's a good jest Master Thomas but you can't raise a rebellion stuck in here!" Quintana laughed.

"Can you lead an army of rats and lice against Henry," scoffed Bos.

"Or maybe turn yourself into a bat and fly to Richard de la Pole through the bars of our dungeon's window!" Prometheus said, his great shoulders shaking with mirth.

"Perhaps I will, for I am Merlin reborn and I will place a new Arthur on the throne of England," said Thomas indignantly but the others continued to howl with laughter, tears rolling down their filthy cheeks, until each man remembered the hopelessness of his own situation.

4

WESTMINSTER HALL

The prisoners' sullen silence persisted for hours so, with nothing else to occupy his mind, Thomas began to think about the girl who'd aided him the previous night. The little trollop had claimed her sister had shared the king's bed and the more he considered Quintana's story the more he became convinced that he'd almost bedded Anne Boleyn, the younger sister of the king's mistress Mary Boleyn, but his thoughts were interrupted by the opening of the cell's heavy wooden door. Three brutish men entered the dungeon and without warning began to beat the prisoners, delivering bone-cracking blows with their stout wooden clubs.

"Back you turds from the arses of diseased dogs, make way for the King's Officer!" spluttered the fatter of the gaolers. Once the prisoners had been cowed, a man wearing an expensive fur trimmed cloak stepped cautiously into the dungeon. He held a pomander under his nose and placed his feet carefully to avoid the reeking pools of urine and piles of excrement that littered the stone floor.

"Which one of you abominable creatures is the warlock? I'm commanded by the Lord Chancellor to take the man named Thomas Devilstone to the Court of King's Bench at Westminster where he must answer for his crimes," said the visitor.

At the sound of his name Thomas looked up and he recognised the man at once. It was Richard Rich, one of the pack of unscrupulous lawyers Cardinal Wolsey used to hunt down his enemies and tear them to pieces, sometimes literally. Thomas knew Lord Rich often applied the instruments of torture with his own hand and had a particular fondness for the rack.

"I'm Thomas Devilstone and I demand to know why I'm being held in this noxious midden?" Thomas replied angrily. The gaolers raised their clubs to deliver the painful retribution such impudence deserved but Rich shook his head.

"You're here because the king desires it, so what price your witchcraft now?" said the lawyer, with barely concealed glee.

"I'm no witch," Thomas repeated. "All I seek is the wisdom of the ancient philosophers, is it a crime to seek such knowledge?"

"That is precisely what His Majesty's court is waiting to decide, now make haste, your judges do not like to be kept waiting," replied Rich with a menacing smile.

"I am to be tried this day? But this is villainy! I've had no time to engage an attorney or prepare my defence!" Thomas protested.

"Fear not, you'll get a fair trial before they find you guilty," sneered Rich and he ordered the gaolers to bring the manacled warlock to the tumbrel waiting in the court-yard without delay. The fattest turnkey went to unfasten the prisoner's chains from the ring in the wall and the stink of the gaoler's unwashed flesh caught in Thomas' throat. Whilst he coughed and spluttered, the gaoler hauled Thomas to his feet and began pushing him roughly towards the dungeon's door.

"Mind your manners you bastard son of gong farmer's daughter! I'm Sir Thomas Devilstone of Tynedale, I'm a veteran of Flodden under the protection of the Lord Warden of the Marches and I demand to be given the treatment due to my rank!" Thomas cried but the gaoler, thinking he was dealing with a foppish, dissolute courtier, merely replied with a mocking laugh. The smirking man quickly regretted his mistake when his prisoner suddenly turned and smashed his manacled wrists into the gaoler's face, removing several of his rotting teeth.

Lord Rich cried out in terror, and fled towards the cell door, but the two other gaolers were skilled in the art of disabling a prisoner and before Thomas could at-tack the lawyer they'd bludgeoned him to the floor. Whilst Thomas gasped for breath, the gaolers dragged him up a long flight of stone stairs to the courtyard. Still groaning Thomas was slung into a cart, guarded by four yeomen officers of the court dressed in a scarlet livery and armed with halberds, as if he were no more than a sack of mil-dewed flour destined for the pig trough. Rich watched the scene and smiled with satisfaction before climbing into a comfortable litter slung between two sleek black horses.

"Bastard took out four of Perkin's teeth so watch him," said the fat gaoler to the sergeant in charge of Lord Rich's escort.

"He'd better not try any tricks with me," replied the sergeant and for emphasis he brandished his halberd over Thomas' recumbent form.

"Hear me well scum, cause me any trouble and you'll go to The Devil with your cock in your hand!" said the sergeant as he held the razor sharp blade dangerously close to Thomas' groin. Thomas still had no wind to reply and before he could recover the cart had lumbered out of the prison's courtyard and into Farringdon Street.

The early spring sunshine was uncharacteristically warm and the little procession soon attracted a large group of spectators. Thomas braced himself for the onslaught of stones, mud and insults that were usually hurled at prisoners being taken for trial but he was surprised by the crowd's good humour. As they passed The Horn Tavern, merchants eating their breakfasts of ale and cheese raised a toast. As the cart trundled through the filth and mire of Fleet Street, apprentices looked up from their labours and gave a loud huzzah. Along The Strand, cooks and kitchen maids waved and blew kisses in his direction. Thomas was utterly mystified by his celebrity until an old woman scuttled up to the cart.

"Bless you sir," said the crone.

"For what?" replied Thomas, trying to keep his balance as cart bounced over a particular bone jarring collection of ruts and potholes.

"For killing Pynch, I was there when you sent that thieving swine to hell and all East Cheap thanks you for it," said the elderly woman, her wizened face beaming with delight.

"Always glad to be of service, but are you quite sure it was me, I thought it was a demon summoned from The Pit who did for Pynch?" said Thomas. He was careful to avoid any admission of guilt, as this hag might be one of Wolsey's paid stooges.

"A demon that you summoned," the woman cackled and she tossed a dried white rose into the straw at the bottom of Thomas' cart.

"None of that mother, we can't have you passing flowers to prisoners, especially ones accused of treachery and witchcraft. Now be off with you or you'll find yourself dangling from the gallows alongside your lover boy," said the court yeoman and he threw the flower into the mud. The crone questioned the sergeant's parentage but she wisely withdrew into the safety of the crowd leaving Thomas to wonder if their meeting had been coincidence or something more meaningful.

The guards may have chased off the crone but they couldn't prevent the huge crowd from following the cart all the way to Westminster. At intervals Lord Rich would poke his head from between his litter's silk curtains to threaten the mob with all manner of painful punishment but Thomas' growing band of supporters steadfastly refused to disperse. Instead they started to sing scurrilous songs accusing Cardinal Wolsey and his servants of all manner of unnatural practices.

Thomas happily led the crowd in their singing and gave a speech urging his followers to resist the tyranny of corrupt clergymen, though he was careful not to say anything that might be considered treason against the king. By the time the cart reached the gateway to the Palace of Westminster, the procession looked like a Bartholomew's Day Fair. Street vendors sold ale to the crowd, acrobats performed tricks and cutpurses silently relieved the richer spectators of their cash. The sentries that guarded the entrance to the palace stared incredulously at the throng that approached them until an exasperated Lord Rich bawled at the captain of the guard.

"Captain, disperse these riotous peasants immediately!" cried the red faced Rich, "The king's justice must not be mocked in this way!"

"At once My Lord," said the captain who lost no time in summoning the rest of his company from the guardroom. The captain's men formed a hedge of steel halberds in front of the palace's gatehouse. This manoeuvre was greeted by howls of protest from the crowd and for a moment, Thomas thought the mob might snatch him from the cart and carry him away to safety. Then someone took a step back and one by one Thomas's supporters drifted away, like pieces of chaff carried off by the wind. As soon as his fickle followers had abandoned their hero, the cart was allowed into the oldest and most derelict of King Henry's palaces.

A few years ago a fire had burned the royal apartments to the ground so the king now preferred to live in his new palace at Greenwich, but the clerics and clerks that carried on the business of government were still lodged at Westminster. The teeth-numbing squeaks of the cart's wooden wheels rattling over the courtyard's cobblestones, only served to remind Thomas that once he'd been welcomed into all Henry's palace by lutes and minstrels. Yet even though he'd returned to Westminster as prisoner he refused to be disheartened by the reversal of his fortunes. He damned Wolsey for a knave and resolved to face his accusers with the defiance and dignity that marked a true Englishman.

The cart stopped outside Westminster Hall, which stood between Edward the Confessor's great abbey church and the river Thames. The medieval hall was home to the highest law courts in England and the steps in front of the entrance were filled with petitioners and pettifoggers busily preparing their cases. Despite the previous crowd's interest in Thomas' procession through the streets, this gaggle of lawyers and their clients were too concerned with their own affairs to pay him any notice.

"Bring the prisoner inside at once, His Eminence does not like to sit in judgement beyond eleven of the clock and it is already past nine," Rich barked to the escort.

"I would hate to inconvenience My Lord Wolsey so I'll gladly take my leave and call another day, now if you would just free me from these chains. I'll be off," said Thomas, holding up his manacled wrists, but the guards failed to see the joke. One of yeomen, standing behind the tumbrel, rammed the butt end of his halberd into the prisoner's back pushing him off balance. Thomas toppled out of the cart and landed face down in a pile of steaming manure.

"You should be thankful, that shit is fresh from the arse of the cardinal's own mule so it's truly blessed," laughed the guard but this time it was Rich who failed to see the joke.

"Enough! Clean that filth from the prisoner's visage at once and be quick about it, the court is waiting," barked the lawyer and he disappeared inside the hall.

Five minutes later Thomas, still dripping from the buckets of water tipped over his head was led into the largest, and busiest, room he'd ever seen. Not even the great banqueting hall at Alnwick Castle could compare with the majesty of Westminster, where every stone declared that this was the seat of Henry's power. The roof, supported by mighty hammer beams, soared above Thomas' head like the vault of heaven whilst the brightly coloured flags decorating the walls seemed to glow like the banners of the angelic host.

The hall itself was divided into different courts by a number of moveable wooden partitions that could be re-arranged to create larger or smaller spaces as necessary. Between these makeshift courts, lawyers scurried about consulting papers, searching for witnesses and cursing the inefficiency of their clerks. The passages were crowded but, like the throng on the steps outside the hall, those inside seemed oblivious to the dead man walking amongst them.

The escorts led Thomas to the court of the King's Bench at far end of the hall. The judges' seating, which gave this court its name, was placed on a dais below an enormous arched window. This seat was separated from the rest of the court by the King's Table, which was covered in a cloth of green and white silk. Flanking the dais were large wooden stands containing several tiers of seats. The first tier on the left was reserved for the jury, but the rest of the seating was open to the public. The escorts manhandled their prisoner towards a second smaller dais in front of the King's Table. This platform was surrounded on three sides by a simple wooden bar. Thomas stood behind this crude balustrade and waited calmly for the proceedings to begin.

News that a trial for something more interesting than debt or detinue was about to start soon reached the ears of others in the hall. Law students, lawyers and even witnesses in other cases began scrambling for a seat in the Court of the King's Bench and the ushers had to use their staffs to stop latecomers from forcing their way in. Once filled with spectators, the court took on the air of an unruly schoolroom. Some of the audience pointed at Thomas and laughed whilst others poured ink down the collars of their unsuspecting colleagues or tried to snatch the square scholars' caps from one another's heads. Not even the arrival of the twelve jurors and the nine solemn faced judges could quell the crowd's excited chatter.

Thomas watched impassively as the white robed, black-capped judges took their seats on the bench. He didn't recognise most of the learned men who were to sit in judgement upon him but he couldn't fail to identify the man in red robes who occupied the central seat. It was Cardinal Wolsey. In his capacity as Lord Chancellor, Wolsey normally sat in the Court of Chancery, which heard civil rather than criminal cases, but no one would question the right of Henry's chief minister to preside over a different court, especially in a case of treason, if he wanted. Once seated, Wolsey carefully adjusted the scarlet cardinal's robes that he habitually wore, even when sitting as a secular judge.

Fearing the worst, Thomas looked around the court to see if an advocate had been appointed to help him plead his case but no one approached the bar where he stood. In that moment, he knew he had no friends in Westminster save the lice that infested his skin. Only these bloodsucking vermin would be glad to see their host spared the gallows so if he were to stand any chance of speaking in his own defence, he had to seize the initiative. Realising he was about to plead for his life, Thomas took a deep breath, spread his arms wide and spoke like Cato in the Roman senate demanding that Carthage must be destroyed.

"My Lords I must protest, My treatment at the hands of the king's officers has been outrageous, I've been assaulted, refused an attorney and given no time to prepare my case. Does the king know of the injustices being committed in his name? Is our Sovereign Lord Henry a foreign tyrant or a King of England sworn to uphold the rights and privileges of free born Englishmen?" said Thomas. He spoke in a strong, clear voice and the crowd were delighted by the prisoner's pugnacious courage. They cheered and applauded Thomas loudly but the cardinal, whose face had turned as red as his scarlet robes, exploded with rage.

"Silence traitor! You're not permitted to speak in this court save to answer the lawful questions asked by your prosecutors," Wolsey boomed.

"I may not speak in my defence? Even Pilate did not deny our Lord Jesus the chance to defend himself," said Thomas.

"Our Lord's name must not be allowed to pass through the lips of a traitor, heretic and necromancer, only an attorney may speak on his behalf," cried a white haired judge, covering his ears like an apothecary who fears the mandrake's screams.

"But I've not been allowed to engage an attorney," insisted Thomas.

"Have you the money to pay an attorney?" Wolsey asked and Thomas shook his head. "Then the prisoner will remain silent or he will be removed and his case tried in absentia. The clerk will now read the charges."

Wolsey waved his hand and a shrivelled old scribe, who sat hunched behind a small desk below the King's Table, began to read from a parchment.

"Thomas Devilstone, formerly of the parish of Dilston in the Franchise of Tynedale," intoned the clerk, "you are hereby charged with the grave and heinous crimes of heresy, necromancy and high treason contrary to laws of God and your king. The details thereof are ..."

The clerk paused to clear his throat.

"... That firstly, on numerous occasions, you did summon demons from the deepest pits of hell to instruct you in the black arts of the warlock and aid you in your treason against your lawful king Henry Octavius. Secondly that in summoning said demons you committed the most serious acts of blasphemy and sacrilege against the Holy Name of our Blessed Saviour the Lord Jesus Christ. Thirdly, that by summoning said demons you have shown that you hold the most dangerous and heretical views contrary to the wisdom of Holy Mother Church. Fourthly..."

By now Thomas had stopped listening but the clerk continued to list the prisoner's alleged offences, including the precise times and dates when he'd summoned the servants of Beelzebub. In his flat monotone, which somehow made the crimes seem more lurid, the clerk described how Thomas had danced with the five legged beast *Buer* when the sun was in the house of Sagittarius, cavorted with the four headed demon *Asmodeus* when the sun was in Aquarius and so on. As each President of Hell was named, the crowd gasped whilst the judges crossed themselves and muttered silent prayers lest their souls be imperilled by merely hearing the demons' blasphemous titles. Thomas even glimpsed a judge kissing one of the amulets he'd made several months ago.

"These are your crimes," said the clerk, "how do you plead?"

"I will not dignify such an outrageous abuse of the king's justice with a plea. I freely admit that I've studied the wisdom of the ancients but only to aid the king in his search for an heir, no more and no less. If this be treason than call me traitor!" Thomas declared. Again the crowd cheered and again the cardinal was not amused.

"Enter a plea of not guilty and call the witness," Wolsey muttered to the clerk who obediently wrote in his ledger and gestured to an usher standing in the corner of the courtroom. The usher opened a door in the partition and an apple cheeked, buxom, young maiden entered the court.

"Stand there and take the oath," said the usher pointing to the far corner of the King's table. The girl did as she was told and stared demurely at the floor as she mumbled her promise to tell the truth before God.

"State your name witness," said the cardinal.

"They call me Joan of Cheapside," the girl said sweetly. Cheap is the word, thought Thomas.

"Are you engaged in honest work?" Wolsey added kindly.

"I am, my father died of the sweating sickness some years back so I help my mother keep our shop. We sell gloves and ever so nice they are. We only use the very best calf and kid skin so they're even worthy of such noble hands as yours My Lord," said the girl and she ended her advertisement with a little curtsy. Thomas rolled his eyes to heaven.

He'd heard of the professional 'men of straw' who strolled between the courts of Westminster Hall with a corn stalk in their shoe to show their willingness to bear false witness but he'd never dreamed there were also women of straw. He wondered how much the trollop had been paid to perjure herself but it must have been a pretty penny for Joan of Cheapside seemed to be an accomplished liar. Having won the judges' hearts with the story of her tragic childhood, she fluttered her eyelashes and brushed her flaxen hair from her face at exactly the right moments to beguile the jurymen.

"Mistress Joan," said Wolsey kindly, "please tell the court exactly what you observed on the night of St Joseph's day last."

"Well your honour," said the girl, "I went to the common beyond Aldgate looking for mushrooms. It was just before dawn, that's the best time for mushrooms, and I saw a very queer light coming from behind some hawthorn trees. I was afraid but something drew me towards that coppice. When I got to the trees, and saw what was going on, I wanted to run away as fast as my legs would carry me but I was as helpless as a pet bird tied by a thread. Oh sir, please don't make say any more, it was so horrible I can't bear to speak of it."

Joan gave a little sob to lend weight to her calumny and the crowd gave a deep sigh of sympathy for the innocent maiden's plight.

"You must go on my dear, your God and your king command it," said Wolsey pressing his fingers together in a gesture of quiet meditation. The spectators leaned forward in their seats in anticipation of what the girl was about to say and they were not disappointed.

"Very well, if I must speak then so be it. I saw a man dressed in a long black robe standing before a large wooden cross that was as tall as a cherry tree. The man looked like one of the black friars of St Dominic but he was no priest because the cross was upside down and ... it was on fire."

Joan paused for effect and the crowd dutifully sucked in their breath.

"You see, no Christian would burn the symbol of our salvation, the prisoner is clearly guilty and I say he should burn at the sake to teach all heretics that the fires of hell await them beyond the grave!" said one of the judges. The crowd roared their approval but the cardinal raised his hand for silence.

"You must allow the witness to finish her testimony, pray go on my dear," insisted Wolsey. The girl nodded and continued her story.

"The man had a long wand in his hand and he used it to draw a circle on the ground whilst he muttered an incantation in a strange language. In the next moment, a column of red smoke began to rise from the centre of the circle and, as I watched, it began to take the form of a magical beast."

"The man had opened a gate of hell and released a demon!" cried another of the judges.

"That was exactly it!" agreed the girl. "The smoke became a hideous demon, with the horned head and cloven hooves of a goat, but it smelled worse than any goat."

"Baphomet, the demonic beast worshipped by the disgraced Templars!" shrieked a third judge.

"But who was the man in the robe who summoned this fiend?" asked Wolsey barely able to contain his own prurient excitement.

"It was him over there," said the girl and she pointed directly at Thomas.

"Then what happened?" said another of the judges breathlessly.

"Oh but it is too shameful to relate," wailed the girl with false modesty.

"You must tell us," said the judge who had little flecks of spittle forming at the corners of his mouth. "Come, have courage my dear!"

The girl took a deep breath and began again:

"The man in the black robe caught sight of me hiding in the bushes. He looked at me with eyes that shone yellow, like the eyes of a dog. I couldn't look away, he held me in his thrall. He spoke no words but I could hear his voice in my head. He ordered me to step forward and I could do nothing but obey. He bade me disrobe and my fingers obeyed his silent command even though my modesty urged me to resist. Slowly I unlaced my bodice and my petticoats and shed my garments one by one until I stood in that glade as naked as the day I was born."

The girl paused and rubbed her hands slowly over her ample breasts and slim waist to show just how much pleasure the sight of her naked form could excite in any male creature, natural or supernatural. At least two of the elderly judges cried out at thought of a young girl standing naked and helpless in front of a burning cross and a lascivious demon.

"And then?" croaked a judge.

"The man in the robe ordered the demon to ravish me," sighed the girl, "I had to give myself to Satan in all his wickedness. He even made me ... kiss The Devil's Lance!"

The crowd erupted into pandemonium. Half the spectators crowed with delight at the girl's lewd tale whilst others insisted the satanic fornicator must suffer death this very day for corrupting such an innocent maiden.

"What nonsense is this? This harlot is clearly lying! How much has she been paid for her testimony?" yelled Thomas, trying to make himself heard over the uproar. Unfortunately for him, the veracity of the girl's testimony was utterly irrelevant for the crowd had thoroughly enjoyed her story. They stamped their feet on the wooden platforms and cheered until the din threatened to disrupt the business in all the other courts.

"Silence, or I shall have the court cleared!" bellowed Wolsey and his imperious voice echoing around the hall's ancient stones had the desired effect. Fearing they might miss more of the girl's highly colourful story, the crowd settled back into their seats.

"Pray continue," insisted Wolsey once order had returned.

"As the demon sated his lust, I was seized by the madness of Venus and I don't know quite what happened after that," said the girl in a hushed whisper. "But I remember hearing the man in the robe whispering with the demon. They were plotting to sacrifice me to The Devil and in exchange for my soul Satan would make Queen Catherine cease her monthly courses so she would become barren before her time."

"Treason!" cried one of the judges leaping to his feet and pointing an accusing finger at Thomas, "Clearly the prisoner has plotted against the natural fortune of his sovereign and the safety of the realm! No wonder the Queen cannot bear a healthy child if warlocks such as he cast their wicked spells upon her!"

"This is ridiculous! If I'd sacrificed this whore how come she's standing here? And why would I wish the queen to become barren? How would I profit from such wickedness?" Thomas countered.

"You were paid by the agents of France or the House of York," retorted Wolsey accusingly.

"Then where's your evidence?" cried Thomas holding his arms wide so the crowd could see he was dressed in rags but Wolsey raised his hand to signify the trial was at an end.

"Enough, there is nothing more to be said. The accused's guilt is confirmed by the testimony of the witness and she may go," said Wolsey. The girl curtsied and flounced from the room, clearly pleased with her performance. Thomas wondered if she knew that her lies had condemned him to a brutal and painful death. Most probably she did and she didn't care.

"The jury is instructed to find the prisoner Thomas Devilstone guilty on all charges," continued Wolsey, addressing the jury's nervous looking foreman. The other judges on the bench nodded their agreement and Thomas knew he was doomed. The niceties of legal procedure were maintained, and the jury was allowed to retire to consider their verdict, but the outcome was never in doubt. No juror would dare disobey the cardinal or they too would hang. After less than a quarter of an hour the jurymen filed back into court and pronounced the prisoner guilty of conspiring with evil spirits to prevent the Queen's conception of a child, a crime that was nothing short of High Treason.

"The punishment for traitors has been established by common practice since the days of King Edward Primus and it is my solemn duty to pass sentence," said Wolsey with a noticeable air of satisfaction.

"It is the order of this court that the prisoner Thomas Devilstone be detained at His Majesty's pleasure until the appointed day when he shall suffer execution in a manner befitting a necromancer, heretic and traitor. On that day he shall be drawn on a hurdle to Smithfield and there hanged by the neck till he be half dead. He shall then be cut down alive, his privy parts shall be cut off, his belly ripped asunder, his bowels drawn from his body and burnt whilst he still lives. His corpse shall be divided into four quarters, one quarter to be set up over each of the four gates of the city of London and his head set upon London Bridge until it doth corrupt and decay. Officers of the court, do your duty."

The moment Wolsey finished passing sentence the crowd became a baying mob. The lawyers, students and other spectators stood on the benches and howled for the prisoner to be taken outside immediately and dismembered in the Palace Yard, lest he use his powers of witchcraft to turn into a bat-winged angel of Hell and fly from the king's justice. Fortunately for Thomas, the court officers ignored the crowd's pleas but they took tight hold of their prisoner's arms, just in case.

5

THE TOWER OF LONDON

With the sound of the crowd's blood lust ringing in his ears, Thomas was led from the court but he was not returned to the Fleet Prison. Instead he was loaded with more chains, bundled through a side door and taken to The King's Stairs, the river jetty that served Westminster Palace. Here a small barge, painted in the green and white livery of the Tudors, waited to convey him to a more secure place of imprisonment - The Tower of London.

As the bargemen rowed the boat out into the Thames, Thomas' mind began to spin like the eddies formed by their gaily painted oars. If he could reach Southwark perhaps he could disappear into the slums and hovels on the south bank of the Thames like the Nubian he'd met in the Fleet Prison but though the river here was narrower than at Tilbury, his chances of reaching the opposite bank by swimming were just as remote. If he tried to leap over the boat's side his guards would hack him to pieces before he reached the gunwale and even if he evaded their weapons the heavy chains that secured his wrists and ankles would send him straight to the bottom of the river.

Yet Thomas could hardly complain that his sentence was unjust or undeserved. The trial may have been a sham, and he sincerely doubted that the girl had really seen what she'd claimed to have seen, but he *was* guilty of casting spells to raise demons in the coppice beyond Aldersgate that night. In fact Thomas had cast great many spells, on a great many occasions, but he'd never burned a holy cross, still less ravished a naked virgin in front of a voyeuristic, goat-headed demon.

His purpose in performing the ritual that had sealed his doom was to try and summon the demon *Astaroth*, the bat-winged, dragon-riding, serpent-bearer who must answer any question asked by a necromancer. Thomas had hoped to force this fiend to explain why the astrological charts he'd prepared with such care had failed to reveal the truth about Queen Catherine's false pregnancy. Nevertheless, though he'd performed the spell and spoken the incantation exactly as described in his *grimoire*, the only thing that had appeared in the coppice had been a rather nervous badger.

Though angry at the spell's failure, he'd not been surprised when yet another demon had refused to answer his summons. During his years studying the Dark Arts, both he and Agrippa had performed hundreds of similar rituals without the slightest hint of success but this final fiasco had been the last straw. As he'd stood alone in the coppice, chilled by the cold light of dawn, he'd finally realised that his tutor's rejection of the occult had been the right choice after all. There and then, he too had resolved to abandon his studies and devote himself to more earthly, and more profitable, pursuits.

After the debacle of that last spell, Thomas had returned to his apartments in the king's palace at Greenwich but he'd known he would have to leave London as soon as possible if he hoped to keep a whole skin. His only chance of survival was to join the last Yorkist pretender to the English throne who'd established a court of Yorkist exiles in the free Bishopric of Metz but at least Thomas knew this city well. He and Agrippa had spent two years there during their travels, and so he'd decided to travel to Burgundy and offer his services to the 'White Rose'.

With the king still distracted by the queen's false pregnancy Thomas reckoned he'd have a few days grace before Henry could be persuaded to sign his former favourite's death warrant. Thomas vowed to use what time he had to settle his affairs and slip quietly out of London but that very night an anonymous note, warning him that Wolsey's men were about to arrest *the king's warlock* had been slipped under his door. Without a second thought, Thomas had snatched up the sword his father had bequeathed him, stuffed his most precious *grimoire* into the lining of his cloak and fled into the labyrinth of tenements to the east of St Paul's Cathedral.

Besides the warning, the note had urged Thomas to *meet with friends at The Boar's Head in East Cheap* but fearing a trap he'd preferred to make his own way out of the city. He'd sold his rings and other jewellery to raise the money for his passage but the first captain he'd approached had cheated him of his gold. The few shillings Thomas had managed to keep had soon been spent and he'd been forced to approach the moneylender Pynch. If only he'd chosen to trust the author of the note he might be on a ship bound for the continent instead of sitting in a barge heading for The Tower.

"Cheer up," said one of the yeoman, noticing the strange look on Thomas' face. "Tomorrow's Ash Wednesday, the beginning of Lent, so they won't chop off your head for at least another forty days."

"Even when we do cut off his head why should he worry?" said another guard mischievously. "He's a powerful wizard so all he has to do is pick up his head and sew it back on!"

"That's as maybe," said a third guard joining in the fun, "but he's also sentenced to be quartered so if we've cut off his arms, how can he pick up his head!"

The boatmen burst into laughter but Thomas ignored them, he was too busy trying to think of a way out of his predicament. Slowly the boat drew nearer to the grey walled fortress he'd struggled so hard to avoid and after a few more minutes they reached The Tower's Water Gate, the entrance reserved for traitors under sentence of death. There was an agonising screech of wood scraping against ancient stone as the gate's portcullis was raised.

The barge passed under the quay called the King's Wharf and entered the moat that surrounded The Tower's outer ward, here a second portcullis guarded the entrance to the inner ward. This too was raised and the barge passed into a stone chamber beneath the massive bastion of the aptly named St Thomas' Tower. The lapping of the oily water and the hollow splashes of the oars echoed eerily around the weed choked vault, making Thomas feel he was being rowed across the Styx to suffer all the torments of Tartarus.

As he climbed out of the boat, Thomas wondered what it would be like to feel the hangman's rope slowly choking the life from his body, or the cold steel of the executioner's knife slicing through his genitals. Yet for all his fears, his arrival was a curiously pleasant experience. He was greeted by no less a person than Sir William Kingston, the Constable of The Tower, whom Thomas had glimpsed on the battlefield of Flodden. Though Sir William didn't recognised his new prisoner, he did treat Thomas as if he were his honoured guest.

Sir William ordered Thomas' chains to be removed, he was allowed to wash and given his pick of clothing from a large wooden chest. Thomas picked out a white linen shirt, smart green doublet, matching breeches and bright red hose but he insisted on keeping his old cloak. Sir William had no objection though he ordered the garment to be searched. Thomas held his breath as a warder ran his fingers along the hem and seams but he need not have worried. The gaoler found no hidden dagger or other weapon so he handed the garment back to Thomas.

If he was surprised at being given such a warm welcome, he was even more astonished by his lodgings. Instead of being cast into a stygian cell, Thomas was taken to a light and airy chamber high in the Beauchamp Tower. The room measured a dozen paces across and boasted three tall, loophole windows in vaulted bays. The windows were unglazed but shuttered and a fire burned in the grate so the room felt warm and dry. The furniture consisted of a bed, table and chair, and though rushlights rather than candles burned in the sconces the room was luxurious compared to The Fleet's pestilential dungeon. Thomas asked his gaolers if all prisoners were so fortunate but the warder would only mumble that the proper fees had been paid then withdrew, locking the door behind him.

Once Thomas was alone he strolled to the nearest window and peered out. The Beauchamp Tower was located on the western side of the fortress and formed part of the wall that surrounded the inner ward. From this vantage point he could see across the narrow outer ward to a second wall and beyond that there was the moat. He was just a two hundred feet from freedom but to escape he would have to widen the windows, climb down fifty feet of ice smooth wall, scale the outer ward's equally un-climbable parapets and swim across the foetid waters of the moat. Moreover he would have to accomplish all these tasks unseen by The Tower's ever-watchful yeomen warders.

Cursing his luck, Thomas turned away from the window and stretched out on the bed to think. For a few hours he amused himself by incinerating lice in the rushlight by his bed and as each verminous insect popped in the flame, a new plan of escape flashed into his mind. There were as many ways to leave a prison as to enter it but the greatest obstacle to his freedom was the fact he was alone. Without allies he couldn't bribe guards, smuggle disguises into his cell or steal keys and he began to wish that Bos, Prometheus and Quintana were with him. Together, the four of them might fight their way to freedom but as far as he knew his former cellmates were still rotting in The Fleet's dungeons.

Having exhausted the supply of lice large enough to catch, Thomas tried to sleep but he'd barely closed his eyes when he heard the sound of a key turning in the cell door's lock. He was about to tell his visitor to go to hell but before he could speak a warder ushered an attractive young woman through the door. The girl wore an expensive gown of dark red velvet over a kirtle of crimson silk and her black woollen cloak was trimmed with white fox fur. Delicate gold chains hung about her slender neck and her embroidered French hood was studded with pearls. Thomas recognised her at once, it was the girl who'd sheltered him, albeit briefly, during his rooftop flight across Cheapside. As the girl dismissed the warder from the cell, Thomas rose from his bed and made a polite bow.

"Mistress Anne Boleyn, you do me great honour by your presence," he said and the girl blushed.

"So you've discovered my name and I've discovered yours, indeed I knew it the moment I laid eyes on you in my chamber, you're the notorious wizard Thomas Devilstone," she said.

"I'm flattered you know me Mistress Anne but to what do I the owe the pleasure of this visit?" Thomas asked. He wasn't surprised the girl had recognised him as he'd been well-known at court but he did wonder if she'd come to enquire about her missing necklaces. If she wanted them back, she would have to ask the light-fingered constables of Tilbury.

"I must beg your pardon but I have a request which, if you see fit to grant, would earn my eternal gratitude," she said hopefully.

"Forgive me Mistress but how would your gratitude profit me? Can your thanks free me from this cell before I am butchered?" Thomas replied.

"Maybe it can, as you know my father is not without some influence at court and at the very least he can make your stay here more comfortable. It was Lord Boleyn who paid to have your fetters removed and to be lodged here, rather than in a dungeon. Even if he fails to secure your release, my father can have your executioners bribed so your death will be quick and painless," Anne boasted.

"That's hardly a great comfort and does Lord Boleyn know I was in your bedchamber the other night?" said Thomas.

"No but it wouldn't matter if he did. He hates Wolsey and he'll aid any enemy of the cardinal, even one condemned for sorcery, so your life need not end on the scaffold. My father and I have need of your special talents and if you can cast a certain spell for us we will secure your release and pardon," she said. Thomas was about to point out if he possessed any magical powers he would have used them weeks ago to aid his escape but he needed friends and if there was the slightest chance the scheming Lord Boleyn could help him, he had to listen to what his youngest daughter had to say.

Much to Thomas' surprise, Anne confirmed Quintana's story. She admitted that her older sister now carried the king's bastard but far from securing the ambitious

Lord Boleyn's position at court Mary's pregnancy had ruined her father's plans. Lord Boleyn had intended that his eldest daughter should supplant Catherine of Aragon in both Henry's bed and on the throne but the king had been happy to keep Mary as his mistress and had steadfastly refused to put aside his Spanish wife. Though Mary's pregnancy now made it impossible for her to remain at court, Lord Boleyn had a second daughter and he was determined that she should succeed where her sister had failed.

"I've already told you, it's been foretold that I'm to be Henry's queen and mother of his heir but my father fears that spells have been cast that blind Henry to the will of God. Why else would he remain wedded to a barren Spanish sow? But, if you could break these spells and help me fulfil my destiny, my father's gratitude would know no bounds. I know it will be difficult to cast such a spell in this dreadful place, but you can teach me the secret knowledge so I may break the curses myself," said Anne and as she finished speaking Thomas felt the green shoots of his hope wither and die.

The girl was clearly deranged and Thomas tried to tell her that it took years of painstaking study to learn the dark arts of necromancy but Anne held up her hand for silence. She was wearing the same white gloves she'd worn when they'd first met but now she slowly removed them. For a moment Thomas failed to understand the significance of her gesture but his mouth fell open in surprise when he realised that Mistress Anne Boleyn had six fingers on her left hand.

"You have the mark of a witch," Thomas gasped and he couldn't help but stare at the extra digit that protruded from the lowest joint of Anne's little finger. It was short and stubby but it had a fingernail and a knuckle.

"Yes I have the mark of one who's been chosen by Hecate but not the power and I don't know why. I've studied the famous *grimoires* till I can recite the incantations in my sleep but I can never cast spells that work. Perhaps with your help I can learn," Anne replied hopefully.

"Given time I'm sure I could teach you all I know but I'm to be sliced like an Easter ham once Lent is passed, Do you really think you can win the heart of a king in forty days?" said Thomas ruefully.

"Love is a thunderbolt and Henry is a man of passion, both strike quickly," said Anne with a shrug but Thomas was under no such illusion.

Even if he performed the proper rituals immediately, he knew that any spell was bound to fail and his head would be rotting on a spike long before Anne Boleyn could drag the king to her bed, let alone to the altar. Yet it also occurred to him that possessing a genuine ability to command supernatural forces didn't matter. As long as Anne *believed* he was a powerful necromancer, he could bend her actions to his will just as effectively as if he'd cast a spell. Moreover, if he was to stand any chance of escaping The Tower, he needed someone who could enter and leave Henry's fortress at will.

"Very well, My Lady, you have a bargain. I'll help you win Henry's heart and a crown but to secure the love of a king will not be easy. I'll need certain items and their price will be high," said Thomas.

"Higher than the cost of the three gold chains missing from my chamber?" Anne said mischievously.

"Consider those a first payment and before I can begin to unlock the gates to a kingdom, I'll need a second," Thomas replied and he told Anne that he wouldn't be able to cast such a momentous spell without the help of his assistants who still languished in The Fleet. When Anne looked at him in confusion, he insisted that for the spell to work he needed his apprentices to bury certain magical amulets in three different places but at exactly the same time. It was all nonsense but a plan was beginning to form in Thomas' mind and he would need the men in The Fleet to ensure its success.

Despite her claim to have studied magic Anne believed his lie without question, her only concern was how to secure the men's freedom but Thomas assured her that nothing could be easier if Lord Boleyn was prepared to spend a little money. All her father had to do was bribe the Warden of the Fleet to record in his ledgers that these three prisoners had died of the fever that infected every gaol and no one would mourn, or even notice, the deaths of three insignificant foreigners. Once they were officially 'dead' it would be a simple matter to smuggle these men to a discreet inn, such as The Tabard in Southwark, and have them wait there for further instructions.

Clapping her hands in delight, Anne readily agreed to the plan and she listened carefully as Thomas told her all the things he would need in order to cast the spell properly. He also instructed his new acolyte as to which apothecaries could supply the different items and made her repeat the list until she'd memorised everything. When Thomas was satisfied, Anne threw her arms around his neck and kissed him but, just as before, she preferred to play the coquette rather than the courtesan. When Thomas tried to pull her closer, she wriggled free of his arms and scampered to the door.

"Not yet, first you must cast the spell to help me win Henry's love. Only when I'm queen will you have the reward your proud manhood desires," she said cryptically and before Thomas could stop her she'd called for the warder to let her out. Thomas watched her leave and noted that she didn't look back or offer any promise that she'd keep her side of the bargain. In that moment, Thomas knew he was being deceived. As soon as she had the king between her legs, Mistress Boleyn would forget him and his only reward would be to die a hideous death.

Night fell and as the lonely hours passed, Thomas became utterly convinced that the Boleyns' promise of rescue was a complete fiction and as soon as he'd cast the spell they'd stand by whilst his death sentence was carried out. His reasoning was simple: if by some miracle Anne received a proposal of marriage from Henry, Thomas would have to die to ensure his silence as any suspicion of witchcraft would send Anne and her father to their deaths. If Lord Boleyn was equal to his reputation, he'd probably have Thomas' tongue cut out so he couldn't shout any accusations from the steps of the scaffold. On the other hand, if the king refused to take Anne as his bride, the vengeful Boleyns would let Thomas hang as punishment for his failure.

Whichever way he looked, Thomas saw an open grave in front of him but he had no intention of trusting his life to a man prepared to sacrifice his daughters' virtue on the altar of his own ambition. Provided Lord Boleyn freed the three men he'd met in The Fleet, Thomas could engineer his own escape and in spite of their earlier mockery, he felt sure that Quintana, Prometheus and Bos would feel bound by the rules of honour to help him.

Once his 'apprentices' were safely lodged at The Tabard, Thomas could send them details of his escape plan but if he wanted to keep his intentions hidden from Lord Boleyn this wouldn't be easy. Encoding his message, using a letter or number cipher, would alert Lord Boleyn that Thomas was up to something, moreover, he'd have to send the key to any such code in advance of the letter. He could ask Anne to deliver the key separately from the message but, if the whole purpose of the cipher was to keep Lord Boleyn from knowing Thomas' plans, entrusting the man's daughter with the means to decode his encrypted messages would render the entire operation utterly pointless.

The only way Thomas could be sure Anne wouldn't betray him to her father was to convince her that any letter she carried contained nothing but vital instructions on how to complete the spell, yet Prometheus, Bos and Quintana had to be able to understand the true meaning without the aid of the cipher's key. The alternative was to find a different messenger but, locked in his cell, he had no hope of finding anyone else to deliver his letters, coded or otherwise. All the next day, Thomas cudgelled his brains in an attempt to unravel this conundrum and he found the solution in what he'd learned from the German magician, cryptographer and Bishop of Wurzburg Johannes Trithemius.

As part of his apprenticeship with Agrippa, Thomas had studied Trithemius' book *Steganographia* which described how anyone could conceal secret messages in plain sight. Trithemius had certainly practised what he'd preached and he'd been so successful in applying his principles to his book, it had been banned by the Holy Inquisition. The pope's pious inquisitors couldn't see past the 'magic spells' that promised to compel demons into carrying secret messages on behalf of the necromancer who'd summoned them but, for those with the wits to understand the book's hidden meaning, this learned work was actually a complete guide to creating codes and ciphers that didn't need a key.

The simplest of Trithemius' devices was to draw an innocent looking picture so Thomas begged to be allowed to have quills, inks and paper. A few days later The Constable of the Tower, in the hope his prisoner might want to write a confession, granted the request and Thomas spent the hours waiting for Anne's return working on an intricate drawing that combined elements of both The Nativity and The Crucifixion.

Slowly and carefully, he drew the three magi carrying their gifts of gold, frankincense and myrrh to the holy stable. He also drew the Rock of Calvary, with its three crosses but added some details that did not appear in the gospels. To the left of the stable, Thomas drew the Tower of London with The Devil imprisoned in a dungeon beneath its stone walls. He also depicted the kings Caspar, Balthazar and Melchior wearing the habits of Christian friars instead of the robes of eastern princes and their faces bore more than a passing resemblance to Bos, Quintana and Prometheus. Finally he added a fourth monk with his cowl raised so his face couldn't be seen. Thomas was no artist but he became so engrossed in his labours he didn't hear Sir William Kingston enter his cell.

"What are you doing prisoner," said Sir William and before Thomas could answer, The Constable of the Tower had snatched up the drawing. Sir William studied the picture closely and demanded an immediate explanation of its meaning or Thomas would be sent to the rack.

"There's no need for torture My Lord I'll gladly enlighten you," said Thomas hurriedly and he quickly explained that because he had no property to speak of, he had nothing to pay for a priest to say a mass for his soul after his execution. He'd therefore drawn this picture in the hope that the Canons of Aldgate could make a woodcut and produce prints that could be sold to pilgrims visiting The Confessor's tomb in Westminster Abbey.

"It's my earnest wish that any money raised will be used for the relief of the poor and for a mass to be sung on the anniversary of my death," Thomas added and he lowered his head to convince The Constable of his contrition. Sir William grunted his acceptance of the story but he continued to study the picture carefully. After an agonising silence, he asked why the magi were dressed as monks rather than as kings of the east and Thomas replied that his intention was to show that the great mendicant orders of Augustinians, Dominicans, Franciscans and Carmelites were the legitimate descendants of Christ's apostles but still Sir William wasn't entirely satisfied.

"And why is Satan imprisoned in *my* Tower of London? Are you dissatisfied with your lodgings, do you wish to complain of your treatment here?" he snapped.

"Not at all My Lord but it's not Satan in The Tower of London, it's King Herod in the Antonia Fortress. I've never been to Jerusalem and I don't know what Herod's palace looks like so I've drawn this royal castle to represent Herod's abode," said Thomas, feigning indignance at Sir William's failure to recognise his artistic talents. Try as he might The Constable couldn't see any hidden meaning in the picture, and he could hardly object to a condemned prisoner trying to make his peace with God, so he returned the drawing to Thomas.

"Here, continue with your work, but you'd better finish quickly. Holy Week begins soon and when Eastertide has passed, you'll go to the scaffold," said Sir William and he strode from the cell.

6

SOUTHWARK

The day after Thomas had completed his picture Anne returned. In truth, he was beginning to doubt he'd ever see her again but it was a measure of the Boleyn family's desperation that she'd brought everything he'd asked for hidden in special pockets sewn into her voluminous petticoats. Thomas dared not ask what it had cost to bribe the warders not to search her, perhaps her high birth had been enough, all he knew was that he now had everything he needed.

There was a bag of coarse grained saltpetre, a pound of lard, a jar of Spanish syrup, a long length of match cord and three short lengths of 'black match', that is strips of paper which had been soaked in an elixir of gunpowder and rolled into fuses. Most importantly of all, Anne had also brought a small cage containing a live bat, a pestle, a mortar and a little wooden jewellery box. Thomas told Anne to place the items on his bed whilst he dragged the chamber's table into the centre of the room.

"My apprentices, are they safe?" Thomas asked, when he was satisfied the table was aligned with the four cardinal points of the compass.

"It cost my father ten pounds of pepper to bribe the Warden of the Fleet but the world now thinks your men's souls are with God and their bodies buried in the Smithfield plague pit," she replied.

"Good, then we can start to guide Cupid's arrow to King Henry's heart," said Thomas happily.

He placed the saltpetre, syrup, lard and the cage containing the bat at the four different corners of the chamber's table, explaining that each item represented one of the four elements of fire, water earth and air. He then placed the mortar and pestle in the centre of the table and coiled the match cord into a loop. Placing the cord around the mortar's earthenware bowl, he told Anne that this arrangement represented the alchemical symbol for the female principle, that is to say herself as the subject of the charm. In fact Thomas needed none of these items for the spell but he did require them for his own escape and he'd no intention of revealing their true purpose to anyone.

Fortunately Anne didn't question his actions and with the table prepared, Thomas opened the jewellery box she'd brought. Inside was a velvet pouch containing a letter B, made from pure gold, with three freshwater pearls, on little gold chains, dangling beneath. On the back of the B, the names ANNE and HENRY had been engraved and the jewel was attached to a long pearl necklace of incalculable value. For a moment Thomas couldn't speak as he admired the exquisite craftsmanship.

"Will it do? It was made by the goldsmiths of St Pauls, just as you instructed," Anne asked nervously.

"It's perfect," said Thomas. Anne breathed a sigh of relief and listened intently as her teacher told her that the gold represented eternity, as it was the only metal that time couldn't corrupt, whilst the three pearls stood for obedience, fidelity and modesty, the chief virtues of a wife. Thomas insisted that they were there to remind Anne that she must not take the king to her bed until he'd made her his bride but once again this had nothing to do with the spell. Thomas merely wanted to punish the lustful usurper who'd abandoned him by making him wait as long as possible for his prize.

"And the B is for my name," said Anne hopefully.

"No, the B stands for *Bel*, the demon who rules men's passions, and it's merely a happy accident that your family name also begins with this letter. Ordinarily, you must inscribe the name of *Bel*, your name and the name of your desired lover on the shoulder blade of a capon and burn it whilst speaking the spell. However, to win a king's love, I needed an amulet more suited to royalty than chicken bones so I asked for this jewel to be made. Now we need one more thing before we can begin," said Thomas and he carefully began to open the seams of his old cloak.

His weeks living as an outlaw had robbed Thomas of the jewelled rings on his fingers, the gold chains around his neck and his father's sword, but his most valuable possession was still safely hidden in his cloak. When he'd fled from the king's palace weeks ago, he'd been sure to take his copy of *The Munich Handbook of Demonic Magic* with him and whilst in hiding he'd sewn its pages into his cloak. The fine vellum on which the book had been printed was as soft as Irish linen and the warder who had searched Thomas on his arrival at The Tower hadn't detected his garment's hidden riches.

This *grimoire* contained everything a sorcerer needed to know about conjuring spirits, casting spells and fashioning charms but it wasn't particularly rare. Most serious students of Natural Philosophy had a copy in their libraries but Thomas' edition was unique because it'd once belonged to Leonardo da Vinci and its margins were full of the artist's designs for new weapons of war. To protect his inventions, Leonardo had described their construction in an impenetrable code, which Thomas had yet to decipher otherwise he'd have sold the secrets years ago, but for the time being this did not matter. All he needed was the original authors' advice to the lovelorn.

One by one, Thomas retrieved the thin sheets of vellum and placed them in the right order. When the book was reassembled, he found the pages devoted to love charms and began to study the magic symbol required by Anne's spell. When he was satisfied, he took a blank sheet of paper and a quill, left over from his recent labours, and drew a large shield. Inside this escutcheon, he drew a single vertical band bisected by sixteen horizontal bands. After consulting the handbook again, Thomas wrote one of the spell's magic words in each alternate horizontal band. These were:

AYSEL CASTYEL LAMISYEL RABAM ERLAIN
OLAM BELAM

Where the blank horizontal bands crossed the vertical band, he wrote the letters A-B-E-L-A-N, but in the twelfth band he wrote the word LEO, the astrological sign associated with kingship and England. When he'd finished, he unfastened Anne's jewel from the necklace, wrapped it in the paper and placed it in the mortar. Finally he went to the fireplace, took a burning splint from the grate and touched it to the paper. Anne gasped as it burst into flame but Thomas ignored her and concentrated on reciting the proper incantation:

> *I command the spirit BEL,*
> *Not to rest until he causes the king's heart to*
> *burn with desire for his servant ANNE.*
> *May it be that HENRY cannot sleep, wake or*
> *do anything until ANNE fulfils his desire.*
> *As the Lord of Hosts commands Lucifer,*
> *so I command thee.*
> *Let it be so.*

As Thomas finished speaking, the flame flickered and died, leaving the golden B surrounded by a pile of smouldering white ash. Thomas quickly retrieved the jewel, placed it carefully in Anne's hand and closed her fingers around it before using the pestle to grind the ash into a fine powder. He then took the mortar to the window and blew the powdered ash into the night. Only now did he allow Anne to look at the jewel and she saw that, apart from a few flecks of soot, it was undamaged.

"It's a miracle!" she whispered.

"You must wear the jewel on your body and never take it off until the king is yours," said Thomas as he reattached the jewel to the necklace and as Anne obligingly lifted her hood, he fastened it around her long, slender neck.

"That's all, the king is mine?" she whispered, admiring the amulet that now graced her bosom.

"Not quite, you must take a letter to my apprentices, it contains coded instructions telling them where they must bury the three charms that will seal the king inside the spell's triangle of power," said Thomas and he insisted that unless his men inscribed the alchemical symbol for the masculine principle on the very face of England, they could not hope to influence its king. Anne begged him to tell her what these amulets were but Thomas was adamant that such secrets could only be revealed to those who'd been initiated into the higher levels of arcane knowledge or the charms would lose their power. Once again he was speaking the purest moonshine but Anne believed him implicitly.

"I'll do as you ask," she said fingering the jewel around her neck and taking the coded picture that Thomas had placed inside an oilcloth wallet.

"Good, once the charms are buried the king will lose his heart to you. When this will be I cannot say but Henry won't be able to escape his destiny," said Thomas. Anne squeaked with delight, pressed the wallet to her heart and called for the warder to let her out of the cell. As she flounced through the door, Thomas noted that she'd said nothing about when he could expect to be freed but it didn't matter. If the rest of his plan succeeded, he'd be safe in Flanders long before Anne realised magic spells had about as much effect on a king's heart as a woman's tears.

In Southwark, the three prisoners released from The Fleet could scarcely believe their luck. Without any warning they'd been snatched from their dungeon and placed in a covered cart but instead of being taken to the scaffold at Tyburn or Smithfield, the tumbrel had trundled over London Bridge and deposited them outside The Tabard Inn. Their gaolers only words of explanation had been to tell them that everyone thought they were dead of *Aryotitus Fever* and they should wait at the inn until they heard from the man who'd secured their release. In the meantime their lodgings had been paid for and they should keep out of sight or they really would suffer a cruel and painful death.

Once the cart had disappeared Quintana's first reaction was to take the first ship for France they could find but Prometheus and Bos felt they were honour bound to wait, as instructed, for their mysterious benefactor. In the end Quintana agreed to stay with the others at the inn, at least until after Easter. The men were installed in a room at the top of the inn but they heard nothing more until the Monday after Easter Sunday, when a bellman announcing the day's news called out the name of Thomas Devilstone.

"Harken, Harken!" cried the bellman, "I have news of the execution of the evil witch and foul traitor Thomas Devilstone!"

"Devilstone, isn't that the man who clobbered our gaoler?" said Bos, opening the garret's single grimy window and peering into the street below.

"On the morrow, the magus, heretic and traitor Thomas Devilstone will be drawn through the city on a hurdle. He shall be taken from The Tower to Smithfield, and there suffer in life all the torments that await him beyond the grave. The king doth desire that all loyal subjects not engaged in urgent business give their attendance to witness the death of this foul traitor and so be instructed by his fate," bawled the bellman

"So another would-be rebel dies a pointless death, what of it?" Quintana replied.

"Perhaps it was Thomas who secured our release. If it was, it's our Christian duty to help him or risk eternal damnation," said Bos.

"Let him help himself, let him conjure a spirit to smite the headsman as the axe is about to fall and carry him to safety," countered Quintana.

"The magi of Nubia are given power to help others, not themselves, is it likely to be any different here? I say the Frisian is right if? Thomas came to our aid only a low born coward and a knave would abandon him," said Prometheus.

"A moment, my honourable African elephant, we don't actually know it was this man who got us out of that hell hole and if it was him why hasn't he sent us a message?

Even if we do owe him our lives, what could we do? It would take an army to storm The Tower," said Quintana. Prometheus had to agree that the three of them had more chance of getting into heaven than The Tower of London but at that moment there was a knock at their door and a grubby boy entered the room.

"I've a letter for a Nubian," said the boy holding out an oilcloth wallet.

"Be off with you," said Prometheus, for they had no money to pay a messenger.

"Listen chum, I've been given a whole shilling to deliver this and deliver it I shall so take it and go to The Devil." said the urchin. The boy tossed the wallet onto the Nubian's bed and ran off. With a shrug Prometheus opened the packet and held up Thomas' drawing for the others to see.

"The magi at the crucifixion?" said Bos looking at the strange picture, "Why would anyone send us a picture of the magi at Easter?"

"Magi... the bellman called Thomas a magus this must be a message from him!" said Prometheus clapping a hand to his forehead.

"I see nothing, why hasn't he made his meaning clear?" said Quintana.

"And have every warder and constable between here and The Tower learn how he means to escape? No, I'm certain there's hidden meaning in this drawing and it's meant for us alone." said Bos but it was Prometheus who spotted the resemblance between the magi 's faces and their own.

"By the burning fire of The Great St Anthony, that man looks like me and the others look like you two. Now, look closely at the castle behind the stable there's a devil seated in a tower of stone, devil ... stone ... Devilstone! And not *a* tower but *the* Tower. Thomas Devilstone is imprisoned in the Tower of London and he will die now Easter has passed," he cried.

"But we know all this! What we don't know is how to get Thomas out before the king's headsman turns his tripes into bratwurst," said Bos angrily.

"You're right Frisian," said Prometheus sadly. "There must be more meaning in this picture but I confess I'm too blind to see it."

"I can," said Quintana quietly.

"I see you're a papist poltroon," muttered Bos.

"We're shown in the picture dressed as monks, that means Thomas wants us to disguise ourselves as friars and come to The Tower to hear his final confession," Quintana said triumphantly.

"By the Pyramids of Meroe you've solved the riddle Portugee! But we must hurry, if Thomas dies tomorrow we must find monks' habits and be at The Tower before nightfall," said Prometheus.

"What do you mean we? You go if you like but as I've solved the riddle I consider my debt of honour has been paid in full. I'm taking the next ship that sails from this godforsaken, rain-soaked island and King Henry can kiss my good Catholic arse goodbye," insisted Quintana.

"Have you no Christian decency? Are you the priest on the road to Jericho who refused to help the dying man?" said Bos accusingly.

"Thomas isn't lying in the road he's behind high walls and locked doors that are guarded by a hundred armed men," protested Quintana.

"Nevertheless you're coming with us whether you like it or not, or so help me I'll send you to France stuffed in a barrel!" said Bos.

"Besides, you're already a dead man so what have you got to lose?" said Prometheus. Quintana opened his mouth to protest he had a great deal to lose if they were caught but it was clear the ex-boxer and former priest intended to pummel his body and his conscience until he agreed.

"Oh very well but if this bastard Devilstone is a rich man I want half of any reward he offers. Remember it was me who solved the riddle!" said Quintana.

Though it was early in the morning when the men set out on their quest it took a surprisingly long time to procure monks' habits, even in a city as vast as England's capital. Like monks everywhere, those friars who followed their calling in London spun their own wool, weaved their own cloth and sewed it into garments behind the walls of their monasteries, so whilst there were plenty of haberdashers and drapers in the city, not one had a monk's habit for sale.

The three men wandered through the streets around St Paul's until Prometheus hit upon a solution to their problem. If they stripped naked and presented themselves at the door of a priory, they could claim to be poor sailors who'd been set upon by thieves and robbed of everything they owned. They could ask the monks for the loan of habits to hide their shame whilst they returned to their ship and promise to return the clothes once they were aboard. It was a good plan but even so they had to try three different monasteries before they found an abbot innocent enough to take pity on them. By the time they'd dressed in their disguises and arrived at The Tower, the curfew bell was sounding.

"Just twelve hours before Thomas dies," said Quintana as they approached the bastion that guarded the bridge over The Tower of London's moat.

"Let me do the talking," said Bos, "I trained for Holy Orders and I can speak the language of the clergy. You two, just try and walk religiously."

"How can anyone walk religiously?" protested Quintana but Bos did not reply. He was too busy looking at a yeoman warder standing in the archway of The Tower's outer gate. The man was watching the approaching 'priests' with deep suspicion.

Whilst Bos, Prometheus and Quintana were searching London for monks' habits, Sir William Kingston was telling Thomas that he had twenty four hours to make his peace with God before the court's terrible sentence was carried out. Thomas accepted the news calmly but begged to be allowed to confess to his own priests who were certain to present themselves once they'd heard the date for his execution had been set. As Thomas had been a model prisoner, and his courage had greatly impressed

Sir William, The Constable granted the condemned man his last request.

Thomas maintained his air of fortitude until Sir William had left but as soon as his gaoler had gone he set to work. He retrieved the saltpetre, lard and jar of syrup that Anne had brought then used the pestle and mortar to mash these ingredients into a thick dough. Once this was done, he divided the glutinous lump into three strips and rolled each strip loosely around one of the black matches. Finally he wrapped each of these large, if crude, candles in squares of hessian cut from his bed's mattress. The task passed several hours but when he'd finished all he could do was sit in his lonely cell to await the arrival of his confessors.

"Halt who goes there?" said the warder guarding The Tower's outer gate.

"Be at peace my son. We are poor friars come to the hear the confession of the prisoner Thomas Devilstone," said Bos solemnly. His deep, booming voice sounded sufficiently holy for the warder to fetch his sergeant.

"Why does it need three of you to hear one man's confession?" said the sergeant.

"Surely you know that this warlock is possessed of powerful magic?" said Bos earnestly. "It will take the combined prayers of no less than three holy clerics to tame the demons that he will surely send against us and even then I am not confident that all of us will survive. We must pray to St Anthony who battled with demons in the desert..."

"Yes, Yes, save your babbling for the pulpit Father but tell me what's in those bundles?" interrupted the sergeant and he pointed at the three cross shaped parcels, each wrapped in rags and bound with leather thongs, which the friars carried over their shoulders.

"They're roods, our wooden crosses that will be our only weapon against the armies of Satan for no demon can bear to be in sight of the symbol of Our Lord's suffering," said Bos reverently and he unwrapped a corner of one of the parcels so the sergeant could see the end of a crudely sawn piece of wood.

"Ask them how can we be sure they're really friars," said the yeoman warder eager to ingratiate himself with his sergeant.

"Imbecile," replied the sergeant, "Can't you see these men are wearing the habits of the Franciscans and carrying crosses?"

"Do not be so harsh your subordinate My Son, the simpleton is right to be suspicious but there's an easy way to be sure, fetch a bible or some other writing and I will read it to you," Bos suggested.

"He's got a point there," said the younger yeoman leaning on his spear, "Only the clergy can read, I mean you're a sergeant, and you can't read."

"I don't need to ask them to read, you dolt! If you were a sergeant instead of a turd, you'd know that Sir William has already told me to expect three friars to hear the witch's confession." snapped the sergeant. He turned to the monks and handed Bos a small wooden board upon which the word *Octavius* had been burned with a hot iron.

He told them that this was the night's password, and if the friars showed it at each of the gates the sentries would let them through without question, however they had to hurry as the curfew was about to begin.

"You have the thanks of us all, my son," said Bos trying not to grin.

"God be with you Father and make sure the evil bastard gets what's coming to him!" said the sergeant as he waved the party through the gate. With a sigh of relief the three men passed through the gates of the Lion and Middle Towers to the causeway that crossed the moat.

At the far end of causeway was the Byward Tower where Bos had to show his pass a third time to gain entry to the outer ward. This was a narrow killing zone between the fortress' two curtain walls and any attackers that reached this point would find themselves assailed from above by all manner of missiles. Quintana shivered at the thought of being shot through with arrows, crushed by stones or scalded to death by the boiling water defenders could pour down from the tops of both walls but nobody questioned the right of three friars to enter the king's fortress. At the Wakefield Tower, Bos again showed his token to the warders and they opened a small postern that led to the inner ward.

The sergeant in charge of this gate also detailed one of his men to escort the three priests to The Beauchamp Tower where the condemned man was being held. Thomas' chamber was guarded a gruff looking veteran who sported a long grey beard and a broad bladed partisan. Prometheus thought the spear was too long to be of much use in the small rooms and narrow spiral stairways of the Beauchamp Tower, nevertheless he grasped the crucifix he carried a little tighter. If it came to a fight, the symbol of Christ's victory over the grave might be his only weapon.

The grizzled warder examined Bos' pass and grudgingly he unlocked the cell. As the door creaked open, Bos and the others were surprised to see a comfortable room with a fire burning in the grate. Thomas was sitting at a table with his back to the doorway, and seemed to be busy feeding titbits to a caged bird. Another warder was in the room, seated on a chair by the fire. A patch covered this man's eye and his spear rested lazily against his shoulder. The one-eyed warder stood up when the friars entered the cell but the prisoner carried on feeding his pet.

"On your feet witch, these holy men are here to save your soul, not that you deserve it you black hearted bastard." snapped the grizzled warder. Slowly, Thomas turned to look at his visitors but said nothing. Bos made the sign of the cross and turned to the warders.

"You may leave us. A confession, even a witch's confession, is for the ears of God alone," he said to them however the half-blind guard made no effort to leave the cell. He merely looked at the Frisian and narrowed his one remaining eye.

"I'm not sure we can do that Father," he said. "We hang this bastard in the morning and I'm supposed to make sure he don't cheat the scaffold by hanging his-self."

"Very well, you may stay if you wish but you do so in peril of your soul. The witch may appear contrite but he's sure to summon many hideous demons to his aid and we may have to battle with all the legions of Hell before this night is over," said Bos. Both warders looked at each other nervously and Prometheus pressed home the friars' advantage.

"I fear your paltry partisans will be of no use against The Great Marquis Sabnock who commands fifty legions of The Damned. The slightest wound from his sword will fill with devilish maggots that gnaw a man's flesh from his bones whilst he still lives and it is said that the screams from any mortal man wounded by The Great Marquis Sabnock would chill the heart of Satan himself," the Nubian added gleefully. At this news, the one-eyed warder 's face turned as white as his colleague's beard and he took a step back towards the cell door.

"As you wish, Father, but I'll have to lock the door… just in case," said the one eyed warder, his voice trembling with terror.

"You must do your duty my son, and you can trust us to do ours. May God bless you and keep you for there is bound to be great evil abroad this night," said Bos kindly. The warders scurried from the cell crossing themselves furiously. As soon as they'd left, the priests threw back their cowls and grinned at Thomas.

"By all the saints you got my message!" said Thomas. He spoke in a whisper but nothing could hide his delight at seeing Bos, Quintana and Prometheus.

"Did you think we weren't coming?" laughed the Nubian.

"I admit I was beginning to think perhaps my picture had been lost or misunderstood," said Thomas.

"I swear by the Queen of Spain's tits you're no Leonardo but at least I had the wit to work out your meaning, I hope you'll remember that!" Quintana said proudly.

"So what do we do now?" said Bos.

"For the moment we pray," said Thomas with a smile and he carefully outlined his plan. When he'd finished, Bos unwrapped his bundle. The woollen wrapping turned out to be a spare disguise for Thomas and as well as concealing its true purpose, the cloth had hidden two swords with a piece of wood tied between their crossguards so the weapons appeared to be a crucifix. Bos untied the wood and handed one sword to Thomas who took it gratefully. The blade was dull and pitted with rust but it felt good to have a weapon in his hand again. Prometheus and Quintana also unwrapped their swords, which had been similarly disguised as crosses, and when all four men were armed Bos began to pray. In a voice loud enough for the warders to hear, the ex-priest spoke the words of the prayer to drive demons from the possessed.

Is it not written, that it is by the finger of God
that I drive out demons and the kingdom of God shall
come upon you. For you cannot drink from the cup
of the Lord and also from the cup of demons. You cannot
partake of the table of the Lord and of the table of demons.
Yet are we who travel the paths of light not stronger than
he who walks in darkness?

The warders outside the cell heard Bos' Latin and though they did not understand the words, they felt much better. They felt certain the holy men would weave a web of prayer around the witch that would be far stronger than any iron chains or stone walls. Soon it would be morning, the headsman would dispatch Thomas Devilstone's corrupt soul to hell and the world would be a safer place for good Christian folk. The warders looked at each other and breathed a sigh of relief.

Bos' prayers continued until darkness fell whereupon Quintana called through the door's little window to request a light for the cell's candles. The grizzled warder duly fetched a rushlight but he was careful to pass it through the tiny window's bars rather than open the cell door. He may have been old but he was wise to most tricks his prisoners tried to play. As the light flared in the cell, the monks' prayers began again and the guards settled down for a comfortable night.

The first indication something was wrong was the strange hissing that sounded like bacon frying in a pan. The guards thought perhaps the friars were cooking their supper but then the screaming began.

7

THE KING'S WHARF

"Oh dear God ... no ... please no!" shrieked a voice from inside Thomas' cell. To the nervous warders outside, it sounded as if the speaker was suffering all the torments of the Holy Inquisition and as the friars' cries grew louder the elderly guards grasped their spears more tightly.

"In the name of the Lord Jesus Christ ... back ... back ... you fiend!" wailed another voice from the cell.

"By the power of Christ I compel thee to return to The Pit!" cried a third voice as great clouds of purple smoke began to creep under the cell door. The warders looked at each other, wide eyed with fright, as the foul smelling smoke slowly filled the passageway. The stench was worse than a cartload of rotten eggs cracked all at once and in the next moment the befouled air was riven by the sounds of clashing swords.

"Do not open the door, we're doing battle with the Great Marquis Sabnock himself, keep the door firmly shut until he's defeated!" cried one of the friars from inside the cell. The warders were only too happy to oblige, no power on earth would induce them to open the cell's door but as a thick billow of smoke wafted through the tiny window, a bat flew through the bars into the stairway. The terrified creature fluttered and swooped between the warders as it tried to find a way out, whilst the equally terrified men screamed and waved their arms to drive the hellish vermin away. In answer to their piteous screams, Bos' face appeared at the barred window.

"By all the saints he's cunning, the Great Marquis Sabnock has turned himself into a bat to escape us. Where is he can you see him?" Bos asked urgently.

"He's out here, the demon is attacking us!" screamed the warders.

"Don't let him bite you, if The Great Marquis drinks your blood, you'll become a slave of Satan for all time. Open the door and let us out, we'll use the power of Christ to recapture this Prince of Darkness!" Bos said. The friar's words were exactly what the warders wanted to hear. They knew they could not defeat a fiendish Great Lord of Hell, even one who had taken the form of a bat, so they forgot the priest's earlier instruction and gratefully unlocked the cell door. Almost before the key had turned, the door burst open and the coughing, spluttering friars burst into the passageway. In the confusion the warders did not notice that four monks, not three, had emerged from the cell.

"Leave us... let us face this peril alone, be gone I say or you'll be damned for all eternity!" Bos roared. He stood in the passageway holding his sword in his huge fist and looking like the vengeful St Boniface before the pagan oak. The sight only added to the warders' panic. Calling loudly to St Michael to save them, the petrified guards threw down their weapons and ran down the spiral stair.

"Come on, we mustn't let the other guards gather their wits or they'll discover they've been tricked by nothing more than a saltpetre candle and a terrified bat!" said Thomas and he followed the fleeing warders down the stairs shouting strange incantations as he did so. Their luck held until the four friars reached the centre of the darkened inner ward but before the fugitives could reach the gateway to the outer ward, they were confronted by a loose skirmish line of yeomen warders advancing cautiously across the grass towards them.

"By the blood stained bollocks of the Blessed Abelard, we're trapped!" Bos cried.

"Get back, behind me," snapped Thomas as he fumbled for the second of his smoke bombs. Once he'd pulled the candle free of his robe he took hold of the match cord, which he'd tied around his waist in imitation of a friar's cincture, and blew on the end. The cord glowed red, for he'd had the good sense to set it smouldering before leaving the warmth of his cell, and as soon as he touched it to the greasy candle's black match, the powder-encrusted paper began to fizz.

"May I?" Prometheus asked, holding out his hand.

"With pleasure," replied Thomas and he handed the spluttering candle to the Nubian who promptly hurled it into the night sky. The bomb spiralled through the darkness, scattering a trail of sparks like a tiny comet, and landed on the grass behind the warders. A moment later the advancing yeomen were engulfed in more clouds of thick, purple smoke.

"The wizard has opened another portal to The Pit! You men must surround this new gateway and stop Lucifer's fire-breathing dragons from leaving Hell. You must defy their flesh-ripping claws and sulphurous breath, you must smite the legions of Beelzebub that will surely follow. Have courage or we're all damned!" Quintana cried at the confused yeomen staggering out of the fog. The yeoman stopped in their tracks. They looked at the crazed hooded monks in front of them, then glanced at the billowing clouds of purple smoke behind.

"We can't fight Satan's armies!" One of the yeomen shouted and that was a signal for the rout to begin. The elderly, corpulent warders threw away their weapons and ran for to the safety of the White Tower, the great stone keep at the centre of the fortress, and the sound of their hobnailed boots clattering on the donjon's wooden stairs was quickly followed by the slam of a heavy door.

The four monks looked at each other in triumph but there was no time to celebrate their victory. Thomas only had one more candle and they still had to reach the outer ward and cross the moat. Bos grinned and told the others to follow him whilst he repeated his performance of a deranged priest exorcising demons. Thomas and the others were only too happy to stay behind the Frisian as the giant, red beard-ed ex-priest ran towards the postern in the Wakefield Tower. Holding his sword high in one hand and the wooden token with the password in the other Bos screamed at the bemused warders guarding the gateway to run for their lives.

"In the name of St Michael slayer-of-demons you must flee! The Devil himself has been unleashed and The Constable has given orders all men must retreat into the safety of the White Tower or perish!" Bos yelled. The two warders recognised the priest they'd admitted a few hours earlier and they knew better than to disobey a man of God, or the Constable's password, so they too gratefully abandoned their post and joined their fellows in the headlong flight into the keep.

As soon as the guards had disappeared into the night, the fugitives ran to open the gate that led to the Outer Ward. The postern was fastened with locks, and they had no key, but the large main gate was secured with a heavy wooden beam that sat in two iron brackets. The seasoned oak was as strong as steel, and would have withstood any battering from outside, but Prometheus and Bos easily lifted the timber out of its brackets and cast it aside. As they did so, Quintana and Thomas hauled open the gates and they all ran into the outer ward.

"Just the outer wall and the moat to cross," said Bos and he turned to lead his companions back the way they'd entered but Thomas stopped him.

"That way, we'll be caught quicker than a drunken bishop catches the pox. Even if the warders at the outer towers have run away, we've no keys to open the gates so follow me," said Thomas urgently and without another word he set off at a sprint in the opposite direction to The Tower's barbican.

The others couldn't fault Thomas' logic so they followed him to the Cradle Tower, a small bastion in the southeastern corner of the outer walls, which guarded a postern that opened onto a narrow bridge over the moat. At the other end of this wooden trestle was the King's Wharf and beyond that was the River Thames. The Cradle Tower had been built to serve as the king's private entrance to his royal fortress and it was manned at all times by two of The Tower garrison's most trustworthy men. The commotion from the inner ward had alerted these two sentries who'd abandoned their supper to investigate and they gruffly challenged the four rapidly approaching monks.

"In the name of the king stand fast and identify yourselves," shouted the first warder, levelling his halberd at Thomas' chest.

"We're poor servants of Christ fighting all the furies of Hell, now stand aside for we must fetch help from the Church of St Catherine!" yelled Thomas and he ran straight at the confused sentry. The yeoman was loath to cut down a friar, even one apparently out of his wits, so he hesitated and as a reward for his piety Thomas knocked the man's spear aside and smashed the pommel of his sword into his face. The second warder was so astonished at the sight of a priest clubbing his comrade to the ground, he failed to notice Prometheus' haymaking punch heading towards his chin. The Nubian's fist landed on the man's jaw with a smack and the second warder fell to the ground like bag of wet washing. With both sentries silenced, Quintana began to search them for the keys.

"Don't bother, the keys to all the gates and posterns are handed to the Constable at sunset," said Thomas calmly but the others looked at him in horror.

"If we can't get out why in the name of Martin Luther's whore of a mother did you bring us here? We'd have been better off trying to bluff our way through the main gate!" cried Quintana.

"I hope you know what you're doing Englishman because we have company," said Bos, pointing at the lines of flickering torches moving along the inner and outer walls' walkways.

"Inside!" replied Thomas and he bundled his companions into the Cradle Tower's guardroom. The small gloomy chamber behind the open door had been furnished with a crude wooden table, several long wooden benches and a ladder that led to a trapdoor in the vaulted roof. After using the table and benches to barricade the door, the four men climbed the ladder, pushed open the trapdoor at the top and scrambled onto the tower's parapet.

"Now what, it's too far too jump to the bridge, we'll have to dive into the moat," said Bos peering over the battlements.

"I'm not swimming any moat, I'm a king and kings do not flap about in water like common fish. Besides it stinks worse than a diseased whore's pisspot," said Prometheus wrinkling his nose in regal disgust at the stench rising from the moat.

"You won't have to swim," Thomas promised but for the moment he had no idea of how they were to reach the bridge. He had hoped to pull up the ladder from the guardroom and use it to climb down to the bridge but the bottom rungs had been chained to an iron ring in the floor and there was no time to wrench it free. The Cradle Tower's guards, who'd now recovered their wits, were yelling for their colleagues to come to their aid and their cries were answered by more shouts from The Tower's inner ward.

"It seems as if our beef eating foes have at last realised they've been tricked and I reckon we have about three minutes to get off this parapet or we're all dead," said Quintana grimly.

"Give me your cinctures," said Thomas and snatching hold of the cords he quickly knotted them into a rope. He fastened one end to the parapet and tossed the loose end into the darkness.

"After you Englishman, I'd hate to be the one to snap such a slender thread or encounter any guards on the King's Wharf," said Prometheus politely. Thomas didn't hesitate, he climbed over the wall and lowered himself to the bridge below.

Despite the darkness, Thomas could see the King's Wharf at the far end of the bridge. He knew this broad, cobbled quay was cut off from the rest of London's waterfront by high wooden palisades and blockhouses at each end so, gripping his sword tightly, he walked cautiously along the bridge. When no challenge came, Thomas guessed the watchmen who were supposed to patrol the docks and warehouses were lying drunk in their blockhouse so he signalled to the others that it was safe to descend. A minute later, the four men had joined him by one of the derricks that leaned into the dark like a giant heron hunting for lampreys.

"So where's the boat?" said Thomas expectantly.

"What boat?" queried Bos.

"Your drawing didn't show any boat," added Prometheus.

"I'm Portuguese, saltwater runs in my veins and I can sail anything that floats but you never said anything about a boat," countered Quintana.

"But how, in the name of Beelzebub's great hairy arse, are we supposed to get to France or Flanders without a boat?" Thomas cried in exasperation. Without some sort of vessel the four men were trapped on the waterfront and the shouts from The Tower were getting louder. In another minute the keys to the postern would have been fetched from The Constable's office and the quayside would be swarming with heavily armed men.

"Perhaps I can help, Master Thomas," said a soft voice with a heavy German accent.

The four fugitives spun on their heels and saw a small man emerge from the shadows. He was aged about forty but stood no higher than Thomas' shoulder. His clean-shaven face was full and round but his build was slim and he had the graceful walk of a dancing master. The man was clearly not from The Tower's guardroom or the city's nightwatch because he wore a long black merchant's cloak wrapped tightly around his shoulders and a plain black bonnet was crammed on his head.

"Who calls my name?" said Thomas pointing his sword at the man.

"I'm Hans Nagel, the trumpet player," said the man, spreading his arms wide in friendship, but before he could say another word Thomas leapt at him, his sword flashing in the moonlight. Taken by surprise, Nagel stepped back in terror and slipped on a pile of dung. The slip saved his life, the sword sliced only air but as Nagel sprawled across the damp cobbles his opponent quickly recovered his balance. In the blink of an eye Thomas was standing astride Nagel's chest with his sword's point pressed against the helpless man's throat.

"I know your name Nagel, you were one of Wolsey's spies and you're supposed to be dead!" Thomas bellowed and he lifted his sword to strike the cowering Nagel's head from his shoulders.

"In the name of God's Mercy wait, you know only half the story, Wolsey's not my true master, I now serve the exiled Yorkist prince Richard de la Pole, he heard of your plight and sent me to bring you to the safety of Metz. I sent the note warning of your arrest and I paid the crone who gave you the white rose, What's more I have a Hansa ship waiting at The Steelyard," Nagel pleaded.

"I'm very grateful to be sure but, if you have a boat, why in the name of the king's piss-stained codpiece didn't you bring it here?" said Thomas angrily but he lowered his sword.

"A boat would be of no use now because the tide is almost at full ebb. Look, see for yourself," said Nagel nervously struggling to his feet. The trumpet player ushered the men to a flight of stone steps that should have led to the river's edge but the waters had receded so far all the men could see was a wide ribbon of stinking ooze disappearing into the darkness. Before anyone could stop him, Nagel had skipped down the stairs and leapt onto the reeking mud.

"I can show you the way across the mudflats but we must go now," Nagel cried.

Realising they had no choice Thomas and the others followed the little trumpet player down the steps but the moment they stepped onto the mud, they sank up to their ankles in loathsome, cloying filth. Walking over the tidal river bed was impossible so, like giant eels, they slid and slithered across the slime. Nagel led them to another flight of steps, two hundred yards up river of the King's Wharf, where the escapees hauled themselves out of the quagmire and onto another quayside.

The five men lay on the cobbles panting for breath and staring at The Tower of London's western ramparts. They'd succeeded in escaping from the fortress but they were still inside London's city walls and a long way from safety. Indeed, the men had barely recovered their wind before an elderly watchman, who'd seen the mudlarks crawl from the river like Grendel's Mother, began ringing a large brass bell. The fugitives groaned. The alarm would bring both the pursuing warders and the city's nightwatch to this part of the waterfront in a matter of minutes.

"We'll be safe once we reach The Steelyard, follow me!" Nagel cried and he took to his heels. Once again Thomas and the others had little choice but to obey so, with their sodden monks' robes flapping around their ankles, they ran after the trumpet player.

The Steelyard lay beyond London Bridge, where the little River Walbrook flowed into the Thames, and since the time of King Edward it's docks and warehouses had been owned by the Hanseatic League. The dues and tolls paid by these shrewd German merchants put so much money in royal coffers, their trading station had been granted the same privileges as a free city, its borders were held to be inviolate and no king dared let his constables enter, even in pursuit of outlaws. Thomas and the other's would be safe behind The Steelyard's walls but as they reached London Bridge their way was blocked by a band of the nightwatch emerging from an alley.

"It is them, and they still blaspheme against Christ by wearing the garb of holy orders, bring crosses, bind them with prayer, make sure the wizards do not use their magic to escape us again!" screeched the watchmen's captain and he pointed the torch he was carrying at the sacrilegious monks.

The men of the nightwatch were not professional soldiers or yeomen warders, they were a citizen militia made up of superstitious craftsmen and shopkeepers so instead of surrounding the fugitives with a ring of steel and calling on them to surrender, they began to sing the words of *The Magnificat*. This craven piety was their downfall. If they'd attacked at once they'd have easily overpowered the escaped prisoners but when Thomas and the others saw their opponents' reluctance to fight they shouted blood-curdling battle cries and charged.

"In Satan's name I curse you! At The Dark Lord's bidding you shall be flayed alive and buried up to your neck in salt so rats can gnaw at your face and crows peck at your eyes for all eternity!" Thomas cried as he ran towards the watchmen's leader.

The astonished captain, a potter by trade, saw this demonic friar bearing down on him and soiled himself. Despite the discomfort of his piss-soaked hose, the petrified potter dropped his torch and ran for his life. In a trice Thomas had retrieved the last of his homemade candles from beneath his habit, lit the match from the fallen torch and hurled the fizzing, spitting firework into the mob. As before the burning saltpetre, lard and sugar filled the street with choking smoke that smelled like roasted flesh and the terrified watchmen truly believed they were staring into The Abyss.

"Here me you lackwit peasants, we can open the gates of hell whenever we choose and release the Nine Legions of the Damned to drag you all to Hades!" Prometheus cried and he swung his sword at a tanner who'd had the temerity to stand his ground. The giant Nubian's blow neatly severed his opponent's arm at the elbow and a great gout of blood spewed the night sky.

Quintana deftly sliced open the belly of a fat fishmonger whilst Bos, his eyes blazing like a Viking, found himself facing two hedge-layers armed with long, rusty billhooks. Undaunted Bos threw back his cowl and roared his battle cry 'better dead than a slave' which in the strange guttural language of the Frisians sounded like Satan's own speech. The sight of a red-bearded leviathan emerging from purple smoke and bellowing foul curses in a demonic tongue, was enough to put the hedge-layers and the rest of the nightwatch to flight.

"Tell me Englishman, how did you manage to think of such a vile torture as being skinned alive and buried in salt?" said Bos as he watched the defeated men disappear into the darkened alleyways.

"He knows the fate that awaits Lutheran heretics like you," said Quintana wiping his sword on the dead fishmonger's apron but Prometheus insisted there was no time for jests and urged Nagel, to take them all to The Steelyard before the night watch returned in greater numbers. Pausing only to relieve the dead men of their purses, the five fugitives set off again and they soon reached the high brick wall that surrounded Hansa trading station. Nagel hammered on the large wooden gate with the hilt of his dagger and bawled some words of German. A moment later the gate opened, Nagel tossed a purse of money at the gatekeeper and bundled the others inside.

In the growing light of the dawn sky, Thomas and the others could see a jumble of half-timbered warehouses facing a stone dock. A wooden jetty had been built at right angles to the quayside and the men were much relieved to see it extended beyond the tidal mud to a large, three masted kogge with a broad, rounded hull and high castles that towered over her bow and stern. The Hansa's red and white striped pennant flew from the ship's central main mast and Nagel lost no time in ushering everyone aboard. Once on deck, Nagel pressed another purse into the captain's grubby hand and if the ship's master was alarmed by the arrival of five monks covered in mud and gore, he kept silent.

"You're just in time, the tide's turned and there's a fair wind, now get under cover and keep out of sight until we're safe at sea," said the captain, jerking his thumb towards the ship's bow and the high, covered forecastle. The ship may have been sailing under a German flag but it's master spoke in the thick burr of East Anglia.

"I thank you for waiting Master Shobery, but if you'd left without us my employer would've fed you to the crows," snapped Nagel but the captain wasn't listening, he was too busy ordering his men to untie ropes, unfurl sails and push the ship away from the jetty with long wooden poles. Slowly the stout little ship, which was named *The Steffen*, drifted into the river's current and joined the other traffic on the river. Their departure was not a moment too soon. As they approached London Bridge the pursuing warders, now accompanied by the men from half the city's nightwatch, began to swarm towards the fortified gatehouse over the central arch.

"Will they bar the bridge?" Bos asked Nagel.

"Have no fear, this ship carries half a dozen cannon but a Hansa flag is worth more than twenty culverins and no one will dare stop us," said Nagel yet he still insisted that his passengers should do as the captain ordered and go below decks. Their pursuers would have no idea which, if any, of the dozen ships sailing east on the strengthening morning tide, might be carrying fugitives to freedom but four monks, standing on deck covered in mud and blood, would be sure to give the game away.

The passengers did as they were asked and made themselves comfortable in the cramped, stifling crew cabin below the forecastle's deck. Just as Nagel had promised, the bridge master dared not prevent a Hansa ship from passing freely down the Thames so the boom and drawbridge that could have barred their way remained open. *The Steffen* sailed through London Bridge accompanied by nothing more than a few startled moorhens and the mournful gaze of executed criminals' severed heads, impaled on the spikes adorning the bridge's gatehouse.

A few hours later the pantomime was repeated at Tilbury and the passengers remained hidden whilst an official looking launch approached the kogge to ask the master his destination and cargo. Captain Shobery declared that he was bound for Ghent with a load of English wool and claimed the protection of the Hanseatic League whereupon the launch scuttled back into Tilbury's harbour. *The Steffen* slid slowly past the hulks moored on the mudflats but their guns stayed silent and once they'd left these obstacles behind, nothing could stop the kogge from reaching the open sea. Thomas and the others should have felt elated that they'd successfully escaped a cardinal's wrath and a king's dungeon but they didn't care, they were all fast asleep.

8

THE GERMAN OCEAN

When they woke it was noon and *The Steffen* was slicing cheerfully through the white-capped waves of the German Ocean. A sailor passed the word it was safe to come on deck and brought fresh clothes, the passengers gratefully swapped their filthy habits for the garb of simple seamen and left the cramped confines of the forecastle. They stood in the ship's prow, letting the salt water sting their faces. After their long weeks of imprisonment the fresh sea air and warm spring sunshine were as welcome as the promise of salvation. At first the men could only congratulate themselves on the success of their escape but it wasn't long before they began to ask Nagel some searching questions.

"So was it chance or God who brought you to our aid last night," said Bos.

"Neither, it was Richard de la Pole, exiled Duke of Suffolk, Prince of the House of York and rightful king of England who ordered me to find the famous astrologer

Thomas Devilstone and bring him safely to Metz," replied Nagel's proudly.

"That's very Christian of him, tell your master we're most grateful," said Quintana watching a seagull soar lazily over the wave tops but Thomas, who'd been unusually silent, suddenly drew his sword and before the others could stop him, he had the tip pointed at their rescuer's throat.

"You're all too trusting, what you don't know is that Cardinal Wolsey once sent a trumpet player named Hans Nagel to spy on the Yorkist pretender but he disappeared. So is this man really Hans Nagel or is he an impostor sent to trap us? Speak, you've exactly one minute to convince me you're not playing some sort of double game before I spill your guts over this nicely scrubbed deck," said Thomas and the steel in his voice was as sharp as the sword in his hand. Nagel turned white with fear as he looked into Thomas' cold grey eyes but from somewhere he found the strength to speak.

"You've no need to fear me Master Thomas, I hate Wolsey as much as any man. The cardinal caught me seducing one of his married servants and threatened to have the public hangman brand me with red hot irons unless I became his agent," said Nagel and without any further prompting he told Thomas the full story.

As it was not unusual for minstrels and troubadours to travel between different cities in search of work, Wolsey had used one of his servants to trap and recruit Nagel, along with an ageing singer named Petrus Alamire. Having ensnared the two musicians Wolsey had sent them to

Metz with orders to uncover Yorkist plots to invade England but once again Nagel and Petrus' weakness for sins of the flesh had been their undoing. The two spies had been unmasked barely a month after their arrival at the Yorkist court-in-exile but, instead of hanging them, de la Pole had decided to play Cardinal Wolsey at his own game. The White Rose had persuaded Nagel and Alamire to work for him and had sent them back to London to spy on their former masters.

The two musicians had proved to be better spies for the House of York than for the House of Tudor and for almost two years they'd travelled between the two rival courts, betraying King Henry's secrets to Richard de la Pole and passing misleading information about Yorkist plots to Wolsey. By the time the cardinal had realised his agents were playing him false Nagel and Alamire were back in Metz so, carefully masking his suspicions, he'd sent convivial letters asking them to return. The letters fooled no one. Sensing their luck was running out, the two spies had wisely refused to leave the safety of de la Pole's castle.

Cardinal Wolsey, as artful as ever, had hidden this fiasco from the king by lying. He'd told Henry that Nagel and Petrus' failure to return from Metz could only mean they'd been arrested and hanged by de la Pole. For a while, the brutal execution of two 'innocent' musicians by evil Yorkists had been the talk of Henry's court but the lurid story had soon been forgotten. Nevertheless Nagel and Alamire had continued to serve the House of York in various capacities and when de la Pole found himself in need of Thomas' unique talents, he'd sent his trusted trumpet player to fetch him.

"It had been four years since I'd been in London, so there was little danger I'd be recognised, but before I could reach you, I learned that you were about to be arrested. All I could do was send the warning note and, though you didn't come to The Boar's Head as I asked, I continued to hope. When I heard you'd been arrested for the murder of Wolsey's henchmen, I realised there was a slim chance I might be able to free you and bring you to Metz after all," said Nagel glancing at Thomas' sword which was still pointed at his gullet.

"But why go to all that trouble? What can Thomas offer this White Rose that other men can't?" Quintana asked.

"The White Rose has vowed to end Henry VIII's tyranny once and for all and as we speak he's raising a great army to recover his lost throne but he needs a man with knowledge of the stars to find the right day for his invasion. Thomas will study the heavens and find a propitious day with favourable winds, tides and other good omens," Nagel declared and at last Thomas sheathed his sword.

"So it would seem that your master and I are destined to make common cause, for I was already on my way to Burgundy when I was taken by King Henry's men. Now it's also my solemn vow to see that great Welsh wine-sack hanging from a Tyburn gibbet and I'll rejoice when white roses bloom once more in England!" Thomas declared but now it was Prometheus' turn to look perplexed.

"Very poetic Thomas, but Henry is your anointed king and you forget that I too have been chosen by God to wear a crown. For that reason alone I can't permit you to aid a rebellion against another Christian monarch without placing my own soul in mortal peril," he said. Prometheus' stern expression convinced everyone that the Nubian would happily throw Thomas overboard unless all talk of rebellion was abandoned but the Englishman had no intention of conceding defeat.

"A king is nothing more than the strongest brigand in the band and if the robber chief becomes a cruel tyrant then his fellow thieves have every right to depose him," Thomas said in his defence.

"You're wrong Thomas, only God can take away what has been given by God," Prometheus insisted and he folded his huge arms across his chest so he looked like an Arabian jinn but Thomas was not to be deterred.

"Not so long ago we were all sitting in the shadow of the gallows but God has favoured us since we met so perhaps we're to be the instruments of God's will. What's more I can prove to you that Henry is a false king who cannot command the loyalty of good Christians," Thomas replied but before he could explain how the House of York's heirs had been cheated of their throne, there was a cry of alarm from the masthead.

"Sail astern!" hollered the lookout and every man on board ran to the ship's rail to get a better look at the small but sleek, square rigged vessel that seemed to be following them.

"By the barnacles on King Neptune's balls she's a balinger," cursed one the sailors shielding his eyes from the sun's glare with a weather beaten hand. Thomas scoffed at the threat from such a small boat but the sailor informed the passengers that balingers were coastal craft and didn't normally venture this far out to sea unless they were up to no good. Nagel asked the sailor if they could outrun their pursuers but the seaman shook his head and assured them a balinger could run down a kogge faster than a greyhound coursing a hare but another sailor was more hopeful.

"Don't listen to that gloomy old sod, he's not had a good word to say about anything these last twenty years! To be sure a balinger's faster than a kogge in daylight but it will be dark in a few hours, perhaps we can lose her during the night," said the more optimistic seaman. The captain seemed to have heard him and ordered his crew to put on more sail in an attempt to outpace their shadow.

The kogge duly increased her speed but she was built to carry Flemish cloth and Rhenish wine safely rather than quickly. The heavy cargo ship couldn't outrun the sleeker balinger and by the time the sun touched the horizon, the gap between the two vessels had closed to a few hundred yards. There could be no doubt that the balinger's crew had hostile intentions so *The Steffen's* captain summoned his men to the main deck and addressed them from the stern castle's rail.

"Those bastards mean to take this ship, so I want every man armed and ready. If they try and jump us during the night we'll give them such a hot welcome the fires of hell will be a blessed relief!" said Captain Shobery. Nagel tried to protest that his orders shouldn't apply to passengers but no one was listening. The main deck of *The Steffen* had become a hive of muffled activity as the crew loaded their cannon with a lethal mix of nails, sharp stones and anything else that could shred human flesh.

"If there's a fight, stay out of it Thomas you hold the fate of kingdoms in your hand and you're too valuable to be killed in some pointless skirmish," said Nagel, taking hold of the Englishman's sleeve.

"What are you talking about trumpet player, I won't run from a fight!" Thomas said.

"But you must, the White Rose knows you have Leonardo's notebook with the secrets of the war machines and he has great need of one of these devices. Build it, help him regain his throne and Richard will reward you above all other men," Nagel whispered. This revelation left Thomas more than a little shocked. Ever since he'd taken the book from the dying Leonardo's study, he'd been careful to tell no one he possessed the precious volume, let alone what it contained, and he couldn't begin to fathom how the White Rose had learned of his secret. He could feel the book, wrapped in cloth and hidden in his shirt, but for the moment he thought it prudent to keep Nagel guessing.

"Maybe I have it and maybe I don't. You must forgive my reticence, Master Nagel, but by your own admission you've taken Wolsey's gold in the past so, until I can be sure where your true loyalties lie, I shall keep what I know to myself," he said and before the musician could protest, Thomas had joined the other men sharpening their weapons.

The ship was soon filled with the sound of whetstones scraping against steel as every man aboard knew that his life depended on the sharpness of both his wits and his blade. Once their swords, boarding axes and halberds had been honed as keen as razors, the crew hid and waited whilst the shadows cast by the ship's masts lengthened and faded into the night. The sky became lit by myriad stars but there was no moon and the darkness magnified the sounds of creaking spars, flapping canvas and rushing water that were the only noises disturbing the night time ocean.

After an hour, those with the sharpest ears heard a faint change in the sound of the waves breaking along the ship's side. The surf's cheerful chatter was being answered by a similar sound off *The Steffen's* port beam and Thomas watched a ripple of hand signals spread along the lines of sailors crouched behind the ship's gunwale. With his heart pounding, Thomas peered through a knothole in the planks and saw the balinger silhouetted against the starry sky. Inch by inch, the pirate boat drew alongside until the two vessels were sailing parallel with each other, less than a rope's length apart.

"Now!" yelled Captain Shobery and the stillness of the night was shattered by hellish thunderclaps. Like wyverns spitting death, fire leapt from the muzzles of *The Steffen's* two port-side canon and in the brief moment that the pirate ship was illuminated, Thomas saw its deck was crammed with armed men. Suddenly there was a third explosion as the kogge's masthead gun sprayed the balinger with another deadly rain of shot and the night became filled with screams and curses of broken men.

"Board 'em!" yelled Shobery and a dozen grappling irons flew through air to land on the pirate ship's deck.

Some *The Steffen's* crew heaved on the grapnel ropes whilst the others loosed arrows or hauled lanterns to the mast-head to spill an eerie yellow light over both vessels.

Like scorpions in a death dance the two enemies became locked together whereupon the men on the kogge gave a great cheer and leapt aboard the pirate boat. Thomas landed on the balinger's deck near its bow and he immediately dropped into a crouch as one of the pirates, blood streaming down his lacerated face, emerged from the shadows. The brute thrust a short boarding pike at where he thought his enemy's head should be but the point passed harmlessly through empty air. In reply Thomas sprang forward, swung his sword and smashed the pike's steel tip from its shaft. The pirate stared at the emasculated tip of his weapon and dropped the useless length of wood.

"Quarter!" he screamed but Thomas was deaf to his pleas, again the sword flashed and the pirate's head was separated from his neck. Elsewhere, Thomas' companions were enjoying similar success. The hatred and rage they'd felt for their gaolers was now turned against the pirates and the men of the balinger were doomed. Bos smashed a great antique battle-axe into one man's skull whilst Prometheus eviscerated another with a deft sweep of his sword. Quintana fenced awhile with a foe before running the man through and once they'd dealt with these opponents they despatched three more pirates with the same ruthless efficiency of a warrener killing rabbits.

The Steffen's crew had the advantage of complete surprise and the presence of four seasoned swordsmen in their ranks ensured the result of the battle was never in doubt. Within minutes, the balinger's narrow deck had become slippery with blood and whilst the smell of spilt entrails served to embolden the attackers it spread fear among the attacked. The pirate chief, dressed in a scarlet cloak, tried to rally his men and make a last stand in his boat's stern but when he saw only Thomas and his companions standing in front of him, he threw sword to the deck and raised his hands.

The victors fell upon the only surviving pirate, trussed him like a chicken and dragged the brigand back on board *The Steffen*, whilst the rest of the kogge's crew heaved the dead into the sea and searched for plunder. Apart from a few kegs of maggoty salt pork, the balinger's hold was empty but despite the lack of loot the sailors were still well pleased with their night's work. When sold the captured boat would earn each sailor a handsome prize, enough to keep a poor seaman in beer until his liver rotted clean away.

"Are you insane Thomas? The conquest of England is more important than capturing this leaky tub," Nagel cried when he saw the man he'd risked life and limb to save clambering over *The Steffen's* side. The trumpet player was standing on the main deck and though he was holding a sword in his hand and sweating it was clear he'd taken no part in the fighting.

"By the untouched tits of Saint Cecilia, you mewl like an old woman, would you have me do nothing and wait to be captured? Anyway, look what we've found, I'll wager this poor fish hoped to find more than wool aboard this ship so let's see what he knows," said Thomas pointing at the pirate chief who'd been deposited at the feet of Captain Shobery.

Having finished their search of the balinger, *The Steffen's* crew crowded around the pirate chief shouting and jeering at the helpless prisoner. Several of their sailors showed what they thought of pirates by punching and kicking the man until his face was a pulp of blood and bruises.

"Hang the miserable bastard," the sailors cried and the captain was about to order the prisoner to be strung up, as the laws of the sea demanded, when Thomas intervened. He wanted to know why the pirates had chosen to attack a vessel under the protection of The Hanseatic League and offered to plead with the captain of *The Steffen* on the prisoner's behalf if he told the truth. The pirate chief glanced around him nervously and spoke.

"My name is William Callice and I was an honest Kent smuggler until a man with a warrant bearing Cardinal Wolsey's own seal offered us twenty shillings apiece if we boarded a Hansa ship called *The Steffen* heading for the Rhine and killed the four fugitives from the King's Justice on board."

"By all the herring in Frau Luther's barrel, I didn't think the cardinal would let us go so easily," muttered Bos grimly.

"So rather than risk The League's wrath, Wolsey has used pirates as his assassins!" said Prometheus.

"I thought a priest was meant to reform sinners not employ them," added Quintana.

"Have you done with him?" asked Captain Shobery and when Thomas nodded, he gave the order for Callice to be hanged.

"You promised …" cried the pirate but his words were cut short by a noose thrown around his neck.

"I lied," said Thomas with a shrug. With the rope tight around his throat, Callice could only gurgle with rage as four burly seamen seized him and held him tight whilst the rope's loose end was passed through a block attached to the mast. A moment later the sailors' jeers and catcalls reached a crescendo as Callice was hauled off the deck and began to kick away what remained of his miserable life. The smuggler was strong, and he fought valiantly against the inevitable, but eventually his face turned blue, his eyes bulged from his head and his swollen tongue lolled from his mouth.

"That's it, he's turned off, shall we cut him down?" a sailor asked the captain.

"No. Leave him for the gulls, perhaps they can stomach a rat's flesh, said Shobery. Nagel certainly couldn't. In death the pirate chief had fouled himself and the dead man's ordure started dripping onto the deck. The stench and the rolling of the ship in the swell sent the trumpet player running for the ship's rail.

The Steffen sailed beneath its gruesome banner all the way to the mouth of the Rhine and just as Shobery had supposed, the seagulls had no compunction about consuming a pirate's flesh. As the kogge entered the great river's estuary, a flock of flying vermin wheeled and screeched around the masthead as they fought to peck at Callice's dangling corpse.

The river now seemed to lose its way in the labyrinth of reed filled channels that formed the Rhine's vast estuary but ships like Hansa kogges had been specifically designed for such waters. *The Steffen* slipped easily over the treacherous shoals and sandbanks and soon entered the broad channel of the River Waal. Beyond the Hansa town of Nijmegen, the Waal joined the other branches of the estuary to form the Lower Rhine.

It was here the seagull's razor sharp beaks severed the last tendons holding William Callice's head to his body. Without warning, the dead pirate's rotting remains fell to the deck and the putrefying corpse burst, spilling maggoty, stinking entrails over the spotless planks. The crew had to use shovels to dump the grisly remains over the side yet Thomas watched the pirate's mangled corpse disappear beneath the river's murky water and felt a great sense of relief. Now he could begin his revenge

Thomas plan was simple: he would use *The Munich Handbook* to recover all he'd lost but he would not rely on the magical spells and enchantments contained in its pages. Instead he would use the designs Leonardo da Vinci had sketched in the *grimoire's* margins and end papers to build the war machines that would restore Richard de la Pole to the throne of England.

All that stood between him and the gratitude of the House of York was the code Leonardo had used to keep the method of each invention's construction secret so, whilst the others idled away the journey, Thomas excused himself and set to work to unravel the conundrum. For hours he sat in the forecastle's cramped cabin studying the sepia diagrams and symbols however nothing he tried revealed the answer to the cipher. After two days, Thomas decided he needed a break from his labours so he ventured on deck and saw that *The Steffen* was approaching the Rhine city of Coblenz.

As he emerged into the spring sunshine Thomas found Bos, Prometheus and Quintana leaning on the ship's rail. He wished them good day but instead of returning his greeting the others informed him that they'd decided to leave *The Steffen* as soon as the ship stopped to take on supplies. Despite the injustices inflicted upon them by King Henry and Cardinal Wolsey none of Thomas companions had any wish to fight for an English rebel, instead they planned to join one of the mercenary bands that served The Holy Roman Empire's innumerable bishops and princelings. They invited Thomas to come with them but, whatever his decision, they were determined to leave the ship at Coblenz.

"The prophet Samuel says that the sin of rebellion is worse than the sin of witchcraft," said Bos, conveniently forgetting the part he'd played in his homeland's revolt against the Hapsburg Emperor.

"And the *Book of Proverbs* teaches that an evil man seeketh only rebellion," added Prometheus. Even Quintana was loathe to risk his neck in any foolhardy venture that promised great danger and little profit but Thomas had not only had he grown fond of the three men, he knew that their help could be invaluable. He therefore did his best to persuade them to stay, at least as far as Metz.

"I can't force you join me but I can promise great riches once Richard regains his throne and make no mistake, this is no rebellion. Richard de la Pole is England's lawful king and we'll be doing God's work," said Thomas and he told his comrades how the House of York had lost the throne of England.

Fifteen years before Thomas had been born, Richard III, the last Yorkist king of England, had been defeated and killed at the Battle of Bosworth Field. After the battle, the victorious Henry Tudor, father of Henry VIII, had found the crown of England hanging in a thorn bush, whereupon he'd placed the golden circlet around his head and declared himself King Henry VII.

Henry VII's grandfather, Own Tudor, had been a lowly Master of the Royal Wardrobe but his marriage to the widow of Henry V, the French princess Katherine of Valois, had plunged this obscure Welsh family into the dynastic bloodbath fought by the rival royal Houses of Lancaster and York. After two generations of bitter civil war Henry Tudor, by virtue of his mother's descent from the dukes of Lancaster had emerged as the Lancastrian claimant to the throne and his forces had met the army of his Yorkist rival Richard IIII at the Battle of Bosworth. On the eve of the battle the childless Richard had named his eldest nephew, John de la Pole Earl of Lincoln, as his successor.

Like their uncle, the four de la Pole brothers could trace their lineage from two royal princes, the Duke of

York and the Duke of Clarence, and thus they had a good deal more royal blood in their veins than the Tudors who could claim only one, but after Richard III's death John and his three brothers had accepted Henry VII as their sovereign. Unfortunately, the new Tudor king was deeply mistrustful of anyone with Yorkist blood in their veins and had conducted a calculated campaign to provoke the de la Poles into rebellion. The scheme had worked. Barely two years after Bosworth, John de la Pole had raised the Yorkist standard once more but he'd been killed at the Battle of Stoke Field and the Yorkist claim had passed to his younger brother Edmund.

Edmund had escaped into exile after the disaster of Stoke but the persecution of the House of York did not cease even after the first Tudor king had died. Henry VII's son, Henry VIII, tricked Edmund de la Pole into returning home and despite the promise of a full pardon, the moment Edmund had set foot in England he'd been arrested and executed. Soon afterwards, Henry had William, the third de la Pole brother, arrested and imprisoned in The Tower of London on false charges of treason. William had never been seen again so of the four de la Pole brothers, only Richard remained.

"So you see my friends, Richard de la Pole has far better claim to the throne than the murderous Tudors and if all this is not enough to convince you that the White Rose's cause is just remember that Henry VIII married his brother's widow, which is a union forbidden by scripture. The Tudors have therefore broken faith with God so all good Christians have a duty to oppose them," said Thomas. The Lutheran Bos and the Orthodox Prometheus were both familiar with the teachings of Leviticus and they had to agree that Henry VIII's claim to the throne was at least no better than that of Richard de la Pole, but Quintana was more concerned with the rewards Thomas promised.

"You say that this White Rose is descended from kings and queens, but how is a penniless exile going to raise any army?" he said. Thomas had to admit he did not know but Nagel supplied the missing information.

"The White Rose has the wealth of Burgundy and France at his disposal," said the trumpet player and he continued Thomas' story. After the deaths and imprisonment of his brothers, Richard de la Pole had fled to the Flemish city of Mechelen where his aunt Margaret of York, widow of the Duke of Burgundy and a wealthy Yorkist heiress, ruled the Low Countries as Dowager Duchess. The House of York's elderly matriarch had welcomed her nephew warmly, given him the title of White Rose and made him swear never to abandon his family's claim to the crown of England.

Margaret had died soon after Richard's arrival and though she'd left her nephew a wealthy man he needed a powerful ally to reconquer his lost kingdom. Richard had therefore sought an alliance with the French king Louis XII who'd been delighted to foment trouble in England. Louis had given Richard an army to wrest the English throne from the Tudors but, whilst the White Rose waited at St Malo for a favourable wind, the French king had unexpectedly made peace with Henry. As a condition of that peace, the last Yorkist claimant to the English throne had been ordered to leave France but Louis had softened the blow by providing the White Rose with a generous pension. French gold had allowed de la Pole to build *La Haute Pierre*, a large palace in the heart of Metz.

Richard de la Pole had soon established a glittering Yorkist court-in-exile in this a fee city on the border of France and the Holy Roman Empire but he'd never forgotten the vow he'd made to his aunt and he'd continued trying to enlist French support to recover his throne. After Louis' death Richard had repeatedly petitioned the new king, Francis I, to provide him with another army to invade England whilst on the other side of The Channel, Henry VIII had become obsessed with ending the Yorkist threat by wiping out the de la Poles once and for all.

"Henry ordered his Lord Chancellor, Cardinal Wolsey, to murder the White Rose and though all the assassins sent by the Tudors have failed Henry's sure to keep trying until one succeeds. Only when the Tudors are cast down and the House of York rules England will honest men like Richard de la Pole feel safe," said Nagel.

"He has my sympathy but what do you want us to do about it?" said Quintana who'd listened to the history lesson with polite detachment, his only concern was to put as many miles as possible between himself and the king who wanted his head.

"You've said that you wish to sell your martial services to some great lord of The Empire but you won't get rich chasing poachers and guarding wine cellars. On the other hand those who fight loyally for the White Rose will be given their castles and great estates," said Nagel but Quintana still wasn't satisfied. He reminded Nagel that every Yorkist plot had ended in failure and the only reward received by defeated rebels was death.

"Nevertheless Richard will be king and, what's more, I can show you how I will lead his armies to victory," said Thomas and before the others could stop him he had disappeared into the forecastle's cabin.

9

METZ

Thomas returned to his bewildered companions a few moments later and he was carrying his copy of *The Munich Handbook*. Holding up the book so everyone could see, he quickly thumbed through the pages to show them Leonardo's designs for armoured wagons, giant crossbows multi barrelled cannon and boats that could sail underwater.

"With such weapons I can make whomsoever I choose king of England and those who join me will win more titles than Columbus and more wealth than da Gama. Moreover these machines can do much more than conquer England for Richard de la Pole!" Thomas said triumphantly and with growing excitement he promised that Leonardo's war machines could help Prometheus take back Nubia from the Funj, or drive the Hapsburgs from Bos' homeland. If they wished, they could even spread the word of Luther all the way to the gates of Rome.

"Do you know how to build these contraptions?" Bos asked suspiciously.

"And if you do, will they work?" Prometheus said.

"I do and they will," Thomas lied. Bos and Prometheus looked at each other and after a brief conversation between themselves the Nubian spoke.

"Very well Englishman, Bos and I will go with you on the condition that you build more of these weapons of war to help us end the tyrannies in our homelands," Prometheus said quietly.

"What about you Portugee, you're lucky that your homeland is at peace so will you continue into Germany or return to Portugal?" Bos added. In reply Quintana spat over the side, he'd no intention of going back to Lisbon, where several jealous husbands were waiting to avenge insults to their wives' honour, but he didn't relish the prospect of venturing into the heart of The Hapsburg's German Empire alone.

"Do you expect me to die of boredom guarding some cabbage eating count's crumbling castle whilst you all become rich in England? I want my share so I'm coming too, but first I'm going to find something to eat," he said. The others laughed and together they went in search of breakfast.

At Coblenz, *The Steffen* left the Rhine and joined the Moselle, a river which led into the heart of Burgundy. At first the river flowed lazily through narrow looping gorges with vineyards marching down the steeply sided hills to the water's edge, like Malcolm's army coming to drink.

The tops of the highest hills were crowned by fairy-tale castles with tall slender towers whilst prosperous towns crowded the slopes beneath their walls. Beyond the ancient city of Trier, the Moselle entered a wider valley, filled with broad water meadows and sleepy villages, and Thomas' first site of their destination was the great square monolith of Metz's cathedral.

For the last few miles of the journey, *The Steffen's* progress was slowed by crowds of gaily painted barges bringing a cornucopia of goods to Metz's numerous markets. A customs post at the city's water gate was collecting tolls and the labyrinthine processes of officialdom created a long queue of river traffic. Fortunately, the red and white Hansa flag speeded *The Steffen's* passage through the throng and by midmorning on the fourteenth day of their voyage, Shobery moored his vessel in the shadow of the huge cathedral which rose up from the quayside like a great gothic cliff.

The wharfs of Metz were as busy as those of London and crowded with boatmen cursing in all the tongues of Catholic Christendom. Bos, Prometheus and Quintana were excited at the prospect of exploring a new city but this wasn't Thomas' first visit. Whilst he was apprenticed to Agrippa, his master had taken a position as legal advisor to Metz's council so master and pupil had spent two years living here. During his stay, Thomas had seen Richard de la Pole several times, usually at one of the city's numerous tournaments and festivals, but he'd never met the White Rose in person.

He asked Nagel how long it would take to be granted an audience with the Yorkist Prince. The trumpet player didn't know but he planned to call on Petrus Alamire, the second of Wolsey's turncoat spies, who still had the White Rose's favour. Alamire would be able to arrange a prompt introduction so as soon the gangplank had been lowered, Thomas and the others set off through the thronging streets.

Alamire lived on the other side of the city, close to Metz's German Gate. It wasn't far but their journey took the five men through a large market square where half a dozen heavily armed soldiers, dressed entirely in black, had gathered on the steps of a church. The sight of their broad brimmed hats, square cut beards, voluminous sleeved doublets and baggy breeches made Thomas think they must be German *landsknechts* but he knew men in imperial service rarely wore black.

In fact, to shock peaceful citizens and thumb their noses at The Emperor's laws dictating what the lowborn could wear, the bloodthirsty German mercenaries called *landsknechts* habitually wore the most colourful and outrageous costumes their tailors could devise. Huge hats decorated with enormous feathers, tight doublets with slashed sleeves, beribboned breeches, striped hose and obscene codpieces all made from contrasting colours were the norm but whilst the cutthroats in Metz's market square wore the same style of clothing as imperial *landsknechts*, their hats, doublets, breeches and hose were all entirely black. Even their armour had been blackened with soot.

"The Black Band! I fought these murderous scum in Frisia and I prayed never to meet them again," hissed Bos as he caught sight of the soldiers

"Have no fear, the men of the Black Band have abandoned The Holy Roman Emperor and now serve the White Rose as his personal guard," soothed Nagel.

"They don't look like a royal guard, they look like mountebanks at a hiring fair," said Prometheus looking at the men with disgust. Four of the soldiers were lolling idly against halberds decorated with fox tails fastened below the axe blades. The fifth was beating an enormous drum whilst a sixth was haranguing passers-by, boasting loudly of the loot he'd won, and the women he'd ploughed, during his many campaigns with the Black Band.

"They're recruiting, I told you the White Rose is mustering an army and these are the men who will drive the Tudors from England," said Nagel.

"The White Rose at the head of the Black Band, what a colourful war this shall be!" said Quintana. The men lingered awhile to watch the wide-eyed barrow boys and costers who'd stopped to listen to the recruiting sergeant. Thomas and the others had seen enough of war to know the reality of life on campaign was a world away from the tall tales the sergeant was telling, yet each man felt his soul stirred by the call to arms.

The cathedral bells summoning the city's monks to their noonday prayers broke the spell and Nagel hurried the men away. Twenty minutes' later they arrived at a tall, half-timbered tenement with upper storeys that leaned precariously over the street. A large wooden trumpet hung from chains attached to one of the first floor's overhanging beams and for those who had their letters there was an engraved brass plaque by the door. The plaque declared that this was the place of business of Petrus Alamire, composer, copyist and doctor in the craft of mining. Nagel bundled the men inside.

The shop's interior smelled pleasantly of vellum and freshly ground inks. The shelves lining the walls were piled high with scrolled manuscripts and more parchments were pinned to a long string that cut the room in half like a curtain. Thomas glanced at the beautifully illuminated pages that had been hung from the string to dry. With great skill, an artist had decorated each page with exquisite miniatures depicting heraldic beasts, scenes from the bible and other vignettes. There were no words written on the vellum only the strange symbols belonging to the language of musicians.

There was a curved window to one side of the door and in this bay was a large lectern angled to make the most of the natural light. The lectern hid whoever was seated behind it but Thomas could see the feathery tip of a goose quill dancing above its topmost edge. Nagel coughed politely and a surprised, owl-like face appeared. The face was round and friendly and belonged to a plump man his fifties. He wore a simple black bonnet on his head from which wisps of grey hair escaped like smoke from a draughty inglenook. The man also wore two circles of glass, held together by a wire frame, clamped to his nose. Thomas had heard of these instruments, which could restore sight to a blind man but he had never seen such wizardry.

"I have returned Master Alamire and I've brought the alchemist named Thomas Devilstone as we agreed," said

Nagel with a polite bow. Petrus looked at his guests and beamed with delight.

"Master Thomas Devilstone, I am delighted to make your acquaintance," he said in good, if heavily accented, English. "I once had the pleasure of meeting your tutor, tell me is he well?"

"As far as I know Master Agrippa is still in Geneva," said Thomas with more than a hint of sadness. He still regretted their bitter parting and at times he missed the wisdom of the great magus.

"Forgive me, I was forgetting your paths had diverged, he went to the Swiss Cantons while you returned to England where the Tudor usurper and his dastardly cardinal have served you ill but enough of idle gossip. You're among friends here in Metz and the White Rose is eager to meet you. The Lord Richard feels every moment England groans under the Tudor yoke is like a stroke of the lash to his own back, so come, we will hasten to Haute Pierre without delay," said Petrus.

The old man put down his quill and snatched up a cloak. As he wrapped the threadbare cloth around his hunched shoulders, Nagel hustled Thomas and the others outside. Much to their annoyance, the little party had to retrace their steps across the city but, as they walked, Thomas introduced his companions and asked if they could serve as his assistants. Petrus confirmed that the White Rose welcomed any man who could wield a sword and who hated the Tudors.

De la Pole's palace lay in the west of the city and occupied a pleasant, open space between the River Moselle and

Metz's citadel. The site had once been home to the Abbey of St Symphorien, a daughter convent of the cathedral, but more than half a century ago the French king's army had destroyed its cloisters and chapels during a vicious siege. The ruins had been left untouched until the Cathedral Chapter had leased the site to Richard de la Pole.

It was a condition of the lease that the derelict buildings were restored but instead of a humble monastery, the White Rose had built a palace fit for an exiled king. La Haute Pierre now boasted a wide moat, spanned by a wooden drawbridge, and a high curtain wall complete with turrets and a gatehouse. From the outside, the palace looked like a smaller version of the Tower of London and the sight made Thomas and the others nervous. Having spent many months casting charts and spells to aid a Tudor king, Thomas felt somewhat apprehensive about entering the last stronghold of the House of York. Similarly, after their recent incarceration, Prometheus and Quintana were reluctant to enter another English fortress.

Even Bos, whose unshakeable belief he was predestined to enter heaven was better protection than any armour, felt unsure of himself. He eyed Haute Pierre's sentries, who were dressed in the hated black livery, with pure loathing as he remembered the men, women and children cruelly slaughtered by the Black Band during the Frisian Wars. Yet, in spite of their misgivings, each man understood that if the White Rose was victorious, he would reward his most faithful servants with land, wealth and titles. Eventually, the lure of Yorkist gold and Thomas' promises of future glories were enough to quieten their fears and the four men followed Nagel and Petrus into the palace of La Haute Pierre.

Beyond the gatehouse was an enormous open courtyard several hundred feet across but instead of a single keep or donjon at the centre there were four square buildings that looked more like rich merchants' houses than military barracks. Between these buildings and the high curtain wall there were wide swards of grass, each edged with a line of trees along each side. In times of peace, the fine ladies of the court would stroll along these shady avenues whilst minstrels played lutes and their lovers recited poetry but the White Rose was preparing for war, not peace.

All around the courtyard, groups of sweating men in braies and shirtsleeves were being trained in the use of a variety of weapons. Some were fencing with giant double-handed swords whilst others learned to handle the eight-foot long poleaxes called halberds. On one side of the courtyard, a hundred new recruits were being drilled in the use of even longer pikes and beyond them, twenty arquebusiers were practising with their devilish handguns. As men of war themselves, Thomas and the others had a keen interest in the new firearms so they insisted on stopping to watch the handgunners discharge their weapons.

After loading their arquebuses with powder and shot, each gunner braced his weapon against his hip and squeezed a serpent shaped lever. The lever pressed a glowing match cord against the touchhole in the gun's breech, there was a loud hissing sound as the charge of powder took fire and the gun roared into life. A moment later, the courtyard was filled with great clouds of smoke and the wooden post, that served as a target, shattered as a score of iron balls smashed it to splinters. Nagel's guests looked at the devastation with professional appreciation and asked if they could fire the weapons themselves but Petrus insisted there was no time.

"Come, we must hurry, the White Rose does not like to be kept waiting," he said. The musician hurried his guests towards the largest of the courtyard's four buildings whose façade had been decorated in the fashionable Venetian style. The ground floor boasted an open loggia of rounded arches and Corinthian pillars, the second floor featured balconies with Turkish balustrades and an elaborate Moorish spire topped each lancet window on the highest floor. Between the windows, which had been glazed with expensive Murano glass, the walls were decorated with brightly coloured tiles arranged in geometric patterns.

Behind the central arch of the loggia, two black-clad sentries stood by a pair of bronze doors decorated with scenes of David, Saul and other biblical kings smiting their enemies. Petrus muttered a few words and the sentries permitted them to enter the richly furnished antechamber to La Haute Pierre's great hall. Once again de la Pole's preference for lavish luxury over military necessity was in evidence and the visitors marvelled at the rich tapestries that hung from the walls and the oriental rugs, not rushes, which carpeted the polished stone floors.

"Who says rebellion ne'er doth prosper?" whispered Quintana staring at the luxurious furnishings appreciatively.

"Truly, the White Rose knows how to live like a king," agreed Prometheus.

"Bah, Our Lord teaches that we should not gather treasures on earth where moth and rust doth corrupt," sniffed Bos.

"And where thieves break through and steal," added Prometheus out loud, but in their minds all four men were imagining how victory in battle could lead to such wealth for themselves.

Their daydreams were interrupted by the arrival of de la Pole's steward. This tall, thin servant was dressed in the white and mulberry livery of the House of York and he told Petrus that his master had given strict instructions to allow no one into the great hall until he'd finished his supper. Thomas protested that his visit was in answer to the White Rose's urgent and personal invitation but the steward insisted his master could not be disturbed. After several minutes of fruitless argument, Petrus' pleas for patience carried the debate and the visitors reluctantly agreed to wait.

The great hall of Haute Pierre was a large wood-panelled chamber decorated with magnificent frescos depicting Yorkist victories over their Lancastrian and Tudor enemies. The hall could seat more than a hundred and fifty people but Richard de la Pole was dining with just two other men. On his left sat the Bavarian soldier of fortune Georg Langenmantel who was a seasoned veteran of the

Black Band and de la Pole's most trusted lieutenant. On his right sat John Stewart, Duke of Albany and Earl of March. Though Albany was a Scot, with his own claim to the throne of the Stewart kings, he'd been driven into exile by the intrigues of Henry VIII and he had as much reason to hate the Tudors as his host.

They sat at the high table, at the far end of the hall from the cavernous fireplace and despite the paucity of diners, their meal had been a sumptuous affair. Rare delicacies such as sugared lampreys, spiced larks and roast swan had been eaten off golden plates and the best Burgundian wines had filled their jewelled goblets. As a final refinement, the diners did not stab their meat with the points of their daggers, as was the usual German or English custom. Instead, they followed the new Italian practice of placing their food in their mouths with little silver forks.

In spite of such a rich diet, the forty five year old Richard de la Pole was still slim and athletic. As well as a tall and sturdy frame, the White Rose was blessed with a handsome face, lively brown eyes and a full head of wavy, chestnut coloured hair, which he kept as neatly trimmed as his full, red beard. At first sight, the casual observer might be forgiven for thinking that he and Albany were brothers as the Englishman was barely four years older than the Scot and both princes carried themselves with the same air of regal arrogance common to those with blue blood filling their veins.

Like his counterpart, Albany wore his auburn coloured hair and beard cut short however his eyes were blue and his mouth was thin, almost cruel, compared to de la

Pole's full and generous lips. The two exiled princes also dressed alike, each favouring the latest French fashion for tightly fitting, striped silk doublets decorated with pearls and embellished with baggy slashed sleeves. Albany had arrived at Haute Pierre exactly six months after de la Pole's visit to the king of France and besides an entourage of fifty Scots men-at-arms, he'd brought letters from Francis asking the Yorkist prince to accept the Scottish duke as the French King's ambassador.

The White Rose had no objection to Albany's appointment but he was angered by Francis' insistence that the Scot should be given full details of his invasion plans as well as command of any French forces sent to aid a Yorkist restoration. No doubt the French king hoped that their mutual loathing for the Welsh Tudors would reconcile these hereditary enemies, and France would win two allies for the price of a single army, but this reasoned logic did nothing to soothe de la Pole's sense of irritation. Francis' letter had made him feel like a wife ordered to take her husband's mistress as her maid and Albany's proud and condescending manner did nothing to help the situation.

This feeling of enmity was mutual. Though Albany was also a royal duke forced to flee his homeland by Tudor plots, he couldn't respect his host whom he regarded as an upstart. The White Rose's ancestors had been wool merchants whereas royal blood had flowed through his family's veins for generations. Moreover, as heir presumptive to the Scottish throne, Albany had ruled Scotland as regent for the twelve-year-old James V until Margaret Tudor, the young Scottish king's mother and older sister of the English king Henry VIII, had forced him into exile. Albany had immediately sought French support for his restoration and the wily Francis had agreed, on condition he joined de la Pole.

Reluctantly Albany had travelled to Metz as Francis' emissary but ever since his arrival the two pretenders had been arguing over the most effective strategy for their joint invasion. De la Pole was convinced that they should first capture London by sailing up the Thames and taking the Tudor capital by surprise. Once Henry had been defeated, de la Pole promised to use the power of English arms to drive Margaret from Scotland. Albany however, had insisted that Edinburgh should be their primary objective. After weeks of wrangling, the White Rose had reached the end of his patience and in desperation he'd tried to win Albany 's backing for his plans with this sumptuous feast.

"Your scheme is daring, that I'll admit, but I repeat it's doomed to failure. If Henry has ships at Deptford or Tilbury he can block any hostile attempt to sail up the Thames and seize London," said Albany, stroking his neatly clipped beard with his long, ducal fingers.

"As I have already explained, at length My Lord Albany, my spies assure me that the only ships in Henry's navy are broken down hulks awaiting repair," countered de la Pole.

"And what of Henry's sister Margaret, won't she come to her brother's aid? My Scottish countrymen have no love for their Welsh Queen but they need no excuse to fight the English. Land anywhere in England and you'll have an army of 30,000 Scots crossing the border within the week but if I rule in Edinburgh your northern flank will be protected," said Albany

"The northern earls will crush any Scots invasion just as they did at Flodden a decade ago, but the situation is entirely different in the south. Do I have to say it again My Lord Albany? Henry is bankrupt and London is defenceless. After his last French fiasco, the English army is disbanded, Henry has no money to raise another and his ships are in port for want of gold to repair them. That's why we must strike at England's capital now, before it is too late!" said de la Pole angrily.

"Henry still has his trained bands and militias to guard London. On the other hand, a landing at Dunbar will force the Tudor whore and her treacherous allies to abandon Edinburgh. Surely you see the sense of my stratagem? To save his sister's honour, Henry will be forced to march north with every man he can muster and once we have crushed his army at Newcastle or Carlisle our road to London will be open." Albany replied.

"Dammit Albany, I'll have my throne with or without you and if you don't support me in this you'll see hell before you see Scotland again!" De la Pole thundered and he slammed his fist on the table so hard an exquisitely chased silver flagon toppled over. For a heartbeat Albany had the feeling that his host would order Langenmantel to plunge his dagger into his guest's throat but a nervous knock and the slow opening of the great hall's door let the evil humour out of the chamber.

"Forgive the intrusion My Lord but there are men without who insist on seeing you immediately, they say they have come from England and must discuss matters of great importance," said de la Pole's steward timidly.

"Well who are they, am I to guess their names?" bellowed de la Pole.

The steward bowed low and announced that Petrus Alamire wished to present Sir Thomas Devilstone of Tynedale to his Royal Highness Richard IV. The White Rose's expression changed the instant he heard Thomas' name and his own regal title, he beamed a great smile of welcome and ordered the steward to show them in at once. Moments later, Thomas and his companions were standing before the White Rose telling him the story of their escape from The Tower of London, the fight with Wolsey's pirates and their arrival at Haute Pierre. Hearing how they'd made Henry and Wolsey look foolish further restored de la Pole's good humour and even the normally saturnine Albany was impressed.

"You've done well Petrus, for I have great need of Master Thomas' services, however I must speak to him in private so you and your companions may withdraw," said de la Pole. He turned to his captain and ordered him to find food and lodgings for Bos, Prometheus and Quintana. Langenmantel obediently rose from his chair, wished his master a good night and ushered the other guests away. Albany also rose to leave but de la Pole insisted that the duke remain. When the three men were alone, he turned to Thomas and looked at him like a hungry child.

"Do you have it?" he whispered.

"Have what, My Lord?" said Thomas, glancing at Albany.

"Do you have da Vinci's notebook with his secret designs for weapons of war. You may speak freely for My Lord Albany, though a Scot, is to be trusted." said de la Pole breathlessly. Thomas ignored the look of pure rage in Albany's eyes and retrieved the oilcloth packet from beneath his shirt.

"I do have it My Lord," he said. De la Pole saw the packet in Thomas' hand and gave a great whoop of delight.

"God's Hooks is that it? Oh I how I've dreamed of this day, for you see Master Thomas I've brought you to Metz to build one of these marvellous machines for my invasion. Da Vinci's genius shall be reborn in you and with your help I shall regain my throne," he cried.

"Indeed My Lord and I've journeyed to Metz for precisely this purpose," said Thomas with a bow but de la Pole was now addressing his Scottish guest.

"Now Albany, you'll see why my plan to seize London can't fail. Master Thomas shall build the same ship that Leonardo designed for the Venetian Doge. Such a ship can travel under the water enabling my army to sail unseen into the Tudor whoremonger's stronghold!" the White Rose declared and Thomas felt his heart miss a beat.

Though he'd boasted to Quintana and the others that he could build such a vessel Thomas had never imagined he would have to do so. He'd been sure that de la Pole would want him to construct one of the giant crossbows or organ guns that da Vinci had designed for the dukes of Milan, not something as ambitious as an underwater boat.

Whilst de la Pole continued to extol the virtues of submarine travel to the highly sceptical Duke of Albany, Thomas turned over the drawing of the turtle shaped vessel in his mind. There'd be problems of course, but the more he thought about it, the more he realised that there was nothing in the laws of nature which said a boat *couldn't* sail beneath the waves and if he succeeded his name would be mentioned in the same breath as Archimedes of Syracuse, Hero of Alexander and even Leonardo himself.

"We shall appear before Westminster like Excalibur rising from the lake and when Henry sees that ruin awaits him, he'll foul himself with fear but he'll be dead before his groom-of-the-stool can wipe his master's poxed, purple arse!" De la Pole ranted.

"A boat that can sail under the water, are you mad?" scoffed Albany. De la Pole opened his mouth to berate his guest but Thomas interrupted him.

"Is the turtle or the oyster mad? They can survive at great depths safe in their shells so why not a man or even an army of men? It is simply a matter of constructing a shell large enough for the purpose it is to serve," he said but Albany was in no mood to be mollified.

"I've heard enough, if your best stratagem is to pretend to be a haddock then I want nothing more to do with your lunatic scheme. I'll return to Paris at once and I'll inform Francis that his beloved White Rose has lost his petals!" Albany cried and he rose angrily from his chair. De la Pole opened his mouth to curse the duke for a craven Scots poltroon but Thomas raised his hand for silence.

"I find your lack of faith disturbing but understandable My Lord Albany, yet I can assure you such a boat can be built and if you doubt my word I'm quite willing to take a test. If I'm lying, my sin of calumny will be known to the demon Abrasax, Prince of Lies, so tonight, at midnight, I'll summon this demon and you may ask him if I speak the truth," he said quietly.

Albany stared nervously at Thomas and wondered what manner of man could talk of the Black Arts so casually. Like most good Christians, the duke believed implicitly in the existence of Satan and the power of necromancers like Thomas Devilstone to converse with the Dark Lord's minions. However the thought of evil spirits being released from the sulphurous pit turned the duke's blood to water and his air of disinterested pride vanished faster than a drunkard's gold in a tavern.

"You can really do such a thing?" whispered Albany in a thin reedy voice.

"He can and you'll see for yourself unless you lack the courage," said de la Pole who was thoroughly enjoying the duke's discomfort. Albany's eyes darted around the room but he knew he was trapped. If he refused to witness the summoning of a demon he'd be branded a coward and henceforward he'd never command the respect of his enemies let alone his friends.

"Very well, until midnight," said Albany swallowing hard.

10

THE PENTAGRAM

Thomas requested the use of the tallest tower in Haute Pierre for the ceremony and the grateful de la Pole offered his necromancer the guards' chamber in the outer wall's north turret. This proved to be more than suitable and Thomas' new patron also sent servants to the markets to fetch the items needed for the spell. These included a robe, cowl and gloves made from red satin, a bible, a live cockerel, tailor's chalk, a brazier, herbs, needles, thread, a wand of seasoned elderwood three feet long and a dozen candles, ideally made from the rendered fat of a hanged man. As such candles could not be procured in time Thomas assured de la Pole that ordinary beeswax candles would do.

Whilst the servants searched the city's apothecaries, Thomas prepared the chamber. The room was emptied of all furniture, except two chairs, and the stone walls and wooden floor scrubbed clean. Once this was done, he spent the rest of the day chalking magical symbols on the floorboards, arranging candles and praying loudly for the strength to summon Abrasax. It was not that he expected he'd need divine protection but he could not be sure who might be listening at the keyhole. To add to the deception, he refused all offers of food and drink saying that, like St Anthony, he was purifying his body for only the pure could survive an encounter with The Devil.

Just before midnight Thomas lit the candles and brazier he'd placed at precise points on the chalk symbols. He then dressed in his scarlet robes and sprinkled some of the dried herbs over the brazier's glowing coals. Once this was done, all he could do was wait for his acolytes and a few minutes' later he heard voices arguing outside the chamber.

"I've changed my mind, I'll have nothing to do with this wickedness and I demand you put an end to this foul outrage at once!" Albany said in a quavering, high-pitched squeak.

"Cease your cowardly prating. You agreed to come and you'll have proof that I'm destined to rule England," replied the gruffer voice of Richard de la Pole. The next moment, the door opened to reveal the protesting guest and his host. Albany took one look inside the dimly lit room, which now had the appearance of a shrine to Satan, and screamed in terror. He turned to flee back down the stairs but de la Pole had a dagger pointed at his guest's heart. Again Albany cried out in fear.

"All regicides shall be cursed, if you murder me, you will be broken on the wheel and after death you shall suffer the worst torments of hell for all time," he wailed.

"So help me I'll fillet you like a Scotch kipper, unless you shut up and go inside!" growled de la Pole and he prodded Albany in the ribs with the point of his dagger. With a last howl of despair Albany crossed himself and stepped over the threshold. The room smelled strongly of exotic herbs and the only light was from the flickering candles but Albany could see the ghostly figure of Thomas, holding his wand of elderwood, standing motionless in the centre of the room. Dressed in his scarlet robes, and with his face obscured by the cowl, he looked like an abomination of a monk in Holy Orders.

"Please be seated My Lords," Thomas said calmly and he pointed his wand at the chairs he'd placed at the centre of the two, five pointed stars he'd drawn on the floor. A candle burned at the point of each star and beneath each candlestick was a page torn from a bible. The spaces inside the star's points were filled with astrological and alchemical symbols. Albany whimpered but he sat on one of the chairs whilst de la Pole took the other.

"You're both quite safe inside Solomon's Shield but it's of the utmost importance that neither of you move outside its protection during the ceremony. Only those initiated into the highest orders of the Secret Arts may stand outside the star when Abrasax is abroad, ordinary men will be torn to shreds by this vengeful demon's spurs and their souls dragged to eternal damnation," Thomas warned.

"We will obey Master Necromancer, now, is the hour propitious?" whispered de la Pole excitedly.

"It is and I shall begin," said Thomas and he placed the tip of his wand in the burning brazier. He left it there for several minutes whilst he recited a prayer in Hebrew. When the room was filled with the bitter perfume of smouldering elderwood he removed the wand from the hot coals and used the charred tip to complete the third magical star he'd drawn on the floor.

Earlier, Thomas had sketched a chalk circle about six feet across and within this ring he'd marked out another five pointed pentacle with three parallel lines through its centre. Where the two outer lines touched the ring he'd drawn the symbol for one of the four elements of earth, air, fire and water. At each end of the central line he'd drawn a Greek cross surrounded by three dots. Now, to complete the symbol, Thomas used the charred end of the wand to draw the Greek letter ω at the point where each of the parallel lines touched the pentagon at the centre of the pentacle. When he was satisfied, he placed a square object, covered by a black velvet cloth, in the pentacle's exact centre and after reciting a prayer he removed the cloth to reveal a cage containing a sleepy, rather mangy cockerel.

"You'll remember My Lords, that Abrasax is a demon of the First Principle and destined to rule all three hundred and sixty five heavens, just as you are destined to rule your kingdoms, but though he's a powerful demon in Hell, here on Earth he can only survive by entering the body of a chicken. Abrasax will therefore speak to us through this humble creature." said Thomas solemnly. Albany glanced at the cockerel. Anything less demonic could hardly be imagined but he was so terrified by the site of the shadowy robed figure standing before him he dared not speak.

"Are you ready to embark on the dangerous road that leads to the gates of The Abyss?" Thomas asked. When both Albany and de la Pole nodded dumbly Thomas went back to the brazier and filled an iron pail with glowing embers and ash. He carried the pail to the cage and stood over it whilst the bemused capon clucked and fluttered its wings. When the bird fell silent he began to chant:

> *Ho! Sax, Amun, Sax, Abrasax,*
> *For thou art the moon, the chief of the stars,*
> *he that did form them,*
> *Listen to the things that I have said, follow the*
> *words of my mouth, reveal thyself to me,*
> *Than, Thana, Thanatha, otherwise Thei,*
> *for this is thy correct name.*

When he'd finished the incantation Thomas took a shovel full of hot ash from the pail and sprinkled it the over the cage as a priest sprinkles holy water in a blessing. The room was filled with the acrid stench of burnt feathers and the pleasant aroma of roast chicken. The poor cockerel began to shriek and claw at its cage as the hot ashes singed its flesh but the necromancer was merciless.

"Silence Demon Abrasax! Such pain from earthly fire is nothing compared to the pain of the fires of hell from which I now release you. Be grateful for this brief respite from your torment and in payment for your moment of blessed relief I command you to answer my questions!" Thomas cried as he opened the cage and took hold of the cockerel by its spurs.

The bird squawked and flapped in annoyance as Thomas held it upside down in his right hand whilst extending the fore and index fingers of his left hand in a V shape in front of the creature's beak. He began to moan softly then slowly moved his outstretched fingers towards the cockerel's eyes The bird fixed its gaze on the approaching hand ... it became calm ... then completely still. Gently Thomas laid the bird on the floor in front of the cage where it remained utterly motionless.

"Understand this Demon Abrasax, I have the power of the Holy Spirit to release you from your torment but I will only do so if you answer my questions truthfully," Thomas whispered. The recumbent cockerel clucked once but otherwise it remained completely still.

"I now control Abrasax but he'll only answer yes or no to three questions. He'll cry out if forced to reveal the truth he guards so jealously but remain silent in the presence of any lie. So, My Lord Albany, ask what you will," Thomas announced to his astonished audience.

"Is it ... is it possible for a boat to sail under the water?" stammered Albany.

"Answer Demon Abrasax!" commanded Thomas and he stroked the bird in one smooth movement from its head to its tail. The cockerel squawked loudly then fell silent.

"Abrasax answers yes," said Thomas.

"Can the magician Thomas Devilstone construct such a vessel?" croaked the duke. His mouth was so dry with terror he could barely speak.

"Answer Demon Abrasax!" said Thomas and he stroked the bird again. The cockerel duly squawked, and fell silent a second time.

"Again Abrasax answers yes," said Thomas.

"Will the bitch-whore Margaret Tudor still rule in Scotland at the year's end?" said Albany, gripping the chair's arms with whitened knuckles.

"Answer Demon Abrasax!" commanded Thomas and he stroked the bird a third time but now the cockerel was silent.

"Abrasax answers no. Now my Lord de la Pole you too are permitted three questions but no more," said Thomas.

"Will the Tudor usurpers prosper?" said de la Pole eagerly. The bird was silent.

"Will I regain my crown?" he asked. The bird squawked.

"Do you speak the truth?" he said. Again the bird squawked. De la Pole begged to be allowed a fourth question but Thomas refused and shut the door of the bird's cage.

"You've answered well Demon Abrasax, I shall now release you until I summon you again. Return from whence you came and rejoice that one day the love of the Lord Jesus will free you from your torment forever," said Thomas soothingly and he snapped his fingers. The cockerel revived from its trance and apart from a few charred feathers seemed to be none the worse for its ordeal.

"Are you satisfied Albany? Even the powers of hell are certain I will regain my throne!" cried de la Pole triumphantly.

Albany did not know what to think. Had the chicken really been possessed by a demon from hell? Or was the necromancer standing before him merely a crude mountebank who had duped the credulous White Rose by telling him exactly what he wanted to hear? All that was certain was that Richard de la Pole was a madman and only a fool argued with a madman.

"I should report you to the Holy Inquisition for your foul heresy but even King Saul consulted the Witch of Endor. Very well, let Master Thomas construct his underwater ship. When it returns from the deep safely, I shall be convinced of the truth of what I've seen in this chamber. For now, it's late and I wish to retire to my bed. Please release me from this diabolical place or do you mean to hold me here by spells and enchantments?" said Albany.

"You're free to leave, Abrasax has returned to The Pit and all danger has passed," said Thomas. With great sigh of relief Albany rose from his chair and left the room with as much dignity as he could muster. Thomas and de la Pole listened to the sound of the Duke scurrying down the tower's stairs as fast as his noble legs would carry him and laughed. The White Rose felt utterly elated, as if he'd finally conquered a chaste maiden. Not only had he confounded the Duke of Albany, he was certain the illustrious name of Richard de la Pole was now known and feared in all nine circles of Hell.

"You've done well my friend and when I am king I shall make you Archbishop of Canterbury!" he said, clapping Thomas on the back.

"You do me great honour, My Lord, but to serve my lawful king is reward enough," Thomas replied with a polite bow but beneath his hood he smiled to himself. Sending chickens into a trance using only his fingers was a trick known to every peasant poultry farmer whilst the needle concealed in his satin glove's fingertip had been sufficient to make the creature squawk on demand. Incredibly these simple devices had deceived not one but two princes of the Royal Blood.

After the success of the ritual to summon Abrasax, the White Rose immediately appointed Thomas his official court astrologer and alchemist at a generous salary of twelve guilders a month. He was given new clothes, lavish apartments and all the paraphernalia a student of the Secret Arts required. In just a few short days, Thomas had recovered all he'd lost and all he had to do in return was build Leonardo da Vinci's underwater craft as soon as possible. The only cloud on his horizon was the fact that he still couldn't decipher the complex code that held the secrets of the boat's construction.

During *The Steffen's* journey up the Moselle Thomas had continued to try to make sense of the strange symbols that the great artist had scrawled across the margins of *The Munich Handbook* but Leonardo's mysterious language had remained as impenetrable as Egyptian hieroglyphics. At least de la Pole had given his new alchemist a week to prepare the drawings the shipwrights who'd build the vessel would need so, alone in his chamber, Thomas carefully laid out the unbound pages of *The Munich Handbook* on a table and prayed to the ghost of the great cryptologist Johannes Trithemius to help him crack the da Vinci code.

The leaves of vellum had acquired a few more stains during their journey to Metz but the sepia symbols and drawings were still clearly visible. The sketches of the undersea boat showed the craft as if it had been taken apart, as well as complete, but the pictures gave no clue as to how the different parts fitted together. The diagrams either omitted crucial details or showed things that were so evidently wrong Thomas assumed the errors were deliberate and just another way Leonardo protected his secrets. The more he stared at the pages, the more he appreciated the enormity of his task but he refused to be discouraged.

He decided to begin with first principles so he drew simple charts to show the frequency of each symbol in the hope he could discover the signs that represented common letters such as 'e' and 's'. During his travels, Thomas had learned French, Latin, Italian and several other languages but after two days he had to admit defeat. If the original language was Italian, the code seemed to use a dialect that was completely unknown to him. Next he tried to apply Trithemius' *Tabula Recta* and when this failed he moved to *Polybius' Square* but nothing seemed to work. The days slipped by and by the end of the week he was no nearer to unravelling the code than when he'd started.

For the first time since he'd left London, Thomas began to feel desperate. If he couldn't read the code, he couldn't build the boat and kings, even in exile, usually punished those who failed them with extreme cruelty. By the morning of the last day he could think of nothing except that the cipher's key might be written in invisible ink and that this ink would be revealed by the bright morning sunlight. Hardly daring to hope, he held one of the vellum pages up to his chamber's window and, like St Paul on the road to Damascus, the scales fell from his eyes. There was no secret ink, there was no cipher, there was only the reflection of the page in the window's glass and it was that which showed that the da Vince code was nothing more than mirror writing.

For a moment Thomas could scarcely breathe he was so excited but he quickly recovered his wits and sent a serving wench to fetch a proper mirror. Ten agonising minutes later, the maid returned with a looking glass. Thomas snatched if from her hand, tossed the bewildered girl a penny and dismissed her from the room. As soon as he was alone he held the polished surface over a page of the book and the code melted away like a debtor's friends. Thomas could now look into the mind of Leonardo da Vinci and the first thing he read confirmed that the code and the misleading drawings were designed to protect the secret of the master's inventions. In a note scrawled beneath the undersea boat, da Vinci informed his students that *he did not wish to make war more terrifying or allow men to make their assassinations on the bottom of the ocean.*

Thomas ignored the warning and gradually unravelled the secrets of constructing the marvellous boat. Just as he'd told Albany, Leonardo had designed a watertight shell with two long, thin bladders that could be filled with air. Inflating or deflating these air bags would allow the vessel to float just below the surface. The turtle shaped craft had a squat tower, which remained above the water so the helmsman could see where he was going, and was propelled by two paddles shaped like a frog's webbed feet. There was also a rudder at the stern and a pair of square boards projecting from each side of the bow like a seal's flippers. According to the decoded notes, altering these flippers' angle of pitch would drive the vessel deeper under the waves or back to the surface.

The paddles, rudder and flippers were operated by a system of cranks and levers that filled most of the boat's interior, however another drawing showed a different method of propulsion using oars protruding from the hull through waterproof gaskets. Thomas reckoned these would be much easier to make than the paddles, and create more room inside the vessel to carry fully armed soldiers, so he decided his vessel would use oars.

Besides construction and propulsion the greatest problem of underwater travel was how to let men breathe beneath the waves so Leonardo's boat showed a system of flexible snorkels attached to floats on the surface of the water. The ends of these airlines were disguised as a driftwood but the more Thomas considered this solution, the less convinced he became of its practicality. Leonardo had designed his craft to attack Turkish ships threatening Venice and whilst such a device might work well in the still waters of the Venetian lagoon, in a fast flowing river like the Thames a large log floating *upstream* would be spotted immediately.

For this reason, Thomas decided to discard the helmsman's tower and the leather air bags as these would be far too visible from a riverbank. Instead he decided to incorporate two lead lined tanks in the upper hull, just above the line of oars. These could be fitted with simple brewer's taps and filled by the pressure of the surrounding water when necessary. Once full, the tanks' weight would submerge the boat but careful calculation would be needed to ensure it sank to the required depth, not plummet to the bottom. There'd be no way to empty the tanks once underwater but Thomas was certain he could devise a way to use detachable stone ballast to refloat the vessel.

He also decided to provide a Gutenberg periscope for the helmsman. The famous printer had invented this device to allow pilgrims to catch a glimpse of sacred statues being paraded around the streets of Bamberg during religious festivals and Thomas reckoned it would be a simple matter to incorporate one into his vessel. However, Gutenberg couldn't help with the problem of air supply.

If Thomas' boat couldn't use snorkels, his only other option was to find a method to produce the clean air that all land creatures needed. How to do this was a question that had perplexed students of the Natural Sciences for centuries and during his apprenticeship Thomas had assisted Agrippa in several experiments designed to isolate this 'quintessence of air'. By placing rats and mice in sealed glass jars and watching them expire, they'd deduced that the act of breathing must extract something from the air and once this substance had been exhausted what remained was toxic to life. They'd repeated their experiment, placing various concoctions in the jar with the rats, in the hope these elixirs would purify the air but the animals continued to suffocate.

Thomas felt sure that Leonardo must have been aware of this problem and had devised some way to overcome it other than a snorkel. If da Vinci had indeed discovered the secret of purifying air, then it had to be contained in his notes so Thomas returned to the pages of *The Munich Handbook*. He studied the diagrams and text until he found the answer in a short monograph on mining. For some reason, Leonardo had turned his skills to the problems of rescuing miners from deep shafts where the air had become foul and had suggested heating saltpetre would release the fabled 'quintessence of air'. The saltpetre, Leonardo claimed, would not only produce clean air to breath, it would remove the poisoned atmosphere from a mine – or an underwater boat.

Thomas could barely believe his luck and resolved to test the theory without delay. He sent for a flask of saltpetre and, as this mineral was used to make gunpowder, de la Pole's gunners had a plentiful supply. He also called for two rats, two wide-necked glass wine jars and a length of twine. Again the castle had no shortage of rats, jars or string and these were delivered to Thomas' chamber within the hour. He placed the caged rats and the other items on a table and covered them with a red cloth and when all was ready, he sent for Bos, Quintana and Prometheus.

Exactly as Nagel had promised, Thomas' companions had been welcomed by de la Pole, and had been appointed sergeants in the Black Band, so he was not surprised when the three men appeared at his door dressed in the black livery of their new employer. Chillingly, Quintana and Prometheus looked perfectly at home in the garb of ruthless mercenaries and even Bos had reconciled himself to wearing the uniform of his hated enemies if it served a higher purpose. The men greeted each other warmly and were in good spirits until Thomas began to explain the White Rose' plan to row an army up the Thames in boats that could travel underwater.

"By the big black beard on the Queen of Spain's mother surely you jest?" said Quintana incredulously.

"Have you lost your wits in the few days you've been absent from our sobering presence?" Prometheus added.

"Are you planning to use witchcraft? I've warned you before Englishman, I'll have no part in any compact with Satan or his servants. Have you forgotten that the Lord Jesus preferred to walk over stormy seas, not under them?" Bos said disapprovingly but Thomas insisted such a thing was possible and did not require anyone to sell his soul to The Devil.

"I can assure you witchcraft has nothing to do with building an undersea boat. When a barrel of wine falls off a quayside and floats just below the water's surface is it magic or the work of Satan? No, it's simply the nature of things. All we need to do is build a barrel large enough to take thirty men into the heart of London and seal it so water cannot enter. Can that be so hard?"

"If water cannot enter then neither can air and after a few minutes, anyone inside your ship of fools will die," countered Bos.

"The Frisian is right, no man can remain alive for long once he's been shut inside a barrel. Have you forgotten that the infidel Turks use this as a way to execute those who have offended their Sultan," said Prometheus sternly.

"But I can show you how it *can* be done" said Thomas with a smile. The others looked at each other in disbelief as their friend went to the table at the far end of the room and removed the red cloth that covered the cages with a flourish. The rats squeaked at the sudden arrival of daylight and began to scrabble at the floors of their tiny prisons.

"Rats, glass jars what's all this junk?" enquired Bos, looking at the equipment suspiciously.

"Now gentlemen, for the first time in history, I shall demonstrate how rats may survive in a sinking ship," said Thomas with a broad grin.

The experiment was relatively simple. First, Thomas took a small copper jug and heated it in the fire, before filling it with some saltpetre. The hot metal caused the grains to give off barely visible fumes and Thomas quickly placed the jug in one of the glass jars with one of the rats. So the animal didn't knock over the jug, Thomas tied one end of a length of twine around its belly and the other to the jar's cork so the creature hung in mid-air over the jug of smouldering saltpetre.

In the second jar, he placed the second rat suspended from its cork like the other but without the saltpetre. He then sealed both jars with candlewax poured over the corks. When all was done, Thomas and the others settled down to watch. At first both animals writhed and wriggled as they tried to free themselves from their glass coffins but gradually the movements of the second rat became sluggish then stopped. The dead rat hung limply from its rope like a hanged man but the first rat continued to struggle long after the demise of the other.

"What sorcery is this, why does one of these vermin die and the other live?" Bos gasped.

"The saltpetre releases the quintessence of air when heated," explained Thomas but even he could scarcely believe the success of his experiment. He'd duped both de la Pole and Albany with his faked necromancy but here there was no trickery or deceit. He'd managed to make fresh air and with this secret he could sail a vessel underwater all the way to the New World if he wanted.

"My God Thomas, you are indeed a marvel, with such knowledge think what we can steal," said Quintana appreciatively

"Then you'll all join me?" Thomas asked.

"I've no love of the water but the poet Virgil teaches us that fortune favours the brave," added Prometheus.

"And God said unto Noah build me an ark, for you alone are righteous in this generation," said Bos.

11

THE BOAT

The White Rose needed no experiments or justification through scripture to convince him that his plan could not fail. He'd already made detailed plans for his submarine fleet and his strategy called for at least four boats, each capable of carrying thirty men beneath the Thames.

The crew of one boat would seize the king's palace at Greenwich whilst the second proceeded to Westminster to capture Henry's seat of government. The men in the third boat would lay siege to The Tower of London, to prevent the garrison coming to the king's aid, whilst the crew of the fourth vessel would seize St Paul's Cathedral and proclaim the restoration of the House of York. With the centres of Tudor power neutralised, de la Pole and the rest of his invasion force would proceed up the Thames in normal ships and arrive a few hours later.

As soon as Thomas presented his design for the underwater boat, the delighted de la Pole ordered work to begin. The wooden stalls of Haute Pierre's stables were removed to create workshops and the best shipwrights and chandlers hired from the city's boatyards. The workmen looked at each other and rolled their eyes heavenward as Thomas explained his drawings. To a man, the carpenters and tanners believed the boat would be a death trap but if a group of crazy Englishmen wanted to drown themselves in the Moselle who were they to try and stop them? De la Pole paid well and had promised every man an extra purse of florins if they finished the boat by St Benedict's Day.

Besides paying generous wages, de la Pole tried to keep his plans secret by making his workmen swear terrible oaths but there was little that could be done to disguise the sounds of hammering and sawing that the echoed around the castle's wall. Worse still, the White Rose's neighbours began to complain to the city authorities about the foul smells that came from the vats of boiling glue and pitch set up in the castle's courtyard. De la Pole had to resort to colossal bribes and threats of retribution from the French king to quieten the city council but in spite of these problems the boat slowly began to take shape.

Surprisingly, building the vessel proved to be quite simple and even fitting the buoyancy tanks required no greater skills than those already possessed by any competent boatbuilder. The vessel's frame was a series of circular wooden ribs of diminishing sizes fastened to two curved keels, an upper and a lower, with the largest of these ribs in the centre. Planks were steamed, bent to fit around the ribs and nailed 'clinker fashion' to the ribs. These 'strakes' were caulked with oakum, and covered with a leather skin before the whole structure was coated with pitch. This created a watertight cylinder fifty feet long with tapered ends at the bow and the stern.

"It looks like a turd," said Quintana disapprovingly as he and the others surveyed the completed hull.

"That should come as a relief, as you're used to being in the shit," said Prometheus.

"It's a coffin and we are doomed for the Leviathan is a monster of the abyss and God shall break it in pieces," said Bos, ominously.

"But God is to be praised for having made all things, including the Leviathan, so come let us finish God's work," countered Thomas.

With the hull complete, the shipwrights set about fitting the taps to the flotation tanks. De la Pole had agreed with Thomas that the underwater boats should be taken across the channel aboard larger ships and launched once they'd reached the mouth of the Thames. As each boat's entrance hatch only had to remain above water long enough for the crew to board, the valves to flood the tanks could be no more complicated than brewer's spigots, which could be opened by turning a simple handle. Thomas ordered three of these spigots to fitted along the side of each tank and another in the top. Without this fourth tap the pressure of air inside the tanks would prevent them from filling. The extra tap would also give the man opening them a measure of control and more time to clamber back inside.

It seemed like sacrilege to deliberately puncture such a precisely built craft but Thomas insisted the workmen bore more holes along the hull's centreline for the boat's oars. He'd calculated nine pairs of oars, each rowed by three men, would be sufficient to propel the vessel at sufficient speed to counter the river's current. The rowers would also serve as marines to assault the bastions of Tudor power whilst a captain, a bosun-sergeant and a helmsman completed the crew. It was Prometheus who raised the question of how Thomas intended to raise the vessel once it had submerged, whereupon the new Noah proudly revealed his system to use heavy millstones as counterweights to the water in the tanks. The stones would be fastened to the boat's keel and when it was time to attack, the weights would be detached so the lightened craft bobbed back to the surface like a cork.

The equally sceptical Quintana asked how the crew could release these millstones from inside the boat whilst it was still submerged. Thomas smiled and showed him several large wooden plugs shaped like inverted mushrooms. Each millstone rested on the broad cap of its plug whilst the stem fitted tightly into a hole drilled through the boat's keel. The plugs were held firmly in place by cross-pegs so, by using mallets and spikes, they could be knocked out of the keel from the inside. The air inside the craft would prevent water rushing in whilst new plugs were hammered into the holes.

Bos pointed out that, with the millstones detached, the vessel could not submerge for a second time but Thomas remarked that if their attack failed this would be the least of their worries. With the ballast tanks, millstones and oars now finished enormous wheels, eight feet in diameter, were fitted to the trestles which had supported the craft during its construction so it could be dragged to the river. The boat was now ready for its maiden voyage and, just as de la Pole had ordered, the final nail had been hammered into place on St Benedict's Eve.

Though St Benedict was the man who'd urged monks to live a life of poverty, chastity and obedience, the men of Haute Pierre marked his feast day with a great banquet to celebrate the completion of the vessel. Tables were set up in the stable yard and those that had laboured long and hard ate and drank in the shadow of their strange looking ship. Thomas and his companions joined Richard de la Pole and the Duke of Albany at the table of honour and whilst the Scottish duke eyed the vessel with a look of deep suspicion the White Rose was overjoyed with his completed craft. He asked how soon the other ships of his underwater fleet could be ready and Thomas informed him that if the first boat tested successfully, the other three could be completed in a matter of weeks.

"You've done well Master Thomas but she needs a name," said de la Pole as he chewed roasted meat from a large mutton bone.

"Might I suggest *The Hippocamp*, after the merhorses that pulled Poseidon's chariot?" said Thomas.

"Splendid! A toast gentleman, to *The Hippocamp*, the boat that shall carry my army into our enemy's capital just as Odysseus' wooden horse carried the Greek heroes into Troy," said de la Pole happily. He tossed the remains of the mutton leg he'd been eating to one of his hunting dogs, raised his wine cup and took a long drink.

"If I remember Homer, not one of Odysseus' men returned to Ithaca alive, all of them perished because their captain had angered the gods," replied Albany as he reluctantly raised his own cup.

"God's Hooks Albany, you're as miserable as one of your Scottish summers! When *The Hippocamp* completes her maiden voyage you'll see for yourself that the success of our mission is no longer in doubt. Be sure to tell the king of France that when you see him," said de la Pole.

"And when shall you launch your expensive coffin?" Albany replied.

"There's no time like the present, we shall take to the water at first light tomorrow. I trust that is possible?" said de la Pole to Thomas.

"As you wish My Lord and with God's will we shall prevail," Thomas replied but he also offered a silent prayer to Poseidon to bless their endeavour.

The revelry continued until midnight when Richard de la Pole retired to his chamber. One by one, his guests followed their host's example until only the potboys clearing away the wreckage of the feast were left in the stable yard. Thomas also returned to his apartments but he had no intention of sleeping. If he was to give a full demonstration of *The Hippocamp's* capabilities he needed an ample supply of saltpetre but he also thought it prudent to try and preserve his secret of purifying foul air for as long as possible. He therefore decided to smuggle a keg of 'Chinese salt', which he'd acquired from the castle's gunners a few days earlier, on to the boat under cover of darkness.

By the time de la Pole's servants had finished their work, the moon had risen but with everyone in the castle now sleeping off the excesses of the last few hours, Thomas decided it was safe enough to proceed. He made his way to the stable yard as quickly as he could and stepped into the silent night air. In the moon's silvery light, *The Hippocamp* looked like a giant grey seal basking on a rocky beach and its architect couldn't help admiring his vessel before climbing the ladder and scrambling inside. It took a moment for his eyes to adjust to the blackness of the boat's interior but just enough moonlight entered the open hatch for Thomas to see what he was doing.

He soon found the small triangular cabinet he'd had fitted in the boat's pointed stern and opened the metal grate that formed the lid. The cupboard was lined with thick sheets of *amiantus*, the alchemist's cloth that wouldn't burn. Thomas had heard stories that this material was woven from the fur of the salamander and that Persian emperors had wiped their mouths with *amiantus* napkins that were cleaned by throwing them in a sacred fire. Whatever the truth of these tales, the fabric was costly and difficult to procure but one of Metz's armourers, who lined breastplates and helmets with this cloth to keep warm skin away from cold metal, supplied him with enough for his needs.

An iron tray, set just below the lid, divided the cupboard into two compartments. Thomas had told the carpenters who'd made this cabinet that it was meant to be filled with red hot stones to keep the crew warm in the icy waters of the German Ocean but its true purpose would only be revealed when the boat was submerged. Once the air began to turn stale, Thomas would fill the iron tray with saltpetre and the heat from the stones underneath would slowly release the quintessence of air from the white crystals. Satisfied everything had been completed according his instructions, Thomas placed the keg of saltpetre next to the cabinet and returned to the hatch.

He emerged to see a figure standing in the shadow of the vessel's stern. At first Thomas thought it was a groom sweeping the stable yard but as the man turned, the moonlight flashed on the thin Spanish sword in his hand. Cursing all saboteurs Thomas drew his own sword, dropped to his belly and started to crawl along the deck. As silently as a dying man's whisper, he wormed his way towards the rear of the boat and when he was directly behind the stranger, he pounced. He landed lightly but as he hit the ground, his foot slipped on a greasy bone abandoned by one of de la Pole's dogs. Thomas went sprawling over the flagstones, his sword clattered into the shadows and before he could recover his wits the stranger had his rapier's point pricking the Englishman's throat.

"What are you doing here necromancer? Speak or I'll spit you like a spatchcock," hissed the Duke of Albany. His eyes burned bright with hatred and Thomas had no doubt that the duke would carry out his threat but his Border ancestry would not let him submit to a Scottish nobleman without a fight.

"I might ask you the same thing, I was checking the boat was ready for launching but you've no business here," he said angrily. Albany's reply was equally irate and he reminded Thomas that the king of France had entrusted him with ensuring victory in their joint war against the Tudors.

"No business have I? That jackanapes de la Pole has not the wit to set a guard and I saw you carry a barrel of gunpowder inside your infernal craft. So tell me, witch, do you mean to destroy your own diabolical contraption? Are you still loyal to your old Tudor masters or do you now take your orders from Satan alone?" snapped Albany and he pressed the point of his sword into the skin of his captive's throat. Thomas felt a trickle of warm blood run down his neck and in his rage at being trapped by a Scot, the Englishman's wounded pride overcame his prudence.

"You witless popinjay, it wasn't gunpowder, it was Chinese salt! I've uncovered the secret of using saltpetre to purify the air inside the boat whilst it travels underwater and without my discovery de la Pole and his entire invasion are doomed," Thomas boasted. At first Albany refused to believe him and he accused the English wizard of casting more spells to deceive the credulous Yorkist prince. It was only when Thomas pointed out that he'd also be aboard *The Hippocamp* during its maiden voyage, and he'd no intention of committing suicide, that Albany relented.

"Very well sorcerer, but I'll keep my eye on you and at the first signs of treachery I'll have you sent to the scaffold. Just to make sure I'll set my own men to keep watch," he said as he sheathed his sword. Without another word the Scottish duke walked away to fetch his sentries, leaving Thomas to nurse the cut on his neck and wonder why

Albany needed to place a guard on *The Hippocamp* when it had been built inside a castle garrisoned by the most feared mercenary army in Christendom.

True to his word Albany placed a dozen of his men around *The Hippocamp*. They remained at their posts until cockcrow but as soon as the sun was up Thomas was back in the stable yard supervising the loading of red hot stones into the special cabinet. By now the shipwrights knew better than to ask the mad English alchemist to explain his hare-brained instructions. Nevertheless, Thomas insisted on maintaining the fiction that some form of heating was absolutely necessary, or the crew would die of cold when they descended into the freezing depths of the river, and an open fire was out of the question.

Once the stones had been loaded, waggoners hitched teams of oxen to the wheeled trestle carrying *The Hippocamp* and slowly the sullen beasts dragged the underwater boat over the castle's drawbridge towards the river. De la Pole, Albany and Thomas led the procession on horseback whilst Bos, Prometheus, Quintana, a company of the Black Band and Albany's sleepy entourage followed behind on foot. Prometheus imagined he was watching the sarcophagus of an ancient pharaoh being dragged to a pyramid whilst Quintana and Bos had the uneasy feeling they were seeing their own coffin being hauled to a watery sepulchre.

The hundred yards of ground between Haute Pierre and the Moselle were marshy so wooden planks had to be laid under the cart's wheels to form a trackway. Inch by inch, the oxen dragged the boat to a shallow sloping spot by the water's edge where, using a rich blend of curses and whips, the drovers goaded their animals into the water. When *The Hippocamp's* prow was in the river, the beasts were finally relieved of their burden and led away. Now shipwrights armed with axes clambered over the cart and hacked through the ropes that tied the boat to the trestles. The whole structure shuddered as *The Hippocamp* slid gracefully into the Moselle and just as Thomas had calculated, the boat settled with its waterline just above the taps in the sides of the flotation tanks.

The river here was broad, deep and slow so *The Hippocamp* could be held in the slack water by a simple mudweight until the shipwrights had transformed the wheeled trestle into a jetty. Whilst de la Pole, Thomas and Albany ate a hearty breakfast brought from the castle's kitchens in wicker baskets, the workmen pushed the oversized cart further into the river, fastened it to wooden posts driven into the mud and nailed planks across the trestles so *The Hippocamp's* admiral could walk to his flagship with dry feet. However, Richard de la Pole was somewhat reluctant to be the first aboard such a strange vessel, so the honour was offered to its inventor.

Thomas didn't need to be asked twice, eager to explore his boat, he ran along the improvised jetty and clambered inside. The interior smelled pleasantly of new leather and freshly sawed pinewood. There was also an eerie silence as the water that surrounded three quarters of the hull dampened any noise from outside. Once he was used to the sensation he found the quietness created a strange air of calm and he wondered if this was how unborn babies felt in the womb. More importantly, the silence meant he could listen for leaks. He held his breath and listened hard but there was no telltale sound of dripping water.

To make sure the boat was watertight, Thomas carefully ran his fingers along each seam of the planking and around the sleeve of each oar. Despite the heat radiating from the cabinet, the wood and leather felt reassuringly cold and dry to the touch. He waited a few more minutes and checked again but the boatbuilders had done their work well and *The Hippocamp* was as dry as a Lutheran sermon. Scarcely able to contain his excitement, Thomas pushed his head and shoulders through the hatchway and called to Richard de la Pole and the Duke of Albany who were who were waiting patiently at the far end of the jetty.

"It's quite safe, she's watertight and floats well, would you care to join me My Lords?" Thomas shouted happily. De la Pole looked at the Scottish duke but Albany shook his head. Nothing on the face of the earth would force him to step inside the Englishman's aquatic mausoleum.

"I can watch you drown from here My Lord, but please do not let my good sense keep you from your watery grave," said Albany dryly.

"I see you're a man destined to follow, never lead, but the future belongs to men who know no fear!" cried de la Pole with ill-disguised disgust and he ordered Bos, Quintana and Prometheus to follow him aboard. His newly promoted captains hesitated but after each man had crossed himself and said a silent prayer, they all clambered inside the boat. One by one they struggled through the open hatch and joined Thomas who was lighting a bees-wax candle in a lantern placed in the bow. The single wick provided just enough illumination for the men to see what they were doing and the flickering light cast eerie shadows on *The Hippocamp's* wooden walls.

"So this is how Jonah must have felt inside the body of the whale," mused Bos as he squeezed his enormous bulk onto one of the rowing benches. Though the interior was intended to carry thirty fully armed men, she felt cramped with just five people aboard.

"Are we really below the surface, can we go deeper?" asked de la Pole, as he examined the fine craftsmanship of Metz's boatbuilders. Despite the lack of space she seemed solid and stable.

"The water level is just above our heads and if we sink to the bottom there should be ten or twelve feet of river above us. All that needs to be done is flood the tanks," said Thomas confidently.

"Are you sure we can rise again?" said de la Pole, and when *The Hippocamp's* architect confirmed that they could, he rashly insisted that the craft was fully sub-merged without delay. Bos, Prometheus and Quintana looked at each other anxiously but Thomas assured them they were in no danger and climbed out of the boat to open the taps.

Once back on deck Thomas could see the spigots just below the waterline and the river felt bitterly cold as reached down to open them. Just as he predicted, the air inside the tanks prevented them from filling until he'd also opened the tap on the top. As soon as he'd done this, he heard a rush of air being expelled through the upper taps and he scrambled back inside as quickly as he could. As he shut the hatch and sealed it tight, the boat quivered as if it was unsure as to what to do.

"It will take a few practice voyages to calculate the weight needed to make the vessel sink to the required depth so for now I merely propose to make a simple descent and return to the surface," said Thomas but no one replied, the others were all too busy holding their breath.

There was a creak and a groan as the weight of water began to press against the new planking then the men inside felt a sudden sensation of falling. After a few seconds, *The Hippocamp* settled in the mud at the bottom of the Moselle and Thomas invited the White Rose to look through the boat's periscope. All that de la Pole could see was brown murky water and strands of weed waving gently in the sluggish current but there was no denying that they were truly below the river's surface. The men looked at each other with a mix of terror and elation. Until now, no man had ever enslaved a god but they had triumphed over Poseidon.

"Not even Moses could lead the Israelites under the waves," whispered Bos.

"How long can we stay submerged?" asked de la Pole scarcely able to believe he was at the bottom of the river.

"For as long as we like, Thomas has discovered a way to make the air we breathe," said Prometheus.

"By using a powder made from dried piss," added Quintana.

"Allow me to demonstrate My Lord," said Thomas eagerly. He clambered over the rowing benches to the cabinet of hot stones, opened the keg he'd left behind earlier and scattered several large handfuls of the Chinese salt onto the hot iron pan. In the gloom de la Pole could see the pile of coarse grains begin to smoke.

"Heating Chinese salt releases the quintessence of air," Thomas said proudly except this time the saltpetre released a lot more than air. For a moment the mineral behaved as it had in the glass jars, quietly smouldering and releasing the precious aether that sustained life, but then there was a blinding flash and *The Hippocamp* began to fill with dense choking smoke. Seconds later the boat's pitch and resin soaked planks caught fire.

The previous serene calm inside *The Hippocamp* was instantly replaced by a pandemonium of panic as the five men tried to beat out the flames but it was too late. The slender pinewood strakes, already labouring under the unnatural stresses of being bent around *The Hippocamp's* curved ribs, suddenly burst apart with a loud crack. The force of the break ruptured the boat's leather skin and water began to pour through the hole. The flood extinguished the flames but did nothing to lessen the peril facing the men trapped inside the doomed vessel.

"In the name of God Almighty get us back to the surface before we all drown!" roared de la Pole.

"Thomas, release the weights, the rest of you, help me try and plug the breach," barked Quintana, who was ripping off his shirt and stuffing it into the hole in the planking. The others scrambled to help him whilst

Thomas found the mallet to knock out the pegs holding the weights to the keel. The bottom of the boat was already awash and as Thomas felt for the first peg, the others trod on his hands. After a few heart stopping seconds he found the peg and struck it as hard as he could but the muddy water in the bottom of the boat was a foot deep and it cushioned each blow.

The deluge of water and the shouting of his companions didn't help but after three waterlogged strikes Thomas managed to knock out the peg that held the stern weight. Instantly the rear of the boat began to rise sending all the men tumbling into the bow. As the boat slowly stood on its nose, the cabinet in the stern burst open, the hot stones fell into the flooded keel with hiss and the resulting steam extinguished the lantern. Now Thomas had to search for the peg holding the bow weight in total darkness

It took a dozen attempts but at last the peg gave way and the boat was free of its anchors. The men felt the vessel rise and when they were sure they'd broached the surface Bos wrenched the entrance hatch open. A shaft of sunlight showed they had indeed returned from the depths but the boat was still filling rapidly with water. Bos climbed out and hauled de la Pole through the hatch as if he were a spent fish. Prometheus followed but before Quintana and Thomas could escape, the water pouring through the shattered planks finally claimed *The Hippocamp* for Poseidon.

The boat began to return, bow first, to the bottom of the Moselle. Water now poured through the open hatch as well has the punctured hull, which hastened the stricken vessel's descent into the deep. Try as they might, Thomas and Quintana couldn't clamber their way to the hatch and they were forced to retreat to a pocket of air trapped in the stern. For a moment they were safe but the water kept on rising. They had barely a minute before they drowned.

"Can you swim?" gasped Quintana, Thomas nodded. "Good, take a deep breath and follow me!"

Both men closed their eyes, filled their lungs with air and dived beneath the oily brown water. Blind, chilled to the marrow and half drowned the two men had to feel their way, hand-over-hand, to the spot where they thought the opening to the entrance hatch would be but all they found were solid wood planks. Thomas tried to fight his growing sense of desperation, he felt as if his lungs were on fire, his head swam with dizziness and he knew that if he lost consciousness he'd die but the lack of air only served to increase his sense of panic and disorientation.

In the final moment before death Thomas could feel the hands of river demons clawing at him but he felt no fear and he gratefully surrendered to the inevitable. He let his body go limp, so the ghostly *nixe* could carry him to Hell, but instead of a blast of red hot brimstone he felt the cold rush of fresh air on his face. Without thinking he opened his mouth to suck in air only for his body to be seized by paroxysms of coughing and retching as his stomach and lungs tried to eject several pints of river water at the same time. Eventually the spasm passed and he realised he was lying on grass. Hardly daring to hope he was in Elysium rather than Tartarus, he opened his eyes and saw blue skies.

"He lives," said Quintana.

"Then he has you to thank for his life Portugee," said Bos.

"What happened? I thought it was all over for me," Thomas croaked.

"Quintana got you out but perhaps it would have been better if we'd all drowned," said Prometheus grimly. Thomas raised himself onto one elbow and saw that he and his companions were surrounded by the men of the Black Band and each of de la Pole's cutthroats was holding a sword or a long wooden quarterstaff. The White Rose, who was looking less like a king and more like a drowned daisy, stood flanked by his men and his face was the same colour as his mulberry banner.

"Assassins! I see it all now. You were sent to wreck my schemes and murder your rightful king, who paid you? Was it Henry? Tell me and I'll make your death swift but hold your tongue and you'll spend weeks in agony before I grant you the mercy of the grave," he shrieked.

"I'm no assassin, it was sabotage! Someone changed my keg of saltpetre for one of gunpowder and in the darkness I didn't notice. Whoever did that destroyed your ship not I," spluttered Thomas.

"Silence! I know you and your fellow warlocks have bewitched me but I'll make sure you miserable traitors suffer the fate of all those who make a pact with Satan," De la Pole raged. Thomas and Quintana, lying half-drowned on the grass, could say nothing in their own defence but Prometheus and Bos leapt to their feet, balled their huge fists and prepared to fight.

"We're not witches, we're baptised Christians who live to serve The Lord of Light not the King of Darkness," cried Prometheus.

"And we'll prove our innocence before God in a trial by combat," growled Bos forgetting that he and his companions were unarmed whilst de la Pole's men carried long halberds with lethal blades.

"Do you think me a fool? With my own eyes, I saw the sorcerer Devilstone raise the demon Abrasax from The Pit!" De la Pole bellowed and he ordered the men of the Black Band to arrest the warlocks.

Though de la Pole's men were hampered by their master's order to take the wizards alive, there was never any doubt about the outcome of the fight. Bos and Prometheus managed to bloody the noses and black the eyes of many of their former comrades but in the end the Black band's superior numbers and stout ash staves carried the day. Bos and Prometheus were clubbed into insensibility whilst Thomas and Quintana were too weak to put up anything but a token resistance.

"Take them to the dungeons at the *pont des Morts* and summon the Cathedral Chapter. The Bishop of St Etienne shall decide these heretics' fate but first we shall give them a taste of the everlasting pain that awaits him in Hell," ordered de la Pole but Thomas and the others weren't listening. The storm of vicious blows unleashed upon the prisoners' heads had knocked them all utterly senseless.

12

THE PONT DES MORTS

Thomas was woken by a strange tickling sensation. Painfully, he opened his eyes and saw a large black rat licking the dried blood that encrusted his temple. Choking back his feelings of revulsion, he lay motionless and tried to decide if the verminous creature was real or a nightmare. The rat carried on lapping at the crusted gore oblivious to his gaze. Finally Thomas could bear it no longer, he gave a cry of disgust and lashed out at the hateful animal. The blow catapulted the rat into the shadows and with a squeak of annoyance it scuttled away through a crack in the wall.

Nursing his ringing head, and thanking God that his limbs had not been chained to the wall, Thomas sat up and tried to make sense of his surroundings. He was imprisoned in a small stone vault with a curved roof and an iron grill for a door. The cell was roughly eight feet long by six feet wide but it wasn't high enough to allow a grown man to stand. There was nothing inside, except a thin carpet of reeking straw, and though it was much smaller than the cell he'd shared in The Fleet, the damp air and foetid stench were identical. Slowly and painfully he crawled to the grating at the front of the cell and peered into the gloom. It was only now that he realised this dungeon wasn't just a place of incarceration, it was also a place of unimaginable suffering.

In the flickering light of the room's torches, Thomas could see several terrifying tools of the witch-finder's trade. To the left was a rack, encrusted with the dried blood and body fluids of its victims, as well as a brazier used to heat the 'Spanish spiders' that tore nipples from women's breasts and shredded men's privy parts. To the right was a wooden chair studded with rows of short spikes and behind this throne of pain was an enormous wooden drum, large enough for two men to stand inside. The drum was attached to a wooden boom and it took a while for Thomas to realise that he wasn't looking at a torture device but a crane. What this machine was meant to lift he couldn't tell because the chain hanging from the crane's boom disappeared through an iron grating in the floor.

If the function of the crane remained a mystery the purpose of the two smaller winches in the centre of the room was all too clear. These windlasses, together with their cats' cradle of ropes and pulleys, were the *strappado* and during his travels Thomas had been told how the Holy Inquisition used this device to suspend heretics in mid-air in a variety of excruciating positions. The gradual dislocation of the victim's limbs was usually enough to secure a full confession but this version of the *strappado* had an unusual refinement. A blunt wooden pyramid, about eighteen inches high at its point, had been fixed to an oak frame placed between the two winches. Together the pyramid and frame stood about the height of a man's shoulder and Thomas noticed that both were stained black with blood.

Shuddering at the sight, Thomas crawled away from the door. The twisted fiends who'd built this dungeon must have known that placing the instruments of pain in full view of their victims would be enough to persuade many prisoners to talk but Thomas was determined not to lapse into the agony of despair. Instead, he forced himself to concentrate on how he could survive the nightmare to come but his thoughts were interrupted by the sound of a lock being unfastened.

On the far side of the chamber a heavy oak door opened and a short but powerfully built brute of a man entered. His head and chin were completely hairless and he wore nothing but grimy breeches, a sleeveless leather jerkin and wooden sabots. He was followed by a second turnkey who had the identical build and grubby clothes of his colleague but in contrast to the first gaoler this man had long, greasy hair and a huge black beard matted with filth and half chewed food. In desperation Thomas lay face down in the straw and pretended to be unconscious.

"Have your senses returned, you cursed English warlock?" said the bald gaoler staring at Thomas' prostrate form. When the prisoner remained motionless, the hairy gaoler handed his bald colleague a short pike, taken from a rack on the chamber's wall and, with a malevolence born of pure evil, the bald gaoler thrust the blade through the cell door's bars. Though blunt and rusted, the spear's point easily sliced through the flesh of Thomas shoulder, causing him to cry out in pain.

"So you're alive, that's good 'cos we've something very special for you, something that makes cocksucking servants of Satan scream a lot louder than a little tickle from my old pig sticker," said the bald gaoler, patting his pike lovingly. Thomas continued to groan and nurse the deep gash in his upper arm, whereupon the hairy gaoler spat into the straw in disgust.

"Be silent, you mewl like a beggar bitch about to whelp yet you have nothing to moan about. His Grace the bishop is coming to listen to your sins in person and the old lecher usually only stirs himself when we have a plump young wench to put to the question. So think yourself honoured that a prince of the church wishes to hear you confess," said the hirsute torturer.

"I'll confess nothing except that it's men's nature to seek knowledge. Only the dull and slow witted mistake wisdom for witchcraft and all I've ever been is a student of the Natural Philosophies," growled Thomas.

"Bravely spoken but I've heard many brave speeches in here. Now, aren't you interested in how we persuade foul witches to reveal their dastardly pacts with The Devil?" said the bald gaoler.

"Be warned, those who persecute the righteous shall themselves suffer the most bestial cruelties and I will gladly follow in the footsteps of Socrates and Hypatia who suffered martyrdom in the cause of Truth," Thomas declared defiantly.

"Say what you like, words make no difference, you'll vomit up all your secrets once we start to play with our favourite toy," said the hairy gaoler and the two brutes walked to the *strappado* in the centre of the torture chamber. Like sailors preparing their vessel for sea, the gaolers began to make adjustments to the device's ropes and pulleys and when they were satisfied they carefully explained each item's function to their victim.

"We tie your arms and legs to these ropes, haul you up then lower your naked backside slowly onto this pyramid. 'Ere, you're not a sodomite are you? We don't use this on sodomites 'cos they like something big and hard shoved up their arses!" cried the bald gaoler and he roared with laughter.

"They call it the Judas Cradle but it should be named Eve's Punishment 'cos they scream like a whore giving birth to her first bastard," added the hairy gaoler. Once again the two men howled with delight but their mirth was interrupted by a voice from outside summoning them to other duties. Reluctantly, the gaolers abandoned their baiting of Thomas and went to do their master's bidding.

"Think on what awaits you when we return, you English bastard, but don't worry, we'll be back soon and we'll make sure you don't die too quickly, the bishop likes his fun," sneered the bald gaoler and the two turnkeys left the dungeon leaving their prisoner alone with the Judas Cradle. Thomas felt the cold sweat of fear run down his back as he wondered how long a man could endure such agony.

The terrifying vision of being slowly spitted like a suckling pig plagued Thomas' thoughts until the gaolers returned an hour later and this time they were not alone. The turnkeys escorted a dozen clerics from the Cathedral Chapter into the torture chamber, led by Jean de Lorraine Bishop of Metz and the White Rose Richard de la Pole.

All the inquisitors, including de la Pole, were dressed in simple monks' habits of black wool, with the hoods pulled over their heads to obscure their faces. Like a snake stalking its prey, the file of holy men slithered into the chamber and coiled itself around the Judas Cradle. As the monks formed their sinister circle, they chanted psalms to protect themselves from evil but once they were in position the singing abruptly ceased. For several minutes the monks stood motionless, letting their silent prayers sow the seeds of fear in their victim's soul. Eventually, the fattest of the monks, whom Thomas assumed to be the bishop, began to speak.

"In the year of Our Lord 1484, the Holy Father Innocent VIII issued the bull *Summis Desiderantes Affectibus*, which commanded all Christians to root out the foul practice of witchcraft and correct, imprison, punish and chastise such persons," said the bishop solemnly. Thomas, sitting in his cell, listened to the bishop repeat the papal declaration of war on witches and snorted with contempt.

"You would obey a pope who thought nothing of committing the sin of simony and who fathered a dozen bastard children?" Thomas declared. For a moment the bishop was so angry at his prisoner's impudence he could only stare at Thomas with cold, merciless eyes but he soon found his tongue and he began to list the charges that had been levied against the English wizard.

"So, Thomas Devilstone, you see fit to add slander and sacrilege to the list of your many and varied sins. Don't think that we in Metz have forgotten how you and your master Agrippa once bewitched a similar court of enquiry to secure the release of another of your coven yet even this is not the worst of your crimes. Today you must answer the charges that you bewitched a prince of the royal blood and so, by means of necromancy, forced him to construct a diabolical boat to travel under the water. Moreover, once you'd built such a vessel, you cast more spells that forced the royal personage of Richard de la Pole to enter so you could assassinate him by means of gunpowder," said the bishop.

"And how would blowing myself to smithereens serve Satan?" Thomas said sarcastically.

"The Devil protects his own, however God saw fit to save his servant Richard and deliver his assassin into our hands instead. It's clear to us you have returned to Metz to conquer this city for Satan but we may yet be merciful. Confess your sins, name the others who conspired with you and you shall all be strangled before your bodies are burned. Yet if you keep silent, you shall suffer all the torments that can be applied to frail human flesh. How do you answer witch?" said the bishop

"I answer by accusing you, John of Lorraine, of being nothing but a debauched French catspaw who's squandered the wealth of his benefices on whores and high living! Now you must sell your soul to settle your debts but a mere bishop doesn't frighten me. I've been tried by a cardinal and he was twice the whore-mongering poltroon you are," said Thomas. Beneath his hood the bishop was speechless with rage so Richard de la Pole took up the cudgel of justice.

"My Lord Bishop, you have my sworn statement that I watched this man force a demon named Abrasax to inhabit the body of a chicken. His guilt is therefore not in doubt and you must proceed to his torture so we may have proof that all Tudor kings have obtained their crowns by witchcraft. This warlock's confession that he used the Black Arts to maintain Henry on the throne will show all true Englishmen they must acknowledge me as their lawful king! Now you may begin," said the White Rose and he pointed to the two turnkeys, who knew better than to shirk their duty.

The gaolers lost no time in hauling Thomas from his cell and dragging him to the Judas Cradle where they began to beat him savagely with long wooden staves. The gaoler's blows continued until their prisoner had been bludgeoned into at least temporary submission and as Thomas lay in the filthy straw, groaning and gasping for breath, they stripped him naked. Finally, whilst the bishop crossed himself and the monks chanted prayers for the salvation of the damned, the metal fetters attached to the ends of the *strappado's* ropes were fastened around Thomas' waist, wrists and ankles.

"This is your last chance witch, confess or suffer unimaginable pain," said the bishop. Thomas couldn't have spoken even if he'd wanted too and in the next moment he felt the rusty manacles bite into his flesh as his naked body was lifted off the floor. He gritted his teeth as the waves of pain washed over him but far worse was to come.

"Confess, or feel the embrace of Judas!" repeated the bishop.

"I bet you like to watch your priests plough your choirboys, you sick bastard!" Thomas shouted hoarsely. In reply the bishop crossed himself and gave the order. With a creak of pulleys and a squeal of ropes the gaolers lowered their prisoner towards the blunt spike positioned directly below his backside and Thomas felt the point of pyramid slowly part his buttocks. In the next instant its wooden tip entered his body.

As the weight of his own flesh conspired with the Judas Cradle to tear apart the most intimate parts of his anatomy, Thomas cold do nothing but cry out in pain. He tried to arch his back, clench his muscles and twist his body to alleviate the agony but every movement only increased the pitiless torture. Perspiration poured down his naked skin and screams flew from his mouth in a ceaseless psalm of pain. As the torment continued, his oaths and curses were quickly reduced to bestial shrieks and howls but at last de la Pole called a halt and Thomas felt himself lifted into the air.

"You fool, what's King Henry to you? The Tudor usurper sentenced you to death so revenge yourself on your betrayer! Name Henry as the as the chief witch of England and you'll die quickly but keep silent and you'll drown in a bottomless ocean of pain," whispered the White Rose. Thomas tried to reply that he thought all kings were the servants of The Devil but before he could speak, the door of the torture chamber crashed open and the Duke of Albany entered. The Scottish duke was accompanied by four of his liveried attendants and before anyone could protest, he'd tossed a blue leather pouch, decorated with French *fleur de lys*, at de la Pole's feet.

"As you're busy I'll spare you the trouble of reading the French king's latest letters, suffices to say that Francis has ordered us both to cancel our planned invasion immediately and march south with as many men as we can muster," said the Scottish duke.

"What!" cried the White Rose.

"You've dallied too long, My Lord, and now it's Francis' turn to fear for his throne. A week ago the king's rebel cousin, the Duke of Bourbon, crossed the Italian frontier at the head of an army of Spanish and imperial mercenaries. Bourbon has already proclaimed himself King of France and laid siege to Marseilles but Francis is moving swiftly to crush this rebellion. He's planning to raise the royal standard at Lyon and his liege lords have been ordered to join him there as soon as possible. Those that delay will be declared traitor and their lands will pass to the crown forthwith," replied Albany, whose French wife owned vast estates in the Auvergne.

De la Pole could only stare at the leather pouch at his feet. A few hours ago he'd been preparing to lead of one of the most audacious military operations in history but now his dreams of recovering his throne were dead, drowned in the murky waters of the Moselle. The king who'd promised his support had betrayed him and the alchemist in whom he'd placed his trust was now naked and hanging by his ankles like a plucked chicken in a market. Albany saw the look of rage in de la Pole's face and though he didn't show any similar emotion, he was as angry as the White Rose.

"Had we sailed for Dunbar a month ago we'd be beyond the reach of the French king by now, but thanks to your stubbornness we must fight Francis' war in the south if we are to retain any hope of his favour," the Scottish duke said bitterly but de la Pole ignored him and turned to Thomas.

"So your dastardly scheme becomes clear. Henry paid you to delay my invasion, knowing full well that Bourbon's rebellion would force the French king to abandon me. Now tell this Scotch viper that it was your witchcraft that caused my plan to fail or suffer more of this," said de la Pole and he signalled to the gaolers to lower their prisoner onto the Judas Cradle once more. Seconds later a shaft of unbelievable pain shot through Thomas' insides and his screams of agony became louder as the wooden pyramid penetrated his body again, but still he wouldn't submit. Albany began to protest that there was no time for de la Pole to continue enjoying himself and insisted that they prepared to march at once. Reluctantly de la Pole told the gaolers to raise Thomas into the air.

"I offered to serve you and your cursed House of York in good faith but now, I swear by the broken bones of St Barnabas, I'll not rest until I've trampled every white rose into the dust!" he said in a voice cracking with pain.

"Shall we continue the torture, My Lord?" said the bald gaoler eagerly but de la Pole shook his head.

"No, though I'm loathe to admit it, My Lord Albany's right and we must pursue this matter on my return. Place the witch and his familiars in the cage, make sure they suffer but keep them alive," growled de la Pole. Without another word, the White Rose, Albany and the clerics left the dungeon but Thomas' torturers did not free their prisoner from the *strappado* immediately. Instead they left him suspended above the Judas Cradle whilst they opened the grating in the torture chamber's floor and climbed into the crane's enormous drum.

The drum was actually a treadwheel and slowly it began to turn but whatever it was on the other end of the chain that passed through the floor's opening had to be heavy as it took the combined weight and strength of both turnkeys to lift it. Sweating and panting with the effort, the gaolers laboured until the topmost bars of an iron cage, about six feet square, appeared. When the cage's roof was level with the chamber's floor, the gaolers secured the treadwheel, released Thomas from the *strappado* and dragged him to his new prison. After unlocking a door in the cage's roof, the gaolers tipped Thomas inside as if he were the contents of a chamber pot being poured into a gutter.

Battered and bruised, Thomas lay on the cage's iron barred floor moaning whilst the hairy turnkey refastened the cage's locks and the bald gaoler returned to the treadwheel. With the cage secured, the hairy gaoler shouted something through the trapdoor before joining his colleague in the drum. A moment later the cage, with Thomas inside, descended into a second torch lit vault immediately below the torture chamber. Here men in the black and white livery of Metz's city guard opened an identical iron grating so the cage could continue its journey. The tiny metal cell finally emerged into daylight whereupon it stopped, leaving Thomas suspended beneath an arch of the *pont des Morts*.

The walls of Metz encompassed several islands in the Moselle and the fortified 'Bridge of the Dead' joined the large Island of Chambière to the river's northern bank. The sinister name was derived from the practice of drowning criminals beneath the *pont des Morts'* and the torture chamber was part of the barbican built over the bridge's central span. Mercifully, the gaolers had obeyed de la Pole's instructions and left the cage suspended twenty feet above the water but for several hours Thomas could do nothing but nurse his injuries. He was covered in cuts and bruises, and his backside ached liked he'd been ravished by a dozen lecherous abbots, but at least no bones had been broken.

For several hours the worst he had to suffer were the curious stares of the pedestrians and boatmen passing over, or under, the *pont des Morts* but the curfew bells ringing across the city brought him fresh suffering. Shortly after the barbican's gates had been closed for the night the iron grate above the cage was opened and Thomas saw the familiar faces of his gaolers looking down at him.

"Good evening, my little spatchcock," cooed the bald gaoler. "How's your arse?"

"If only you had a prick you could go and plough your mother!" spat Thomas.

"But if I had no prick I couldn't do this," said the bald gaoler who promptly dropped his filthy breeches and released a shower of steaming piss into the cage.

"You foul, stinking bastard!" screamed Thomas.

"Such ingratitude, you must've been parched sitting out in the sun all day so I merely gave you something to drink but you must be hungry as well as thirsty. Are you hungry?" asked the bald gaoler whereupon the two turnkeys picked up a large wooden vat they'd brought with them and tipped its contents through the hole in the bridge's roadway. A deluge of rotting entrails and putrid kitchen waste cascaded over Thomas whilst the gaolers roared with laughter.

"Did you enjoy your meal? And what would could be better to go with such fine victuals than some pleasurable company?" said the bearded gaoler. Thomas braced himself for a shower rats or some other vermin but instead he felt the cage move upwards. This time it was raised to the level of the bridge where the door in the roof was opened once more.

In the bottom of the cage, Thomas couldn't see what was going on but it seemed as if a riot had broken out above his head. The air was filled with the sound of cursing and in the next moment three men were tipped head first into Thomas' prison. Despite the bruises, dried blood and encrusted filth that covered their faces he recognised the new arrivals at once, they were Bos, Prometheus and Quintana.

"So you too have been put to the torture," said Quintana, eyeing Thomas' battered, naked body, but there was no hint of kindness or sympathy in his voice.

"You see now that the Left Hand Path leads to pain and death," groaned Bos miserably but the Nubian was more forgiving.

"Leave him be, it seems to me he's suffered enough. Have you forgotten that we all followed him to Metz willingly and we're no worse off now than before we met him. Besides, if he escaped The Fleet and the Tower of London then this chicken coop should present no problem. So Thomas, can you release us from this cage?" Prometheus said hopefully.

"I will not die here because I've sworn a solemn oath to revenge myself on the prince of lies who calls himself the White Rose!" said Thomas hoarsely.

"By the looks of things you couldn't revenge yourself on a dog that had pissed over your boots," said Quintana with as much humour as he could muster.

"Your tortures are but a warning of the torments that await all sinners in Hell, you must repent and leave vengeance to The Almighty," said Bos eyeing the Englishman's battered body. Thomas ignored the Frisian and insisted that he'd not rest until his enemies had been defeated but even Prometheus urged the Englishman to put all thoughts of revenge out of his mind, at least for the time being.

"You're a remarkable man Thomas," said the Nubian. "Most of us can make an enemy of one king but you've managed to incur the wrath of two!"

13

THE CAGE

With four men imprisoned in the tiny cage there was no room to lie down or stand up. All the prisoners could do was sit with their legs dangling between the bars of the cage's floor and with each hour that passed their torments increased.

When the sun rose they had to endure the steady stream of rocks and refuse dropped through the grating above their heads. In the evening they were plagued by the bites of gnats and mosquitoes that clouded around them and when the sun set, the damp rising from the river seemed to chill the very marrow of their tortured bones. Thomas suffered worst of all. Having been thrown into the cage naked, he had no clothes to protect him from the day's fierce heat or the night's cold air and he soon developed a fever. After five days his condition suddenly worsened and the others realised the shadow of death was upon them all.

"We can't stay here, the Englishman won't last much longer," said Bos.

"I'm all right," Thomas whispered but it was clear that he wasn't. Some of his deeper wounds had failed to close and his blood was slowly being poisoned by the filth that fell from above.

"Bravely spoken but I've grown tired of these lodgings and intend to quit this address forthwith," said Quintana with a weak smile. "Now how shall we take our leave, by road or river?"

Unfortunately their situation seemed hopeless. They had no tools to pick the locks that fastened the cage's door or money to bribe the guards and not even the combined strength of Bos and Prometheus could bend the solid iron bars. Even if they could escape their prison, they would have to climb up the chain that attached the cage to the bridge, open another locked grating and force the wooden gates of the barbican that barred their way to freedom. Yet, unbeknown to them all, they still had allies in Metz. On the morning of the sixth day, after the merchants and drovers had made their way into the city, a familiar face appeared at the iron grating in the bridge.

"Thomas, are you there?" hissed the visitor. The Englishman was faint with hunger and fever but he opened his eyes and saw the face of Hans Nagel looking down at him.

"Trumpet player! What in the name of de la Pole's stinking codpiece brings you here? Do you still serve the White Rose? Have you come to report my suffering to that pus-sucking viper? God's blood if I were free of this cage, I'd wring your scrawny neck," he said weakly. The other prisoners were about to spit their own curses at Nagel but he begged to be allowed to speak.

"Hear me out, you must be mindful that all is not as it seems. I'm here to help you escape, as I helped you once before, but I can't explain now. The few florins I paid the sentries will turn their heads for no more than a minute so take this, put your faith in the power of the onager and when you're free, meet me at the Lazar House on the Isle of Ghosts," hissed Nagel.

From his previous time in the city Thomas knew that the Isle of Ghosts was a small, wooded islet that lay a few hundred yards downstream of the *pont des Morts*. He also remembered that its only inhabitants were lepers. The other prisoners cried out in horror at thought of taking refuge among those cursed with a disease that putrefied a victim's flesh whilst they still lived but Nagel wouldn't listen to their protests.

"There's no danger," the trumpet player insisted and he dropped a heavy package through the grate. The object landed on the cage's roof and was retrieved by Prometheus who stared at it in bewilderment. Nagel had given them a length of stout silk cord wrapped around a short iron rod, as thick as a constable's staff but no longer than a man's forearm. At first examination neither item seemed to be of any use in their current predicament but before they could ask the trumpet player to explain further, he'd vanished into the crowd crossing the bridge.

"What's the good of this?" said Quintana examining the cord. "Even if we could break out of the cage the rope is too short to reach anywhere and what in the name of the King of Spain's great hairy bollocks did Nagel mean by trusting in the power of the onager?"

"To The Devil with ghosts and onagers, whatever they are, we should not trust a trumpet player who produces nothing but wind for a living," muttered Bos whereupon Prometheus burst out laughing.

"I'm surprised you've not heard of the wild desert asses that are as stubborn as a Lutheran cleric and smell just as bad. Onagers have a kick as powerful as their odour, so the beasts have given their name to a type of catapult. My father used these war machines to great effect during his wars with Funj," he chuckled

Prometheus described how, during one battle with the invaders, boulders hurled by onagers had scattered his father's enemies like flocks of frightened quail and if only the Nubians had possessed more of these catapults, which drew their power from coils of twisted rope, their homeland might still be Christian. The others protested that ancient siege engines would be of little help in escaping from a cage hanging below a bridge but Prometheus insisted that the same power of twisted rope could open their prison. All they had to do was tie the silk cord around two of the cage's bars and use the iron rod as a lever to wind the loop ever tighter.

To raise their spirits higher, the prisoners could actually see the Isle of Ghosts that lay in the main channel of the Moselle between the fortified bridges of the *pont des Morts* and the *pont Ysfroy*. This narrow islet was little more than a waterlogged mound of trees and reeds but it seemed to call to the prisoners like the Isle of the Blessed called to ancient Greek heroes. Tall thickets of willow and alder hid the leper house from view but if Thomas and the others could escape from the cage they could reach it by the long causeway that joined the Isle of Ghosts to the larger Island of Chambière.

The prospect of escape seemed to revive Thomas a little but having discovered the secret of freeing themselves from the cage they had to wait until nightfall before they could put Prometheus' theory into practice. With agonising slowness, the sun crept across the cloudless summer sky and whilst they waited they had to endure another day of being pelted with taunts and garbage. At last the city's curfew bells sounded and the barbican's gates were closed. The footsteps of the sentries faded into the night and as soon as the prisoners heard nothing but silence they set about their task.

As quietly as he could, Quintana tied the silk cord around two bars in the middle of one of the cage's sides then Bos and Prometheus used the rod to twist the loop ever smaller. Miraculously, the solid iron that had refused to budge when pulled by human muscle alone opened as easily as an eager bride's legs on her wedding night. When the first two bars had been forced apart, they repeated the process with adjacent bars until the gap was wide enough for even the Nubian to pass through.

"Now what? Even if we can climb up the chain, there are a dozen more obstacles in our way once we reach the bridge," said Prometheus, as he stared nervously into the black waters of the Moselle that churned twenty feet below the cage.

"Then we must swim to this Isle of Ghosts, if the plunge into the river doesn't kill us," said Quintana but Prometheus insisted there had to be another way.

"Do you fear the living dead that dwell on the island of lepers?" scoffed Bos.

"I fear nothing but I've told you before, I was born in a desert and I'd no need to learn swimming!" snapped Prometheus. Bos began to protest that the Nubian had managed to escape the underwater boat but Prometheus insisted there was a great deal of difference between scrambling a few yards to the shore and swimming half a mile through treacherous currents.

"Not only that, we could break our necks jumping into the river... and it's dark ... and what about the Englishman? He's in no condition to leap into freezing water," added Prometheus and he pointed at Thomas who was sitting forlornly in a corner of the cage. His face was the colour of ash, and he was both shivering and sweating with fever, but there was also a look of grim determination in his eyes.

"Don't worry about me, if I have to crawl through all nine circles of Hell to revenge myself on Richard de la Pole I'll do it," he said hoarsely.

"Good, because we can't wait for morning when our gaolers will see what we've done to their nice shiny cage," said Quintana and without a second thought he leapt into empty space. For a heartbeat there was silence then a faint splash announced the Portugee had reached the water.

"He's a madman!" said Prometheus leaning through the gap in the bars to watch Quintana's fall.

"Mad or not we must follow," said Bos and he gave the Nubian a hefty shove. Taken by surprise, Prometheus lost his grip on the bars, toppled forwards and fell. His arms whirled like windmills, and his feet flailed as if he was trying to run up invisible stairs, before he too disappeared into the water.

"Are you sure you can make this leap Englishman?" said the Frisian. Thomas nodded but in truth he was nearing the end of his strength.

"We'll jump together and I'll use Nagel's cord to pull you to the island," said Bos and before Thomas could protest, the Frisian had tied the cord around their wrists. As soon as he'd done this, he climbed through the gap in the bars and balanced on the iron beam that formed the outside edge of the cage's floor. Summoning the last of his strength, Thomas forced his quaking limbs to follow. With both men standing precariously on one side of the cage, it tipped alarmingly and before they could change their minds they'd been pitched into the night.

For a brief moment, the cold air rushed against Thomas' naked skin then the suffocating waters close over his head like the lid of a coffin. As the muddy river filled his mouth and nostrils for the second time in a month, he thought he was back in the sinking *Hippocamp*, yet the memory only served to remind him that if he could survive one drowning he could survive another. He felt a tug on his wrist as the cord tightened and he kicked his legs. Together, the two men clawed their way to the surface and managed to seize a lungful of precious air before the powerful current caught them.

The weight of water sent the men tumbling down river, tossing them around like a terrier playing with two dead rabbits. Somehow Bos managed to keep them both afloat and in his delirium Thomas prayed to any god who would listen to guide these poor sinners to dry land. After what seemed like an eternity, his prayers were answered. An eddy pushed the two half-drowned fugitives towards the shallow water around the Isle of Ghosts and Thomas felt mud under his bare feet. Though still half submerged, he managed to crawl into the reeds at the water's edge but here his strength gave out.

"I can make it," Thomas insisted but Bos had to drag the exhausted Englishman through the reeds and over-hanging trees into a muddy clearing where they lay on the wet, spongy ground gasping for breath. Fortune had at least guided them to their destination, and the trees hid them from the eyes of the sentries on the city's bridges, but a voice from the darkness made Bos sit up with a start.

"Frisian, is that you? It's me, Quintana, and I've caught the biggest, blackest fish you ever saw!" said the Portugee and he crawled into the boggy glade closely followed by Prometheus. They were both dripping wet, and covered in cuts and bruises, but even though it was only the Nubian's pride that had been seriously hurt, Prometheus was not in a forgiving mood.

"You stupid, murderous, bastard son of Japheth, what d'you mean by pushing me into the river? I'm a prince not a pike fish, I could've drowned!" Prometheus hissed.

"You ungrateful son of Ham, I saved your life, if I'd left you in the cage you'd be dead by nightfall," said Bos indignantly. Both men struggled to their feet and they would have come to blows had not Quintana quickly placed himself between them.

"Perhaps we're already dead and we've passed into Hell but if we'd crossed rivers of burning brimstone we'd all feel a lot warmer than we do now," he said but Bos and Prometheus continued to threaten each other with extreme violence until the Portugee pointed out they were risking certain capture unless they put as much distance as possible between themselves and the city of Metz before sunrise. Reluctantly the two men admitted the folly of fighting each other and, with peace restored, they began to discuss what to do next.

"Do we wait for Nagel or do we strike out on our own? The lepers must keep a boat somewhere on this miserable mudflat and we can use it to get away before anyone finds us," said Bos.

"I also vote we abandon Nagel," said Prometheus slowly nodding his head. "By his own admission the trumpet player has spied for the House of Tudor and the House of York and by helping us escape he's betrayed them both so who knows where his loyalties truly lie?"

"I agree Nagel's not to be trusted so, whatever he's up to, I say to The Devil with Tudors, Yorkists and trumpet players, let's seek our fortunes elsewhere," said Quintana.

The Portugee suggested that as they could no longer fight for the French king, or his ally Richard de la Pole, they should revive their original plan and offer their martial skills to one of the German princelings who always needed good men to keep their mutinous peasants under control. Prometheus agreed they must abandon their former employers but insisted they'd make more money by enlisting with one of the imperial mercenary captains helping the rebel Duke of Bourbon besiege Marseille. Even Bos agreed that their brightest future lay with the pike squares.

"I'll never forget what the imperial *landsknechts* did to my homeland, so I have no love for The Empire or its Hapsburg Emperor, but if there's no other way to keep body and soul together I'll go with you. Did not Our Lord say that we must render unto Caesar that which is Caesar's?" said Bos.

"I've no idea what you're talking about Frisian, all I know is an imperial guilder will buy as much wine and as many women as a French florin so I'm all for joining the imperial *fähnleins* wherever they're headed," said Quintana.

"So we'll forget the quarrels of English kings and head for Marseille to sign with an imperial captain. If our friend wishes to continue his fight with the White Rose that'll be his choice and though I've no wish to let the injuries we've suffered go unavenged, a feud between Englishmen was never our concern," said Prometheus and he turned to look at Thomas who'd yet to offer his views on their future. It was only then that the three men realised that the Englishman had passed out.

Prometheus knelt beside Thomas to check his pulse and breathing, both were weak and he was shivering with fever. The Nubian shook his head and announced there was nothing he could do, unless the Englishman was taken to the leper house and left in the care of the monks he'd die. The others didn't hesitate, Bos helped Prometheus pick up the unconscious Thomas and, with Quintana leading the way, they set off through the undergrowth. Fortunately, the Isle of Ghosts measured just a few hundred yards from end to end and it didn't take them long to find the leper hospital.

A century ago, during an outbreak of plague, Metz's bishop had decreed that anyone who fell sick must be cared for outside the city walls. To comply with their bishop's instructions, monks from the city's Abbey of St Nicholas had turned an abandoned watermill, on a nameless islet in the Moselle, into an infirmary and once the plague had abated this hospital had become a refuge for the city's lepers. A few years later, the islet's crumbling mill house had been rebuilt, consecrated as a chapel to St Lazarus and surrounded by a high wall with only a single narrow gateway. Behind this rampart against infection lived a score of unfortunate souls, with two elderly friars to minister to their needs, and ever since its occupation by the lepers the islet had been known as the Isle of Ghosts.

Few healthy folk dared to venture across the weed encrusted, wooden causeway that was the only way to get on or off the Isle of Ghosts with dry feet so Bos, Quintana and Prometheus met no one as they carried the insensible Thomas through the marshy woodland. After a short walk, they emerged from the alders to see the leper house standing in the middle of an open patch of bog. A muddy path led from the hospital's gate to the end of the causeway and through a gap in the trees, the men could see the broad channel of the Moselle that separated the Isle of Ghosts from the Island of Chambière. At the far end of the causeway Metz's city walls rose out of the mud like a sheer cliff.

Suddenly the clouds in the night sky parted, bathing the Lazar House's in ethereal moonlight, and for a brief moment the three men felt like Percival gazing on the castle of the Fisher King. Fearful that Nagel could have laid a trap, they waited until the clearing had returned to darkness before carrying the unconscious Thomas through the reeds to the hospital's entrance. Two burning torches had been placed in sconces on either side of the doorway and in their flickering light the men could see a green cross of St Lazarus, patron saint of lepers, had been daubed on the door's worm-eaten planks. They could also see a frayed bell rope disappearing into a hole between the moss-covered stones.

Prometheus and Bos laid their burden by the door whilst Quintana pulled on the rope. From deep inside the hospital a bell rang as if sounding a death knell for their souls. Alarmed by the noise, the three men sprinted back to the safety of the trees but there was no sign of anyone from de la Pole's Black Band or the city's nightwatch. The clanging of the bell eventually gave way to the sound of iron bolts being slid back and the door creaked on its hinges. The graves of the dead being opened on Judgement Day would make just such a noise but in the silence that followed St Peter didn't blow his last trumpet. Instead a small, pale faced friar appeared in the doorway.

"Come my friends, it's quite safe and I'll need your help to carry this sick man inside," called the friar kindly but the men hiding in the thicket hesitated. They all knew that those cursed with leprosy were driven from towns and villages with sticks and stones, forbidden to beg by the roadside and even refused entry into ordinary churches. They all feared the disease far more than they feared any king or his army but they couldn't abandon their patient until he was safe from the White Rose. As quickly as they could, they carried Thomas into the leper house but they'd barely stepped over the threshold before the wooden door slammed shut and Hans Nagel stepped out of the shadows.

"Open that door trumpet player or I'll rip you apart with my bare hands!" Bos roared.

"Why so hostile Frisian?" said Nagel cheerfully. "I'm alone, unarmed and I've helped you escape from certain death not once but twice!"

"All we know is that you're not to be trusted and we've only brought Thomas here because he needs a physician but we intend to leave at once," said Quintana.

"And if you try to stop us, we'll kill you," said Prometheus with a shrug.

"I'm afraid you'll have to stay. If you don't, you'll be recaptured and returned to your cage as soon as the sun rises but here you're perfectly safe," insisted Nagel.

"After all who'd think of looking for the living on the Isle of Ghosts?" added the friar who'd opened the door.

"It is not discovery that concerns us, it's the risk of becoming lepers if we remain here," protested Quintana, whereupon the friar gave a little laugh and informed his guests that leprosy was a gift from God because those who suffered on earth would be spared the pain of purgatory after death.

"Only those whom God chooses are blessed with the noble disease so you may remain in this house without fear," said the friar as he covered Thomas' naked body with his cloak. The others were far from convinced by his logic but they couldn't deny that the friar seemed to be perfectly healthy.

Bos, Prometheus and Quintana looked at each other as they tried to make up their minds. Wherever Nagel's loyalties lay, he certainly spoke the truth about their prospects of escape. At daybreak, the city watch would begin searching for them and they'd be lucky if their freedom lasted until sunset. Eventually Bos announced that if Jesus could keep company with lepers so could he. Cursing him for a pious fool, the others agreed to stay and they helped the Frisian carry Thomas, who'd remained comatose throughout the debate, across the leper house's large and muddy courtyard.

The friar led the way through a chaos of vegetable patches, beehives, pigsties and chicken runs to the only stone structure inside the walls. This building, which served as a chapel, dormitory and hospital, was constructed from large cobbles collected from the riverbed and thatched with reeds cut from its banks. Beneath the apex of the steeply pitched roof were two thin, lancet windows and below these was a rounded arched door. Much to the men's discomfort, the black openings of the chapel's windows and doorway, set against the wall of pale cobbles, looked like the face of a dying man screaming in fear of Hell.

The interior of the building comprised of a single, large, rectangular room with rushes on the floor and rows of wooden cots arranged along the two long walls. Each bunk contained a pile of rags that murmured softly in fitful sleep. The remains of a fire glowed mournfully in the centre of the room and a wisp of smoke curled towards a hole in the thatch. The smell of wood smoke mixed with the stench of unwashed, putrefying flesh was indescribable but the men followed the monk to the eastern end of the room where a crude wooden table served as a simple altar. There was no altar cloth but there was a gold cross, flanked by a pair of equally expensive candlesticks. A priest was kneeling in front of the cross, his hands clasped in prayer.

"Father Sebastian," said Nagel with a polite cough.

"Who disturbs me at this holy hour?" said the priest in a cracked reedy voice. He spoke in French, but his accent was unmistakeably English.

"Our guests have arrived, including our friend from England, alas he's sick and in need of your care." whispered Nagel. The priest quickly finished his devotions and dismissed the other friar, who gratefully scurried away to his bed. As Nagel helped Father Sebastian rise from his knees the altar candles illuminated the elderly priest's face and the new arrivals could see he was ancient.

Apart from being as old as Abraham, Father Sebastian was small and thin with a gaunt, deeply lined face that had the same colour as burr walnut. His few strands of grey hair clung to his otherwise bald head like wisps of cloud around a bare mountain top, but his eyes were bright and alert. His dress was similar to that of a hospitaller knight but instead of the white cross of St John, his coarse black habit had the green cross of St Lazarus stitched to one shoulder. The priest greeted his visitors warmly before turning to examine Thomas. After a few moments, he announced that although the patient was gravely ill, he would recover if given the proper care.

"He has a high fever and must be kept warm, has he suffered much?" Father Sebastian asked as Bos and Prometheus carried Thomas to a spare cot on the far side of the dormitory.

"He's been put to the Judas Cradle and exposed in the iron cage below the Bridge of the Dead, all at the express order of the White Rose," said Bos as Thomas was laid on the cot's rat chewed, straw filled mattress and covered with threadbare blankets.

"That's truly an outrage, Thomas Devilstone is a good man, righteous in the eyes of God," said Father Sebastian shaking his head. "I remember meeting him on his first visit to Metz. He and his master understood that leprosy is not carried by demons or an evil miasma and wished to learn more of my experiences treating the sick in the hope they could discover an elixir to cure the disease. I believe they had high hopes for the healing properties of quicksilver."

"Judging by the occupants of these cots they laboured in vain," said Prometheus who knew only death could relieve the suffering of lepers.

"Nevertheless I thank them for their efforts but enough of such talk. Thomas needs rest and you must also be tired. Stay here for as long as you like and if you'd prefer to sleep in one of the barns I'll quite understand," said

Father Sebastian. The exhausted men gratefully accepted the monk's offer and retreated to a byre on the opposite side of the courtyard. There were no beds but the piles of hay and straw that littered the floor were dry and as soon as the men lay down they were asleep.

14

THE LAZAR HOUSE

At dawn the following day, the fugitives were woken by the sound of church bells ringing across the city and they guessed the call to arms meant their escape had at last been discovered. Once the tocsins had fallen silent, the men listened to the faint shouts of a large crowd gathering on the other side of the river until Nagel arrived with boiled eggs, bread and cheese for their breakfast.

"Your departure has caused quite a stir Everyone is saying the Graoully has eaten you!" Nagel said excitedly as he handed out the food to his guests.

"The what?" said Bos filling his mouth with cheese.

"The Graoully is the monstrous dragon cast out of Metz by St Clement," said Nagel and he gleefully began to describe the fearsome beast.

The Graoully was a gigantic, two-legged wyvern with leathery scales, bat-like wings, a pointed tail and breath so foul it poisoned the land for miles around. This monster had lived in the city's ruined Roman amphitheatre until

St Clement had arrived in the city with a promise to send it back to Satan if the pagan Messines embraced Christ. The terrified citizens had happily agreed so the saint had commanded the Graoully to 'reside in a place where neither men nor beasts could dwell'. As soon as Clement had finished his prayer, the monster had fled into the watery depths of the Moselle.

"A silly story to scare fools and fishwives," sniffed Bos.

"Perhaps, but people are saying the English sorcerer summoned the Graoully to free him from his cage. That suits our purpose admirably," replied Nagel and he told the men that their former gaolers had been threatened with their own rack unless they confessed to aiding the prisoners' escape. The cowardly brutes had begged for mercy and had sworn by everything they held holy that they'd seen the monster rise up from the river and bend apart the cage's iron bars with its talons. They also swore that the wizard could not control the creature he'd released from the river and it had devoured everyone inside the cage before returning to the water.

"Ha! Do these poltroons really believe Thomas could summon a dragon? I'll wager those guards were lying to save their skins," said Prometheus.

"Of course they were, but with everyone thinking you've all been eaten by a ravenous beast, the city watch won't search for you too hard, will they?" said Nagel with a smile and the others roared with laughter. The thought of the superstitious constables believing their prisoners had perished in the belly of a dragon brought tears of mirth rolling down their cheeks. Nagel also had good news about

Thomas, his fever hadn't worsened during the night and Father Sebastian felt sure the Englishman would make a speedy recovery provided he received plenty of rest and lots of good food. Happily the barns and larders of the leper house were well stocked with fresh bread, meat and vegetables.

Just as Nagel had promised none of the city watch, or any of the Black Band, dared search the Isle of Ghosts, especially as everyone in the city had become convinced that the prisoners had been eaten by a monster. After a few desultory patrols, the hunt was abandoned and the citizens began to prepare for the departure of the Black Band. De la Pole and his men left for the war in the south by the city's St Barbara gate, which was on the opposite side of Metz to the Isle of Ghosts, but the fugitives in the leper house could hear the sound their enemy's fifes and drums grow ever fainter.

Whilst their persecutor was marching to the French king's muster at Lyon, the fugitives slowly recovered their strength and after a week on the Isle of Ghosts everyone, including Thomas, was healthier than they'd ever been. Realising that the time had come for his guests to leave, Father Sebastian summoned them all to a council of war and they met in the small, curtained cubicle at the far end of the chapel from the altar. This sparsely furnished room served as Father Sebastian's private apartments and behind the tattered curtain was a cot, some stools and a small table.

"I allow myself a little privacy so I may read and meditate without disturbing the sick. You must forgive the poverty of my quarters but please make yourselves comfortable as best you can. Now my friends, I've recently received news from London, and we'll we have much to discuss once you've heard it, but first please allow me to tell you my story," said the priest.

Whilst his visitors perched uncomfortably on the crude furniture, Father Sebastian revealed that he too was an Englishman who'd once held high office at the Tudor court. Shortly after the coronation of Henry VIII, he'd been appointed to the College of the King's Chaplains and, as a trusted member of the royal household, the new king had often sought the elderly priest's advice on important matters of state. However Father Sebastian's loyalty and sound advice had not protected him from the king's wrath. After nearly three years of faithful service, he'd been summarily dismissed from his post, charged with treason and sent to The Tower.

"Like Joseph in Egypt, I was cast into prison even though I'd committed no crime and I've no doubt that it was Cardinal Wolsey who turned the king against me," said Father Sebastian angrily. "You see gentlemen, I'm a man of peace but the king had set his mind on a war to win back the French crown. I tried to persuade Henry to abandon his vainglorious dreams of conquest but Wolsey encouraged the king in his foolish ambition as a means of furthering his own career. In a matter of months, Wolsey had driven all those who'd favoured peace with France into exile, obscurity or The Tower and had it not been for the queen, I'd have ended my days on the scaffold."

The priest's eyes clouded with tears as he told the others of how Catherine of Aragon had persuaded Henry to let him spend his last years abroad, nursing the lepers of Burgundy as penance for his error, and how Henry had only agreed because he'd believed he was sending his former advisor to a slow and painful death. Despite the king's malicious hopes, Father Sebastian had grown old in the service of the sick but now the shadow of death was finally upon him, his dearest wish was to return home.

"Daily I pray to God to let me see England again but until Wolsey is dead or banished from Henry's realm, not even my bones will be allowed to rest in my native land," said Father Sebastian miserably. He ended his tale with tears streaming down his cheeks and a harsh bitterness in his voice.

"Don't forget that I too was brought low by Wolsey's schemes so every man here has suffered at the hands of this corrupt prince of the church," cried Nagel. The others assured him that none of them had forgotten the catalogue of injustices that they'd all endured at the hands of Cardinal Wolsey but they were eager to hear the news from London and urged the priest to continue. Father Sebastian blew his nose on his habit and smiled as he exploded his mine.

"You will be delighted to know, my friends, that our beloved Cardinal Wolsey is standing on the edge of the abyss and all because King Henry's one eyed serpent is searching for a new Eden to corrupt and destroy," said Father Sebastian gleefully.

When his guests looked confused the priest explained that Wolsey's potentially fatal dilemma stemmed from Henry's need to divorce the barren Catherine of Aragon and marry the more fecund Anne Boleyn. To free the king from his marriage, Cardinal Wolsey had to present a petition to Pope Clement asking for a decree of annulment, on the grounds Catherine had once been betrothed to Henry's dead brother. This earlier betrothal, though never consummated, made Henry's marriage bigamous under church law but Wolsey's duplicitous diplomacy, especially concerning France, had deeply angered the pope. Thanks to the cardinal's intrigues, Pope Clement would never grant any request made by Wolsey on behalf of the English king, whatever its theological merits.

"So you see my friends, God has placed the means to end our exile within our grasp. Wolsey must fall but Henry is reluctant to lose the only priest who dares to put his king before his God. It therefore falls to us to help the king push Wolsey off the cliff!" cried Father Sebastian happily.

"Cliffs ... serpents ... Eden ... you speak in riddles priest, why can't you say clearly what you mean?" complained Bos but it was Nagel who answered the Frisian's question.

The trumpet player declared that ever since Henry had been crowned, he'd feared a Yorkist restoration so Wolsey's chief task as Lord Chancellor had been to track down and murder every Yorkist heir. Wolsey had been very successful in this task, and only Richard de la Pole had escaped his net, but in the last five years every assassin the cardinal had sent to Metz had been unmasked. However if Thomas, Bos, Prometheus and Quintana could succeed where Wolsey had failed, Henry would take this as a sign that God wanted him to dismiss his murderous cardinal. Wolsey would be banished, or executed, whilst the successful assassins would be swiftly restored to royal favour.

"Don't you see? The death of the White Rose will free Henry from the twin threats to his throne and he'll surely reward those who wielded the knife!" Nagel cried triumphantly and he looked disappointed when the others failed to share his enthusiasm for de la Pole's assassination.

"God's Truth you exasperate us Nagel, first you urge us to join the White Rose and now you want us to kill him, which is it you really want?" Bos said angrily.

"A jilted lover could not be more contrary, or more murderous," agreed Quintana.

"Indeed you have more twists and turns than one of your sackbuts," added Prometheus.

"So tell us, truthfully, are you for Tudor or York?" said Thomas. Nagel shuffled his feet nervously as the others continued to insist that he reveal his real motives for aiding their escapes from both The Tower and the cage. At first the terrified trumpet player tried to avoid answering their barrage of questions but Father Sebastian urged him to speak.

"Very well, since you ask, I'm loyal only to Father Sebastian, as he's the only man who's ever shown me any kindness, and in return I've sworn to help him get back to England," he said tearfully. This failed to satisfy his interrogators and they demanded to know more of Nagel's history. Again the trumpet player refused to speak so, much to his embarrassment, Father Sebastian finished his tale.

The priest told his guests that shortly after Nagel's arrival in Metz, the trumpet player had been caught sodomising one of de la Pole's squires. Dragged in front of the outraged White Rose, Nagel admitted that Wolsey had sent him to spy on the exiled Yorkist prince and he would've died on the Judas Cradle had he not bought his life with an offer to change sides and become a double spy. The wily de la Pole had immediately realised Nagel's value to the Yorkist cause and had secured a pardon for his secular crimes from Metz's bishop. However the bishop had insisted that Nagel must also seek both absolution for his mortal sins and a cure for his 'sickness' from Father Sebastian.

"Wait a minute, you told us it was your seduction of Wolsey's married servant that got you into this mess in the first place," cried Bos.

"That's true but I didn't say it was a married woman," said Nagel, blushing with shame. Bos opened his mouth to quote Leviticus but Father Sebastian held up his hand for silence.

"All that's now past and with The Lord Jesus' help our friend has learned to control his unnatural appetites, so if God has forgiven him so should we," said the priest but this did little to quiet his guests' confusion. On the one hand Father Sebastian seemed to be a devout and pious Christian yet he was also happy to ignore The Bible's teachings when it suited him. Not only was he willing to forgive Nagel's unpardonable sins, he was urging his guests to break God's commandment forbidding murder. For several minutes the men sat in uncomfortable silence as each man searched his own conscience. Finally Thomas burst into laughter.

"By the great pus-filled warts on Lucifer's arse what a band of sinners we are!" he cried. "Each of us has been touched by The Devil and our only way back to God is through a garden of thorns. Very well Father, I'll pluck your White Rose and when you get to heaven be sure to tell The Almighty it was me, Thomas Devilstone, who decided the fate of kingdoms and empires!"

It took a while for Thomas to convince the others that the assassination of the White Rose would bring them the riches and revenge they all craved but in the end he succeeded. He reminded Bos that Richard de la Pole now led the Black Band, the same army of cutthroats that had devastated his Frisian homeland, and he owed it to his slaughtered countrymen to cut the new head off this brutal hydra. Similarly, he convinced Prometheus that the indignity of imprisoning a prince of the royal House of Nubia in a cage could only be avenged by extinguishing the royal House of York.

Finally, only Quintana remained aloof from the conspiracy and he insisted that their original plan of joining the imperial army besieging Marseille would fulfil both their ambitions. Firstly any brave man could help himself to as much plunder as he could carry once the city had fallen and secondly any failure to raise the siege would result in de la Pole's disgrace and ruin. Thomas countered by insisting that Quintana's best chance of becoming rich and, more importantly, surviving long enough to enjoy his new found wealth, lay in England with the gratitude and pardon of the English king. Eventually sheer weight of numbers carried the day and Quintana threw up his hands in weary resignation

"Oh very well, I suppose you fools need a man with something other than rocks in his head to keep you out of trouble. Besides, you've all forgotten that we're still sitting on a mudflat in the middle of the Moselle? So until we escape from Metz any talk of future riches is purest moonshine," he said.

"Fear not, I have a plan for you to leave Metz by the *pont Ysfroy* and I promise that no sentry will stop you." said Father Sebastian with a toothless grin. The old monk stood up and disappeared behind his cubicle's curtain. He returned a few minutes later, tossed a pile of dirty rags onto the floor and told his guests that lepers could enter or leave the city unmolested during the hour before sunrise or the hour after sunset. If they dressed in these rags and presented themselves at the appropriate time the sentries were duty bound to let them pass.

"For it is written in the Book of Leviticus that the leper shall wear garb that has been rent and torn asunder, and though his hair shall be loose, he shall put a covering upon his visage, and wherever he so goeth, he shall cry unclean," said Bos, picking up some of the tattered clothing.

"Wear the garb of a leper? By the empty tomb of St Lazarus you can't mean it, we'll surely be struck down with the disease," gasped Quintana, looking at the dirty beeches and soiled cloaks but Father Sebastian reminded him that the afflicted could only be chosen by God and the alternative was to face certain death in de la Pole's cage. Eventually Quintana had to admit that disguise was the best way to leave the city.

"I'll take you to the bridge and vouch for you. If you're questioned, say you're travelling to the Shrine of Our Lady at Benoite de Vaux to bathe in the healing waters. I can't leave the city but Nagel will be with you and he knows every byway between here and the Alps" said Father Sebastian as he showed the men how to wind thin strips of cloth around their limbs and tie a veil around their heads so that the biblical prohibition on a lepers revealing their disfigured faces would be observed. After the men had finished dressing they wrapped spare clothing in bundles, which they tied to pilgrim's staffs, and once their disguises were complete Father Sebastian stepped back to admire his handiwork.

"Excellent, you'd all fool St Lazarus himself! But we must leave immediately for once the sun dips below the horizon no leper may be abroad," said the priest as he collected his own staff and a rattle from beneath his cot. A few minutes later the little party left the hospital and though the priest whispered words of encouragement the men began to sweat with fear and loathing. The musty bandages covering their faces smelled of death and despite Father Sebastian's earlier assurances, the fugitives were convinced that the evil of leprosy would soon start to poison their blood.

As lepers were forbidden to possess boats the only way off the Isle of Ghosts, without swimming, was over the broken down causeway that linked the Lazar House with the rest of Metz and at the far end of this pontoon, a track followed the narrow strip of mud that lay between the river and Metz's northern walls. This section of the city's ramparts ran all the way to the eastern end of the Island of Chambière where the great stone bridge of the *pont Ysfroy* spanned the Moselle's main channel. If the fugitives could reach the other side of this fortified crossing they'd be free.

The sky shone red with the first glow of sunset as Father Sebastian and his lepers hurried across the causeway. They quickly found the track across the mudflats and set off for the *pont Ysfroy* but as they neared the bridge a group of fishermen, setting eel nets at the water's edge, barred their way. At the sound of Father Sebastian's rattle the frightened fishermen began to shout curses and throw stones but if they thought the lepers would flee from their barrage they were mistaken. Father Sebastian damned them all for cowardly brutes and, like Moses parting the Red Sea, he ushered his charges through the mob, cracking fishermen's heads with his staff as they went.

"Why is it that wherever we go people through things at us?" muttered Bos as they climbed the eel fishers' slippery wooden ladders that led to the bridge but no one was listening, the others were too busy looking at the their last obstacle to freedom.

Like the *pont des Morts*, the *pont Ysfroy* was protected by a barbican built over the bridge's central arch. There were two pairs of gates, divided by a portcullis, but until the curfew bell sounded all the barriers would remain open. As most men of martial spirit had left the city with Richard de la Pole's Black Band, the barbican was guarded by just two dotards who were leaning on their halberds dozing until the sound of Father Francis' rattle and cry of 'unclean' spurred them into life.

"Lepers! Don't come any further, keep back I say!" growled the more senile of the two sentries and he lowered his poleaxe. Behind their veils the lepers held their breath. They were just yards from safety but one word out of place would mean discovery and death.

"Calm yourself my son, I'm Father Sebastian of the Lazar House on the Isle of Ghosts and these men wish to take the holy waters at Benoite de Vaux. I've brought them to the city gate at dusk as the law permits, now let these dying men go in peace," said the priest but neither sentry was satisfied. Whilst the senile sentry kept his halberd levelled at Father Sebastian's chest his comrade, who still possessed some sense of duty, stepped forward to examine the lepers. Though he was careful not to stand too close to the diseased wretches, he peered at their rags and sniffed the air suspiciously.

"There's evil abroad Father, are these men sure they want to be outside the walls after dark? The Graoully was seen in the west of the city not six nights ago. They say it bent open the iron cage below the *Pont des Morts* and devoured the four men inside. The Isle of Ghosts is close by so surely you heard the prisoners' screams as the beast consumed them?" he said.

"Alas my hearing is not what it was and I heard nothing," said Father Sebastian truthfully so the sentry told him the story of the English wizard who'd come to Metz and spent weeks training the city's dragon to swallow him yet keep him alive in its belly.

When Father Sebastian asked why anyone would want to do such a thing, the sentry insisted that the warlock wished to kidnap the English rebel prince who lived in the palace of Haute Pierre and carry him back to England, just as Jonah was carried to Ashdod, where he'd be surrendered to his enemy the English king. Apparently, the sorcerer had made at least one successful voyage inside the beast but when summoned to the cage the Graoully had turned on its master and eaten him. Father Sebastian dismissed the story as nonsense but the older sentry insisted his colleague was speaking the gospel truth.

"My cousin who guards the *Pont des Morts* says he actually heard the prisoners' limbs snap as the monster ground his bones like grist under a millstone," he said.

"A fitting end for any necromancer to be sure but whilst I'm grateful for the warning these men must make their journey tonight. See how the disease is so advanced in this wretch his skin has turned black," said Father Sebastian and he opened the bandages wrapped around the Nubian's shins. Prometheus' legs had been cut quite badly during his swim to the Isle of Ghosts and though his wounds had almost healed, his dark African skin was still covered crusted with scabs. The sight convinced the sentries that the man's flesh was rotting on his bones and they recoiled in horror.

"Be off with you and never set foot in Metz again!" the sentries cried and they covered their mouths and noses with their cloaks as the lepers shuffled by. Father Sebastian began to tell the gatekeepers why he wasn't going with the doomed men but the curfew bell was sounding and the sentries were too busy securing the city for the night to pay any more attention to the ramblings of an ancient priest. As the lepers reached the far end of the bridge, Thomas glanced back to see Father Sebastian waving farewell, a few seconds later he was lost from sight as the city's gates were slammed shut.

"I wouldn't like to be in those guards' shoes when they discover they've been gulled so easily," chuckled Quintana as the lepers trudged off down the road.

"Will Father Sebastian suffer when they find out who we were?" asked Prometheus anxiously but Nagel put his concerns to rest.

"I doubt it, he's survived so long amongst the damned no one will dare risk his immortal soul by laying hands on a man so favoured by God but we must make haste. To kill our quarry we'll first have to catch him and de la Pole has a good start," said the trumpet player and he suggested that the quickest route south would be to head for Nancy and then follow the old Roman road to Lyons.

Though Richard de la Pole had marched the Black Band out of Metz some days ago, five men alone could travel much faster than an entire army and the assassins set off in the full confidence that they'd soon run their fox to earth. Their spirits soared even higher once they'd discarded their lepers' rags and though Father Sebastian hadn't been able to give them any money there were plenty of poorly guarded barns and chicken coops along the way. With fresh clothes on their backs and their bellies full of stolen eggs, their only problem was finding a way to kill the White Rose.

"It'll be difficult to get close to him, our faces are too well known," said Bos.

"Then we must fashion new disguises and prepare a trap," offered Quintana.

"I agree but what shall we use as bait?" Thomas added.

"We must discover his secret vices for no man is safe from himself," said Prometheus and he asked Nagel, who'd been longest in the White Rose's household, for details of their enemy's appetites.

The trumpet player didn't hesitate to tell them that Richard de la Pole had a weakness for women and though the others had seen scant evidence of the White Rose's philandering during their time in Metz, Nagel assured them that his former master's love affairs had once been the scandal of the city. One of the White Rose's most notorious liaisons had been with the wife of a goldsmith and like David pursuing Bathsheba, he'd seduced the woman by contriving to have her husband sent away. Cunningly, de la Pole had commissioned several fine pieces of jewellery from the man he intended to cuckold, which meant the goldsmith had to travel to Paris to buy materials.

With her husband gone, the goldsmith's wanton wife happily surrendered to the handsome, wealthy and highborn Englishman. After the White Rose had robbed the woman of her virtue, he'd boasted about his conquest and when the goldsmith returned, his outraged friends had told the man about his faithless wife. Most husbands would have thrown the trollop into the street but, fearing the wrath of an exiled king, the goldsmith did nothing. De la Pole therefore continued the affair quite openly, until the city's scolds and busybodies insisted that Metz's bishop took action.

Much to the consternation of the goldsmith, the bishop didn't prosecute de la Pole, instead he issued warrants for the arrest of the cuckolded husband for failing to control his wife and summoned his sluttish spouse to answer for her adultery. Not wishing to be branded with hot irons and placed in the pillory, the woman had fled to the safety of her lover's castle but the goldsmith had been sent to prison for several months. The day after his release, the goldsmith and de la Pole had met in the street and the two rivals had fought like thieves, much to the amusement of a large crowd that had gathered, but before any serious wounds could be inflicted the city guards had arrested them both.

Again no action was taken against de la Pole but this time the bishop ruled that the wife must be returned to her husband, provided that the goldsmith swore on the holy relics of St Stephen and St Clement not to beat her too hard. The goldsmith had refused to take such an oath so he was promptly banished from Metz. The goldsmith's wife was also banished and she fled to the nearby town of Toul but she remained de la Pole's mistress until her death a few years later.

"But if the stupid whore's dead, how can she help us?" Bos said when Nagel had finished his story.

"Her death doesn't mean de la Pole has lost his natural desires, so all we have to do is find another willing to sacrifice her virtue in a noble cause and whilst de la Pole is distracted by her charms, we'll strike," said Quintana with a knowing smile.

"And where will we find such a Delilah?" said Prometheus.

"That won't be difficult, every whore in France will be making for the king's muster at Lyon," said Thomas. "If we fill a bawdy house with fine lusty trollops it won't be long before the White Rose pays us a visit and a man is never more vulnerable than when he's in the arms of Venus!"

15

LYON

Thomas and his companions made good progress by following the Roman road that linked Nancy with Lyon. Even after centuries of neglect, this ancient highway was in a better condition than the muddy tracks of England or Germany and the travellers even began to enjoy the journey. The early summer weather was fine and warm, the roadside inns were plentiful and their cellars full of good food and wine. Moreover, there was an abundance of innocent wayfarers to provide the cash they needed to pay for proper board and lodgings.

For weeks, the French king's captains had been pasting recruiting notices on the walls of inns and taverns across France. Now the roads to Lyon were crowded with runaway ploughboys and fugitive apprentices, all eager to win fame and fortune in King Francis' army. From somewhere, Quintana procured a pack of cards and fleeced these lambs by engaging them in games of *primero* and *piquet*. Thomas told fortunes and sold the necessary charms, fashioned from twigs and dried grass, to protect against the death or injury in battle he confidently predicted.

For his part Prometheus resumed his boxing career and challenged the braver bucks to wager on bareknuckle bouts, which he invariably won. Even Bos contributed to their reserves of cash by preaching hell-fire sermons warning of the dangers of popery and passing round his hat. Thomas was surprised that so many of their fellow travellers were eager to embrace the new religion of Luther as most of the people on the road were French and France was the First Daughter of the Roman Church. The French king was also a devout Catholic and his ally the pope had declared Lutheranism to be heresy, nevertheless Bos drew increasingly large audiences at each inn where they stopped.

Some of the most ardent members of Bos' congregation were veterans of France's endless wars with the Hapsburg kingdoms of Germany, Spain, Sicily and Italy - four crowns now united in the single person of the Holy Roman Emperor Charles V. These grizzled warriors had known glorious victories at Mézières and Marignano and crushing defeats at Bicocca and Sesia. Yet despite the dangers of battle these men gladly continued in the profession of arms. No peasant ever became rich but a pikeman, halberdier or arquebusier could win enough loot to retire and, whatever their past sins, Bos' preaching assured them of a place in heaven if only they had faith in their own salvation.

There were not just eager tyros and battle hardened veterans heading for Lyon. Just as a rotting carcass attracts swarms of flies, the king's muster brought forth the *tross* an unruly caravan of pedlars, sutlers and merchants who clogged the road with their lumbering wagons and in their wake came gaggles of beggarly women with brattish children clinging to their dust-caked skirts. South of Dijon the numbers of the *trossen* were swelled by scores of thieves and whores also hoping to profit from the business of war and the would-be assassins gratefully hid themselves in this throng.

The men arrived at their destination at the end of July and they were amazed to discover that France's ancient capital had adopted a younger sister. The original Lyon of brick and stone still stood on the peninsular formed by the meeting of the rivers Rhone and Saone but, on the flat plain to the east of the Rhone, a new city of wood and canvas had been born. The French camp's hundreds of white tents and brightly coloured pavilions had been laid out like a permanent settlement, complete with broad streets, narrow alleys and open squares, and like any other city this temporary metropolis thronged with people.

The cries of merchants selling their wares, sergeants drilling their men and whores plying their trade mingled in the warm air and drifted over the valley floor like a swarm of angry bees. The panorama of sights and sounds was strangely intoxicating and for several minutes Thomas and others could only stand at the side of the road, staring at the tented Sodom stretched out before them.

"And it came to pass that God destroyed the cities of the plain for their wickedness," muttered Bos.

"But he remembered the righteousness of Abraham and brought him out of the wicked city," countered Prometheus.

"To Hell with Abraham and every righteous hypocrite who ever walked the earth, there's a lot of money in those tents and I intend to have my share," said Quintana, licking his lips in anticipation.

"We won't get rich looking like this and if we plan to open a brothel fit for a king we'll need more than just new garb," said Thomas waving a hand over the rags he was wearing. He and the others had barely noticed that the journey from Metz had reduced their clothing to tatters and they now looked more like the wretched lepers they'd left behind than the prosperous whoremasters they hoped to become.

"Telling fortunes and playing cards will take too long to raise enough money to buy everything we need but what happened to your *grimoire* Thomas? Perhaps you could use it to find great wealth," said Nagel hopefully but Thomas shook his head. Though *The Munich Handbook* offered plenty of spells that promised to lead a necromancer to riches hidden in the earth, he'd left the book in his chamber at Haute Pierre.

"As far as I know the White Rose now has *The Munich Handbook* and considering it's brought us nothing but disaster perhaps it's for the best," he said bitterly. However, whilst Thomas no longer valued the book's impotent magic spells, he couldn't forget that it had been sabotage rather than a flaw in his design that had sunk *The Hippocamp*. Prometheus agreed that Leonardo's irreplaceable drawings could have been sold or pawned for a handsome sum if the book hadn't been left behind but Bos was delighted that the evil *grimoire* had been lost.

"It was a tool of Satan and no good could ever come from its possession," he said firmly and the debate continued until Quintana suggested an alternative way to raise some money.

"If we can find the sutleress called Mistress Kleber she might give us credit. She and I have done business before and she knows me well," he said confidently.

"If she knows you well, the only thing you'll get is her boot up your arse," said Bos.

"And even if she's here, how will we find her in this labyrinth of wood and cloth?" said Prometheus but Quintana was quite certain he could find the mysterious woman.

"You'll always find Kleber where there's most money's to be made, so I reckon she'll have bribed the Camp Provost for a pitch in the middle of the camp," he said and before the others could protest, he'd set off down one of the tented streets. The others sighed and trudged after him.

The Portugee led his companions through the dusty alleys between the tents where all the equipment and supplies required by an army on campaign were offered for sale. In one part of the camp, tailors stitched the garish doublets and breeches favoured by men at war whilst cobblers sold new shoes from long poles carried on their shoulders. Elsewhere, armourers forged steel helmets and breastplates, blacksmiths shoed horses and sharpened

swords and apothecaries sold the medicines and oint-
ments that promised to cure everything from warts to a
gangrenous limb.

Besides these specialist artisans there were the tents
belonging to the cooks and general traders called sutlers who, for a price, provided the army's ordinary rank
and file with everything else they needed. Some sutlers
were veterans, men too old or too crippled to fight but
who still yearned for the excitement and freedom of life
on campaign. Others were widows or deserted wives
who'd become sutleresses simply to earn a living but
the woman they were looking for was none of these.
According to Quintana, Mistress Kleber had joined the
tross to escape the boredom of the marriage bed and
had quickly become notorious for driving the hardest
of bargains.

The maze of tented streets met at a broad square in the
centre of the camp that served as both a market place and
a parade ground. Dozens of brightly coloured flags had
been planted around the edge of the square and each banner was accompanied by a drummer, a fifer and a sergeant.
Like rival traders in a street market, the battle scarred sergeants competed with each other for recruits by shouting
inflated promises of wealth and glory whilst their musicians played stirring martial tunes. The scene looked like a
village hiring fair but instead of reapers and cowherds, the
sergeants wanted men skilled in the art of splitting skulls
with heavy halberds, piercing ribs with eighteen foot pikes
or slitting open stomachs with the razor sharp 'cat-skin-
ner' swords called *katzbalgers*.

Ignoring several invitations to join various regiments, Quintana asked a young ensign if he knew where Mistress Kleber was to be found and to the others' surprise, the boy pointed to a large red pavilion on the opposite side of the square. Outside this tent, groups of customers were examining heaps of clothing, weapons and armour piled high on trestle tables but the centrepiece of Mistress Kleber's bazaar was an immense iron cauldron that hung from a stout wooden beam as thick as a man's arm. A grubby boy tended the blazing fire beneath the steaming pot whilst the woman herself served the queue of men waiting for bowls of her piping hot stew.

"Mistress Kleber, you're looking as young and as beautiful as ever!" cried Quintana but the woman was not in the first flush of youth. She was nearly sixty years old, her skin was waxy and pale and her hair was as grey as the ash beneath her cauldron. Despite her trade, she was thin, almost skeletal, and her face was lined with a scowl as bitter as the black bread she handed out with her potage.

"Such smooth talk can only come from the tongue of a blind man or a lying, Portugee bastard, so what do you want Quintana!" she said, without look up from her pot.

"Your hand in marriage," said Quintana dropping to one knee and seizing the woman's arm. The crone turned to look at him, smiled and spat on the ground in disgust.

"Judging by the rags you wear I'm still much too good for you. Now enough of your jests, tell me what you want or piss off," she said snatching her hand away.

"I want to borrow some money and I've always paid my debts, to you at least," said Quintana rising to his feet.

Mistress Kleber put down her ladle, wiped her hands on her filthy apron and looked at the dishevelled group with a disapproving eye.

"The last time we met you said you'd return rich but I see you still keep the company of thieves, vagabonds and heathen blackamoors! The French King's captains won't want an infidel savage in their ranks so my advice to you is find some other war in which to get yourself killed," she said.

Quintana winced as he saw Prometheus frown and he quickly informed the sutleress that the Nubian was a baptised Christian who'd be sitting at God's right hand whilst she was in Purgatory serving soup to lost souls. Kleber was unimpressed and was about to reply with another stream of insults when Thomas hurriedly intervened. He explained that he and his companions wished to set up in business and needed to borrow fifty livres to buy a tent, wagon, stock and clothes more befitting merchants of quality.

"Fifty livres? That's a king's ransom and the camp already has so many sutlers a poor old woman can't make an honest living," sniffed Mistress Kleber.

"Who said anything about an honest living? We intend to deal in whores," said Thomas but the old woman merely laughed out loud.

"You fools, you'll starve in a week! There are already plenty of whores here," she said.

Undeterred Quintana returned to the fray and pointed out that common streetwalkers were good enough for common soldiers but the noble lords who'd left high born wives and sweethearts at home wouldn't be content to plough a furrow that had been worked by a hundred others. However they planned to supply only the finest female flesh and ensure their favours were reserved for men of gentle birth. He also assured Kleber that rich noblemen would pay handsomely for such women and they'd pay her back double what had they'd borrowed within three months. Kleber rubbed her bristled chin and thought for a moment. She agreed it was a generous offer but she insisted on something to guarantee the loan.

"I'll lend you the money but in return I want a few hours alone with him," she said, staring at Thomas with hunger in her eyes.

"Me!" the object of her lust gasped and he began to feel the bile rise in his throat.

"Yes you, my old bones haven't been ridden in years and I want a good long hack. Besides, if you're going into the whoring business it will be useful experience!" laughed the crone and before Thomas could declare he'd rather return to the cage his companions bundled him to one side.

"I won't whore myself like an East Cheap cokenay!" Thomas protested.

"So you're quite happy to be a pimp but you refuse to get your hands dirty?" said Bos sternly.

"It's not my hands I'm worried about," snapped Thomas.

"There's more cluck in an old hen than a young chicken!" said Prometheus with a broad grin.

"And you might find you have a taste for well-seasoned fowl," said Quintana.

"Foul is the word, she must be a hundred years old! She'll be as dry as a crypt and you might as well ask me to put my manhood in a cheese-grater!" cried Thomas but the others refused listen to his pleas. Eventually he had no choice but to surrender however he demanded a bottle of aquavit to put the fire of passion in his belly.

"It's a bargain Mistress Kleber, our young friend promises to ride you straight to the arms of Venus this very night," said Quintana happily when they returned to the cauldron.

"Good, now go and bathe him, I like my men to smell as sweet as a primrose not stink like a Saracen's arsehole," said Kleber. Once again, Thomas was marched away and whilst the prospective lover bathed in the river, Nagel used the last of their spare cash to buy a flask of brandy. He returned to see Thomas emerge from the water covered in frothy soapwort and looking like Aphrodite rising from the foam. The Englishman rinsed the suds from his hair, climbed on to the riverbank and without bothering to dress he snatched the flask from Nagel's hand.

"You'd better get me drunker than Irish lord at Christmas or the deal's off," said Thomas taking a long greedy pull from the flask. The fiery liquid burnt his throat and made his eyes water but he felt a little better. The others urged him to take care but Thomas ignored them and took another swig.

"Not too much, you don't want to spoil your magnificent gifts," said Nagel, eyeing Thomas' naked form.

"You needn't worry, all Englishmen can take their drink, you could drown me in beer and I'll still be able to tup the old crone till her eyes pop," said Thomas, but despite his boast it was a decidedly tipsy Englishman that staggered to his place of execution. Night had fallen, which was a blessing, and the old woman had done her best to make herself presentable. She had donned a wig of long golden hair, rouged her lips and cheeks and changed her apron. Unfortunately the flickering candlelight made her look less like a blushing young maid and more like a demon in a passion play.

"Ah my love," she cooed as Thomas was brought into her presence. Quintana and the others could barely contain their laughter as the aged cook planted a clumsy wet kiss on Thomas' lips.

"I think I am going to be sick," muttered Thomas drunkenly as he felt the stubble of the old woman's chin scratch against his cheek.

"Fear not, I have a physick to cure you," replied Kleber and she dragged her reluctant lover into the tent. As Thomas disappeared inside the others looked at each other and wondered whether or not to rescue their friend but in the next moment they were all shaking with laughter.

"She'll eat him alive!" chuckled Bos.

"With some of her stew and black bread!" laughed Prometheus.

"Come on, let's listen to Cupid's chorus," said Quintana and he led the others around the back of the tent. The canvas was no barrier to any sound and they could hear every word being said.

"Oh you are such a pretty boy and I know what boys like to play with, undo my bodice," said the voice of Mistress Kleber. There was a disgusted grunt from Thomas.

"Do you like my poonts, pretty boy?" said Mistress Kleber eagerly.

"Oh yes, very nice," said Thomas without enthusiasm.

"Hold them, oh but your hands are cold, I know where I can warm them..."

"Jesus and all the saints, slow down mistress, I beg you!" said Thomas.

"Feel me there, just there ..."

"Ugh!" said Thomas in a voice that sounded like the mewling of a strangled cat.

"Now take me ... ride me ... plough me deep!"

Outside the tent, the audience could bear no more. Stuffing their fists in their mouths they ran from the scene and when they were at a safe distance they collapsed into paroxysms of mirth. It took several minutes for their laughter to subside but once they'd recovered their composure the four men retreated to Mistress Kleber's cauldron to warm themselves and wait for Leander to return to Abydos. It was long after midnight when the bedraggled lover appeared at the fireside and though he was desperate to forget the last few hours, the others tormented Thomas with questions until he begged for mercy.

"By the blood stained hands of St Dominic you're worse than Torquemada! Very well, if you must know, her skin was like leather, her tits like empty wine skins and her coney would make Lucifer himself vomit up his own intestines. That's my last word, except to say that whatever debt I may have owed you all for getting you into this mess is now paid," Thomas told his inquisitors.

"Do you think you may have left her with child?" giggled Nagel but Thomas ignored him, wrapped himself in a borrowed blanket and refused to say another word.

When they woke the next morning, Mistress Kleber was as good as her word and fetched the fifty livres Thomas had asked for from a large iron bound chest. The Englishman had evidently done his work well as she radiated good humour and chattered like a novice nun as the men picked out new clothes from her extensive stock of second hand breeches, doublets and hose. The men had already decided that a recreation of an Ottoman Sultan's seraglio would attract wealthy customers such as Richard de la Pole and so they chose to dress as *Phanariots.*

In contrast to the flamboyant German *landsknechts,* these Greek merchants wore drab, ankle length tunics gathered at the waist by a simple sash. Plain white shirts, knee length breeches and woollen stockings were worn beneath these tunics whilst a long, loose fitting coat was worn over the top. A broad brimmed beret completed the costume and though Greek Christians were forbidden to carry weapons in their native Constantinople, Thomas and his companions equipped themselves with the new rapier swords that were much favoured by Spanish merchants. Where Mistress Kleber had acquired such items was a mystery but their new clothes disguised the men's identities perfectly and their patron eyed her clients with satisfaction. She even shed a tear when she saw Thomas.

After saying their farewells, the four 'Greeks' strode off to spend more of their borrowed gold and their first purchases were the wagon and tents they'd need for themselves and their girls. Being late arrivals these necessities were in short supply but Quintana beat down the extortionate prices by threatening to have Bos and Prometheus beat up the different vendors. When it came to furnishing their travelling temple to Aphrodite, they bought damask silks, oriental carpets, Turkish divans and a pair of 'marble' pillars made from wood and plaster. These would form the centrepiece of an erotic masque their harlots would perform to help their customers make their selection.

After a few days hard bargaining, the new bawds had everything they needed except their trollops but they didn't have to look too far to find them. An outbreak of the Neapolitan pox had forced the burghers of Lyon to close the city's brothels and whilst dozens of homeless harlots had migrated to the French army's camp, many pimps had forbidden their girls to consort with soldiers. Despite the rich profits to be made, these whoremasters feared that their strumpets would escape their clutches by marrying some amorous arquebusier or priapic pikeman. Though battle usually cut short such unions, the wayward girls' freedom endured long after their husband's death.

Thomas and the others decided to 'rescue' some of these fallen angels by offering them better terms than their current employers. As Bos and Prometheus looked too fearsome, and Nagel looked too puny, it fell to Thomas and Quintana to venture into the city and find suitable candidates. At dusk, dressed in black cloaks and feeling like Romans setting out to abduct Sabine women, the Englishman and the Portugee crossed the bridge over the Saone and entered the old city. As the moon rose, the two men found themselves in a promising alley behind the Basilica of St Martin so they hid in a doorway to await the arrival of Lyon's nightingales. They didn't have to wait long. After half an hour four women entered the alley and began to walk aimlessly up and down the cobbles.

Curiously, the women advertised their trade by wearing the most modest Italian attire. Their heads were covered by waist length shawls of virginal white and their voluminous skirts of yellow linen hid any clue to the tempting curves beneath. Had it not been for the bright colours of their costumes, a passer-by could easily have mistaken these acolytes of Venus for Christian nuns. Having satisfied himself they'd be open to offers, Thomas was about to approach the women when a man entered the alley. At first he thought the stranger might be a customer but there was something about the man's demeanour that suggested otherwise. He had all the grace and refinement of an ox and when the harlots started opening their purses, Thomas guessed he must be their pimp.

The smallest girl, whose name seemed to be Ulla, failed to hand over any cash. She tried to explain she'd been too sick to work but the bovine pimp was in no mood for excuses. He promised to thrash the girl within an inch of her life unless she paid her dues in full and he raised a fist the size and shape of a hambone to add weight to his threat. The girl cowered in fear but the oldest of the harlots came to her rescue.

"God's Wounds Bruno, how can she earn if you leave her looking like a whipped dog? Ulla's been ill with fever but she'll have your money by the end of the week, I swear," snapped the older harlot, pushing the terrified younger girl behind her.

"Sick? She's a lying bitch, only yesterday I saw her making cow eyes at a saddler's apprentice!" roared the pimp. Thomas, watching from the shadows, decided these girls would not hesitate to leave this brute but they'd be no use if they had black eyes and broken teeth. So, before Quintana could stop him, the Englishman stepped into the moonlight.

"Leave off there!" Thomas shouted from across the alley.

"The nightwatch!" cried one of the whores but the pimp ignored her. He paid his bribes regularly so he'd no need to fear Lyon's constables. Instead he turned to face Thomas.

"Who in a pig's arse are you?" said the pimp.

"The man who is going to take away your whores and give them a better life," Thomas replied.

"Is that so and how's a long streak of piss like you going to take my girls?" snorted the pimp.

"In one of two ways, I'll pay you a florin apiece, for fair exchange is no robbery, and take them peaceably or I'll kill you and take them for nothing. Make your choice," said Thomas nonchalantly.

"Then you'll have to kill me 'cos I make no bargains with fancy talking bastards!" sneered the pimp.

"Excellent! I heartily agree with your decision, for I hate parting with money," said Thomas and the pimp suddenly realised the stranger was deadly serious. His dullard's face contorted into a brutish mask and he retrieved the heavy cudgel he always carried beneath his filthy cloak.

"I'll smash you," he said and started to swing the club menacingly. His opponent merely smiled and flicked back his own cloak as if he were about to do nothing more dangerous than relieve himself. The whores gasped as Thomas revealed his own weapon, the long, thin rapier he'd purchased from Mistress Kleber earlier that day. It was almost too easy, yet Thomas delighted in putting on a show of his swordsmanship to impress the girls. The pimp, bellowing like an ogre, hurled himself at Thomas who stepped to one side and slashed at the man's rump. With a gentle whisper, the whip-like Toledo steel sliced through the pimp's beeches and cut a deep gash in his flabby buttocks.

"My final offer is half a florin for each girl or you die," said Thomas.

"Bastard!" screamed the pimp as the pain from his lacerated backside finally penetrated his thick skull. He charged again, holding his cudgel high above his head as if he were about to drive a fence post into the earth. In reply, Thomas casually aimed his rapier at his opponent's throat and lunged. Blinded by pain, rage and the darkness, the pimp ran onto the sword's point and the combined the impetus of his charge and Thomas' thrust pushed the rapier clean through the man's neck. The dying pimp fell to his knees and clawed weakly at the three feet of steel sticking out of his throat. Thomas spat in the man's face, placed a foot on his chest and heaved the weapon free. The death rattle sounded in the pimp's throat and he fell, face-first, into the alleyway's stinking mud.

"Is he dead?" said one of the girls hopefully.

"As dead as a nun's dreams of marriage," said Thomas wiping his sword on the dead man's cloak. As soon as he'd said the words the whores surrounded the corpse and started to rain spittle, kicks and curses onto Bruno's lifeless head.

"Bastard... cuckold... sodomite... Spaniard!" They chorused. Thomas let the women vent their fury on the dead pimp and called to Quintana who'd remained in the doorway watching the spectacle.

"You didn't think to assist me?" he said as the Portugee joined him.

"My crippled grandmother could beat that clumsy oaf, besides I thought you needed the practice," replied Quintana watching the whores desecrate their late pimp's cadaver and feeling a chill of fear run down his spine at their viciousness. It was fully five minutes before the harlot's mouths were dry, and their lexicon of curses exhausted, and only then did they turn their attention to their rescuers.

"So who in the name of St Nicholas are you two?" said the oldest of the whores to Quintana, who was looking at her in the same way a man looks at a horse he's about to buy. The woman was in her late twenties but she still had her looks and Quintana reckoned she had perhaps three or four good years left before her customers went in search of firmer flesh. The three other girls also looked handsome enough to secure a loyal band of high paying regulars and the Portugee began to think they might even make a profit from their venture.

"I am Luis Quintana, a gentleman of Lisbon, and this is Thomas Devilstone, a gentleman of England. There are two more in our company, a Frisian and a Nubian, who are also good Christian men as vigorous and as honourable as us, your humble servants," said the Portugee with a polite bow.

"We're here to make you an offer, my friends and I plan to assemble a caravan of the best courtesans and earn a fine fortune following Francis' army," added Thomas.

"You mean you'll get rich whilst we endure the attention of drunken bakers with tiny cocks and blacksmiths with bad breath?" said the older whore suspiciously.

"By no means, you shall entertain only young and wealthy gentlemen of quality and we propose to divide all profits equally. In return for our shares, my friends and I offer you both our protection and our promise you shall be well treated," replied Thomas.

"What if we refuse?" said the chief whore.

"Then we'll have to tell the nightwatch we saw you kill your pimp. I've no doubt the wretch deserved to die, nevertheless murder is a crime and you'll all be swinging from a gibbet by next eventide," said Quintana sternly. The whores gasped in horror and clutched their dainty throats.

"You bastards! What if we say different? It'll be our word against yours!" said the older whore.

"Who'd believe a harlot, even four harlots, against the testimony of two gentleman such as we?" said Thomas,

"But ladies, we don't wish our bargain to be sealed by threats. We offer you the best of futures, a life in the fresh, free air of the countryside away from the foul stench of the city. Come now, would you rather live as creatures of the night, until your looks desert you or the pox sends you to an early grave? Or would you rather join us and make your fortunes entertaining wealthy, well born warriors just as Briseis entertained Achilles?"

"Remember how we all wanted to go to the camp but Bruno wouldn't let us," whispered Ulla.

"I don't care who rides me are so long as they pay well, said the third trollop.

"But no cripples, I can't abide cripples," said the fourth. Thomas and Quintana repeated their promise that the girls' customers would all be strong, young noblemen, all as skilled in the arts of love as the arts of war, but the older whore insisted on one last condition.

"We'll join you but you must agree that any of us may leave your service whenever we wish. We may be whores but we'll not be slaves," she said.

"We agree gladly, now ladies may we be permitted to know your names?" said Thomas sweeping the hat of his head and bowing low like an Italian courtier. The younger whores giggled as the oldest of them introduced herself as Magda and her companions as Ulla, Maria and Helene. With their bargain sealed, Thomas and Quintana dumped Bruno's corpse in a dark corner of the alley and covered it with refuse. The girls had been living in a shack nearby so they returned to their hovel to retrieve their few possessions and wait for the city's gates to be opened at dawn.

16

MILAN

Though Thomas and Quintana were certain no one would miss the dead pimp, at least until they were all safe in the king's camp across the river, the girls feared that the city's guild of thieves and beggars had already started searching for Bruno's murderers. Unfortunately for the harlots, their fears would not open Lyon's gates any sooner and so the girls spent an anxious few hours waiting for the curfew to be lifted at dawn. To calm their nerves, Quintana invited the girls tell their stories and Magda, the oldest, was only too happy to oblige.

Married at fourteen, and widowed before she was twenty five, Magda been too old to find another husband and had quickly found herself on the streets. Maria and Helene were sisters who'd run away from a drunken father whilst the youngest, Ulla, had been sold into a life of slavery by her peasant father who had too many female mouths to feed. All four of the girls had the raven hair, almond eyes and olive skin of the south and once dressed in fine muslins and silks, they could easily pass for exotic Turkish houris.

At last the sun rose, the morning bells began to ring and the city's gates were opened. Just as Thomas had predicted Bruno's violent death had gone unreported and no one stopped them from leaving the city. The strange company crossed over the Rhone in high spirits but when they arrived at the camp they found the sutlers' tents and pavilions being dismantled and loaded onto wagons. Thomas and Quintana pushed through the crowds of captains and sergeants searching frantically for missing men and arrived at their tent to find Prometheus and Bos had already started packing their gear. Nagel had gone to Mistress Kleber, to find out what was going on, and whilst Thomas was making the introductions the trumpet player returned.

"It seems we've gathered our golden geese not a moment too soon, the king has given orders to march and we must leave within the hour," said Nagel.

By late afternoon, the thirty thousand men of the French king's army were snaking down the Rhone valley like a giant serpent from an ancient myth. The *argoulets*, the light horsemen who scouted the way ahead, darted between coppices and thickets like the serpent's tongue and these were followed by the body of the beast which was made up of four vast pike squares. Though their heavy weapons were carried in the carts of the baggage train, the foot soldiers marched in their battle formations and each square contained more than five thousand pikemen, arquebusiers and halberdiers. Behind the squares came the *sakers*, *bombards* and *culverins* of Fran-

cis' train of artillery and these valuable pieces were protected by squadrons of armoured knights and mounted
men-at-arms, riding in two flanking columns each almost three thousand strong.

Bringing up the rear was the *tross* and the straggling
tail of carts and camp followers now included a passable
imitation of a Turkish harem. Thomas and his travelling
coterie of courtesans rode in two wagons, each pulled by a
pair of mules. The first wagon carried their tent, curtains
and carpet, the second was filled with their clothes, furniture and food. Progress was slow, less than six miles a day,
but whenever the army made camp Quintana bribed the
Camp Provost for a pitch near the noblemen's quarters.
It was a wise strategy and just as they'd hoped, the exotic
delights offered by their *odalisques* proved to be extremely
popular with the army's wealthy gentlemen of quality.

Prometheus and Bos, dressed as an oriental eunuch
and a Circassian slave, turned away anyone who lacked
the money or manners to treat the girls with respect and
even after they'd repaid their debt to Mistress Kleber, their
coffers remained brim full of coins. Their only disappoint-
ment was the fact that their customers did not yet include
the White Rose.

"Will he ever come?" Thomas grumbled as another
day passed without a visit from de la Pole.

"Why should we worry? We're making a fortune from
these French poltroons. I hope this war lasts for ever!"
Quintana countered.

"That's easy for a unrepentant sinner like you to say
but my soul is troubled and I wish this business was over,"

said Bos but Prometheus urged the Frisian to forget his worries.

"It's no sin to slit the throat of a treacherous knave like de la Pole. He didn't think twice about leaving us to die a slow death in that cage so by all the laws of honour we may avenge such an insult with a clear conscience," the Nubian declared but Bos remained troubled.

"It's not killing the White Rose that troubles me, it's the sin of fornication. In Hell fornicators are strung up by their privy parts, their heads immersed in a river of fire and their bodies tormented by the foulest demons until the end of time," he said gloomily whereupon Quintana burst out laughing.

"You fat Frisian fool! If you really knew scripture, your conscience would be clear. Did not Our Lord consort with harlots? Did he not forgive the sins of Mary Magdalene? So calm yourself my friend, what's good enough for Our Saviour is surely good enough for us," he said.

Curiously this argument seemed to satisfy Bos. His mood lightened and he went about his daily tasks with a much happier heart. However, whilst Thomas and the others were making money from the sin of lust, those who hoped to earn a fortune from the sin of wrath were becoming disappointed. Instead of a protracted war of long, lucrative sieges the French king's progress through Provence quickly became a triumphal procession. Each rebel held town and city called upon to surrender did so without the army unsheathing a single sword or shooting a single arrow.

Once a city's gates had been opened, the king rode through the streets at the head of the Black Band, who looked suitably intimidating in their smoke-blackened armour, to receive the citizens' oaths of fealty. Everywhere, Francis was cheered as a liberator who'd freed his people from the imperial catspaw Bourbon. By the time the king reached the main square, the ambitious burghers who'd declared for the rebel duke were waiting for their lawful sovereign wearing hair shirts and with nooses around their necks. Their acts of penance did them no good, Francis was happy to indulge his loyal subjects' demands for swift vengeance and the rebel councillors were summarily hanged, just as Bourbon had executed their predecessors a few weeks earlier.

Richard de la Pole watched each rebel mayor dance beneath the gallows and became convinced that he was being granted a vison of his own victory. He especially appreciated Francis' ruthlessness at dealing with traitors and promised himself that he too would line the roads of his reconquered kingdom with gibbets. Once every Tudor lick-spittle had had his neck stretched, he'd invite Francis to a great feast and they'd drink each other's health from the skulls of their defeated enemies. To add to de la Pole's good humour, Francis had put the Duke of Albany in charge of securing supplies so the Scotsman was busy combing the surrounding countryside for fodder like a lowly ostler.

With no fighting to delay their advance, the French army reached Avignon by mid-September whereupon Bourbon made one last attempt to capture Marseille. The rebel duke desperately needed a port so his imperial allies could resupply his army by sea once the mountain passes to Italy had been closed by winter snow. However, though his bombards quickly breached the city's walls, the defenders beat off every assault and the news that Marseille still held out, urged Francis to drive his men forward. If he could trap Bourbon's demoralised troops against Marseille's walls the war would be won but, despite marching twenty miles a day, he was too late. When the king finally reached the battered city he found nothing but empty trenches and abandoned earthworks.

In the end, Bourbon had lost his nerve and had begun a rapid retreat towards the safety of Hapsburg held Lombardy. Once his last desperate gamble had failed to win Marseille, the rebel duke had become so fearful of being trapped on the French side of the Alps he'd ordered his men to abandon their cumbersome artillery so they could withdraw more quickly. Much to his delight Francis captured a great many *culverins*, *bombards* and other pieces of heavy metal but his men were beginning to grumble. They'd not been allowed to sack a single town or city during their victorious march through Provence and their purses were becoming as empty as their recent victories.

Francis sensed this growing disquiet and promised his men that wealth and glory lay to the east of the Alps, where the fabulous riches of Lombardy could be harvested as easily as ripe quinces. The prospect of spending a comfortable winter enjoying the wine and women of Northern Italy was enough to quell any potential mutiny but to cross the Alps in October was no easy task even for battle hardened veterans. There'd be little fodder for horses or food for his men so the French king divided his army into three columns.

One column, under the Duc de Montmorency, would head south and pursue Bourbon as he followed the coast road through Nice and Savona. Francis himself would lead a second column north to Turin where he'd collect more mercenaries recruited from the Swiss Cantons and renew his alliance with his uncle the Duke of Savoy. Meanwhile, the ageing Marshal Chabannes would take main body of the French army, and the baggage train, into Italy through the *Col de l'Argentière*. Though this was the lowest of the western passes, and the heavy snows of winter had yet to fall, the surrounding mountains rose to heights of more than ten thousand feet and great curtains of rain were blown through the pass by squally winds as cold and as bitter as a wronged wife.

The Col's frequent downpours turned the unpaved mountain road into a morass that clung to boots, wheels and hooves but it was the artillerymen, struggling to haul their heavy cannon through the cloying mud, who had the worst time. Eventually Chabannes, exasperated by his column's lack of progress, ordered everyone in the baggage train to help the gunners heave their pieces over the pass. Thomas and his companions were assigned to a particularly troublesome *saker* whose twelve hundredweight of bronze seemed determined to remain on French soil. For two days they manhandled the gun's black painted carriage along the deeply rutted road but as they neared the summit of the pass, one of the *saker's* wheels became firmly wedged between two rocks.

"By the great grey beards of The Patriarchs, The Israelites in Egyptian bondage did not toil as hard as we do," grumbled Bos as he strained to move the gun's huge wooden wheel.

"The Sons of Jacob had the warm African sun to cheer them but here it's a wonder there's a drop of water left in those damned clouds," grumbled Prometheus glancing at the cold, grey skies overhead.

"Surely if Hannibal could cross these cursed mountains then so can we," insisted Thomas.

"Hannibal didn't have to carry his blessed elephants!" countered Nagel who was sweating from his exertions like a man on the way to the scaffold. An ogre of a master gunner roared at the trumpet player to stop gossiping like a fishwife and fetch handspikes from one of the wagons waiting down the track and though Nagel fetched the heavy crowbars as quickly as he could, another gun captain was losing patience. He threatened to blast the stranded *saker* out of the way with powder.

"Lay a hand on my gun and I'll send you to hell where your mother spreads her legs for the devil's stinking cock!" bawled the master gunner.

"Wished you'd stayed at home Englishman?" Bos grinned as he took a handspike from Nagel and forced it between the rock and the wheel.

"Why can't you conjure a spell to level these mountains, or summon great eagles to carry us to our destination, or at least make the sun come out!" Nagel moaned.

"I wish I had a spell to keep you silent but I told you, the *grimoire* is lost and even if I had it I could no more summon a demon than you could summon a kind word for that gunner," snapped Thomas.

"After three... one, two, three ... heave," bellowed the master gunner. Thomas and Bos put all their weight on their levers as Nagel and the rest of the men hauled on the ropes. The gun seemed to tremble in its cradle as the ropes tightened and it moved a fraction of an inch. A loose pebble skittered down the rain-drenched slope and the gun lurched free.

In this way, Chabannes' column continued its slow progress through the Alps but as the days went by, the army's ranks thinned. Some men, chilled to the marrow by water-logged shoes and sodden cloaks, finally succumbed to the bitter cold. Others, once they'd realised a soldier's life was not full of the riches and adventure they'd been promised simply deserted. A few of these absconders made it back to their farms and workshops but most were quickly recaptured by the provosts and hanged. Their bodies were left dangling by the roadside as food for crows and as a warning to others.

Three weeks after the French army had left Marseille the road finally freed itself from the mountains and entered the broad valley of the River Po. It was as if a sluice gate had opened and Frenchmen poured into Northern Italy like the melt waters of an Alpine river but if Francis' troops expected Italy to be a land of warm sun and gentle breezes they were disappointed. By now it was late October and a Lombard winter could be as cold and miserable as an English summer. The sky remained grey, the wind was full of frost and the leaden clouds poured more rain on the miserable soldiers.

Yet despite the filthy weather there was good news awaiting Francis' army. There was no sign of Bourbon or his imperial allies, so the road to Milan lay open, and by a propitious coincidence King Francis and his army arrived before the gates of the city on the feast day of Saint Francis. It was a good omen and just as at Marseille the French won a bloodless victory. As soon as Francis' pickets had appeared on the horizon the imperial army had fled to Lodi, three day's march to the east, but it wasn't the arrival of the French that had forced Bourbon's second ignominious retreat, it was the arrival of plague.

With the city full of pestilence, Francis had wisely declined to claim his prize in person. Instead, he'd insisted that Milan's city fathers come to him to surrender. The French army had made camp on the eastern bank of the Lambro, a small and sluggish river a healthy two miles from the centre of the plague ravaged city. In the king's sumptuous pavilion of blue silk decorated with golden *fleur-de-lys* the Milanese burghers had fallen to their knees, spat on the portraits of the Sforza dukes and sworn eternal loyalty to their French overlord. In return Francis had graciously accepted their declarations of fealty and promised to spare the city the customary three days' sack.

The kings' clemency may have won him many friends amongst the Milanese but once again his army was denied the chance to plunder. To avert munity Francis had to bribe his men with an extra month's wages and grant them a week's furlough in which to spend their windfall. Thomas and his companions were delighted with the news, a break in the campaign meant there might be a chance that Richard de la Pole would be tempted to sample the delights of their harem. Yet once again, despite of a steady stream of noble customers, there was no sign of the White Rose.

"By the missing nutmegs of The Ethiopian Eunuch, I swear he must prefer the company of men," muttered Prometheus.

"Perhaps he's found God and now spends his time in prayer," suggested Bos.

"More likely he's sick with the Neapolitan pox," snapped Quintana.

"Someone must know something, perhaps our girls can ask among the customers," said Thomas.

For once, the conspirators were in luck and that afternoon the Seigneur de Foix-Lescun and the Duc de Montmorency sent word that they wished to spend an evening in the company of Venus. Both men enjoyed high favour with the king and commanded two of the three battles that made up the left wing of the French army. The third battle was Richard de la Pole's Black Band so if anyone knew what kept the White Rose from indulging his passions it would be these noble Marshals of France.

The girls were excited by the prospect of entertaining such distinguished gentlemen, especially as Lescun and Montmorency were young and handsome with reputations for being athletic lovers. In honour of the occasion, Quintana proposed that they perform the erotic masque called the *Dance of the Seven Gates* and the girls were delighted with his suggestion. The hours passed quickly and the two aristocrats arrived shortly after sunset. Bos and

Prometheus, who were standing guard at the entrance, watched the two marshals meander towards the tents and guessed they'd already spent most of the day drinking.

"Good evening keepers of Cupid's flame, it's my birthday and I want to make merry with your finest harlots," slurred Lescun as he staggered up to the tent.

"Good evening and welcome noble lords, we are indeed most honoured to welcome two Marshals of France to our humble Temple to Venus," said Prometheus bowing low. Montmorency grinned foolishly, handed over a purse of money and the Nubian ushered the men inside.

The tent's interior would have delighted the most fastidious of Turkish sultans. There were soft, intricately woven carpets on the floor and curtains of embroidered silk lined the walls. Between the comfortable divans of gilded wood strewn with silken cushions, were low tables upon which had been placed silver platters piled high with sweetmeats, sherbets and jugs of wine. Braziers full of hot coals warmed the chill night air whilst bowls of rosewater banished the noisome odours of the camp.

Everything had been designed to convince noble customers that they'd entered an oriental harem but at the far end of the chamber stood two incongruous Greek columns with a curtain of purple silk hanging between them. In the soft candlelight, these pillars looked as if they'd been carved from marble but they were nothing more than wood and plaster. The columns would play a central role in the evening's entertainment but they also marked the spot where Thomas and the others had buried the iron bound strongbox that contained the proceeds of their debauchery.

Once Montmorency and Lescun had been relieved of their cloaks they were made welcome by Quintana and Thomas, who were also dressed in the turbans and flowing robes of the east. They invited the noblemen to recline on the divans and help themselves to the refreshments on the tables whilst Nagel, seated cross-legged on a pile of cushions, played soft music on a Turkish *shawm*. When their guests had made themselves comfortable, Quintana clapped his hands and Thomas opened the curtain between the columns to reveal a *tableau vivant* celebrating feminine beauty.

The four girls, fancifully dressed as Turkish *odalisques*, were standing as still as statues and their guests applauded loudly in appreciation of their elegant poses and revealing costumes. Each girl wore a low cut chemise made of coloured silk embroidered with gold thread. These tight fitting blouses were worn above voluminous pantaloons made of gossamer. The thin gauze revealed tantalising glimpses of the girls' smooth and shapely legs, however their heads and faces were covered by tall headdresses and long veils that left only their lustrous eyes showing.

To complete the illusion that their guests were privileged visitors to the sultan's harem, the girls wore silk sashes around their waists, Turkish slippers on their feet and a glittering array of gold bangles and silver bracelets adorned their wrists.

"For your pleasure, your beautiful companions will perform the ancient *Dance of the Seven Gates*, the dance that beguiled Belshazzar at his feast and which Salome performed to ensnare Herod," Quintana announced.

"The dance tells the story of Ishtar, the Babylonian Goddess of Love, and her search in the Realm of Shades for her dead lover Tammuz" added Thomas. "To the enter the underworld, Ishtar had to pass through seven gates and at each gate the Guardians of the Dead demanded she remove an item of clothing, for it is it written that naked we must enter the world and naked we must leave it."

Quintana clapped his hands again and Nagel began to play a haunting melody that seemed to swirl around the tent like smoke from burning incense. As the music played the girls began to dance, slowly at first, twisting their arms and legs and arching their backs into shapes that accentuated their female curves. Montmorency and Lescun watched with open mouths as the girls writhed with sensual delight and as each girl twirled through the Greek pillars she removed part of her clothing.

The first time through the gate, the girls removed their headdresses and let their long black hair tumble down their necks and shoulders, though they kept their faces veiled. The second time they removed their bangles, letting them fall to the floor in a tinkling cascade of gilded metal. At the third passing they kicked off their slippers, at the fourth they took off their veils and at the fifth they stripped the sashes from their waists to reveal the sensuous curves of their hips. Now the girls wore only their chemises and pantaloons.

Still they danced, letting their distinguished audience stroke every inch of their bodies with their eyes. The men were almost helpless with desire when the girls passed through the portico for a sixth time and removed their chemises to reveal breasts as round and as luscious as ripe peaches. The music's tempo became quicker and the dancing more furious as the girls spun and gyrated around the chamber causing their guests to whimper in anticipation.

"The seventh gate, for heaven's sake pass through the seventh gate before we die of unsated lust!" Montmorency croaked. The girls were dancing with such furious abandon, sweat poured between their breasts as they passed through the portal for the last time. As the music reached a crescendo, the girls tore off their pantaloons and at the sight of their completely naked bodies Montmorency and Lescun leapt from their divans. With a great cry of victory, the two nobles disappeared under a forest of nubile female limbs. Thomas, Quintana and Nagel bowed low and withdrew to let their guests take their pleasure in private.

"De la Pole doesn't know what he's missing," chuckled Quintana.

"Then let us hope that they'll tell him," said Thomas counting out the ten golden *livres* that their guests had paid for their entertainment.

The three men joined Prometheus and Bos in a tactical retreat to their private quarters where they remained for several hours. In spite of their prodigious consumption of wine, both Montmorency and Lescun proved equal to their reputations and by the time they took their leave the girls were exhausted. They pleaded to be allowed to rest but Thomas and the others could not wait to learn if their guests had revealed de la Pole' secret.

"Please, Master Thomas, let us sleep. Your questions plague us like the sixty diseases suffered by Ishtar in *The Underworld*," yawned Ulla.

"All we need to know is why is the White Rose living like St Anthony the Hermit, surely one of them said something?" insisted Thomas. Eventually Magda remembered that Lescun had mentioned something about their fellow marshal getting more than his linen washed by one of the camp laundresses called Caterina. The girls swore that was all they'd learned and retired to bed.

The would-be assassins were relieved de la Pole hadn't taken a vow of celibacy, or succumbed to the Florentine vice, but if he was receiving female attention for the price of a clean shirt he'd be unlikely to visit their expensive house of entertainment. Had Catarina's lover been an ordinary man it would have been a simple matter to make the girl vanish. No one would miss a humble laundress but the suspicious de la Pole would be at the very least alarmed by her disappearance and be put on his guard. At worst he would order his men to scour the camp for her.

A detailed search of every tent was the last thing the conspirators needed so Thomas proposed they paid the girl to break off the affair and leave camp. Quintana dismissed the Englishman's idea arguing they could hardly outbid a prince for the girl's affections. Nagel suggested an anonymous letter to the camp provost, accusing the laundress of being an imperial spy, would soon part her from the White Rose but Bos was appalled. The Frisian insisted committing such a sin would not only condemn an innocent girl to a shameful death, it would bring the wrath of God upon them. The debate continued for almost an hour before Prometheus offered a viable solution to their problem.

"This girl might leave camp if she was convinced that her love was doomed," he said thoughtfully.

"And what would make her think that?" replied Nagel.

"Have Thomas tell her fortune," replied Prometheus.

"More magic and superstition, is sorcery any less of a sin than bearing false witness?" said Bos angrily but Thomas quickly grasped the possibilities of the Nubian's idea.

"There'll be no sorcery just a little innocent deception. A parchment with a few signs and symbols drawn on it should be enough to convince an illiterate peasant girl she must cease her sinful fornication and flee for her life," he said excitedly. Quintana also warmed to the scheme and as Bos could offer no better alternative they agreed that Thomas should seek the girl out as soon as the sun was up.

A few hours later Thomas, dressed in his Turkish robes and with a folded piece of parchment hidden in his sash, went in search of de la Pole's laundress. He found her with the other washerwomen, standing in a tub of water, holding her skirts above her knees and trampling dirty breeches and undershirts beneath her dainty feet. She sang happily as she worked and she didn't notice Thomas approach so he watched the girl appreciatively for a moment. She was tall and slender, with wild auburn hair and a pretty face that had yet to be turned florid by her life of drudgery.

"Greetings, My Lady," said Thomas bowing low. The girl looked up and screamed.

"A Turk!" she shrieked. A few of the other washer-women also looked up from their labours but they merely laughed when the saw that the 'Turk' was one of the exotic whoremongers who'd become well known throughout the camp.

"Don't you fret Caterina dear, he's probably come to offer you a more enjoyable way to make money from a man's codpiece!" shouted one of the women.

"What do you want?" said Caterina eyeing her visitor suspiciously. Thomas apologised for startling the girl and quickly told her that he was the seventh son of a seventh son, a man born with the gift of seeing the future in the stars but he was deeply troubled.

"Last night I saw something in the House of Venus that indicated you're in grave danger but clouds covered the heavens before I could divine the proper meaning of my vision. Is there somewhere more private where we can discuss what I saw?" said Thomas urgently. The girl looked shocked but she climbed out of her washtub and thrust her soaking feet into a pair of wooden clogs.

"There is a sutler's tent nearby, it'll be quiet at this time of day, we can talk there," she said nervously. Thomas followed the girl along a muddy path that threaded its way through the laundresses' tents. After a few minutes they arrived at a grubby kiosk, which smelled strongly of wet grass and stale beer. They seated themselves at a crude trestle table and Thomas ordered two tankards of mulled cider from the one-legged sutler.

"You say you've seen something about me in the stars, for god's sake what is it?" said the girl in hoarse whisper.

Thomas held up a finger for silence, reached into his robes and pulled out a piece of parchment. He spread the paper on the table and explained that the series of concentric circles he'd drawn represented different people in Catarina's life whilst the mystical symbols revealed what part those people would play in her future. Thomas sincerely doubted that the girl could read, let alone understand the arcane language of astrology, so he'd drawn the chart to look impressive rather than reveal any occult truth. It didn't matter that the signs were meaningless, Thomas was confident he could invent any meaning he required whatever the girl said in answer to his questions.

"You were born under the sign of the water carrier?" he said, pointing to the astrological sign that best represented the girl's current employment.

"No, I'm a Sagittarius," said the puzzled girl but her astrologer seemed to be delighted by his error. He jabbed his finger at the crossed arrow sign for 'The Archer' and gave a cry of triumph.

"Ah the centaur who was skilled with the bow! At first I could not make sense of the riddle but now I see what the stars were trying to tell me ... and it's just as I feared. Your destiny is to be ruled by an arrow, that is Cupid's arrow. You see that the arrow in the sign of Sagittarius is pointed directly at the sign for the lion. Forgive me for being indelicate, but to those skilled in reading these signs this indicates that you've taken a high born nobleman as a lover, is that true?" he said.

"How could you know that?" gasped Caterina. "Richard told me to tell no one!"

"Those who are highest see furthest so from the vantage point of the heavens all things are visible. All our actions past, present and future, are known to the stars but I see that Fate has not blessed your love for this noble lord. If you stay with him you'll die within the week. Your only chance is to hasten to a nunnery and do penance for your sin of fornication with this man," said Thomas clasping his hands as if in prayer.

"You must be mistaken, is there no other way?" Caterina whimpered.

"There's no mistake. The symbol for Ophiuchus the serpent bearer reveals that the deceiving demon Asphodel is abroad and he's searching for the souls of sinners to take back to Him who reigns over The Inferno. You must therefore leave this camp this very day or suffer a terrible death," repeated Thomas sternly.

"I will, but I must go to Richard and warn him," sobbed the girl.

"Don't go in person, send word that you've repented your sins and joined the Dominican Sisters in their House of Holy Grace but mention no word of our meeting. Speak only of your repentance and your hope that your sacrifice will cleanse both your souls. If you don't do exactly as I say, the next time you see your lover will be in Hell!" said Thomas firmly, whereupon the girl screamed and ran from the tent as fast as her long legs could carry her. The sutler watched her go and was about to box the Turk's ears for upsetting his customers but Thomas tossed a gold florin onto the table before sweeping from the tent with a flourish of his long cloak. The sutler shrugged and pocketed the coin.

"You're too late," said Bos glumly when Thomas announced his success to the others. "Whilst you were playing fast and loose with poor ignorant washerwomen, we've had news. The army has been ordered to march on Pavia."

"Pavia? But I thought Bourbon was at Lodi?" Thomas asked.

"That's as may be but all we know is that we must break camp and move to Pavia at once," said Prometheus with a shrug.

17

PAVIA

A thousand years ago, Pavia had been the capital of the barbarian Lombard Kingdom but its capture by Charlemagne, the first Holy Roman Emperor, had brought the whole of Lombardy under Frankish rule. Long a centre for art and learning, the city had been ruled by a succession of French kings, German emperors and Italian princes, but over the centuries Pavia's wealth and power had been slowly eclipsed by that of nearby Milan. Nevertheless the accession of Charles V, the Hapsburg King of Spain, to the thrones of Germany and Italy had returned Pavia to its previous importance.

The city guarded a strategic bridge over the River Ticino, which carried the main road from the port of Genoa, an imperial ally, north over the Alps. This accident of geography had made Pavia a vital link in the chain that bound the emperor' dominions in Italy, Sicily and Spain to the Hapsburg lands in Germany, Austria and the Low Countries. Following the surrender of

Milan to the French king Francis, the Emperor Charles had ordered Pavia's garrison of 9,000 *landsknecht* mercenaries, led by the Spanish prince Antonio de Leyva, to hold the city at all costs however these men, and Bourbon's army in Lodi, were the only imperial forces south of the Alps. If Francis could defeat them before Charles arrived with reinforcements, the French would be masters of all Italy.

The French marshals Montmorency, Lescun and de la Pole urged their king to ignore Pavia and attack Bourbon at Lodi but Francis had studied the campaigns of Charlemagne. He insisted that Pavia was the key to Italy so, on the morning of the 28th of October 1524, the *Pavesi* awoke to see the vanguard of the French army marching towards their city. Though a siege had been expected, and the imperial defenders had strengthened Pavia's medieval walls with a ring of wooden blockhouses and earthen redoubts, there was panic. Those that could, loaded their possessions onto carts and fled but one after the other the roads out of the city were captured and closed by squadrons of French horsemen.

With Pavia completely surrounded, the French began to seal off the defenders from the outside world by constructing an elaborate network of palisades, ditches and gun pits that covered the flat, open plain beyond the city's walls. These siege works were centred on four fortified strongpoints: the village of San Lanfranco in the west, a group of monasteries known as the Five Abbeys in the east, the ancient bridge over the Ticino in the south and the Castel Mirabello in the north.

Though it had been given the grand title of 'Castel', Mirabello was actually a hunting lodge in the middle of a vast diamond shaped deer park that stretched for three miles to the north of Pavia, and it looked more like a Byzantine chapel than an Italian fortress. There was a squat circular tower capped by a dome at one end and an ornate cathedral-like facade at the other. Its walls were pierced by tall thin windows like a church but, like a castle, Mirabello was surrounded by a rampart of packed earth and a water-filled moat which was spanned by a wooden drawbridge. Despite its name and outward appearance Mirabello had been built to house noblemen in comfort and the lodge's luxurious rooms were quickly seized by the French army's senior commanders.

Once France's noble marshals had taken up residence, the *tross* quickly followed and the Castel Mirabello soon became a rocky island surrounded by a stormy sea of flapping white canvas. Thomas and his fellow assassins erected their travelling seraglio's tents in the middle this maelstrom and with Caterina now in a Milanese nunnery they confidently expected de la Pole to pay them a visit yet, once again, they were confounded. Instead of being garrisoned at Mirabello, The White Rose and his Black Band had been ordered to the fortified village San Lanfranco, where they were to hold themselves in readiness for an attack the ancient walls of Pavia.

Despite his recent victories, the French king knew time was not on his side. His men were being decimated by the diseases that flourished in the incessant autumn rain and they desperately needed to find dry winter quarters inside the city. Francis therefore planned a simultaneous assault, against Pavia's eastern and western defences in the hope of dividing and conquering the imperial defenders.

The assault in the west would be led by the king in person, supported by Marshal Lescun's levies and de la Pole's Black Band. The attack in the east would led by Robert de la Marck Seigneur de la Flourance and, much to de la Pole's annoyance, supported by his old rival the Duke of Albany who'd been temporarily relieved of his fodder gathering duties. The French bombards had been pounding the city walls for days, and the gun captains confidently predicted that two suitable breaches could open at any time, so the king ordered his men to sharpen their swords and prepare for battle.

The White Rose stared appreciatively at the jagged hole in the city wall. The gunners had done their work well and a section of masonry at the furthest point between two of the blockhouses guarding Pavia's western approaches had been reduced to rubble. The dawn mist swirled over the half mile of flat, open ground in front of him and de la Pole shivered, but with excitement not cold. The time for the attack was near and this would be his chance to outshine his Scottish rival once and for all. A page boy appeared leading de la Pole's warhorse by its reins. The White Rose grunted his thanks, mounted his charger and cantered off to join the French army forming up at the edge of the plain.

Francis had deployed his men in three long lines that stretched out along the battlefront. The first line consisted of archers and crossbowmen whose orders were to sweep the defenders from Pavia's walls. The second line consisted of halberdiers and double handed swordsmen who would scythe through any survivors trying to defend the breach. The third line would be made up of the Black Band who would protect the first two lines from any counterattack and offer support where needed.

"Good morning My Lord," said Count Wolf, one of de la Pole's most trusted captains, as the White Rose arrived at his place in the line.

"Good morning Wolf, how are the men?" De la Pole replied cheerfully.

"Their spirits are high and they're eager to start slitting *landsknecht* throats," said Wolf proudly. He was a veteran of the Italian Wars who'd been so long in Italy he'd forgotten he'd been born north of the Alps. Only his ruddy beard and guttural accent indicated his Swiss ancestry.

"With luck we'll be breakfasting inside the city before Albany has finished putting on his best silk breeches," replied de la Pole glancing along the Black Band's well-disciplined ranks. His men's sombre armour and clothing contrasted sharply with the brightly coloured garb of the other French troops but this made his men appear even more terrifying. In the half-light of dawn, The Black Band looked like an army of spectral wraiths summoned from deepest pit of Hell and de la Pole wondered if the necromancer Thomas Devilstone could ever have conjured such a formidable host.

A fanfare of trumpets gave the signal for the assault to begin and the French army began to shuffle forward. De la Pole glanced to his left and saw the royal standard and the banners belonging to the king's personal guard of Scottish nobles fluttering in the breeze. He cursed at the sight, though he admired Francis' courage in leading the assault in person, he was worried by the rashness of the king's gesture. If Francis was killed or captured at Pavia there'd be no Yorkist invasion of England in this or any other year. Putting such thoughts out his mind, de la Pole fixed his eyes on the towers of the sleeping city. Pavia rose from the surrounding plain like a volcanic island in a placid sea and the French army rolled towards it like a fierce ocean storm.

After the men had marched three hundred paces a second fanfare sounded, the lines stopped and the sky turned black as hundreds of bowmen loosed their missiles. Whilst the bowmen fixed fresh arrows and bolts to the strings of their bows and crossbows, the French halberdiers and swordsmen gave a great shout and charged forward. The bowmen quickly loosed a second volley over the heads of their comrades before slinging their bows over their backs, drawing their swords and running after them. De la Pole felt his own men were straining to follow but he held them in check as the king had ordered. The Black Band were Francis' best men and not to be squandered in the first charge. A moment later the White Rose had good reason to thank the king for his foresight.

The attacking Frenchmen were still a hundred paces from the city wall when the blockhouses on either side of breach began to spew flame and fire. The battlefield became engulfed in a fog of smoke as the defenders' hand-guns and cannon let fly a murderous hail of iron balls and stone shot. Under such withering fire, the first wave of the French assault broke. In vain, the survivors tried to find shelter in any small depression in the ground but the blockhouses had been cunningly sited to create a deadly killing field.

Suddenly the battle seemed to draw breath as the imperial gunners paused to reload. The French took the chance to launch another flight of bolts and arrows but they were answered by a second ear splitting roar of guns. Through the smoke, de la Pole's caught sight of the royal banner being waved, this was the signal for the Black Band to join the fray. De la Pole spurred his horse and cantered to the front of his little army.

"Men of the Black Band, we are to be unleashed at last, come let us follow the hounds of Mars and they'll lead us to honour, riches and glory!" he cried. His men raised a great cheer, the fifes and drums struck up the beat and the Black Band set off over the boggy, uneven ground. Their armour clanked and their long pikes clattered together like the bare branches of trees in a winter gale but the lessons learned in months of training kept de la Pole's six thousand men marching in perfect formation. A spent culverin ball splashed into the mud but not a man turned a hair, all their eyes were focused on the smoke that wreathed the breach in Pavia's walls. Beyond that curtain of death was everything a man could wish for and all he had to do to seize it was stay alive.

The White Rose also felt his spirit rejoice in the glory of war. At the head of his men he felt invincible and he began to imagine the lofty spires of Pavia's churches belonged to St Paul's Cathedral and Westminster Abbey. At last he understood why God had led him to this rain soaked corner of Italy. This baptism of blood and fire would forge his Black Band into a mighty army that would conquer England and restore the House of York to the throne of their ancestors.

The sharp cracks of the arquebuses and sonorous booms of the heavy cannon shook de la Pole from his reverie and as the noise of battle grew louder, figures began to emerge from the smoke filled breach. For a heartbeat de la Pole thought the imperial garrison had launched a counterattack and he was about to order his men to lower their pikes to defend against such a charge when he realised the men fleeing for their lives were not German *landsknechts* but French bowmen. In that instant de la Pole realised the assault had failed but he had no intention of turning back without firing a shot.

"Onwards! Don't let these cowardly farmhands shame us into retreat, we're men of the Black Band, we'll not give ground even if we face all the Legions of Hell!" he cried and ordered his pikemen to halt whilst his arquebusiers advanced and fire a volley.

His handgunners roared their battle cry and ran forward whilst their comrades planted their pikes butt first in the ground. When they were fifty paces from the breach, the arquebusiers touched their matches to their weapons. Two hundred handguns roared their defiance and scores of defenders gathering for a counterattack were pitched backwards into the mud. Like rabbits seeking the shelter of a thicket, the arquebusiers quickly retreated behind the forest of pikes to reload and they were not a moment too soon. As the sound of the Black Band's volley died away, a thousand Imperial *landsknechts* came pouring out of the breach. They ran down the rubble piled against the shattered wall brandishing huge double-handed swords and shouting all manner of threats and curses.

"Kill the oath-breakers! They are the Black Band, they are traitors beyond the mercy of God and men!" cried one *landsknecht* captain.

"No quarter for *landsknecht* scum! Show the Emperor's cocksucking, catamites how real men fight!" came de la Pole's reply.

The *landsknechts* rushed at their enemy and began hacking at the hedge of pikes with their long swords, trying to carve a way through the line to the arquebusiers. To meet the danger, de la Pole's own swordsmen rushed between the ranks of pikemen wielding their *katzbalgers*. These short German swords were no more than two feet long and had been designed for use in the press of the melee. So whilst the *landsknechts'* two handed blades quickly became entangled in the pikes, the Black Band's swordsmen used their 'cat skinners' to rip open their opponents' bellies.

The ground in front of the first rank of pikes became sodden with the blood and entrails of the fallen but the *landsknechts* fought back, lopping off pike-heads and pikemen's limbs with their two handed swords as if human bone was mere firewood. Revelling in the slaughter, de la Pole was in the thick of the fighting, using his old fashioned longsword to crush skulls and slice flesh whilst the steel barding around his horse's chest turned countless blows from imperial weapons.

The butchery continued for some minutes but it was stalemate. The Black Band could not pass through the narrow breach without breaking formation and to do so would have been suicide. Equally, the defending *landsknechts* were not strong enough to dislodge the attackers. Eventually a French trumpet sounding the retreat ended the impasse. De la Pole had been in enough battles to know when a fight was lost and though the thought of retreat stuck in his throat, he gave the order for the Black Band to withdraw. However his men did not turn and show their backs to the enemy, instead they dressed their ranks and began to slowly march backwards. It was a remarkable manoeuvre and it allowed the Black Band to salvage some pride from the debacle.

The wind slowly cleared the smoke from the battlefield to reveal the city's defenders standing on the ramparts and the roofs of their blockhouse, cheering and waving their blood stained blades. De la Pole saw one man holding a tattered battle flag and recognised it at once as the ensign of Francis' Scottish Guard. The French king's bodyguard must have been decimated to allow their banner to be lost to the enemy and for a moment the White Rose wondered if Francis was dead but a thunder of hooves to his left announced that the king was alive and still in command of his army. De la Pole watched Francis gallop away with the morning sun glinting off his armour and his royal blue surcoat, adorned with golden fleur-de-lis, streaming behind him.

By now the attackers were out of range of the defenders' guns, there was no loss of honour in resuming a more normal mode of march so de la Pole gave the order and his men swiftly turned about. The assault had lasted less than thirty minutes and had cost the lives of more than eight hundred men, including fifty members of the Black Band, but the comforting news for de la Pole was that the Duke of Albany had fared little better in his assault on the eastern breach. Meanwhile, in the French baggage park at Mirabello, the news of the White Rose's failure to capture the city was greeted with a mixture of dismay and relief.

"If we'd been lucky those imperial *landsknechts* would have done our work for us and we could all have gone home," said Bos ruefully.

"That wouldn't have helped, to reap any reward from the death of the last Yorkist de la Pole must be killed by one of us." said Thomas.

"That's as maybe but for once I agree with the Frisian. I'm growing tired of playing nursemaid to whores. Face it Thomas, your plan to trap de la Pole has failed and we need to think of something else," said Prometheus.

"Our harlots are also growing restless. I don't know what the trouble is but there's bad blood between Ulla and Magda. They used to be thick as thieves but now they barley exchange a polite word." added Quintana.

"Who can fathom the mind of a woman? Sometimes I thank God that I never married," said Nagel shaking his head.

"A surly strumpet is bad for business and if we don't snap them out of it, I'll wager it'll be bad for us all," said Quintana and his warning proved to be prophetic. The next day the cauldron of discontent between the Ulla and Magda boiled over into open war.

It was Thomas who witnessed the fiasco. He was returning to their tent after fetching the day's provisions when he saw a Swiss *reisläufer*, his breeches in his hands, running for his life. A moment later, Ulla tumbled out from under the canvas and hurled an earthenware flagon at the fleeing, half naked soldier. The bottle flew past Thomas' head, missing his face by an inch.

"Get out of here chum, Hell hath no fury like a harlot who wants to be a wife!" the *reisläufer* warned as he ran past. Angered that one of his refined women had been defiled by a common pikeman Thomas reached for his sword to cut the man down but before he could skewer the knave, the man had gone.

"You cheap bastard, you promised to wed me, yet I find you whoring with that diseased trollop!" Ulla shrieked. She was about to continue the chase when Magda sprang from the tent and wrestled her rival to the ground.

"Arsed faced bitch!" spat Ulla as she struggled to free herself from Magda's grasp.

"Watch your tongue dick sucking slut!" retorted Magda and she slapped Ulla hard across her face.

"At least I don't have to get a man blind drunk before he'll lie with me!" Ulla howled and she kicked her opponent in the belly. The warring whores began to roll around in the mud, bellowing curses and trying rake their nails down each other's faces. Their shrieks soon brought a large crowd of spectators and the men added their cheers to the pandemonium. Ulla finally managed to wriggle free of her rival's clutches and a moment later the two women were back on their feet, circling each other like angry tigresses.

"How dare you steal my man, as soon as he'd been paid for flattening this miserable Italian shit pile, we were going to open a tavern together!" Ulla hissed.

"You stupid cow is that what he told you? Don't you know they all say that just to get up your chatte for nothing! Anyway he promised me I could be his *kampfrau* days ago!" Magda spat back.

"Only because you got him pissed! Look at you, you old mare, what man would prefer you to me? How many bastard brats have sucked on your saggy teats?" Ulla retorted.

"At least I have got something a man likes to get hold of, unlike you, you flat chested witch!" Magda growled and she charged at the younger girl but Ulla neatly sidestepped the attack and as the other woman careered passed, she seized a fistful of Magda's chemise. The cloth tore to reveal Magda's magnificent breasts and the crowd roared with delight.

"Give us a squeeze!" cried one admiring onlooker.

"I'll squeeze your foul head back between your mother's shit-stained legs!" bellowed the bare breasted trollop and again the two girls began to grapple. Ulla managed to hook her leg around Magda's ankle and whip her rival's feet from under her. As she lay sprawled in the mud, Ulla sat astride Magda's naked chest, slapping and pummelling her defeated foe like a baker kneading bread.

Thomas realised he had to intervene or Magda wouldn't be able to work for days, perhaps weeks. He was about to step in and break up the fight when he noticed a face in the crowd. He couldn't be sure but he thought it was Georg Langenmantel, de la Pole's chief captain, whom he'd last seen at the Castle of Haute Pierre. His heart missed a beat. Even disguised as a Greek there was a chance he'd be recognised and, at the very least, the White Rose would be put on his guard. Thomas cursed his luck but just as was about to retreat into the crowd the camp provosts arrived.

"Scatter, here come the *rumormeisters*!" said a voice as the two burly watchmen, each carrying the stout wooden truncheons nicknamed 'argument settlers', pushed their way through the throng.

"Hey, you two, cut it out or we'll send you both to the Provost Marshal and he'll kick you out of camp," bellowed one of the watchmen but the battling women seemed oblivious to the watchman's threat and they continued to scratch and claw at each other's faces.

"You've been warned!" said the other watchman and the two constables began to beat the women with their clubs. The trollops howled and screamed with frustrated rage but only Ulla had the good sense to scurry away. The crowd, who had no love authority military or civilian, were happy to cover Ulla's escape but even though she'd driven her rival from the field, Magda refused to surrender.

"Beat a woman would you? You cowardly bastards! Wouldn't your mothers be proud to see you thrash a poor defenceless girl?" cried the aggrieved Magda, picking up a handful of pebbles. She threw the stones at the nearest watchman and one struck him on the cheek.

"You ungrateful cow, we stopped you from getting a real beating, that harlot was tearing you to shreds!" he cried.

"Sod this for a laugh," growled the other watchman and he swung his club at Magda's midriff. She crumpled as the wind was knocked out of her and whilst she writhed in pain the watchmen seized her by her hair.

"I'm with child! If it's stillborn I'll name you as murderer!" Magda wailed.

"Quiet you lying bitch, even if you are about to whelp, which I doubt, we don't need any more brats round here." growled the watchman

The two constables began to drag the shrieking Magda off to the Provost Marshal and, with no more entertainment, the crowd began to drift away. Thomas looked round for Langenmantel but de la Pole's captain had disappeared and Ulla too had vanished. Thomas was relieved but he was also furious. Now the whole camp knew his girls had been consorting with common soldiers in the hope of luring one into marriage. Their reputation as high-class whores was ruined and they'd never see another noble customer, let alone the pretender to the throne of England.

Cursing his luck, Thomas hurried off to find the others and tell them the bad news and, just as he feared, they too weren't pleased.

"So Magda's been kicked out and Ulla's run off with a pikeman, perhaps she was impressed by the length of his weapon," said Quintana but no one laughed.

"We're finished, thanks to those ungrateful sluts no one will come near us now," said Prometheus but Thomas was more hopeful.

"There's still time to salvage something, if de la Pole won't come to our whores why don't we take our whores to him?" He suggested.

"Have you lost your wits Englishman? We'll be recognised at once. The whole point of our charade was to make de la Pole came to us so he'd not be on his guard," protested Bos

"The time for caution has passed and if we escort the girls disguised as Turkish eunuchs, with turbans on our heads and veils over our faces, no one will know who we are. Besides he won't be expecting us as we were all eaten by a dragon in Metz, or had you forgotten?" Thomas said.

"Perhaps the Englishman is right, all we have to do is say our girls are gifts from the French king and once we're inside de la Pole's tent we can run him through and be away before anyone knows he's dead," said Prometheus considering the merits of Thomas plan.

"And if we succeed, how shall we prove to Henry Tudor that we've sent his sworn enemy to The Devil?" said Bos.

"The White Rose wears a ring decorated with the badge of his house. That ring will be enough to convince Henry that the last Yorkist is in his grave. Now if we act before any rumours reach de la Pole we may succeed after all," said Thomas and he went off to find their two remaining girls.

Curiously Marie and Helene seemed not to care about the fate of the two other women. They greeted the news that one had been driven from the camp and the other had disappeared with nothing more than a shrug. On the other hand, they accepted their new commission eagerly. To entertain a king, even a king in exile, was the pinnacle of any courtesan's career and they spent the rest of the day bathing and scenting themselves. Once the sun had set behind the French siege lines, and the slow steady boom of cannon had ceased for the night, Thomas and the others donned their disguises, escorted the giggling girls to a covered mule cart and set off for de la Pole's camp.

18

THE PORTA REPENTINA

After the failure of the French assault on Pavia the Duke of Albany had been sent to besiege the imperial city of Naples, in the hope this would force the emperor to abandon Lombardy entirely in order to defend the capital of his Italian territories. Much to de la Pole's relief, he and the Black Band had been kept at Pavia and ordered to occupy a new camp closer to the king's own quarters inside the deer park. As soon as Albany had left for the south, de la Pole 's men had obediently moved their tents to a spot by the deer park's north western gate called the *Porta Repentina*.

Though de la Pole's new camp was only a mile and a half from the main French baggage park at Castel Mirabello, the walk was quite long enough for the assassin's veils and long robes to become soaked with the sweat of fear. The last time they'd been in the presence of the White Rose he'd condemned them all to death and they couldn't forget the suffering and miserable humiliation of their torture. Yet, strangely, once they'd arrived at the Black Band's camp the dread that had gripped their bowels was replaced by a steely determination to kill their persecutor or die in the attempt.

Unlike the tented city around Castel Mirabello, the Black Band's camp was a more military affair. De la Pole had learned the highly effective tactic of laagering his wagons when in enemy territory so they formed a protective wall around the army's tents. Once lashed together, the wagons turned de la Pole's camp into a fortress, especially as some of the carts had been specially adapted for such use. These wagons had high sides, pierced by loopholes for arquebuses and crossbows, and served as turrets in the camp's wooden wall. To complete this wagon-fort's defences, its only entrance was closed off by a spiked rail, guarded by four mulish members of the Black Band.

"What do you stinking Saracen bastards want?" growled one of the sentries, who was trying to warm himself in front of a glowing brazier.

"We come with a gift for the English noble lord who calls himself the White Rose," said Prometheus bowing low and touching his hand to his chest, chin and forehead in the oriental manner of greeting.

"Hey I know you," said the sentry and the visitors' hearts all missed a beat. "Aren't you the Saracen whoremasters everyone's talking about? The story is you've lost your girls - that was a bit careless of you wasn't it? Take my advice when you catch 'em, give 'em a good thrashing. You know the saying, a woman, a dog and a walnut tree, the more you beat them the better they be!"

"Is it that sod Pieter? Let me get my hands on him, I've been pissing hot coals for weeks thanks to his pox ridden harlots," said a voice from the gloom and a second sentry stepped into the brazier's light.

"No it's not Pieter it's the ones who save their girls for dick-less French dukes," said the first guard.

"Our girls are clean, which is why the king himself has given me the honour of presenting the English Lord with his evening's entertainment," said Prometheus and he signalled to Thomas and Quintana who opened the cart's canvas covers to reveal Marie and Helene. The girls, wearing their veils and revealing costumes, smiled and waved coquettishly at the sentries.

"His Most Catholic Majesty has heard of the great bravery and courage of the English Lord so he has sent this rare and exotic gift by way of thanks," added Prometheus.

"So in return for his assault on the breaches these sluts get to assault his breeches is that it? Lucky English bastard," grumbled the witty if long suffering sentry.

"You'll find his tent in the centre of the camp, you can't miss it," said the other sentry and he helped his comrade move the spiked barrier. The sentries stood back as the cart and its escort trundled into the wagon-fort and once inside the men could see that de la Pole was taking no chances.

A hundred yards beyond the gate was a second ring of carts, identical though much smaller than the first, so the wagon-fort had both an outer ward and a 'citadel'. The outer ward was filled with the ordinary soldiers' tents whilst the officer's luxurious pavilions were pitched inside the citadel. The entrances to the two wagon-forts were linked by a wide-open space, which served the camp as a parade ground, and in the centre of this square of beaten earth was a gibbet displaying the rotting corpse of a hanged man. Around the dead man's neck was a placard bearing the single word SPY.

Prometheus and the others led their cart across the parade ground, pausing only to glance at the dead man swinging lazily from the gallows. When they arrived at the entrance to the citadel their way was barred by yet more guards. Prometheus repeated his story that he came bearing gifts fit for a king in exile but, like Laocoon before the gates of Troy, the guard captain was suspicious.

"I was given no instructions to expect any gift," he said looking closely at the strange party standing before him.

"But that is the nature of a surprise if the recipient is warned of its coming it ceases to be a surprise, now please tell your master his royal gift is waiting and the frost of a November night will not improve its quality." insisted Prometheus. Reluctantly the guard disappeared inside the citadel. He returned a few minutes later looking chastened.

"It seems you are in luck blackamoor, His Majesty is in the mood to accept the French king's gift, you'll find his tent over there," said the captain and he pointed towards de la Pole's huge pavilion.

The White Rose's quarters had been constructed from three large, conical tents made from silk dyed in the Yorkist colours of mulberry and white. The central pavilion was flanked by two smaller tents and these were connected to each other by short canvas corridors. The poles that held up the entire structure were capped with gilded crowns and on either side of the entrance, banners bearing the rose and sun badges of the House of York hung limply from flagpoles planted in the ground.

The whoremasters halted their cart in front of these standards and were greeted by de la Pole's personal steward, who was waiting to receive the White Rose's visitors. Mercifully the man was not the same *major domo* who'd jealously guarded the great hall of Haute Pierre and he didn't recognise the men who helped Helene and Marie climb down from the wagon. However, the steward did look disapprovingly at Thomas and Quintana as they escorted the girls towards the tent. Thomas recognised the look of hunger in the servant's eyes and he couldn't resist taunting the man.

"These houri are extremely skilled in the arts of love, they can take a man inside and make him squeal with pleasure without him moving a muscle," he whispered in the steward's ear.

"Well I hope your tarts don't give my master the pox or all the armies of the sultan won't be able to save you from the White Rose's thorns," he retorted and he followed the whores into the large central tent that served the White Rose as his audience chamber and the captains of the Black Band as their beer hall.

In spite of their veils, the men's noses detected the odours of roast meat and wet dog mingled with the smells of stale wine and unwashed bodies as they entered but despite reeking like a tavern the tent had been furnished in the style of Haute Pierre's great hall. Carpets had been laid over wooden boards that covered the muddy grass and martial banners hung from the canvas roof. Three long trestle tables had been arranged in an open square and behind the high table was an ornate throne. The tent was lit by expensive beeswax candles and heated by braziers full of burning coals.

Just as at Haute Pierre, de la Pole's steward insisted the men wait whilst he fetched his master and he disappeared into the smaller tent to the right, leaving Thomas and Quintana to adjust their disguises and remind themselves of their plan. It was simple enough, after satisfying two lusty wenches, de la Pole was bound to fall into a deep, untroubled sleep and under the pretence of collecting the girls, the murderers would enter their victim's sleeping quarters and strike.

After a few minutes' anxious wait, de la Pole appeared dressed in nothing but a white linen smock embroidered with the golden suns of York. He barely glanced at Thomas and Quintana but he eyed the girls hungrily. With a flourish, Thomas and Quintana removed the girls' cloaks to reveal their ample charms. Marie and Helene had dressed themselves in their tight Turkish costumes that both displayed their beauty to its best advantage and showed they did not carry hidden daggers or other concealed weapons. De la Pole relaxed, he doubted if Wolsey could have hired new assassins and have them reach Italy so soon after the failure of the sorcerer's plot to drown him in the Moselle.

"You say these lovely *houri* are a gift from King Francis?" he said appreciatively.

"The king's own chamberlain visited our humble tent this very afternoon and made the bargain, so these delightful ladies are your companions for the evening. All we ask is that when you've taken your pleasure, you permit them to return to us." said Quintana, trying to sound like a Turkish slave merchant.

"Tell the king I'm delighted with His Majesty's thoughtful gift now leave us," said de la Pole with a wave of his hand. Quintana and Thomas bowed low and shuffled backwards out of the tent. As the steward escorted them through the entrance, Thomas raised his eyes and saw the White Rose, his arms around the girls' waists, disappear into his quarters accompanied by a chorus of girlish giggles.

They emerged into the night air to find Bos, Prometheus and Nagel standing by their cart, feeding handfuls of soggy hay to the mules. Quintana asked the stewards if there was somewhere where they too could refresh themselves, whilst awaiting the girls' return, and the steward pointed to a sutler's tent by the entrance to the inner wagon-fort. The 'Turks' offered their obsequious thanks, strolled over to the tent and sat down at one of the crude wooden tables. A surly serving wench appeared and Bos ordered mugs of strong beer for them all.

"How long do you think he'll take?" said Bos taking a great swig of beer from an earthenware pot.

"Not long, Marie and Helene could exhaust a rhinoceros within the hour and the White Rose is not in the first bloom of youth," replied Quintana.

"But he's an Englishman and any Englishman can make a wench howl like a banshee all night long," protested Thomas, somehow feeling the need to defend his countryman.

"They're more likely to laugh all night long after being tickled by your tiny English carrots but in Portugal we know a trick or two to make our women folk cry for their mothers," said Quintana.

"You mean you don't pay them? Now Frisian women are true ladies. They don't scream like a heretic being persecuted by The Inquisition, they moan softly like the wind whispering through the dunes of the Waddenzee Islands." said Bos as he called for more ale.

"Desert women know it pleases a man to hear their cries of pleasure," said Prometheus wistfully and he poured a great draught of beer down his throat, spilling most of it over his Turkish robes.

Nagel was strangely silent on the subject of pleasing women but the others carried on their discussion, and drank more ale, until the sutler informed his patrons he was closing for the night. As the men left the tent they had to agree that Thomas was right in his assessment of English prowess as de la Pole had still not sent word he'd finished with the girls.

There was nothing to do but stand around the dying fire in front of the sutler's tent and try to keep warm whilst continuing their wait. Slowly the sounds of the camp died away as the men of the Black Band settled down to sleep. Eventually, the only noises that could be heard were the snuffling of the horses in the corrals and the cries of sentries announcing that all was well. As the hours passed the assassins grew impatient and were on the point of putting their plan into action regardless of the situation inside de la Pole's tent when they saw the steward walking towards them.

"My master now wishes to sleep and you may escort the girls away. Please follow me," said the steward and, the Turks obediently followed the servant back to the White Rose's tent.

As they crossed the parade ground each man felt for the dagger hidden in the sashes around their waists and rehearsed the murder in their minds. Whilst Nagel guarded their cart, Prometheus and Bos would silence any servants inside the tent, Quintana would bundle the girls to safety and Thomas would end the aspirations of the House of York forever. With luck, the White Rose would die in silence and his murderers could slip unnoticed out of the camp but if the alarm should be raised, they would strip off their robes and mingle with the hue and cry searching for the assassins.

With their hearts pounding in their chests, the men were ushered inside de la Pole's pavilion but instead of seeing Marie and Helene waiting patiently for them, they were met by a dozen swordsmen and standing at their head was the White Rose. He stood at the front of his men with a great longsword in his hand and a look of triumph on his face.

"You will now do me the honour of ending this charade and remove your turbans so I may see the faces of my assassins," said de la Pole, pointing his sword at the astonished Turks.

"We're betrayed!" roared Bos. He pulled the dagger out of his sash to strike down his enemy but in an instant one of de la Pole's men had a sword point pressed into the neckcloth wound around the Frisian's throat. Bos dropped his blade and raised his hands, the other assassins did likewise whilst de la Pole's men ripped the veils from their faces.

"How did you know?" said Thomas as de la Pole's guards searched each of their prisoners and found the daggers hidden their Turkish sashes. The captain of the guard tossed each dagger on to the nearest table as proof of the captives' guilt.

"Your efforts at disguise have been woefully inadequate. Harem eunuchs in a sutler's tent quaffing ale like Vikings? Don't you know the Turkish religion forbids The Faithful to drink beer or wine?" sneered de la Pole. Thomas rolled his eyes to heaven and cursed himself for making such a simple error. The White Rose saw his would-be murderers' confusion and roared with laughter.

"God's Hooks, you still think you escaped from Metz by your own efforts but it was I who arranged everything!" he cried and he began to boast of the cleverness of his plan to free his own murderers.

De la Pole claimed that, despite the men's crimes, he'd never desired their deaths only their confession that they'd helped the House of Tudor make a pact with The Devil. In fact, the prisoners were far more use to him alive because if Wolsey learned that his assassins were dead or imprisoned he'd be forced to send new murderers whose identities would not be known. It therefore made sense to free Thomas and the others so they could continue with their mission but he couldn't do so openly, as that too would alert Wolsey. He'd therefore sent his most trusted agent to win the prisoners' confidence, help them escape and follow them. Thomas tried to say that though they shared the cardinal's ambition they were not Wolsey's men but de la Pole was in no mood to listen.

"Don't deny it, you were Henry's astrologer and you're still loyal to the usurper so there can be no other explanation for your desire to kill me. However a snake is no danger if you know where it is and happily you made things very easy for my spy. He tells me that an English mountebank, a Nubian savage, a Frisian heretic and an avaricious Portugee have been easier to track than a herd of camelopards walking down The Strand," said de la Pole gleefully.

"A spy following us? We saw no one," growled Prometheus balling his fists in answer to the insults but before he could lash out, Nagel lowered his hands and stepped towards de la Pole.

"I'm almost sorry gentlemen but I told you at the beginning I was loyal to the White Rose," said the trumpet player and he calmly told them how he'd duped them all, including the senile Father Sebastian, into aiding their sworn enemy.

"By the lying eyes of Ephialtes, so it was you who destroyed *The Hippocamp*, you added sulphur and charcoal to transform my elixir of saltpetre into gunpowder!" Thomas cried angrily but Nagel was equally vehement in his denial.

"I most certainly didn't, it was you devils who exploded your own infernal device to send my master to a watery grave, just as your corrupt cardinal ordered," said Nagel indignantly.

"We keep telling you, we're not Wolsey's men," insisted Bos.

"And why would we want to blow ourselves up," protested Quintana.

"Your incompetence is merely proof that Henry can only recruit knaves and village idiots to his cause. No doubt the usurper hoped you'd all drown and take his shameful secrets to the bottom of the river with you," said de la Pole.

"You've made a grave mistake in making enemies of us, we've no love for Henry or Wolsey. They didn't pay us to kill you and we didn't sink our own ship, so if wasn't your pet rat who planted the gunpowder, it was someone else who also wants to kill you or your invasion plans," said Thomas.

"We offered you our swords in good faith for we believed you to be the rightful king of England and we'd have sailed in your infernal boat all the way to London had you so ordered," added Bos.

"It's not us who betrayed you, it was you who betrayed us and traitors must die," spat Prometheus.

"You've turned your loyal servants into the very assassins you've always feared and now you'll have to kill us to stop us," said Quintana.

"Which is exactly what I had in mind, Wolf take these dogs outside and stretch their necks at once!" said de la Pole to his captain and his guards immediately seized hold of the four prisoners. Thomas and the others struggled in a vain attempt to prevent their arms from being pinioned behind their backs but their efforts to delay the inevitable were suddenly interrupted by two high-pitched screams. A moment later, Marie and Helene came running out of de la Pole's private quarters.

"A rat, there's a rat in the tent!" they squealed in unison. The shriek of her shrill female voice distracted the men of the Black Band for the briefest of moments but that was all Thomas and his companions needed.

Quintana drove his knee into the groin of the nearest guard and the man fell to his knees, clutching his crushed manhood and howling in pain. Bos, though his wrists were bound, managed to smash his forehead into another guard's face splintering the man's nose. Thomas twisted himself free of his half tied bonds and began pummelling his captor into insensibility whilst Prometheus, the rage of battle upon him, picked up one of the smaller guards, who still weighed as much as a full barrel of ale, and threw him at two more of his opponents. The three guards tumbled over in a tangled mass of arms and legs and in doing so they knocked over one of the braziers full of glowing coals.

The contents of the brazier tumbled over the sprawling guards scorching their flesh. The stricken men howled in pain and they began brushing the burning coals off their skin but in doing so the red-hot embers fell against the tent's walls and the cloth began to smoulder. A heartbeat later, the tent burst into flame. Marie and Helene screamed and ran for their lives whilst de la Pole's men tried to beat out the flames with their bare hands. Ignoring the fire, Thomas and the others retrieved the daggers that had been taken from them and fell upon their enemies from behind.

Their blades flashed in the orange glow of the strengthening flames, de la Pole's men screamed as their throats were slit and were dead before they knew what was happening. The White Rose was now alone but not defeated and he launched himself at his foes, wielding his sword with the skill of a fencing master. The huge English blade was designed to be used from the saddle, to crush heads and lop the limbs off humble footsoldiers, and it was more than a match for his opponents' daggers.

Even though the White Rose was outnumbered, the reach of his blade easily kept the assassins at bay. Slowly, the fire and the fury of de la Pole's onslaught forced Thomas and the others to retreat towards the tent's entrance, until a great blanket of burning silk detached itself from the tent's roof and fell, like a fiery curtain, between the foes. Prometheus quickly cut away the smouldering cloth but de la Pole had gone, he'd slashed open the back of the tent and slipped away.

"It's over, our phoenix has flown and so must we," said the Nubian bitterly.

"Our only hope is to set fire to as many tents as we can and in the confusion we may also get away," said Quintana. Hurriedly, the Portugee snatched up a fallen sword and tore a strip of cloth from the tent. Tying the rag around the sword's point he plunged the makeshift torch into the flames until it caught fire. The others did likewise and were about to run outside when they saw Thomas hesitate.

"Go on, I'll join you later, *The Munich Handbook* might be somewhere in this tent and this may be my only chance to get it back. I'll meet you at the village of San Genesio, by the north western gate into the deer park, and if I'm not there by daybreak I'm dead," he cried and he began to hack away the burning guy ropes and tent poles that blocked the corridor to de la Pole's private quarters. There was no time to argue, so the others ran from the doomed pavilion and began thrusting their firebrands into the tents surrounding the parade ground.

The smaller tent where the White Rose had entertained Marie and Helene was also full of smoke but Thomas could see a bed surrounded by crumpled clothes in one corner and a wooden strongbox in another. Thanks to the sudden of his flight from the tent, de la Pole had left the key to the chest on a chain fastened to his discarded breeches so Thomas quickly unlocked the box, flung open the lid and began to search through the contents. He tossed embroidered doublets, Spanish novels and fine woollen hose onto the floor but there was no sign of his lost *grimoire*. He cursed angrily to himself, he could hardly believe that de la Pole had destroyed the precious book, or left it behind, yet there seemed to be no other place in the tent to keep anything of value.

The smoke and smell of burning was becoming unbearable and Thomas could hear the sound of drums summoning the Black Band from their slumbers to fight the spreading fire. He stood up and took a last look at the ornately carved chest. At the last moment, inspiration struck him. He dropped to his knees and began to explore every inch of the carved wood with excited fingertips. A minute later, he found the secret catch hidden in the centre of an exquisitely chiselled rose. He pressed it and a small drawer in the base of the chest popped open.

Inside the hidden drawer was the familiar oilcloth wallet. Thomas snatched it up, unwrapped it and gazed upon his lost copy of *The Munich Handbook*. De la Pole had had the book rebound but a quick inspection of the pages revealed da Vinci's priceless drawings and notes were still intact. Thomas was overjoyed to have recovered the precious volume but before he could examine it further a loud crash, indicating the centre tent behind him had collapsed, spurred him into action. He rewrapped the book, stuffed it into his shirt and slashed his way through the tent's cloth walls.

A moment later he'd crawled through the torn fabric and was breathing fresh air. Once outside, he was just a few feet from the inner ring of wagons and without a second thought he dived under the nearest cart. The ground was wet and strewn with refuse but screened by the cart-wheels He could now travel unseen between to any point in the wagon fort's citadel. Using his hands and knees to slither through the mud and garbage he began to crawl away from the burning tent. His only thought was to find a patch of darkness where he could cross to the outer ring of wagons but he hadn't gone far when he saw the shivering figures of Marie and Helene huddled beneath the cart ahead of him.

"Over here, it's me," Thomas hissed. The girls turned and looked at him miserably. Freezing cold and covered in smuts they looked less like harem girls and more like orphans of the storm.

"What's happening, have we done something wrong?" Helene asked.

"No, it's my friends and I who've made a complete bollocks of everything. We've all sworn to kill the man who calls himself the White Rose but now he's vowed to kill us," said Thomas grimly and he quickly explained that their seraglio had been merely a ruse to get close to their target.

"You bastard, you might've told us, we're not in the habit of assisting murderers!" Marie said angrily.

"You have my unending apologies and if we get out of here I'll make it up to you but for now, if you'll excuse me, I have more pressing matters to which I must attend," said Thomas curtly and he was about to crawl away when Helene grabbed his sleeve.

"You're not going to leave us here are you? If they catch us they'll hang us as surely as they'll hang you!" she wailed. Thomas swore under his breath. It would be hard enough for one person to escape, let alone three, but he couldn't leave the girls to the tender mercies of de la Pole's torturers.

"Of course I'm not leaving you but we'll need to change, three Turks running around a French camp will stick out like a beard on a nun," whispered Thomas and he looked around for somewhere where they could steal some new clothes.

They were in luck, the tent a few feet from their hiding place was intact and every man in the Black Band was now fully occupied with fighting the fire. There was a chance the tent was still occupied by some lazy drunkard or sleeping *kampfrau* so Thomas crept forward cautiously, drew his sword as quietly as he could and carefully slit open the canvas. He breathed a sigh of relief when he saw the tent was empty and there was a pile of ebony coloured clothing heaped in one corner. He signalled for the girls to join him and once inside they all dressed in the livery of their enemy. In the darkness, they would easily pass for three of de la Pole's men and so they ventured into the open.

Again fortune was with them, the fire was now threatening the camp's powder store so every available man was busy chopping down tents to create a fire break or hurrying to fetch water. The light from the inferno illuminated a stream of men with buckets running towards the *Repentina* gate a hundred yards from the camp and Thomas guessed they were heading for the little river Naviglio, which lay just outside the deer park's walls. As he waited for a suitable moment to join the exodus of watercarriers leaving the camp, Marie tugged on Thomas' sleeve and pointed to two leather buckets and a small barrel lying under a cart. The pails were full of holes and the keg missing a stave but that didn't matter. Thomas grinned, snatched up the keg for himself and gave the buckets to the girls.

Surrounded by hundreds of other people carrying buckets, barrels and anything else that would hold water, no one paid the fugitives the slightest attention and the throng carried them out of the camp and through the *Repentina* gate like three twigs being swept over a weir. Even at the riverbank they had no difficulty in slipping away into the darkness and they were soon running through the empty fields and pastures that lay beyond the deer park. Breathless with the relief and elation of escape Thomas led Marie and Helene to the village of San Genesio where he'd agreed to meet the others.

19

THE GALLOWS

To Thomas' great relief, Prometheus was already waiting for them whilst Bos and Quintana arrived a short time afterwards. Judging by the fact they were all wearing the same sombre clothing as himself, they too had escaped from the camp disguised as members of the Black Band.

"Was it worth risking your neck for that cursed *grimoire*?" Bos asked when they'd finished congratulating themselves on outwitting de la Pole without the aid of the deceitful Nagel. At the mention of the missing spell-book, Bos, Prometheus and Quintana stared accusingly at Thomas and their unsympathetic expressions quickly convinced him that it might be better to keep quiet about recovering *The Munich Handbook*, at least for the time being.

"It wasn't there," he lied and the others accepted Thomas' fiction with knowing nods of their heads before turning their attention to more pressing matters.

"We can't stay here, de la Pole will soon have every Frenchman who can walk or ride scouring the countryside for us, especially as we've just added sabotage, arson and attempted regicide to our list of crimes," said Quintana brushing the singed hairs from his beard.

"But we can't leave, the White Rose and his snake-tongued slave Nagel must die if our honour is to be restored," Prometheus replied sternly but the Portugee shook his head.

"I think our careers as assassins are over because after tonight it'll take an army to get within a mile of Richard de la Pole, or do my eyes deceive me?" Quintana said and he waved his hand towards the horizon. In the faint glow of the burning camp, the four men could see their dreams of winning the gratitude of an English king, either Tudor or Yorkist, disappearing in the clouds of smoke and flame.

"I fear the Portugee has a point, we've failed and there's nothing more to be done," said Bos and after some thought Prometheus reluctantly conceded that the affair was ended. Even Thomas had to admit that wherever their destiny lay, it could no longer be at Pavia.

"Perhaps you're right but what shall we do now? If the entire French army is after our blood perhaps we'd be safest in imperial territory," he suggested.

"By the blessed tits of the Holy Virgin, that's what I've been saying all along!" Quintana cried.

As Lodi was the nearest city still loyal to the emperor, Thomas thought they should journey there as quickly as possible. Prometheus agreed but added that after Lodi they should continue further east, to Hungary, where they'd be even safer from the intrigues of French kings or English rebels and they could atone for their sins by slaughtering infidel Turks. Bos agreed that any of the Christian princes fighting the Ottoman Turks would welcome their talents but Quintana raised a note of caution. He reminded the others that, wherever they decided to go, they'd need money to get there and the profits from their whoring lay buried beneath their tent in the camp at Mirabello.

"But Mirabello is surrounded by the French army!" Bos protested, Thomas and Prometheus also thought trying to reach their tent would be tantamount to suicide but the Portugee was adamant.

"It would be suicide to abandon so much gold, have you forgotten that we earned a tidy sum from our labours?" Quintana said, whereupon Marie and Helene cried out in indignation.

"You mean *our* labours, and if you plan to abandon us like bastard children you've got another think coming," they said angrily and they added their voices to the heated debate. None of them wanted to abandon their hidden treasure but the gates into the deer park would not be opened until dawn and by then every French picket, scout and sentry would be on the lookout for spies and saboteurs.

In the end, Thomas' argument, that they could return to Mirabello once the tide of war had receded, prevailed and despite Quintana's continued grumbling about the evils of poverty the men agreed to set off for Lodi at once. The two women however had different ideas, they were still wearing the earrings, bangles and other jewellery that the company had bought to adorn their houris' costumes and if they sold just one of these baubles they'd have enough money to return to Marseilles.

As the girls had no desire to remain in Lombardy they offered their erstwhile bawds a bargain, if they could keep the wealth they wore, they'd happily forfeit their share of the buried profits. The men, realising they would have the best of the arrangement, readily agreed and as their roads now took them in opposite directions, they said their goodbyes. Marie and Helene left on good terms, and wished their former employers well, but what had become of Magda and Ulla, no one could say.

Lodi stood at the eastern end of a triangle formed by Milan twenty miles to the north and Pavia twenty miles to the south. With Milan in French hands, and the imperial garrison at Pavia besieged by Francis' army, Lodi was the largest city in Lombardy still loyal to Charles V's Holy Roman Empire and it's walls were defended by 15,000 imperial mercenaries.

These *landsknechts* included the rump of the failed invasion force led by the French rebel the Duke of Bourbon and the Flemish prince the Count of Lannoy. Bourbon had taken much of the blame for the debacle at Marseilles so Lannoy had remained Imperial Viceroy of Naples and Commander in Chief of the Holy Roman Emperor's Italian armies but his men were demoralised and desertions were rife. Realising the fate of Italy could be decided at

Pavia the emperor had promised to send reinforcements to Lannoy as soon as possible and the core of this new army would be 12,000 *landsknechts* under the command of the celebrated mercenary colonel Georg von Frundsberg.

Added to Frundsberg's Germans would be fresh contingents raised from the emperor's Spanish and Italian territories so, in a few weeks, Lannoy would be able to lead an army of more than 30,000 men in a lightning campaign to relieve the 10,000 imperials trapped in Pavia and drive the French back over the Alps. As disease and desertion had also reduced the French army's strength to less than 25,000 men, an imperial victory would be all but certain, provided Pavia's garrison could hold out until Frundsberg arrived.

On the first day of December, Lannoy received news that Frundsberg had left his camp in Bavaria and was making a forced march over the Brenner pass. Later that day, whilst Lannoy's chaplain said Mass for the beginning of Advent, the imperial marshal prayed that the old campaigner his soldiers called *Father of Landsknechts* would survive making such a perilous trip in the depths of winter.

Whilst Lannoy waited patiently for Frundsberg, Thomas and his companions spent a miserable week travelling to Lodi. The sun, when it did bother to shine, was as weak as a faithless husband's excuses whilst the rain lashed them longer and harder than any sergeant's cane. The worst of the storms broke whilst the men were trudging wearily over the flat plain to the south of Lodi. This squall was so violent the men were forced to shelter in a goatherd's hut even though they were barely a mile from the city's gates. Exhausted by their trip, the men had fallen onto the heap of mouldering straw they'd found inside and were soon fast asleep.

How long they'd slept they didn't know but they were roused by strange sounds coming from outside the shack. Fleeting shadows interrupted the sunlight streaming through the gaps in the wooden planking and the men inside heard the whispered sounds of a guttural language that sounded like German. As Thomas and the others sat up and felt for their swords, the hovel's flimsy door crashed open to reveal a huge soldier dressed in the colourful slashed doublet and striped hose of an imperial *landsknecht*. He was holding an arquebus with a smouldering match in its serpent and Thomas had no doubt the gun was loaded with small, sharp pebbles that would be lethal if fired into this confined space.

"Don't shoot we're simple travellers on our way to Lodi," Thomas cried in German but their visitor was staring at Prometheus who sitting in the straw like an enormous Rumpelstiltskin.

"By all the saints in heaven, you don't see many blackamoors in Lombardy so who in the name of St Maurice's big black arse are you?" said the *landsknecht* but before Prometheus could answer, the handgunner realised that all four travellers were dressed entirely in black.

"St Jude's balls! You're wearing the livery of the Black Band!" he exclaimed and he shouted to his comrades to come and help him take charge of the *landsknechts'* hated enemies. Seconds later he was joined by two other men who were also armed with handguns.

"These cowardly scum must have legged it from the French siege works at Pavia," said the second *landsknecht*, staring at the stolen clothing Thomas and the others had neglected to change.

"On your feet you garlic chewing cocksuckers and keep your hands where we can see them or you'll get a barrel full of hot stones up your arse. You're either deserters or spies but one way or another way Frundsberg will have you all dangling from the end of a rope before sunset!"

"Wait, it's true we've come from Pavia and we are spies but we don't serve the French or the Black Band. We've been sent in secret by Henry Octavius, King of England to gather information that may be useful to the emperor," Thomas lied.

"Henry who?" said the handgunner looking at his captives in bewilderment. Thomas sighed and patiently explained that king of England was not only the emperor's ally, he was Charles V's uncle and it was English gold that paid the imperial army's wages. They should therefore be welcomed as friends and comrades-in-arms not treated as prisoners.

The *landsknechts* looked puzzled. They didn't know or care who was king of a fog bound rock lying at the edge of the world but they did know that Sir John Russell, the English king's ambassador to the imperial court, had recently arrived in Lodi with a chest full of gold and a pay parade had been called for the following day. The fact that one of the strangers spoke his German with an English accent was enough to make them hold their fire but it was the bounty of four guilders apiece paid on spies and deserters that persuaded them to take these renegades to their camp.

"If you're friends you'll hand over your swords and come to the camp peaceable," said the third *landsknecht* suspiciously. Quintana began to protest that he'd had enough of being treated like a dog that had eaten it's master's lunch but Thomas assured him that this was precisely what they'd hoped would happen.

"We left Pavia seeking the protection of the imperial army, well we seemed to have found it," he said happily and he handed over his sword.

The others did likewise and a moment later they all stepped into the empty sunshine of an Italian winter's day. Once outside, the four men stood blinking in wonderment at the sight before them. Where last night there'd been nothing but muddy fields and herds of mangy goats, a new tented city had sprouted like a forest of giant mushrooms.

"By the par boiled flesh of Saint Vitus are we following these armies or are these armies following us!" cried Bos.

The host that had arrived during the night were Frundsberg's reinforcements for Lannoy's army but, as Lodi was already full of Spanish and Italian troops, the Germans had been forced to camp outside the city. As was their custom the *landsknechts* had built a wagon-fort, which was almost identical to that of the Black Band, but Bos and the others had been so exhausted they'd slept through the din of tent pegs being hammered into the ground and the clatter of carts being chained together. Their escort was a foraging party, sent to find any stray rabbits or chickens, and whilst Thomas was happy to be taken inside, the others' misgivings returned as they reached the wagon-fort.

"Why are we letting these slow witted sausage chewers do this to us?" Quintana whispered.

"There're only three of them, we could take them easily," added Prometheus.

"He that hath no sword, let him sell his cloak and buy one," said Bos feeling his empty sword belt.

"That's exactly what I plan to do! We said we'd need an army to get close to the White Rose, well… why not an army of imperial *landsknechts*?" Thomas said cryptically.

Bos replied that he thought they'd all agreed to abandon their careers as assassins and make an honourable living slaughtering godless Turks in Hungary but their escort ordered them to keep quiet. Ten minutes later, they were inside the wagon-fort listening to the *landsknechts* explain to their captain how they'd caught four French hens trying to fly their coop.

"Search them, they may be spies or assassins," the captain ordered.

"Of course we're spies and assassins, I keep telling you, we're *your* spies and assassins, pay no heed to these clothes, I'm an English gentleman in the service of the emperor's ally King Henry Tudor," Thomas insisted.

"Chewed her what?" said the mystified captain. The man's shameless ignorance was enough to persuade Thomas that he needed a firmer approach and he rounded on the captain angrily.

"Impudent knave! Insult my king a second time and I'll have your tongue cut out! Now I will say this only more, I bring vital information about the French army for Colonel Frundsberg and I demand to taken to him immediately," he snapped.

"You know Frundsberg?" said the captain whose face had grown visibly paler at the mention of the colonel's name.

"Of course I know him, do you think I'm here to plough your pig faced sister? And as Frundsberg pays you with English gold you'd better tell him I've arrived and look sharp about it," said Thomas.

Despite his confident invocation of the name, Thomas had never heard of Georg von Frundsberg until he'd overheard the colonel mentioned by one of the foraging party who'd taken them prisoner. However, he did know that a threat to their pay was the about only thing that interested a *landsknecht* and the bluff worked better than he'd hoped. The captain ordered his men to take the English spies, if that's what they were, to the colonel without further delay.

Frundsberg's bright red tent was smaller than de la Pole's but it boasted a more impressive array of banners and flags by its entrance. The mercenary colonel's personal standard, quartered yellow and black with a silver heron in the black squares and stylised mountains in the yellow, was planted next to a white flag emblazoned with the red crossed swords of an imperial marshal. A pair of yellow imperial battle flags, decorated with the Hapsburg's double-headed eagle, completed the display.

The middle-aged Frundsberg was sat at a folding table that had been placed outside his tent so he could enjoy the rare winter sunshine. Even seated, it was evident that the

Father of Landsknechts was still a powerful, ruthless man and his thick, square cut beard contrasted the thinning hair on his head. As befitting his rank, the colonel wore three quarter armour and a short cape of orange cloth around his shoulders. A silken red sash, another imperial badge of command, was tied across his polished steel breastplate and his distinctive roman-style helmet, decorated with a plume of red feathers, was placed on the table to one side of the papers he was studying.

Thirty years earlier the colonel had helped the previous Emperor Maximilian create the *landsknechts* to counter the threat of the Swiss mercenary armies employed by the Hapsburg's numerous enemies. Under Frundsberg's command, the emperor's elite body of pikemen, halberdiers, handgunners and swordsmen had quickly surpassed their hated *reisläufer* rivals, in both skill and reputation, and when they weren't in imperial service Frundsberg hired his men to anyone with enough gold to pay them, providing they weren't French or Swiss. After three decades of almost uninterrupted victories, the *landsknechts* had become the most sought after mercenaries in Western Christendom and their name had become a byword for the worst excesses of war.

Having spent more than half of his fifty years in Maximilian's service, the ageing colonel had tried to retire to his Bavarian estates once the old emperor had died but, like Cincinnatus, his devotion to the Holy Roman Empire had brought him back to the battlefield each time the new emperor Charles V had summoned him. Most recently, Charles had bestowed the title of *Highest Field Captain of the Entire German Nation* on Frundsberg and charged him with raising the reinforcements for Lannoy's beleaguered army in Lombardy. Despite the onset of winter, Frundsberg had quickly recruited more than 12,000 veterans to his banner and had crossed the Alps in record time.

There was another man seated at the table in front of the tent, who might have been Frundsberg's slightly younger brother. He too had a full white beard and the tired expression of a man who'd served many powerful masters but instead of armour he was dressed in the long black cloak and square cap, which marked him as a man of letters. Around his neck he wore a heavy gold chain, decorated with red enamel badges displaying three golden lions, alternated with the combined red and white rose of the Tudors. Thomas recognised the man at once. It was Sir John Russell, one of king Henry's most trusted ambassadors and a staunch ally of Cardinal Wolsey.

In his dirty and dishevelled state, Thomas reckoned there was no chance that the ambassador, who'd spent many years at the imperial courts in Spain and Austria, would recognise him as the lowly astrologer whom Wolsey had condemned to death. Nevertheless, he tried to avoid Russell's quizzical stare and concentrated his attention on Frundsberg. Unfortunately, he found little comfort in the colonel's cold expression, there was something of the wolf in Frundsberg's yellowish eyes and Thomas realised this was a man who'd raised himself high by climbing a tower of dead men's bones.

"Who are you and what do you want? Captain Schreiber says you have important news so speak up before

I have you flogged," growled Frundsberg without looking up from his papers. Thomas was about to introduce himself as the man who held the keys to Pavia but Lord Russell spoke first.

"I know this man, he's a rogue and a trickster whose name is Sir Thomas Devilstone and though His Majesty bestowed a knighthood on this scoundrel, he's no gentleman. Why, back in England he's under sentence of death for witchcraft!" Sir John cried and at last Frundsberg looked at his visitor.

"You're Thomas Devilstone? They say Satan himself carried you over the walls of London's Tower and took you to Metz where you were devoured by your own dragon. Is it really you that stands before me or some infernal *doppelgänger* sent to haunt me for my many sins?" Frundsberg asked.

"My Lord, don't believe these tales, they're mere stories to frighten children, but you must believe me when I say that my death sentence was part of an elaborate ruse to help me deceive the White Rose into revealing his secrets," said Thomas and he hurriedly explained that his trial had been a sham to convince Richard de la Pole that Henry's astrologer had fallen from grace and now bore a murderous grudge against the Tudors. However, though this trick had helped Thomas and his three companions infiltrate the Yorkist court, they'd been betrayed, imprisoned and tortured.

"In spite of the injuries we'd suffered, we escaped and vowed to continue with our mission to thwart the pretender's invasion of England. We disguised ourselves and followed the White Rose all the way to Pavia where we spent many weeks spying out of the French siege works. Of course, as soon as we heard that the famous Colonel Frundsberg was on the march we hastened to Lodi to tell you what we know," said Thomas proudly but Russell saw through the outrageous lie immediately.

"I don't believe a word of it! I have the confidence of both The Lord Chancellor Cardinal Wolsey and King Henry and neither told me anything of such a ridiculous stratagem, if you ask me this man is a double spy sent to lay a false trail," snorted Russell but Frundsberg wanted to hear more.

"Very well necromancer, I do need news of the French camp but answer me this, can you prove anything you say? Perhaps my Lord Russell is right and you mean to deceive me with lies, so should I have you flogged as deserters, burned as sorcerers or hanged as spies?

"If you know who I am, you'll know that fate has entrusted to me a copy of *The Munich Handbook* that was once owned by the master Leonardo. I'll swear on this book what I say is true and may God and The Devil tear my soul in two if I lie," said Thomas, ignoring his companions' angry looks.

"I've indeed heard of this book, may I see it?" Frundsberg asked. Thomas quickly retrieved the oilcloth wallet from beneath his shirt, unwrapped the book and placed it on the table. Frundsberg stared at the battered volume, which now smelled strongly of smoke, but he didn't touch it.

"Put it away, I can sense its dark power and I want nothing to do with it," he said quietly. Thomas obediently put the book back in his shirt but he was utterly unprepared for what happened next. Without warning Frundsberg roared for his guards and before Thomas knew what was happening he and the others had been pushed to the ground and trussed like chickens.

"For once, just for once I would like to go somewhere where people are glad to see us!" moaned Bos as he squirmed in the mud.

"Silence, *hexen*, I don't know what enchantments you used to escape Henry Tudor or the White Rose but you'll not escape me. We Germans know how to treat witches, they die!" Frundsberg cried.

"What madness is this? I've come to ensure your victory, Lord Russell, in the king's name I command you to prevent this," Thomas shouted as he struggled against his bonds.

"The king's justice has condemned you for witchcraft and if the good colonel chooses to carry out the sentence I'm powerless to prevent it," said Russell with a triumphant wave of his hand. Thomas bellowed at Russell he was a worse traitor to God than Pontius Pilate but his curses fell on deaf ears. Frundsberg issued more orders to his *trabant* bodyguards; drums beat, trumpets sounded and the entire body of Frundsberg's army began to assemble on the parade ground in front of his tent.

Whilst the *landsknechts* formed up in their different companies, the prisoners were manhandled into a cart that was dragged to the inevitable gallows at the centre of the camp's parade ground. The strengthening morning sun cast the ominous shadow of the gibbet over the prisoners as they tried to make sense of what was going on.

"By all the unholy turds laid in the great cess pit of Great Tartarus, why didn't you leave that damned book to burn to ashes?" Prometheus growled and for once Thomas did not know what to say.

"Tell our judges that we had nothing to do with your necromancy or so help me Thomas I'll crawl from the grave and drag your soul to hell myself!" Bos added but Quintana shook his head.

"He can't do that, there are no judges, Frundsberg has already found us guilty and this is just how the Germans decide sentence," he groaned.

Some years ago the Portugee had fought in the Conquest of Navarre and he'd seen these pike courts before. The mercenary army divided itself into its three battles, the van, the body and the rear, to discuss the matter and whatever sentence two out of the three battles decided was carried out. There were only three crimes, desertion, treachery or stealing from fellow *landsknechts,* and there was no appeal. Thieves and spies were hanged whilst deserters were made to 'run the gauntlet', this involved the prisoner running between two lines of their comrades, who each struck the condemned man in turn.

"What happens if the prisoner survives the gauntlet?" asked Prometheus.

"No one has ever survived," said Quintana darkly.

"I warned you Thomas, the evil of that book has infected us all and now we'll spend eternity in Hell suffering all the dreadful punishments inflicted on godless necromancers!" Bos cried.

"You think on Hell too much Frisian, have you forgotten we are Christians and Jesus died to redeem all our sins? If we truly repent, his blood shed on the cross will secure our passage into heaven," said Prometheus but for all the Nubian's optimistic view of the afterlife, it seemed as if Thomas' revelation that he still owned *The Munich Handbook* had sealed their immediate fate.

Once his men had formed up, Frundsberg told them that the condemned men were powerful sorcerers who'd bewitched two kings of England and he quoted the new teachings of Luther, who at least agreed with the pope on the subject of witches. The former monk had declared that sorcery was a sin against the Second Commandment and all those who practised witchcraft should be burned. Thomas' possession of *The Munich Handbook* was proof of the prisoners' guilt and there was only one possible sentence. All that remained was to decide how the prisoners should die.

"This is ridiculous, may we not defend ourselves?" Bos said.

"I told you, this is a court of law not justice, so we'll be lucky to see nightfall," said Quintana.

"Sweet Merciful Redeemer, I'm a king of Nubia who's escaped the murderous plots of a usurper and a pretender, surely I can't end my days dancing for the entertainment of a bunch of beer swilling, cabbage eating peasants!" Prometheus moaned.

"Well, if you've any suggestions now's the time to speak. Perhaps the Englishman has an idea?" said Quintana but Thomas remained dumbstruck. He couldn't believe that Frundsberg or Russell, who were both under orders to defeat England's enemies in battle, could turn against a man with the vital information they needed to defeat the French. Was the German colonel really so fearful of witches? Was the English ambassador so in thrall to Wolsey? But whatever their motives Thomas couldn't see a way out of the dreadful punishment that was about to befall him and his comrades.

Once Frundsberg had finished his speech, the drums started beating and his men separated into their companies to debate the merits of various punishments. With a curious air of detachment, Thomas and the others sat in their cart and listened to the snatches of the impassioned arguments that reached them. Most of the *landsknechts* regarded running the gauntlet, though a punishment for cowards, still allowed a soldier to die with honour but sorcerers were beyond such mercy and so should suffer hanging, the shameful death reserved for thieves and spies.

As the day wore on Thomas and the others could only be thankful that the German soldiery never considered the papal or Lutheran instruction to burn witches and the prospect of hanging seemed to offer a blessed relief compared to being slowly starved to death in a cage or roasted quickly over an open fire. Escape was impossible, they were surrounded by thousands of heavily armed mercenaries who'd hack them to pieces if they so much as spat outside their cart, and gradually the prisoners became resigned to their fate. The others even forgave Thomas for rescuing his book, as they all knew that the Angel of Death had been stalking them ever since they'd escaped from The Fleet.

According to *landsknecht* custom, any sentence of death had to be carried out before sunset. However, until the matter was decided, the soldiers were excused all but essential duties so the debate continued for as long as possible. Hour after hour, the prisoners sat in miserable silence whilst Frundsberg's men enjoyed their holiday but as the sun touched the horizon, the captains of each battle presented their answers to the camp provost. The decision was unanimous - the sorcerers must hang.

"Fear not, we'll send your immortal souls to God or The Devil without delay so make your peace with one or both. Do any of you wish for a priest?" said the colonel to the condemned men and at last Thomas found his voice.

"You're making a grave mistake Frundsberg. If I die, the information I have dies with me and without it your cause will be lost, as God is my judge ..."

"God's not your judge, I am and I say you hang, you bastard son of Satan. Why even your name, Devilstone, mocks good Christians and declares your allegiance to evil!" Frundsberg cried and he gave the order for the executions to proceed immediately.

To prolong the grisly entertainment, the colonel instructed his hangmen to string the witches up one at a time and that Thomas, as the chief of the coven, should die before the others in case he used his diabolical powers to free his familiars. Frundsberg also told his executioners to bind only the prisoners' arms, so their legs kicking away their last seconds of life would further amuse his men.

"Pray to the Lord Jesus and this day you shall be with him in paradise," said Prometheus as Thomas was dragged from the cart and manhandled to the gallows. As his hands were tied behind his back Thomas looked up at the gibbet, it was a simple affair, two upright posts supported a crossbeam with an iron ring fixed to the centre. A rope had been threaded through the ring with one end fastened to the packsaddle of a mule and the other tied off in noose.

"We will rejoice when we're seated at God's right hand, watching our enemies cast into the abyss!" Bos called as the hangman tied the battered copy of *The Munich Handbook* to a leather thong and hung the fateful book around Thomas' neck.

"Die well!" Quintana shouted as the hangman placed the noose over Thomas' head.

"No true Englishman is afraid to die but I call upon all those present to bear witness that I'm innocent and God has always protected me from the false charges of my enemies ..."

The hangman tightened the noose with a sharp tug that ended Thomas' last words in mid-sentence and from somewhere a priest began to read the words of the Twenty Third Psalm. Before the friar had finished, there was a sharp cry like the crack of a whip and the sound of a hand slapping against the mule's rump. Thomas felt the noose tighten and he was lifted off his feet. Immediately the coarse fibres of the rope began to tear at Thomas' throat and his head began to pound as the flow of blood to his brain was cut off.

The crowd gave a loud, mocking cheer and Thomas tried to reply with a stream of curses that would damn the men who'd unjustly murdered him but the noose choked his words into a meaningless gurgle. In desperation Thomas tried to tense the muscles in his neck to keep his windpipe open but the rope and his own weight had formed an unholy alliance that was slowly throttling him to death.

Though he'd been determined to die with dignity, the last spark of life forced Thomas to struggle against the bonds holding his wrists and kick his legs but this dance of death was so comical, the crowd burst out laughing at the dying man's futile attempts to relieve the pressure on his throat.

The last thing Thomas saw was the smiling face of Sir John Russell standing at the front of the crowd of whooping, jeering *landsknechts*. The last thing he heard was a sharp snap as something broke.

20

LODI

Thomas kept his eyes closed, fearing that if he opened them he'd see an army of devils waiting to cast his soul into a pit of burning brimstone, but as his senses returned he realised he could hear birdsong rather than the wailing of the damned. For a brief moment he believed his innumerable sins had been forgiven and he was in paradise but if this was heaven, it hurt like hell. There were shooting pains in his arms and legs, a dull ache around his throat and his head felt as if he'd been hit in the face with a shovel, yet through the waves of pain came a voice he recognised.

"Thomas, can you hear me, are you alive?" said Prometheus.

"I don't know, if I can hear you perhaps you're also dead," Thomas croaked and he opened his eyes to see his Bos, Prometheus and Quintana looking back at him. He tried to sit up, but his hands were still tied behind his back and he could feel the noose about his neck. At least his head was still attached to his shoulders and as he looked beyond Bos and the others, he saw a solid wall of men, all staring at him in wonder.

"By the Divine Mercy of Lord Jesus he lives!" Prometheus cried and a cheer went up from the crowd.

"It's a miracle, truly you're righteous in the sight of God," added Bos.

"It wasn't your neck that snapped it was the rope," explained Quintana as he cut Thomas' remaining bonds and removed the noose. With a groan, Thomas sat up and touched the angry red mark around his throat. The skin was raw and painful but he was alive. Now Frundsberg and Sir John Russell came to see the miracle for themselves. The colonel stood at Thomas' feet like the Colossus of Rhodes, extended his hand and offered to help Thomas to his feet.

"So Englishman you've survived your own hanging, by all the laws of God and Man you and your companions must be acquitted of all charges. Do you agree My Lord Russell?" he said.

"Wholeheartedly, this man has been judged by God and found innocent. When I return to England the king shall hear of this and I've no doubt he'll restore you to his highest favour," said Sir John. The English ambassador beamed at Thomas, like an indulgent father forgiving a spoilt child, and in honour of Thomas' deliverance he offered to pay, on King Henry's behalf, for a thanksgiving mass to be sung in Lodi cathedral that very day. Unfortunately for Sir John, Thomas was not impressed by this vicarious royal munificence.

"By the great red tits on the whore of Babylon, do you think the screeching of a few ageing eunuchs will excuse your foolishness ? If only you'd listened to me, instead of hanging me up like a string of onions, you'd have learned a great many things that are vital to your cause but now I've a good mind to leave you to wallow in your own ignorance!" Thomas said bitterly but already he was feeling his anger being replaced by sheer relief at having cheated the grave.

"Have a care Englishman, I still command here and I don't offer my friendship lightly," said Frundsberg but he again stretched out his hand. This time Thomas took it and with a roar of approval, the crowd surged forward. Before their colonel could prevent it Thomas, Bos, Prometheus and Quintana had been lifted up and were being carried shoulder high to the nearest sutler's tent.

Inside the canvas tavern, tankards of ale were thrust into the freed prisoners' hands and, despite the bruising around his neck, Thomas greedily poured the beer down his throat as if he was quenching a fire deep in his belly. When the mug was drained he slammed it on the table and called for another… and another. Soon the whole camp was celebrating the Miracle of Lodi with an ocean of beer and it was some time before Thomas and his companions were allowed to rest. Eventually the men whom Frundsberg couldn't hang were given a tent to themselves and left to sleep, but though the hour was late, none of them dared close their eyes.

"What spells and incantations did you use to outwit the grim reaper? I put little trust in spells or prayers but you must've done something to win God's favour," said Quintana as he stared at the canvas roof of their tent and thanked Heaven it was not the wooden lid of a coffin.

"I did nothing, it was pure luck that the rope snapped," said Thomas truthfully but the others insisted he must have called upon some divine or demonic power to save them all from the gallows. In exasperation Thomas repeated that, whilst there were many necromancers who claimed to be able to cheat death, he'd never seen any of them successfully return from the grave or bring a corpse back to life. He also revealed that the authors of the expensive *grimoires* used by such death defying sorcerers deliberately wrote long and complicated spells so they could blame their magic's inevitable failure on the mistakes made by those foolish enough to try and follow their directions.

"Any occult ritual, especially one to open the gates of The Underworld, takes months to prepare but even then it's all a charade," Thomas added bitterly. "All spellbooks warn that if the sorcerer lights a candle on the wrong day, pronounces the words of an incantation at the wrong hour or makes even the smallest error in the position of the stars when he begins his work, then a spell is bound to fail. Thus the fault will be his, not that of the magic, but all spells are impossible to perform exactly as instructed. I know this, because I've tried to harness the hidden forces of nature many times and despite following every instruction to the letter, I've never yet cast a spell that worked as it should."

"That's because you chose to follow Simon the Magus not Simon-Peter the Apostle, yet even in your error God has forgiven you and spared you for some important task. So, Englishman, whatever dark path you may have trodden in the past if you continue to walk in the light my sword will be yours to command," said Bos earnestly.

"The Frisian is right, just as the angel freed St Peter from Herod's dungeon to preach to the gentiles, so God has delivered you from your enemies in order to do great deeds. I may have lost my crown but I've not lost my faith in the Lord Jesus so I too give you my oath, as a prince of the royal blood, that I will follow you faithfully wherever you may lead," added Prometheus.

"For me the only truth is in gold but I'd be a greater fool than these two pious idiots to ignore what I've just seen with my own eyes. After surviving your own hanging your reputation alone will bring you more wealth and honours than any magic spell so, if you'll allow me to gather up the crumbs from under your table, I too will offer you my sword," said Quintana.

Though Thomas was surprised at his comrades' declarations, he gratefully accepted their pledges and with that, the others finally fell into a deep and dreamless sleep. It was ironic, Thomas thought as he lay listening to his comrade's peaceful snores, that he'd wasted so much time and effort trying to summon demons to do his bidding when it was actually far easier to recruit ordinary men.

Having fought numerous battles against papal armies and committed countless acts of sacrilege, Frundsberg's bloodthirsty mercenaries' had been placed beyond God's Grace by a succession of popes, yet their frequent excommunications had done little to curb the *landsknechts* capacity for murder, rape and pillage. However, in spite of their contempt for priests and the Ten Commandments, the men camped outside Lodi were all deeply superstitious and they shared Quintana's belief that the Englishman had been spared for some higher purpose.

As proof of their devotion, Frundsberg's men kept a constant vigil outside Thomas' tent throughout the bitterly cold night and at dawn the next day, when their new messiah rose to answer the call of nature, they greeted him like the multitude that welcomed Jesus into Jerusalem. Surprised and deafened by so many men shouting his name, Thomas begged to be left alone so he could recover from the previous evening's excesses but the crowd ignored his pleas and demanded more miracles. Thomas was only rescued when the captain of Frundsberg's personal guard appeared and presented an invitation for Thomas and his men to join the colonel for breakfast.

A short while later, the half-strangled former sorcerer and his three erstwhile apprentices found themselves breaking bread with the inquisitor who'd sentenced them all to death barely twelve hours ago. Perhaps unsurprisingly, Frundsberg made no mention of the failed execution but he did apologise for the absence of Lord Russell, who'd been called away to a meeting with the Duke of Bourbon. After his steward had placed bread, sausage and ale on the table, the colonel asked Thomas if he was still prepared to reveal what he knew about the French siege works at Pavia.

"Indeed yes My Lord, I bring both news from the besieged city and a request from Cardinal Wolsey," said Thomas trying to lie as convincingly as a genuine ambassador from the Court of St James, but Frundsberg insisted on hearing the French order of battle before granting any favours. Thomas agreed and called for pen and paper so he could draw a map.

At the bottom of his sketch Thomas drew the river Ticino, flowing from left to right, with Pavia on its northern bank. To the north of the city, he drew the misshapen diamond of the deer park and the six gates in the fifteen foot high wall built by the old Visconti dukes. At the apex of the diamond he marked the *Porta Pescarina* and the road linking this entrance with the *Torretta* gate at the diamond's base. Thomas also marked the *Porta Repentina* and *Porta Riazzo* that allowed entry to the park from the west, as well as the *Porta Duo* and *Porta Levrieri* which gave access from the east.

Within this outline, Thomas showed the position of the three largest French camps inside the deer park. First was King Francis' camp, shared by Richard de la Pole and his Black Band, which lay close to the *Porta Repentina*. Second, in the centre of the diamond, was the main French baggage park and noblemen's billets at the Castel Mirabello. Third, between the *Porta Levrieri* and *Torretta* gates, was the camp of Francis' Swiss mercenaries led by the French adventurer the Seigneur de la Flourance.

"Is that it?" Frundsberg asked when he saw that all his old adversaries had taken the field against the emperor but Thomas shook his head.

"Those are the French camps to the north of Pavia but King Francis has also fortified two villages that cover the main western and eastern roads into the city," said Thomas and he marked the positions of San Lanfranco and the Five Abbeys, from where the French king had launched his abortive assault several weeks ago. He also told Frundsberg that San Lanfranco was garrisoned by a rearguard made up of unseasoned Gascon levies led by the king's brother-in-law the Duc d'Alençon, however the siege works protecting the Five Abbeys and the road to Lodi were guarded by more reliable Swiss *reisläufer* whose commander was the king's boyhood companion the Duc de Montmorency.

"Now I've told you what I know, in return His Eminence Cardinal Wolsey begs that you help me kill the White Rose and end the Yorkist plots against England's rightful king forever," said Thomas, trying to maintain the fiction that he had the cardinal's warrant for assassinating the White Rose, but even though Russell wasn't there to challenge his lie, Frundsberg waved his hand dismissively.

"Why should I help you do that? The White Rose is a danger only in Henry's mind and Wolsey fights battles that were won long ago," he snapped but Thomas replied by telling the colonel what he knew about Henry's need to divorce his barren Spanish queen, the emperor's aunt, so he could sire a male heir with a new wife. Frundsberg listened to the story of Henry's dynastic woes with barely concealed boredom but he became more interested when Thomas explained how Henry's codpiece could upset the delicate balance of power between France, England and The Holy Roman Empire.

Repeating what he'd been told by Nagel, Thomas argued that Cardinal Wolsey's constant snubs to papal authority had deeply angered the Vatican and Pope Clement would never grant an annulment of Henry's marriage so long as Wolsey remained in power. As a result of the pope's visceral hatred of Wolsey, Henry had to sacrifice his chief minister in order to win Clement's blessing but a divorce would be a disaster for Frundsberg's paymaster, the Emperor Charles V.

"If Wolsey falls, Catherine of Aragon will be cast aside and England will join France in an alliance against The Holy Roman Empire," said Thomas triumphantly but Frundsberg remained unimpressed.

"In the name of St Boniface's beer-stained beard why would Henry do that? Surely he hates Francis and wants the French throne for himself," said Frundsberg but Thomas had his answer prepared.

He reasoned that if Catherine of Aragon was shamed by a scandalous divorce, the Emperor Charles would have to defend his aunt's honour and declare war on England. As Henry couldn't withstand the combined might of Spain, Italy and The Holy Roman Empire, he'd be forced to seek French help. On the other hand, if de la Pole died at Pavia, Wolsey could take credit for exterminating the House of York and his position at court would become unassailable. If Henry couldn't dismiss the man who'd saved his throne, he couldn't obtain his divorce and Catherine of Aragon would stay queen.

"So, My Lord, as long as Wolsey stays in office, England will remain an imperial ally to confuse and confound our common enemy, the French," he added confidently.

Though it was strange for Thomas to pretend he was trying to save the career of the venal cardinal who'd caused his disgrace and exile, all he needed was for Frundsberg to believe enough of the lie to help him kill de la Pole. Once the White Rose was dead, Thomas could return to England in triumph and reclaim his position at court; then he'd settle with Wolsey. As he imagined the cardinal rotting in a dungeon, Frundsberg considered Thomas' request but though the threat of an Anglo-French alliance was real enough, the colonel was a soldier who had no time for spies and assassins.

"And for slitting a rebel's throat, Henry will reward you with a dukedom, is that at the bottom of all this? Dear God, why is it that the English, can only be trusted to do three things, piss themselves when drunk, catch the pox from diseased whores and plot to kill each other," groaned Frundsberg. Thomas was about to challenge the insult but before he could continue Bos came to his aid.

Between mouthfuls of black bread and spiced sausage, The Frisian reminded the colonel that de la Pole now led the Black Band, who were the *landsknechts'* sworn enemies, so whatever the English king and his cardinal were up to, this was Frundsberg's best chance to punish those treacherous Germans who'd betrayed their oath and abandoned their emperor. Prometheus also added fuel to the fire by remarking that these renegades were the best troops in the French army but, the lion couldn't fight without a head, so if their captain was killed his men would scatter.

Frundsberg frowned. He couldn't fault either the Frisian or the Nubian's logic but it was Quintana who finally persuaded the colonel that the four assassins eating his food and drinking his ale were worthy of his blessing.

"What my friends are saying, My Lord, is that if the Black Band is destroyed, the French will have to raise the siege and acknowledge the emperor as master of Italy. If you give Charles this victory you'll be able to name your own reward and I trust you'll remember those who helped you," said the Portugee and at this Frundsberg threw back his head and laughed like a mule.

"By the poor burned arse of St Lawrence here's one man who speaks words I understand. The Englishman may have more twists than a pig's tail but there's always honesty in a man who fights for gold," he guffawed. Though Frundsberg still refused to condone assassination, he declared he would offer his assistance provided the Englishman pursued his vendetta honourably, on the battlefield, and raised a company to fight at Pavia. Thomas was a little taken aback and pointed out that few Englishmen had ever served as *landsknechts*, and none had led his own *fähnlein*, but Frundsberg assured him that after yesterday's miracle he'd have no trouble attracting recruits.

"A man who's survived his own hanging is a powerful talisman and there are plenty of unsigned men in the camp who'll flock to your banner," the colonel insisted. Thomas protested that there'd be no guarantee he'd meet his enemy on the battlefield but Quintana reminded him of the *landsknecht* custom of rival captains challenging each other to single combat before battle commenced.

"The White Rose can't refuse such a challenge if you're his equal in rank," agreed Prometheus.

"Don't forget you're half his age so you should beat him easily and such a victory is sure to restore your reputation at Henry's court," added Bos. Thomas thought for a moment and decided the others were right. King Henry could hardly refuse to pardon them all if he killed the last Yorkist prince in a chivalrous trial by combat witnessed by two armies.

"Very well My Lord, I'll accept your offer and I promise you this, without de la Pole and his Black Band the French can't hold Pavia and without Pavia they can't hold Italy," said Thomas.

Without further debate, Frundsberg wrote out the *weberpatent* which gave the Thomas the right to recruit up to four hundred unsigned men who were already in the camp or who might arrive later. It also allowed him to appoint sergeants and create his own *fähnlein*, the sacred battle flag of a *landsknecht* company. Having received his commission, Thomas had no doubt about who should serve as his subordinates or the device he should use for his banner and a few hours later he showed his new sergeants a splendid yellow flag with a pugnacious red devil in the centre.

"So you have power to raise devils after all," said Quintana eyeing the banner appreciatively.

"May The Devil bring us luck," added Prometheus and even Bos approved of the device.

"Lucifer was the brightest of angels who was cast out of Heaven for his pride. In our sin, we too are exiles looking for a way back to God so it is fitting that we should be The Devil's Band!" he cried.

The four men agreed to raise their banner and begin recruiting that afternoon but first they had to discard the enemy's black clothing they'd been wearing since their escape from de la Pole's camp. Fortunately, Frundsberg's sutlers were delighted to extend credit to men saved by God from the gallows and after a few hours they were all dressed in a manner more befitting *landsknecht* officers.

Quintana chose a suit of contrasting red and green quarters, colours that honoured the flag of his homeland, whilst Bos favoured the blue and gold stripes used in the banner of East Frisia. Thomas chose a concoction of red and yellow, the livery of St Cuthbert patron of the old Saxon kingdom of Northumbria but Prometheus picked his red and white outfit for no other reason than he liked the colours. As well as contrasting hues, their new clothes sported the slashed sleeves, tight breeches, striped hose and outrageous codpieces that were the badge of the mercenary. Broad brimmed hats, with plumes of brightly coloured ostrich feathers and beards clipped in the square German style completed their costumes.

For side arms Bos, Prometheus and Quintana bought short *katzbalger* swords, which they hung from their belts unsheathed as *landsknecht* custom demanded. Quintana and Bos also purchased sergeant's halberds but Prometheus preferred to wield one of the long, *zweihänder* double-handed swords much favoured by the *doppelsöldners* who volunteered to fight in the front rank of the pike squares in return for double pay. When it came to armour, the others purchased simple iron skullcaps but Thomas, as much to show his rank as for his protection, bought a breastplate with hinged thigh guards and armed himself with a falchion. He was surprised to find a replacement for the distinctive English sword he'd lost so many months ago but he regarded its discovery as a good omen.

Once they were properly equipped, Thomas raised his devil's banner in the parade square and was gratified to see a queue of men quickly form. He glanced along the line of expectant recruits and felt the hairs on the back of his neck tingle with excitement. If he'd spent a year scouring the deepest dungeons in Christendom he couldn't have assembled an uglier array of more villainous soldiery but with Bos, Prometheus and Quintana acting as his sergeants he knew he could lead these thieves and murderers to glory. Quintana was already putting his military experience to good use by examining the weapons each man had brought with him.

Unlike the musters in Metz and Lyon, where every runaway potboy and farmhand had been made welcome, Frundsberg only employed tough, professional soldiers. Whether they fought with pike, halberd, double-handed sword or arquebus, every man had to provide himself with the tools of his trade so the Portugee set himself the task of watching for *doppelgängers*. These men had usually sold their weapons to pay their gaming debts, nevertheless they tried to enlist by borrowing what they needed from those who'd just signed on. By sundown, Quintana had driven a score of these rogues from the line but even without them Thomas had recruited nearly 400 men.

The following day Thomas called for experienced men to volunteer as *doppelsöldners* and organised his company into platoons. These *rotten* consisted of ten ordinary, or six double soldiers, who'd share a tent and a cart for the duration of their contract. Once this had been accomplished, The Devil's Band was ready to take the oath of loyalty to the Holy Roman Emperor Charles V.

At the appointed hour, the other companies gathered on the parade ground and when the entire army was assembled, thirty different coloured *fähnleins* fluttered cheerily in the breeze. Among them was the winged skull of the *Todesengel*, the wolf of the *Kriegshund* and the lightning flash of the *Heiligsturm*. Every one of these companies had a fearsome reputation, yet the men in their ranks looked jealously at their comrades in The Devil's Band and wished they too were led by a hanged man who, it was whispered, also had the power to summon dragons.

While the men waited patiently for the ceremony to begin, Frundsberg's *trabants* erected a ceremonial gateway, consisting of two upright halberds, with a third tied between them to form a crossbar, in the centre of the parade ground whilst their colonel mounted a snow-white charger. Accompanied by the beating of a hundred drums Frundsberg rode along the ranks of his men acknowledging their cheers. At last the drums fell silent and for a moment the only sound was of crows arguing noisily in the leafless trees but then Frundsberg spoke.

"The men of the *Teufel's Bande* will present their arms and take the oath of loyalty to the Holy Roman Emperor Charles of Hapsburg, King of Castile and Leon, King of Aragon and Sicily, King of Naples and Rome, King of Germany and Jerusalem, Lord of the Netherlands and the Americas, Archduke of Austria…"

It took some time to list each of their employer's eighty-six titles, especially as every honour was greeted with more cheering, but eventually the roll was completed and Thomas stepped forward. He raised his hand and swore to 'serve The Emperor well and obey his officers without discussion or delay'. After his men had repeated these words, Thomas led them through the yoke of halberds and they again presented their weapons for inspection. Only if Frundsberg's *trabants* deemed a man fit would he be entered into the official lists and receive a chit for his first month's pay. The *trabants* dismissed a dozen of Thomas' recruits, who slunk away grumbling, but before the others could claim their wages, the drums called the army to attention and Frundsberg began to address his men.

The colonel announced that the Count of Lannoy, the imperial commander-in-chief, had received orders to relieve Pavia immediately so the entire army would march as soon as Christmas and Epiphany had passed. Thomas listened to the impassioned but curiously empty speech and failed to understand the delay. The French had been camped in the freezing mud and rain for nearly two months and, thanks to his efforts, half the Black Band had been without tents for a fortnight. The French army would be bored, cold and vulnerable but Frundsberg and his men, for all their fearsome reputation, seemed happy to postpone the inevitable battle for as long as possible.

Once the parade had been dismissed, and the men had drifted away to empty their newly filled purses into the hands of the camp's whore's and sutlers, it was Quintana who explained that the delay wasn't cowardice but common sense. Mercenary commanders were paid according to how many troops they could keep in the field so if they lost men they also lost money. As most soldiers, from exalted colonels to humble pikemen, followed the drum to get rich most *landsknechts* were happy to avoid battle, until their employers insisted they delivered the war they'd been paid to fight.

"So you see my brave English captain, only a witless fool would risk his neck for an emperor, a king or a pope until it's absolutely necessary," said the Portugee with a smile but Prometheus and Bos were outraged at the suggestion there was no honour in soldiering.

"Love of money is the root of all evil," said Bos but Quintana cursed him for a pious poltroon.

"What's wrong with fighting for cash? You were born a king but the only way a poor man like me can become rich is with a sword in my hand. I'll happily fight Frenchmen for the German Emperor, Tartars for the Tsar of Russia or blue baboons for the King of Ethiopia, but only so long as there's gold in their coffers," he said.

"An interesting philosophy but you've hardly become rich have you?" Prometheus remarked.

"It's true my weakness for pretty faces and pasteboards has emptied my purse many times, so I'm forced to return to soldiering to keep body and soul together but that's another good reason to prefer the safety of a camp to the dangers of a battle," admitted Quintana.

At least the days spent in idleness weren't wasted. Thomas was no stranger to war but the border skirmishes between English and Scots *reivers* were very different to the great battles of Italy and he'd much to learn. The tactics of the pike square, which the *landsknechts* called an *igel* or hedgehog, were relatively simple but took a great deal of practice to perfect.

In battle, ten or more companies came together to form an *igel* with a solid block of three or four thousand pikemen at the centre and the remaining halberdiers, *zweihänder* swordsmen and arquebusiers massed in two or more ranks around the outside. A quarter of each pike square's strength was made up of *doppelsöldners,* identified by the white plumes in their hats, who always formed the front line facing the enemy. As the situation required these men, armed with halberds and handguns as well as double-handed swords, could advance and form a screen of skirmishers or launch the suicidal charges known as the *verlorene haufe*, the forlorn hope.

The rank and file arquebusiers could also leave the safety of the pike square, form 'wings', and fire a volley of shots before retreating behind the *igel's* long spines to reload. When charged by cavalry, or another *igel*, the pikemen would jam the butt ends of their pikes into the ground and lower the points to create a hedge of steel that protected their comrades but, if ordered to attack, the pikes would be raised and these huge formations of infantry would roll towards the enemy like a storm cloud, drums sounding the thunder and handgunners spitting red hot balls of lightning.

At the last moment, the men of the forlorn hope would unfurl their blood red banner, run forward and use their halberds or double handed swords to lop the heads off enemy pikes and pikemen alike. Once two *igels* collided the result was a melee, a murderous trial of strength where the short, round ended, *katzbalger* swords were used to hack away at the crush of men. During the melee, no quarter asked or given and those who fell wounded were trampled into the blood soaked earth.

Whether deployed in attack or defence, the *igel's* strength was its coherence. If its ranks became disordered, the enemy's cavalry or *doppelsöldners* could penetrate the pike block and wreak havoc so the men of each *fähnlein* practised manoeuvring together with constant drill. Fifes, drums and sharp raps across the shins from the sergeants' canes kept the ranks dressed and the files in line until the thousands of men could act as one giant beast without thinking.

Bos and Quintana, who'd experienced this type of fighting before, proved to be excellent sergeants but Prometheus, who was more used to the hit-and-run warfare of the desert, preferred to lead the swashbuckling *doppelsöldners*. Quintana could scarcely believe that the Nubian had volunteered for such dangerous duty but Prometheus was convinced that the length of his time on earth had already been decided by God and hiding from his enemies would not persuade The Almighty to grant him a single extra minute of life.

For his part, Thomas learned how to integrate his company into the pike square or fight in open order but his men's successful performance on the parade ground only added fuel to their captain's impatience. He knew that at any moment the White Rose might be carried off by a culverin ball or succumb to the camp fever that put more men in their graves than any battle, but the feasts of Christmastide passed and still Lannoy refused to budge. It wasn't until the end of January that the imperial commander-in-chief finally obeyed his emperor and gave the order to march.

21

THE FIVE ABBEYS

The 30,000 men of Lannoy's army arrived before the city of Pavia on the 2nd of February 1525 but instead of making an immediate surprise attack on the demoralised French, Lannoy ordered his men to build a huge fortified camp around the *Casa de Levrieri*. This abandoned villa, which lay a mile to the north east of the city, occupied a strategic point overlooking both the *Porta de Levrieri*, the eastern gate into the deer park, and the five fortified monasteries that guarded the road from Pavia to Lodi. Facing Lannoy's 24,000 German and Neapolitan *landsknechts*, supported by 6,000 Spanish horsemen, were 8,000 Swiss *reisläufer*. Of these 5,000, under the Seigneur de la Flourance, were stationed along the eastern walls of the deer park whilst 3,000, under the Duc de Montmorency, garrisoned the Five Abbeys.

Though the imperials boasted overwhelming numbers, Lannoy did not want to waste valuable men in a bloody assault. Instead, like Caesar at Alesia, he decided to besiege the besiegers and use his guns to batter the French into submission. He therefore ordered his men to construct gun-pits, protected by ramparts, palisades, and trenches, and though the frozen earth was as hard as moneylender's heart, the imperial siege works progressed quickly. All the while, their enemies watched the net closing around them and did nothing. Apart from a few lazy cannon shots and some easily repulsed patrols, neither Flourance or Montmorency made any serious attempt to interfere with the construction of the imperial camp.

"Why don't the fools attack whilst we're busy shovelling baskets of frozen shit?" grumbled Bos as he watched a group of his men filling wicker gabions with earth and placing them in the front of the gun pit they were building.

"The French are no fools, they know we outnumber them, so unless Francis can concentrate his entire strength against us any attack will be crushed. On the other hand, if he weakens any point in his own siege lines the imperial garrison will break out," said Prometheus.

"At least it's us giving the orders for a change and I'm delighted to sit on my fat sergeant's arse watching other people work," said Quintana happily but as he spoke, Thomas returned from a meeting of Frundsberg's captains with the last news the Portugee wanted to hear.

"It seems as if the emperor's getting fed up with paying for an army that won't fight, he's demanding something in return for his gold and we have been chosen to supply it," said Thomas excitedly and he informed his sergeants that The Duke of Bourbon was going to lead three *fähnleins* against the fortified abbeys at dusk.

"By the bruised thumbs of the Holy Carpenter how could you do this to me Thomas? We'll all be shot to pieces!" groaned Quintana.

"Cease your mewling Portugee, at least you'll have a chance for your plunder. Papist abbeys are stuffed full of the gold paid by sinners in the hope of buying their way out of Hell," said Bos.

"You speak the truth Frisian, and as the pope of Rome is in schism with the true Pope of Alexandria it will no sin to loot a heretic's church!" said Prometheus with a grin.

"You may plunder all you want but the French are siting big *nachtigall* siege guns in each of the three abbeys opposite our lines and we must make sure these nightingales never sing," said Thomas but that was only part of the reason for the attack. Besides protecting his camp, Lannoy needed to exchange messages with the beleaguered garrison inside Pavia so the raid would be accompanied by a thirty Spanish *ginetes*, light horsemen skilled in irregular warfare.

"This all well and good but does it have to be us?" complained Quintana.

"We've been chosen because The Devil's Band needs to be baptised in blood but don't worry, have you forgotten I bear a charmed life?" said Thomas and the others laughed.

To allow the men time to prepare for the attack, those in the raiding party were excused other duties for the rest of the day and after an afternoon spent sharpening weapons and sleeping, the entire force began to assemble in the imperial trenches closest to the Five Abbeys. Most of the men were armed with swords or halberds but each company's captain also carried several long cloth bags tied around their waists and a pair of lighted slow matches tucked into their hat bands. Quintana asked what these were for but Thomas would only grin and insist that the Portugee be patient.

An hour after sunset the Duke of Bourbon ordered his captains to form their men into a skirmish line that could move quickly and silently over broken ground and whilst this was being done there was a huge explosion from the direction of the *Porta Levrieri*. Bourbon had learned many lessons whilst leading the failed siege of Marseille and he'd arranged for a diversionary artillery barrage to bombard the deer park's eastern gate. The detonation of the mine was the signal for a cacophony of cannon fire to erupt from the imperial gun positions, tongues of flame spat from the earthworks and the air was filled with the whine of iron shot speeding towards the enemy.

Though the imperial guns' target was far to the left of the men waiting in the trenches, each raider ducked instinctively as the cannon and culverin balls sped on their way. When the guns drew breath to reload, Bourbon gave the word and the *landsknechts* scrambled clumsily out of their trenches. The Spanish horsemen galloped away and were quickly lost in the darkness leaving the men on foot to pick their way through the palisades and pits full of sharpened stakes that protected their own camp. Five minutes later, with hearts beating, swords drawn and skin sticky with sweat, the raiders reached the Vernavola river that flowed between the French and imperial lines.

The diversion had worked better than Bourbon dared hope and whilst the Swiss rushed more men to the *Porta Levrieri* in expectation of an attack, the raiding party found an undefended bridge over the Vernavola and crossed to the dead ground between the *Torretta* gate and the Five Abbeys. The guns they had to destroy were in the monasteries of San Giacomo, San Spirito and San Paolo and from here the raiders could attack each abbey's lightly defended western gateway. Thomas and The Devil's Band were ordered to capture the abbey of San Paolo but in the gloomy light of a winter's moon, the darkened abbey looked more like a castle than a House of God.

San Paolo's cloisters were surrounded by a high wall of red brick, topped by swallowtail battlements of white limestone, the octagonal turrets at each corner were pierced by loopholes and the entrance was barred by heavy wooden gates protected by a similarly fortified gatehouse. The Devil's Band had brought ladders but rather than risk scaling the walls Thomas decided on a bold *ruse de guerre*. He formed his men into a column, marched them openly along the road from Pavia and as they approached the abbey's gatehouse he shouted to the sentries, in his best French, that he was bringing reinforcements to help repulse an imminent attack.

The darkness, the continuing imperial barrage and the fact that Thomas' shouts came from a direction supposedly occupied by friendly forces, duped the Swiss sentries completely. They opened the gates and even urged the new arrivals to hurry and join them on the walls facing the imperial lines. Scarcely able to believe his luck, Thomas waved his falchion and four hundred *landsknechts* poured into the abbey like molten metal running into a mould. The Swiss defenders suddenly realised their catastrophic mistake and tried to bar the way but it was too late.

The men of Bos and Prometheus' *rotten* cut down the sentries trying close the gates whilst Thomas and Quintana led the rest of the raiders further into the abbey. The Germans had a special loathing for their Swiss counterparts and slaughtered the sleeping *reisläufer* wherever they found them. Within minutes, the monastery's cloisters and dormitories became filled with the screams of the wounded and dying but Thomas and Quintana ignored these skirmishes and led a squad of thirty men to the open square in front of the monastery's chapel.

A few yards to left of the chapel's bell tower, the Swiss gunners had demolished three sections of the abbey's outer wall and built a long platform of wood and tamped earth behind these openings. The platform measured roughly a hundred feet long by twenty wide, with steeply sloping sides rising eight feet high. The flat top of this low, truncated pyramid had been covered with thick planks of oak that supported three heavy *nachtigall* cannon each weighing sixty hundredweight. The guns' ornately patterned muzzles projected through embrasures protected by earth-filled, wicker gabions and the iron shot was arranged in neat piles behind each brightly painted carriage. The cannons' powder however was stored in covered wagons parked some yards away from the platform.

A dozen Swiss gunners were sheltering behind the powder wagons but Thomas ordered his men to show them no mercy. The *landsknechts* gleefully charged their foes, who defended themselves gallantly with axes and the short gunners' pikes called linstocks, but the raiders had surprise and numbers on their side. The Germans swarmed around each wagon and the Swiss gunners died in a chorus of guttural battle cries but in answer to their comrades' tortured screams, fifty more *reisläufer* came running out of the abbey's church.

As he carried a small keg of powder onto the platform, Thomas saw the danger and shouted to his men to hold off the Swiss counterattack whilst he spiked the guns. His men rushed to obey and the square in front of the chapel's bell tower rapidly became a vision of Armageddon. Elsewhere, the raiders had set fire to the abbey and the burning buildings illuminated the small knots of men fighting desperately for their lives. Swords splintered skulls, halberds sliced off limbs, pikes pierced bellies and though the men of The Devil's Band fought like demons, two Swiss halberdiers managed to cut their way through the melee and climb the steps to the gun platform.

Quintana pursued the Swiss but, before he could cut them down, the first *reisläufer* fell on Thomas, who was busy trying to break open his keg of powder. Quintana shouted a warning just in time, the Englishman ducked behind the nearest gun carriage and his attacker's blade bit into the painted wood instead of his skull. In one swift movement, Thomas had drawn his sword, rolled under the carriage and leapt to his feet before the Swiss halberdier had wrenched his weapon free.

The Englishman's vicious backhand cut caught his opponent on the side of the head and the falchion sliced through human bone as easily as a butcher's cleaver. A bloody chunk of skin and skull went spiralling into the night as the dead man, gore pouring down his lifeless face, slumped over the gun carriage. As soon as he was sure the first *reisläufer* was dead, Thomas turned to look for his second attacker and saw the man lunge at Quintana just as the Portugee clambered onto the platform.

With a litheness learned in the backstreets of Lisbon, Quintana parried the blow with his sword but the Swiss was also no beginner and he managed to trap his enemy's *katzbalger* in the angle between his halberd's axe blade and spear point. With a sharp twist, the *reisläufer's* wrenched the sword from Portugee's hand and it clattered to the floor. Quintana, who was now defenceless, took a step backwards but found himself trapped against another of the guns. The Swiss halberdier grinned maliciously as he prepared to spit his opponent like a suckling pig but his cry of victory turned into a choking gurgle of defeat as Thomas' plunged his falchion between the man's shoulder blades.

"I am in your debt Englishman," said Quintana as the dead *reisläufer* fell at his feet.

"And I yours Portugee but we can repay each other by blowing these guns back to Basel," said Thomas retrieving his sword. He thrust the falchion into his belt before untying the long cloth bags wrapped around his waist and handing them to Quintana. When the Portugee did nothing but stare at the slender sacks in confusion, Thomas told him to fill them with gunpowder from the keg and stuff them into each gun whilst he piled the rest of the powder barrels around the carriages.

Though there was still fighting in other parts of the abbey, the brief but bloody battle of the bell tower had been won and Thomas found his men searching corpses for gold. Unfortunately, the Swiss must have left their florins inside the chapel they'd been using as a barracks as none of the dead men provided anything in the way of loot. Thomas therefore had no trouble persuading the empty handed *landsknechts* to give up their search and help him wedge as many powder barrels as they could under each gun.

Having filled the bags with powder, Quintana rammed them into the guns' breeches and for good measure, packed each muzzle with mud and stones. After priming the touchholes Thomas laid a thin trail of powder along the top of each guns' barrels, taking care to make each fuse slightly longer than the last. Snatching up a gunner's linstock, Thomas ordered his men to take cover and wound the lighted match he carried his hat around the linstock's metal crosspiece. Finally he said a silent prayer to St Barbara, touched the glowing end of the match to each fuse in turn and ran for his life.

With his heart thumping in his chest, Thomas joined his men behind a low wall and watched the sparks on top the guns dance towards the breeches. Slowly each flame crept ever closer to its touchhole then, almost together, the sparks disappeared. For a heartbeat Thomas thought the fuses had been extinguished by the damp night air but in the next instant the coal black sky was shattered by an ear splitting crash and the abbey was lit up by a pillar of boiling fire. In the orange glow, Thomas saw the guns' silhouettes, their massive muzzle burst asunder, rise from their carriages and tumble backwards as if they were no heavier than apple blossom blown across a farmyard.

Bos, who was busy fencing with three Swiss swordsmen, heard the roar of the explosion and looked up to see the tower of flame, fifty feet high, rise from the gun platform. For a heartbeat, he thought that God had appeared to lead his chosen people out of bondage and though the distraction lasted less than a second it was enough for one of his attackers to snatch a wheel-lock pistol from his belt and fire. The pistol's ball struck the Frisian's leg at point blank range and buried itself deep in the muscles of his thigh.

In spite of the shock and pain Bos remained on his feet but the pistoleer's companions saw their opportunity and moved in to finish off the Frisian. Even badly wounded, Bos managed to parry his opponents' cuts and lunges but he was bleeding like headless hen and his strength was ebbing fast. In another minute, Bos would have been swept away by the blizzard of Swiss steel but Prometheus ran to his aid. The Nubian cut down two of the Swiss as if they more nothing more than stalks of wheat then thrust his sword into the pistoleer who was frantically trying to reload his weapon.

"So the ox has had his horns trimmed," said Prometheus as he knelt down to examine the ragged hole in Bos' leg.

"A child's mistake," groaned the Frisian weakly, he tried to stay standing but the pain was too great and with a roar as loud as that of the Minotaur in the Labyrinth he collapsed. Immediately, Prometheus started to tear strips of cloth from the dead *reisläufers'* tunics.

"Don't move or you'll bleed to death and I'm sure St Peter isn't ready to receive Lutheran heretics just yet," he said as he tied the makeshift bandages around Bos' wound and used his dagger as a tourniquet. He twisted the cloths tighter until Bos yelped with pain but the flow of blood ceased.

"Does that feel better?" said the Nubian but Bos didn't reply, he'd passed out. Prometheus cursed the gods of war for their fickleness but imperial casualties had been mercifully few. For the loss of just twenty of their comrades the raiders had slaughtered every defender in the garrison and as a reward for their total victory, Thomas told his men to strip the abbey of everything of value then destroy what they couldn't carry. The chance to plunder was what every man in The Devil's Band had been waiting for and the loudest of the approving cheers came from Quintana.

"C'mon lads, the chapel is sure to be stuffed full of money for the relief of the poor and none are poorer than us, so fetch a barrow and follow me!" he cried. His men quickly found a handcart and eagerly followed their sergeant into the abbey's chapel. The barrow's wooden wheels clattering up the stone steps made a noise loud enough to wake the dead entombed in the chapel's crypt but Quintana emerged a few minutes later with nothing but an angry face and an empty handcart.

"Those thieving, cow-buggering Swiss bastards, they've picked the place clean!" Quintana cried and he kicked a dead Swiss halberdier in disgust just as Prometheus emerged from the darkness.

"I thought I'd find you here, now if you've no use for that cart follow me. That damn fool Frisian has taken a pistol ball in the leg and he lies as senseless as a millstone by the gate," he said urgently. Grumbling at the injustice of being left a pauper, Quintana ordered his men to lend a hand but they wouldn't attend to any of the wounded until they'd finished searching every corpse they could find for rings, coins and anything else of value. The pickings were slim and the dead bodies in the abbey's cloisters and dormitories seemed to be as impoverished as their late comrades by the gun platform.

There could be no doubt that the abbey's gold and silver had been looted by the Swiss months ago, and immediately spent buying whores and wine from the sutlers camped in the French baggage park at Mirabello. Though this knowledge did little to alleviate Quintana's anger, he had the wit to realise that the *reisläufers'* empty purses could only mean that the entire French army hadn't been paid in weeks. Frundsberg was bound to be interested in the news that his enemy was running short of cash so, leaving his men to help Prometheus heave Bos onto their barrow, he went to find Thomas.

Having completed his mission, the captain of The Devil's Band was busy supervising the evacuation of the abbey and he agreed with Quintana that Frundsberg must be told of the Swiss mercenaries' poverty as soon as possible. There was no sign of Bos or Prometheus by the gate so Thomas and Quintana joined their men picking their way over the boggy ground between the French and imperial lines. As they reached the bridge over the Vernavola, a series of explosions from the abbeys of San Spirito and San Giacomo indicated the other companies had also accomplished their tasks.

It was as they crossed the bridge that Thomas and Quintana caught up with Prometheus who was dragging the cart carrying Bos and three other wounded by himself. Forgetting their rank, the two men immediately took hold of the shafts and helped the Nubian haul the barrow across the ditches and craters in front of the imperial lines. On their return, Thomas was summoned to a meeting of captains so it was left to Prometheus and Quintana to carry Bos to his tent. There were plenty of doctors, of varying degrees of skill, in the camp but Prometheus had become an accomplished physician during his long war with the Funj and he knew how clean and close a gunshot wound.

"The Frisian is lucky, the ball didn't sever an artery so if I can remove it and stitch the wound he'll live," said Prometheus and he asked Quintana to buy a bottle of aquavit, a needle, physician's pincers and a catgut crossbow string from the nearest sutler's tent whilst he removed the blood soaked bandages. Without a word Quintana disappeared from the tent and returned some minutes later carrying everything the Nubian needed. With the bandages removed, Prometheus used the aquavit to clean the bloodied flesh but the stinging spirit roused Bos from his slumbers.

"Dear sweet Jesus Christ! What in the name of Pope Julius' puke-stained beard have you done to me?" Bos cried as his senses, and the pain, revived but in the next moment he slumped back on his cot and his whole body began to shake as if possessed by demons.

"Quickly, the angel of death is trying to tear the Frisian's soul from his body, unless we hold him still the ball may move and sever an artery after all!" snapped Prometheus. There was no time to find a length of rope to bind Bos to the cot and the only way to stop him convulsing was for Quintana to sit on his chest. Through the waves of pain Bos could see the Portugee sitting astride him like a catamite trying to satisfy a lazy bishop, which did nothing to put the Frisian at ease.

"What are you doing you foul sodomite," he roared but his curses became nothing more than strangled screams as Prometheus thrust the pincers deep into the wound.

"Is this vengeance for having your liver torn from your body by the eagles' talons," Bos moaned. In his agony the Frisian imagined his physician had been transformed into the Titan of Greek myth but Prometheus ignored him and continued to probe Bos' punctured muscles for the pistol ball. After what seemed like an eternity of torture, the Nubian gave a cry of triumph and pulled the misshapen bullet from the hole in Bos' leg yet, even now, there was no respite for the tormented patient.

"I still have to remove the patches of cloth torn from your breeches and hose, if they stay in the wound your blood will be poisoned and you will die of fever," said Prometheus and he plunged the pincers back into Bos' mangled flesh. As he searched for the grubby bits of cloth, the Frisian howled, screamed and cursed but Quintana's weight and strength held him still. The Nubian kept to his task and eventually pulled out two scraps of bloody fabric, each only slightly larger than a thumbnail.

"Almost finished," he said with satisfaction.

"Who taught you healing, Torquemada the Inquisitor?" Bos cried but there was still more pain to come. The Nubian poured some aquavit into the wound and Bos yelped like a whipped hound.

"The caraway in the spirit will kill any poisons," the Nubian explained but the wound had begun to bleed profusely and had to be closed at once. Ignoring the Frisian's threats to take terrible revenge if he bled to death, Prometheus deftly threaded the needle with a thin length of catgut taken from the unwound bowstring and sewed the wound shut as expertly as a tailor mending a torn coat. When he was done, Bos lay panting and sweating on the cot whilst Quintana dabbed away the gore and bound the stitches with clean bandages.

"Is that supposed to cure me?" Bos said through the mist of sweat and pain that shrouded his body.

"The mother who bore you suffered much more than that little tickle. Besides, your pain will ease in a few days whereas she suffered for years!" replied Quintana. The Frisian said nothing in reply, instead he snatched up the flask of aquavit, took a long draught and let his tortured body relax. In the next moment he was fast asleep.

Whilst Bos was suffering at the hands of his doctor, Thomas and the other captains who'd led the raid were making their report to the imperial commander-in-chief. The Count of Lannoy listened carefully to what his men had to say, especially about the lack of plunder, before awarding them each a bounty of five guilders for a good night's work and dismissing them from his tent.

Lannoy was pleased with the success of the raid, apart from destroying the siege guns threatening his camp, the dashing Spanish horsemen had delivered his letters to the besieged garrison's commander Don Antonio de Leyva and returned with vital information. However, as his captains left to claim their reward, Lannoy could only ponder on the irony that although he served the richest monarch in Christendom, his financial situation was as parlous as that of the French king.

The letters from Spain Lannoy had received the previous day had warned him that the emperor's patience was almost exhausted and His August Majesty would not send any more gold to Italy until the Imperial Army had, at the very least, rescued the 9,000 men of the imperial garrison trapped inside Pavia. Lannoy had angrily tossed the letter into the fire and as the flames consumed the emperor's ill-disguised rebuke, he'd wondered how his star could shine so brightly one moment yet fade so quickly the next.

Like the emperor he served, Lannoy had been born in Flanders and, because both the German Hapsburg emperors and the French Valois kings claimed his homeland, it was inevitable that he should become a soldier. Though his ancestors had fought on the French side at the Battle of Agincourt, Lannoy had chosen the Holy Roman Empire and had entered imperial service during the reign of the old Hapsburg Emperor Maximilian I. The ambitious young man had greatly impressed his patron, who'd made Lannoy a Knight of the Golden Fleece and chief equerry to his grandson the future emperor Charles V.

Lannoy's meteoric rise had continued once Charles had ascended the imperial throne. In rapid succession, the new emperor had appointed his favourite Governor of Tournai, Viceroy of Naples and commander of all the imperial armies in Italy and Lannoy had repaid Charles' faith in him by crushing a French army at the Battle of the Sesia River. This victory had opened the way for the rebel Duke of Bourbon to invade Provence but Sesia had been the imperial army's last success on the battlefield. Bourbon's failure to capture Marseille, followed by the ignominious retreat over the Alps and the abandoning of Milan to the French, meant the imperial army's commander in chief was in danger of losing his lucrative position.

If Lannoy couldn't relieve Pavia, let alone drive Francis and his army out of Italy, his career would be over but he was to loathe risk a full-scale assault on the city. If such an attack failed his own army would be destroyed, the French would finally win control Lombardy and he'd be utterly ruined. On the other hand, if he continued to disobey The Emperor's orders to relieve Pavia, the flow of imperial gold would cease, his unpaid army would mutiny and his disgrace would also be total.

There seemed to be no way out of this impasse and Lannoy knew time was running out. In the dispatches brought from Pavia by the previous night's raid the garrison's commander, de Leyva, had admitted he'd only recently averted a mutiny by melting down church plate to pay his mercenaries. De Leyva had also claimed that had he not committed such sacrilege, his *landsknechts* would have surrendered the city to the French and gone home.

Though Lannoy and de Leyva were both spending gold faster than an old fool married to a young trollop, the revelation that there was nothing worth plundering in the Five Abbeys could only mean that the French king had also seized church plate to pay his men. If Francis was as bankrupt as himself, it followed that neither commander could keep their mercenaries in the field any longer than the other and this gave Lannoy an idea of how he could simultaneously assault Pavia and abandon the siege whilst keeping both his honour and his purse intact.

Instead of a bloody assault on the French siege works, an attack on the enemy camps in the deer park would keep Francis' army occupied whilst Pavia's garrison broke out of the besieged city. Once the two imperial forcers were reunited, they could withdraw to the safety of Lodi and wait for the better weather, and the imperial treasure ships, to arrive in a few months' time.

Even if this strategy failed, and the garrison was forced to surrender, Lannoy reckoned he'd be no worse off than he was now. Having obeyed The Emperor's orders to attack there'd be no need for him to remain at Pavia, he could still withdraw to Lodi in good order and promise to begin the war anew in the spring. Though, in either case, his plan would leave the French in possession of this strategically important city, Lannoy calculated it would be a Pyrrhic victory for his enemies because Francis would find no gold to pay his men or bread to feed them inside Pavia.

With luck, the poverty of the city would force Francis to take his battered army back over the Alps and the more Lannoy thought about his scheme, the more convinced he became of its merits. He decided that the 24th of February, ten days hence, would be the day best suited to his plan's execution as this would give his men plenty of time to prepare whilst the French would be further weakened by disease and desertion. Moreover, apart from being St Matthias' Day and the luckiest day in the Christian year to begin any endeavour, this date was The Emperor Charles V's birthday.

Whilst Lannoy outlined his plan to his colonels, the French Duke of Bourbon, the German warlords George von Frundsberg and Marx Sittich von Ems, and the Neapolitan condottieri the Marquis de Pescara and his cousin the Marquis de Vasto, in another part of the camp Thomas Devilstone sat looking up at the starry winter sky. Algol, The Devil's Star, was shining blood red in the constellation of Perseus and every astrologer knew that this was an omen of confrontation and war.

Algol represented the head of the Medusa, the hideous snake haired female demon killed by the hero Perseus, and though he no longer put any faith in astrology, Thomas wasn't surprised that the appearance of the star heralded the arrival of an ugly old crone at his tent. Several days ago, he'd followed Quintana's advice and paid the beggar woman to carry a message to Richard de la Pole offering to settle their differences by single combat, should the two armies meet in battle. To make sure his intentions were clear Thomas had enclosed a handful of heron feathers with his letter.

The heron was a bird rumoured to be so cowardly it fled from its own shadow and Thomas was certain that the White Rose wouldn't let such an insult go unpunished but the reply wasn't at all what he expected. Without a word, the crone handed him a small wooden casket sealed with wax seals that bore the imprint of a white rose. Thomas tossed the crone a coin and watched her scuttle away into the darkness. As soon as he was alone, he broke the seals and opened the box.

There was no letter inside but the heron feathers had been returned, stuck in a cork and fashioned to resemble a shuttlecock used to play the peasant game of battledore. A man didn't have to be a student of Trithemius to understand de la Pole's meaning, the last prince of the House of York was declining the challenge because he considered the challenger to be too low born. In a rage Thomas threw the shuttlecock to the ground and stamped it into the mud.

22

THE DEER PARK

The powers of recuperation displayed by Bos astonished everyone, including Thomas, and he begged to be told the secret of the medicine Prometheus administered to his patient every day. At first the Nubian would only smile, and say that alchemists were not the only ones who could work magic, but the Englishman persisted. Thomas argued that Prometheus might have need of the same physick one day and there'd be nobody to prepare it if wounds had rendered the Nubian insensible.

Eventually Prometheus relented and, amongst other things, showed Thomas how to make the poultice that prevented wounded men from developing the fever that often killed them. The main ingredients were stale bread and certain spider webs, which were ground up with water to form a thick paste. This glutinous porridge was then placed in an earthenware pot, which was buried close to a regularly used campfire and left in the warm earth for two days. Once the porridge had grown a thin coat of blue-green mould it could be smeared on the wound and covered with clean bandages.

"By the great winged ox of St Luke you have the gift of healing Nubian," said Bos as he took his first steps since being shot and Thomas had to agree that the poultice had worked a genuine miracle.

"I've seen men survive deep wounds only to die of fever within the month," he said admiringly.

"The secret is to apply a fresh poultice every day and use only blue mould not black or red. Blue purifies the blood but other colours are poisonous," Prometheus warned.

"You should sell such secrets to the quacks and sawbones that have slaughtered more men than all the barbarian hordes of Tartary, you'd make a fortune!" said Quintana.

"The power to heal is a gift from God, it shouldn't be bought and sold like a basket of eggs, besides I've already told you that no one trusts the medicines of a stranger," snapped Prometheus but, in spite of this opinion, the men of The Devil's Band were deeply impressed by the Nubian's miraculous salve and they regarded Bos' rapid recovery as further proof that their company was blessed with supernatural good fortune. Their sergeant's return to the ranks was especially timely as the camp was alive with talk that another night assault on the French lines was imminent.

The rumours were confirmed when, on St Matthias' Eve, every man was ordered to stitch a large white square to his clothing, or find a white undershirt to wear, and spend the rest of the day sharpening his weapons.

Prometheus was puzzled by this command but Quintana assured him that it was a simple device to help tell friend from foe in the dark and went back to putting a keen edge on his cat skinner sword.

As the hours passed, the imperial camp became infected with a miasma of excitement as the men of Lannoy's army steeled themselves for battle. Few prayed, most drank and the whores did a brisk trade as hundreds of pikemen, halberdiers and arquebusiers prepared for death by trying to create life. Inevitably, brawls broke out as drunken *landsknechts* fought over wine and women so, to create a distraction, the provosts hanged thirty deserters from a huge triangular gallows. Like gluttons at a feast of death, the crowd of baying, jeering mercenaries thoroughly enjoyed this taste of blood and by sunset the men who made a good living from killing were eager for the real slaughter to begin.

After his challenge to single combat had been refused Thomas was also impatient to meet de la Pole on the battlefield and he answered his summons to a meeting of Frundsberg's captains with alacrity. When he returned an hour later, he gathered The Devil's Band together and explained the forthcoming attack was no mere raid like the assault on the Five Abbeys. Instead they were to be part of a great battle that would shape the future of all Christendom. His men murmured their approval and listened intently as their captain explained how they were to march into history.

Taking a piece of charcoal, Thomas sketched a map on a broad canvas sheet he'd had nailed to the side of a cart. Just as he'd done for Frundsberg, he drew a large diamond to represent the fifteen foot high wall around the deer park, with the besieged city of Pavia at the bottom and the French baggage park at the Castel Mirabello in the middle. At the top of the diamond, close to the *Porta Pescarina*, he marked the point where Spanish sappers had already begun to break down an unguarded section of the wall. At the diamond's western point he marked the French camp by the *Porta Repentina* and at the eastern point he marked the Swiss camp by the *Porta Levrieri*.

Having drawn his map, Thomas told his men that the imperial guns would soon begin bombarding the Five Abbeys but this would be a diversion. Whilst the French and Swiss sheltered from the storm of cannon fire, Lannoy would lead his army of Spaniards, Neapolitans and Germans to the breach in the deer park's northern wall. The actual battle would begin when 3,000 Neapolitan arquebusiers, under the Marquis de Vasto, launched a surprise attack on the Castel Mirabello. Lannoy had become convinced that the French king had recently moved into the comfortable hunting lodge and if the Neapolitans could capture Francis as he slept, the battle would be over before it had begun.

On the other hand, if Francis was elsewhere, de Vasto would hold Mirabello whilst the rest of the imperial army stormed the other French camps. To launch simultaneous attacks on objectives nearly three miles apart, the imperials would be divided into two separate columns. The first column would consist of two Spanish pike squares, led by Pescara and Bourbon, as well as most of the imperial horse commanded in person by the Count of Lannoy. The second column would be made up of two German pike squares, led by Sittich and Frundsberg, supported by the remainder of the cavalry.

While Pescara and Bourbon's *igels* stormed the camp by the *Porta Repentina*, Lannoy's Spanish and Italian horsemen would engage the French knights and mounted men-at-arms. Meanwhile Sittich and Frundsberg's *igels*, including The Devil's Band, would attack the Swiss at the *Porta de Levrieri*. Lannoy's strategy, Thomas told his men, was to pin down the entire French army whilst the imperial garrison inside Pavia broke out of the beleaguered city. At a given signal, their comrades would batter down the *Torretta* gate at the southern tip of the deer park and, if everything went according to plan, all the imperial forces would meet at Mirabello and make an orderly withdrawal to Lodi.

When he'd finished, Thomas let his men discuss the plan for a few minutes. Like all those facing death, his men wanted to know their chances of survival so their captain climbed onto the cart and spoke to reassure them.

"You know me, I was saved from an unjust hanging so I could raise The Devil's Band and there can be no doubt that tomorrow we'll win a great victory at Pavia because all ventures begun on St Matthias' day are blessed," said Thomas and he paused to let a murmur of approval ripple through the ranks of his men. When he was certain he had their full attention, he began again and this time he carefully increased the power and passion in his voice as he spoke.

"After Judas had betrayed Our Lord and hanged himself, Matthias was chosen by lot to join the Apostles. Now you've been chosen to fight for the Holy Roman Emperor, heir of Constantine Equal of the Apostles, and a hanged man will lead you into battle on St Matthias' Day. Could there be any better omens? It's written in the stars that we shall win wealth and glory by the steel in our hands and the courage in our hearts but a greater prize is that the things we do at Pavia will be numbered amongst the deeds of heroes forever. Years from now, we may be mocked for our gouty legs and rheumy eyes but those who think us feeble will fall silent when we strip our sleeves, show our scars and declare that once we marched to Pavia and fought for the emperor upon St Matthias' Day!"

As his men began to shout loud hurrahs, Thomas snatched the hat from his head and waved it in salute. His men replied by calling on The Almighty to help them smite the French, crush the Swiss and punish the hated traitors in the Black Band but their captain said only one silent prayer. Amidst all the cheering Thomas asked the God of Battles to bring him face to face with Richard de la Pole but before he could elaborate on his vow, a messenger arrived with orders for The Devil's Band to join the other companies assembling on the parade ground.

The imperial army was ordered to form up as quietly as possible because the first part of their march would take them close to the Swiss sentries at the *Porta Levrieri*. Though the captains insisted that silence was essential to maintaining the element of surprise their sergeants made a considerable amount of noise by cursing loudly any man whose weapon clattered against his armour. After nearly an hour of feverish, though hushed, preparation the army was ready to move but Lannoy insisted that the men kneel and say a prayer to St Matthias before taking a single step.

As soon as the chaplains had finished their final benediction, the night sky dissolved into a hellish maelstrom of fire, smoke and noise. The barrage continued even after Lannoy had given the order to advance and though the thunderous cannon fire succeeded in covering the sounds of marching men, the flashes of flame from the guns' muzzles illuminated the imperial army as brightly as the Egyptian Pharos lit Alexandria's harbour.

Despite all of Lannoy's careful precautions, the Swiss sentries on the walls of the *Porta Levrieri* couldn't fail to spot twenty thousand men shuffling past their watchtowers and they quickly alerted their colonel. Though only 34, the Seigneur de la Flourance was an experienced and able commander and he immediately sounded the alarm. Within ten minutes his 3,000 Swiss *reisläufer* were formed up on the *Porta Levrieri's* walls, their guns loaded and matches lit. For half an hour Flourance's men waited for an assault on the eastern gate to begin but the Swiss could only stare in bewilderment as the imperial column ignored them and disappeared into the moonless night.

The Seigneur quickly realised that Lannoy was trying to outflank his position and force an entry somewhere else along the deer park's wall. He also reasoned that Lannoy would probably choose to storm the *Porta Pescarina* or *Porta Duo* so he immediately sent a rider to warn King Francis of the danger. Four *landsknecht* pike squares would wreak havoc if they managed to enter the deer park, and only Flourance's Swiss were close enough to reinforce the lightly defended northern gates, so as soon as the messenger had left, the Seigneur gave orders for his men to march.

The Devil's Band were in the van of the column that crept through the wintry countryside as silently as tens of thousands of fully armed men could. Their feet crunched on the frosty earth and their breath hung in great clouds around each man's head. Though their destination was only three miles away, the darkness of the night and the sheer number of men slowed the column's march to a crawl and it took nearly four hours to reach the breach in the wall made by the sappers.

Much to Lannoy's annoyance the gap was far too small to allow an entire army to pass through, so in spite of the cold and their eagerness to slaughter sleeping Frenchmen, the army had to wait whilst the Spanish *gastadores* broke down more masonry. It took another three hours for the sappers to make the original breach wider, and open two additional gaps in the wall, so it was nearly dawn when the Marquis de Vasto climbed onto a pile of rubble to address the Neapolitan arquebusiers who were to attack the Castel Mirabello.

"Listen you men, I am Alfonso, de Avolos, d'Aquini Marquis de Vasto and like you I'm from Naples. Though we may be cold now, I'm going to lead you to a place that's hotter than the mouth of Vesuvius because it's there we'll find fame, glory and plunder! We're to surprise the French king and his noble dukes and marquises as they sleep at Castel Mirabello and if we take them alive we'll share a ransom beyond the avarice of a Persian emperor. So prime your guns, light your matches and follow me!" said de Vasto and he led his men into the breach. Quintana watched the Neapolitans disappear into the dawn mist and cursed his luck.

"Did you hear what that prince of pasta pedlars said? It should be us snatching French fops from their beds and making a fortune not a bunch of Byzantine bandits," he said bitterly but no one was listening because Lannoy had given the signal for the rest of his army to enter the deer park. In spite of the sappers' best efforts, the *igels* still had to break formation to pass through the breaches and it took another thirty minutes for the thousands of men to assemble on the other side of the wall.

The *landsknechts* reformed their squares at the northern edge of a boggy heath that stretched all the way to Pavia three miles to the south. This broad expanse of open grassland was roughly half a mile wide and bordered to the east and west by thick woods. The road that linked the *Porta Pescarina* with the Castel Mirabello and the *Torretta* gate ran through the centre of this heath and disappeared into a bank of fog rising off the marshes. The thick mist muffled sound but there was no mistaking the crack of gunfire that indicated that de Vasto's attack on the hunting lodge had begun.

As Lannoy's plan required, the imperial army now split into two columns. The bulk of the cavalry, followed by Bourbon and Pescara's *igels*, galloped away to attack the French camp at the *Porta Repentina* and were soon hidden from sight as they disappeared into the trees at the western edge of the heath. Meanwhile, Frundsberg's and Sittich's 8,000 German *landsknechts* and Spanish *ginetes* marched east, to attack Flourance's Swiss at the *Porta Levrieri*, and Thomas could only curse as they set off in the one direction that led him away from Richard de la Pole and the Black Band.

To add to his frustration, The Devil's Band had been placed in the rear of Frundsberg's *igel* and despite his promise to his men Thomas was beginning to worry that they'd not be given the chance to draw their swords let alone win fame and glory. His fears grew when the din of battle drifting across the heath suddenly changed, the crack of ordered volleys gave way to sporadic gunshots and the disembodied shouts of men fighting at close quarters became the shrill screams of women.

The new noises coming from the direction of the hunting lodge could only mean that de Vasto's men had captured the French baggage train and any sutler or whore who refused to surrender their wealth was being shot in cold blood. The sound of the Neapolitan victory reminded Quintana that the profits from their bordello still lay buried beneath the tent they'd abandoned two months ago so he left his place in the ranks and ran to speak to Bos and Prometheus.

"Do you hear that? That's the sound of people stealing our money!" Quintana groaned.

"It sounds to me like the souls of the damned being tortured on the other side of the abyss," said Prometheus.

"That could be us lying dead in the mud of Mirabello, truly the wages of sin is death," added Bos.

"So long as those thieving Neapolitan bastards don't get their hands our gold I don't care how they're paid," muttered Quintana but before he could suggest they abandoned the battle, at least temporarily, to dig up their money Thomas ordered them back into line. Still grumbling, Quintana hurried back to his *rotten* and as he disappeared into the ranks Frundsberg ordered his *igel* to prepare for an attack.

Whilst the Spanish cavalry galloped away to guard the imperial column's flanks, Frundsberg's and Sittich's well drilled *landsknechts* clattered to a stop. For a moment there was silence then the siren sounds of drums and fifes came floating out of the fog. As the strange, ethereal music grew louder, Frundsberg's ordered both squares' *doppelsöldners* to advance and form a skirmish line thirty yards in front of each *igels'* spines. Brandishing two-handed swords, halberds and arquebuses, the *landsknechts'* forlorn hope ran forward and as they prepared to greet the Swiss with a storm of hot iron and cold steel, a ghostly forest of pikes began to take shape at the edge of the mist.

In his dreams Richard de la Pole heard the call to arms but before he was properly awake, his page was shaking him.

"An attack, My Lord, there's word from the north gate the imperial army has breached the wall and is marching towards us. There is even talk that the Castle Mirabello has been captured and every man and woman in the baggage train slaughtered!" The boy stammered nervously.

"Murderous cowards, what sort of knave kills unarmed pedlars and helpless women? Well don't just stand there like a moonfaced poltroon, get me dressed," growled the White Rose sleepily.

Whilst the boy fetched his master's armour from its wooden stand in the far corner of the tent, de la Pole rose from his cot and began pulling on his braies and hose. Like King Francis, the Yorkist prince insisted on wearing a full harness of expensive, though outdated, fluted armour as a badge of his rank and though his page worked feverishly to buckle the cowters, pauldrons, vambraces and other metal plates around his body, the complicated task took some minutes to complete.

"Hurry up you sluggard, you're as slow as a sinner's progress through purgatory!" De la Pole bawled but his impatience only made matters worse. In his haste, the boy's fingers struggled to match straps with buckles and his master was only partially encased in steel when Georg Langenmantel and Hans Nagel arrived with more news. The Black Band's senior captain was more concerned about missing his breakfast than the enemy attack but Nagel was deathly white and he was shaking with fear.

"What's the matter trumpet player, you look like a corpse raised from the grave?" De la Pole snapped as his page began to fit greaves and cuisses around his master's legs.

"My Lord, the enemy is everywhere!" Nagel whimpered but Langenmantel dismissed his fear.

"There's no reason to panic there is a general attack but Flourance's Swiss have two imperial pike squares pinned down by the *Porta Levrieri* and though a gang of Neapolitan cutthroats has seized our baggage park at Mirabello the king, praise God, wasn't there. Francis is alive and thirsting for battle so he's ordered all his knights and gendarmes to attack the two *igels* advancing towards us," said the captain.

"Then come Georg, we mustn't keep His Majesty waiting!" De la Pole cried and he snatched his helmet, an old fashioned *armet* with a bulbous visor and three purple plumes, from his page's outstretched hands.

"Wait My Lord, there's one more thing. A new banner has been in the imperial ranks, it shows a dancing devil and the rumour is that the men who follow this *fähnlein* are led by an English sorcerer who survived his own hanging," said Nagel, who knew nothing of Thomas' recent challenge to meet the White Rose in single combat. De la Pole however was unsurprised by the news.

"So the fiend has failed to heed my advice to go home and play battledore. Very well, if God means me to kill him, I shall but I won't stain noble steel with his foul blood. Only iron can kill a witch and I have just the thing!" De la Pole snarled and he went to the rack of weapons on the far side of his tent. With a grunt of satisfaction, he selected a lethal looking raven's beak war hammer, with a flat crushing face on one side of its iron head and a vicious curved spike on the other. After trying a few practice strokes he tied the weapon's long wooden handle to his sword belt with a leather thong and strode towards his tent's entrance.

"But My Lord! What about me? Remember it was I who unmasked the English necromancer's treachery and if he finds me here, he'll kill me," Nagel pleaded. With a snort of contempt Langmantel de la Pole told the spy he'd be quite safe in the French camp with the rest of the whores and left the tent but de la Pole was a little more sympathetic to the musician's concerns.

"Calm yourself, Master Nagel, besides myself and the Black Band there are more than 3,000 fully armed knights between you and Thomas Devisltone so stay here and polish your trumpet, you'll be needing it to celebrate our victory!" de la Pole laughed and he followed his captain outside.

Nagel watched them go and felt a strange sense of foreboding. He was roughly the same age as his master but he began to wonder if he'd lived too long to play the game of crowns that Richard de la Pole enjoyed so much. It took less than a minute for the trumpet player to decide it was high time he left the White Rose's service and, pausing only to fetch his belongs, which were pitifully few, he made his way to the *Porta Repentina*. The deer park's western gate was deserted, as every man in the French camp had rushed to join their king preparing to repel the imperial attack, so no one saw the little trumpet player disappear into the misty Lombard dawn.

Despite the weight of steel around his limbs, the White Rose mounted his waiting horse with graceful ease before snatching his lance from his varlet and galloping away to lead the Black Band into battle. His men had already formed into a square and when they saw the sunburst pennant of the House of York flying from their colonel's lance, they cheered as loudly as if the war had already been won. In reply, the White Rose pointed towards the sunrise and addressed his men.

"Today two suns rise over Pavia, the sun in the heavens and the sun of York! Now we march to fight filthy *landsknechts* and they say that the treacherous English sorcerer that neither the Graoully of Metz or the demon Frundsberg could kill is among them but let's see how this son of Satan fares against our good, honest steel!" De la Pole cried and he gave the signal to advance. Drums beat, fifes played and the men of the Black Band took a pace forward. Soon the 4,000 men under de la Pole's command were marching in perfect step towards the four lines of French cavalry that had already formed up in the open ground half a mile to the east of their camp.

Immediately in front of the French horsemen were six hundred yards of boggy grass and beyond that was the woodland that lay between the *Porta Repentina* and the breach in the deer park wall. Mounted on their richly caparisoned chargers, and wearing full suits of armour covered by surcoats emblazoned with ancient coats of arms, the 3,000 French knights and mounted men-at arms looked as if they were parading for a coronation but as the noble lords waited patiently for an enemy to fight, men on foot carrying blood red banners began to appear at the edge of the trees. These flag bearers were quickly joined by groups of two-handed swordsmen, halberdiers and arquebusiers all wearing white feathers in their broad brimmed hats.

A quarter of a mile away, de la Pole watched the imperial foot soldiers emerge from the wood and realised these men must be the forlorn hope from Pescara and Bourbon's pike squares, sent to pin down the French until the main body of their *igels* arrived, but for the moment neither side could attack the other. The imperial arquebuses didn't have the range to reach their enemy and even *doppelsöldners* wouldn't be so foolish as to challenge a force of armoured horsemen in the open. Equally, it would be madness for the French knights to charge handgunners as old-fashioned armour and aristocratic escutcheons offered little protection against arquebus balls.

Having satisfied himself that the French horsemen were in no immediate danger, de la Pole glanced to his right and saw the captain of a French gun battery guarding the road from the *Porta Repentina* to the Castel Mirabello had also spotted the enemy and had quickly turned several of his lighter pieces to face the wood. Without warning, a dozen French *sakers* and *falconets* fired a volley of shots and though the imperials promptly retreated into the trees, the cypresses and cedars of the wood could not stop solid spheres of iron.

Some balls struck the trees squarely, shattering the bark and heartwood into clouds of lethal splinters. Other shots ricocheted off the trunks and ripped into the huddles of men sheltering from the murderous barrage. The wood had now become a death trap for the imperials and de la

Pole breathed a sigh of relief. The quick thinking of the French gun captain had stopped the advance in its tracks, now he could send the Black Band's own skirmishers into the wood and mop up what was left of the demoralised *landsknechts*.

The White Rose smiled at the thought of the glorious slaughter to come and was about to give the order for his men to attack when a fanfare of trumpets caused him look to the north. To his astonishment, several thousand horsemen, carrying the banners of the Count of Lannoy, had suddenly appeared at the far end of the wood and were forming up in three lines at right angles to the trees. Lesser men would've turned and fled but this was the moment for which the French king had been waiting. Despite taking the French by surprise, Francis knew that the lightly armoured Spanish and Italian horsemen, who wore little more than a helmet and breastplate, would be no match for his fully armoured knights and gendarmes.

Barely able to conceal his eagerness for battle, Francis ordered his knights to drive the imperial cavalry from the field and like a flock of starlings the mass of French horsemen began to metamorphose into new lines that blocked Lannoy's advance. For a minute the two ranks of horsemen did nothing but stare at each other across a quarter of a mile of gently undulating grass but then more trumpets sounded and the French lines lurched forward. Horses whinnied as they felt their rider's spurs prick their flanks but they obediently increased their speed from a walk to a trot and as their canter became a gallop, Lannoy ordered his own men to charge.

Now the dawn became filled with a pandemonium of trumpet calls, thundering horses' hooves and shouted battle cries as the two bodies of horsemen hurtled towards each other. Brightly coloured surcoats and banners streamed in the wind and the first rays of sunlight glinted off steel helmets, swords and spear points. At last moment, the riders lowered their lances and those on foot could only watch in awe as the two armies of centaurs crashed into each other with a noise that sounded like a thousand doors splintering under a thousand battering rams.

Just as Francis had predicted, the lighter Spanish lances shattered on the thick French armour whilst the sheer weight of metal behind their opponents' charge knocked the imperial riders off their horses as easily as small boys with sticks knocked the heads off flowers. Within seconds, hundreds of Spanish and Italian horsemen had been skewered on French lances or had broken their necks as they were bludgeoned from their saddles. Those who survived the initial charge found their razor sharp Toledo blades were easily turned by the French noblemen's armour or shattered by their enemies' heavier longswords. The butchery was brutal but short and after just five minutes of savage hand-to-hand combat the surviving imperial horsemen turned their mounts and fled.

It was a splendid victory and all that remained was for de la Pole to clear the wood of imperial survivors but, before he could give the order, the imperial *igels* under Bourbon and Pescara appeared at the far end of the wood. The front rank of each Spanish pike square was bristling with arquebuses so Francis' knights suddenly found themselves facing a firing squad and not even their own artillery could save them. The French cannon that had bombarded the wood at the start of the battle were forced to remain silent, as the gun captains couldn't open fire without hitting their king.

Unhindered by the presence of friendly troops in their own field of fire, the imperial arquebusiers touched their matches to their handguns. There was a roar of exploding powder and a storm of lead smashed into the bewildered French cavalry. Scores of noble dukes and marquises were toppled backwards out of their saddles or thrown forward as their mounts were shot from under them. In the same instant, the imperial forlorn hope sheltering in the woods emerged from the trees and fell upon the dismounted noblemen. Before the fallen knights could recover, the Spanish and Italian footsoldiers had pinned them to the ground and fired handguns into the visors of their archaic helmets or thrust cheap stilettoes between the plates of their expensive armour.

Yet Bourbon and Pescara didn't have things all their own way. In their haste to plug the gap left by Lannoy's routed cavalry, the imperial squares had become disorganised and many of the surviving French knights managed to penetrate the Spanish pike blocks. Once amongst the pikemen, those on horseback had the advantage and they wrought terrible vengeance on their despised enemies. The French knights' longswords were the perfect weapon for slicing through the skulls of men on foot but the Spanish pikemen's long spears and short *katzbalger* swords were of little use when fighting armoured horsemen at close quarters.

The French king and his Scottish guardsmen found themselves in the middle of this bloody slaughter, and so long as his royal banner continued to fly above the melee Francis might yet carry the day, but half a mile to the south Richard de la Pole could see that the French knights were outnumbered and in grave danger of being surrounded. The Black Band was now the only force that could prevent the king's encirclement but Francis' reckless charge had taken the French knights a long way from de la Pole's pike square and it would be least fifteen minutes before he and his men could join the fight.

There was also a danger that, if the Black Band moved north, imperial reinforcements would emerge from the woods to their right and attack them in the flank or rear but de la Pole didn't hesitate. If his men could rescue Francis, they'd turn disaster into triumph and the French king would be forever in his debt. The White Rose could almost feel the hand of destiny on his shoulder as he ordered his drummers to sound the advance but, wary that Frundsberg and Sittich's 8,000 Germans were still at large somewhere in the deer park, he ordered his men to keep their unwieldy defensive formation.

Slowly, like a great ship under sail, the Black Band's pike square turned north and marched off to help a pretender to the throne of England save a King of France from certain death or capture.

23

BAD WAR

Richard de la Pole was right to be cautious. On the other side of the wood, the pike squares that he feared so much had been fighting Flourance's Swiss for almost an hour and in that time Frundsberg's and Sittich's *landsknechts* had inflicted terrible punishment on their detested rivals. Minute by minute, yard by bloody yard, the imperials had forced the Swiss to retreat leaving hundreds of dead and dying men in their wake. It was only a matter of time before Flourance's dwindling numbers of *reisläufer* finally broke but The Devil's Band had yet to draw their swords or fire a shot.

Whilst other companies' *doppelsöldners* hacked at the Swiss like drunken woodsmen clearing a coppice, The Devil's Band had been held in reserve at the back of Frundsberg's pike square. For a brief moment Thomas thought their chance for glory had come when he saw a group of horsemen riding towards them but as the riders emerged from the mist he could see they were Spanish *ginetes* not French men-at-arms. He guessed the Spaniards were bringing messages from Lannoy on the other side of the wood but though it was clear they'd been in a hard fight Bos was unimpressed.

"Those cowardly Dons run from the enemy like Philistines fleeing Samson, if only our colonel would let us loose, we'd chase those French fornicators all the way back to their Parisian brothels," he said in frustration. Ignoring Bos, the horsemen rode up to Frundsberg and though Thomas couldn't hear what was being said it was clear from the grave expression on their colonel's face that the battle on the other side of the wood wasn't going well. After a few minutes the *ginetes* rode back towards the trees whilst Frundsberg rode straight towards the yellow banner with the red dancing devil.

"Now necromancer, you said you wanted a chance to settle your score with the White Rose, well I'm going to give it to you," said Frundsberg and before Thomas could reply, the colonel had told him that the French king and his entire force of knights were surrounded and fighting for their lives but Richard de la Pole's Black Band was marching to their rescue. To counter this threat, Frundsberg had been ordered to leave Sittich to finish off the Swiss and take his *igel* to reinforce Bourbon and Pescara. However, it would take some time for Frundsberg to extricate his men from the melee and those precious minutes may be decisive.

"You and your men must form a forlorn hope, hasten to the other side of the woods and delay the Black Band until my *igel* can join you and regrow its spines. If you succeed every man in your *fähnlein* will promoted *doppelsöldner*, if you fail The Devil himself won't save you," said Frundsberg gruffly.

"With men such as this I could stop Hannibal crossing the Alps," Thomas boasted. He was barely able to conceal his delight at having his prayers answered but the colonel merely grunted in salute and went off to issue more orders. As Frundsberg rode away, Thomas ordered his pikemen to abandon their cumbersome pikes and arm themselves with arquebuses and other weapons better suited to their mission. There were plenty of discarded swords, handguns and halberds littering the Swiss path of retreat and his men had no trouble in rearming themselves before they sprinted into the trees.

Though the men of The Devil's Band could move much faster without their pikes, it still took ten minutes for them to reach the far side of the wood. When they emerged from the trees, the men in smoke blackened armour were much closer than Thomas had hoped but there was still time to disrupt their advance. A few yards away, there was a drainage ditch running across the open ground in front of the wood and immediately Thomas knew this was where de la Pole could be stopped.

After looting the Swiss dead, more than half his force was now armed with arquebuses so Thomas ordered his men to use this shallow trench as cover and fire from a kneeling position. He also told the handgunners to pair off, then fire and reload in turn, so as to keep up a continuous stream of shot. His men knew better than to disobey a hanged man and they threw themselves into the ditch with scant regard for the eighteen inches of freezing, muddy water at the bottom.

"Men, this our moment for glory, we must delay the Black Band until Frundsberg arrives with our comrades so this ditch will be the line our enemies must not cross. Give no quarter, trust to St Matthias and do not rest until every man in the Black Band lies dead in the mud of Pavia!" Thomas yelled but his voice was almost drowned by the pandemonium of drums, fifes and gunfire that seemed to be getting louder.

Like a great black wave rolling out of a stormy sea the Black Band advanced towards the ditch and all the while the dazzling figure of the White Rose, dressed in his polished steel armour and mounted on a white charger, rode in front of his men urging them to greater efforts. Thomas stared at the figure, and tried to calm his thumping heart that seemed determined to beat its way out of his chest, there could be no mistaking the purple plumes, the golden sun pennant or the white rose badge on the horseman's surcoat.

"Arquebusiers, fire!" roared Thomas.

The White Rose reined in his horse and lifted his visor to getter a better look at the battlefield. He could see his path to the French king was now blocked by a thin line of men sheltering in a ditch. At first he thought they must be deserters who were cowering in the filth of an open drain in a pathetic attempt to save themselves. He smiled as he imagined the Black Band trampling these cowards deeper into a muddy grave of their own making but then he saw the puffs of smoke and the tongues of flame. A heartbeat later the volley fired by The Devil's Band smashed into his men.

The lead bullets punctured the Black Band's steel helmets and breastplates as if they were no thicker than parchment. Men shot in the face or chest died instantly, those hit in the groin or belly were condemned to the agony of a lingering death and amidst the shrieks of these stricken men, de la Pole heard his *destrier* whinny in pain. Without thinking, the White Rose kicked his feet free of the stirrups and rolled out of the saddle just as the horse stumbled and fell. He hit the ground with a bone jarring crash and his head rattled around inside his steel helmet like a pea shaken in a bucket but at least he'd escaped being pinned under the dying animal.

Battered and bruised, de la Pole struggled to his feet and tried to open his visor but the steel had become twisted in the fall. In a furious rage de la Pole tore off the helmet and threw it away before kneeling to examine his stricken charger. A ball had ripped through the animal's chest, piercing its lungs, and the mortally wounded beast was snorting crimson froth from its nostrils.

There was no time to be sentimental, de la Pole drew his sword and sliced through the animal's neck but as he put the horse out its misery, he saw that the men in the ditch had raised a yellow banner with a red devil in the centre. De la Pole roared in anger at the sight of the hateful flag and swore he'd make the sorcerer pay dearly for killing his favourite mount.

"A horse, my mother's eyes for a horse!" de la Pole yelled and the captain named Wolf ran forward to seize a riderless, fully armoured *destrier* that was grazing calmly nearby, despite the hell of battle raging all around.

"Here's a new mount My Lord!" said Wolf breathlessly as he handed the reins to his colonel. With a brief word of thanks de la Pole climbed into the saddle and signalled for the front two ranks of his square to form their own skirmish line.

Immediately two hundred arquebusiers and halberdiers dressed in black armour ran forward and unleashed the spitting cobras of war. Smoke and fire exploded from the Black Band's handguns but their enemies pressed themselves in the mud of the ditch and most of the balls whistled harmlessly over their heads

Cautiously Thomas raised his head and felt a spent ball send his hat spinning through the air but he didn't blink. Instead, he kept his eyes fixed on Richard de la Pole and vowed that only one of them would leave the battlefield alive.

"Return fire!" he yelled and the other half of his arquebusiers spat the poison of the basilisk at their enemies. Once again the men in black cried out in pain as their bodies were smashed into a pulp and their black armour spattered red with blood. However, the rest of de la Pole's square was now just thirty yards from the ditch and the first group of Thomas' handgunners had yet to finish reloading. There would be no time for The Devil's Band to fire a third volley.

Glancing over his shoulder, Thomas saw the first of Frundsberg's banners appear at the edge of the trees a hundred yards behind the ditch. It would take some minutes for the colonel's different *fähnleins* to reform their square, and until this was done their comrades would be as vulnerable as crabs that had just shed their shells, but there was little more Thomas could do. If his men stayed where they were, they'd be trampled to death but if they abandoned the ditch they'd be cut down before they got half way to Frundsberg's rapidly growing square. Even though they were outnumbered ten to one, the Devil's Band had no other option but to attack so Thomas stood up, drew his falchion and pointed the butcher's blade at the Black Band.

"They shall not pass, charge!" he yelled.

"For God and the fallen angels!" came the single reply and the four hundred men of The Devil's Band scrambled out of the ditch.

Though they were covered in mud and filth they looked no less terrifying than Frundsberg's brightly coloured *landsknechts* and they crashed into de la Pole's skirmishers with a noise like a hundred blacksmiths striking a hundred anvils with a hundred heavy iron mauls. Out of the corner of his eye Thomas saw Bos, Prometheus and Quintana leading their *rotten* deep into the melee but the battle quickly became a series of individual duels and Thomas lost sight of both de la Pole and his comrades as a halberdier in black armour stepped in front of him.

The man swung his long poleaxe in a wide arc, daring Thomas to attack, but the Englishman had no time for the formalities of fencing. Instead he dived at the halberdier's legs, pulling his body into a ball as he hit the ground and rolling towards his enemy. It was too late for the halberdier to change his stroke and his blade whistled through empty space before he was sent sprawling by the impact of Thomas' body against his shins. As the halberdier tumbled backwards, Thomas plunged his falchion deep into the man's groin.

Leaping to his feet, Thomas looked around. There was no sign of Bos or Quintana but he saw Prometheus using his long *zweihänder* sword to cleave his way through a group of enemy halberdiers as if they were nothing but prickly gorse bushes in a grassy meadow. The Nubian hardly seemed to break sweat as his enormous sword hacked the heads of halberds and halberdiers alike and as he pruned this hedge of steel he caught sight of Thomas.

"Look to your left that poltroon of a Portugee needs help!" Prometheus bellowed.

As soon as Thomas turned his head, he saw that Quintana was exchanging blows with Richard de la Pole himself and the duellists were less than a twenty yards away. Though the White Rose had lost his helmet, the Portugee had lost his halberd and he was struggling to fight a man on horseback armed only with his short *katzbalger*. The steel skull cap Quintana wore beneath his wide-brimmed hat, offered no protection from the storm of French metal breaking over his head and it was taking all of the Portugee's strength and skill to parry the swingeing cuts from de la Pole's longsword.

As Thomas sprinted to help his comrade, he saw Quintana step inside the arc of de la Pole's blade and thrust his cat skinner at the small strip of unprotected horse flesh below de la Pole's saddle. However, the White Rose had been in too many battles to be caught so easily and he deftly turned his mount so the Portugee's cut landed on the horse's steel barding.

Sensing victory, the White Rose spurred his *destrier* and a ton of metal and horseflesh slammed into Quintana, pushing him backwards. As the Portugee lost his balance, de la Pole smashed his steel plated foot into his opponent's face and Quintana fell to the ground, blood pouring from a deep gash in his forehead. Thomas reached his friend's side just as de la Pole was about to trample his defeated enemy into the mud and he yelled, as loudly he could, in a desperate attempt to distract the White Rose from desecrating Quintana's senseless body.

"Hear me White Rose! I'm Sir Thomas Devilstone, the man you refused to meet in honourable single combat, so now I call you coward, knave and traitor!" he cried. The ruse worked and the insults caused de la Pole to turn his attention to Thomas.

"You dare call yourself knight? For that alone you must die, you cursed child of Lilith, and for your insolence you must suffer a peasant's death," de la Pole sneered as he sheathed his longsword and armed himself with the raven's beak war hammer.

Digging his spurs deep into his horse's flank, de la Pole urged his great *destrier* forward but Thomas stood his ground. He waited until de la Pole raised his hammer to strike, then deftly leapt to one side so the bone-crushing weapon missed him by a hair's breadth. Many men engaged in such an uneven contest would have tried to strike back at their enemy but Thomas knew better. In the skirmishes and blood feuds of the north he'd learned that men fighting in full armour soon exhausted their strength so all he had to do was wait until de la Pole made a mistake.

Just as his father had taught him, Thomas ducked every swing of his enemy's hammer and with each unsuccessful charge de la Pole became a little more tired. All the while Thomas goaded the White Rose with more insults and when de la Pole's rage and fatigue prompted him to make a careless stroke he took his chance. One blow from Thomas' falchion would crush de la Pole's leg armour, snapping the frail bone inside but, as he sprang forward to strike, he stumbled over Quintana's body. In a heartbeat, de la Pole had snatched up a lance that had been planted in the earth and had wheeled his horse to face his nemesis who was lying sprawled in the mud.

"Say your prayers assassin because now you die!" hissed de la Pole as he couched the lance under his arm and aimed its point at his Thomas' chest.

Cursing his luck, Thomas felt in the grass for his dropped sword but grasped only the wooden butt of an abandoned arquebus. There was a glowing match in the serpent so he snatched up the weapon and pressed the snake shaped trigger but the gun's muzzle stayed silent.

"You see, God is with your lawful king!" roared de la Pole in triumph but before he could plunge his lance into his foe there was a loud bang and Thomas saw the

White Rose's unprotected head disappear behind a crimson cloud that spattered his gleaming armour with brains, blood and splinters of bone. Thomas swallowed hard and stared at the gun clutched in his hand, wondering if the damp charge had been slow to take fire but there was no smoke wreathing from its barrel.

When he looked up, he could see the White Rose staring at him with the one sightless eye that remained in his shattered head. As if unwilling to admit the reality of his own death de la Pole's lifeless hands slowly let go of the reins, his corpse toppled from the saddle and his riderless horse galloped away. As it did so Thomas saw Bos standing in front of him, a smoking arquebus in his hand.

"This is no time to lie down, there's a battle to be won, look they're beaten," Bos said and he pointed towards the Black Band's pike square which was slowly retreating. Scarcely able to believe his eyes, Thomas looked around him and saw no sign of the French king's banner. Instead the two imperial *igels* commanded by the Duke of Bourbon and the Marquis de Pescara had joined Frundsberg and the three pike squares were advancing to crush the last remnant of the French army. In the face of overwhelming numbers, the Black Band could do nothing except retreat but they were doing so in good order.

"Wait Frisian, I saw Quintana fall," said Thomas, pointing to their comrade's prostrate body and as he did so, Prometheus emerged from the mist.

"Leave him with me and I'll see what I can do. Unless you want us all to be hanged as deserters, you must lead our men back to Frundsberg," said the Nubian calmly.

Thomas didn't need to be reminded about the savagery of *landsknecht* justice and he ran after Bos who'd already caught up with the rest of The Devil's Band. Together the two men rallied their company, who were still recovering from their fight with de la Pole's forlorn hope, but there was no time to celebrate their victory. Even de Vasto's arquebusiers had left off looting Mirabello to join in the final slaughter and Thomas was determined to secure a fair share of the spoils for himself and his men.

After Francis' standard had fallen, the rest of the French, Gascon and Swiss troops had melted away until only the Black Band remained as an effective fighting force. With de la Pole dead, and the French king's fate unknown, it had fallen to Langenmantel to take charge and he'd promptly ordered his men to withdraw to their wagon fort at the *Porta Repentina.* Here, he hoped to join with other survivors and make a last stand but it was already too late. Whilst Langenmantel tried to make an orderly withdrawal, de Vasto's arquebusiers sniped at his retreating pike square and slowed it down sufficiently for Frundsberg, Bourbon and Pescara's *igels* to surround what was left of the Black Band.

As soon as Langenmantel realised that he and his men were trapped, he ran forward and called on Frundsberg to settle their differences in single combat but the old mercenary colonel had no time for such empty acts of chivalry. With a wave of his hand, the *Father of Landsknechts* ordered his arquebusiers to open fire and the last captain of the Black Band died in a hail of bullets. Not wishing to waste any more precious powder or shot, Frundsberg ordered his halberdiers and swordsmen to finish off the renegades with steel instead of lead and the other colonels followed his example.

Like mastiffs baiting a bull, the different *fähnleins* of each pike square took it in turns to charge the thinning ranks of survivors and though it was only a matter of time before the Black Band was utterly destroyed, none of the condemned men asked for quarter. Having re-joined Frundsberg's *igel* Thomas led The Devil's Band in one such charge and as his men smashed into their enemy, he prayed that Nagel would fall beneath his sword. It was a vain hope and there was no sign of the trumpet player in the piles of black clothed dead that were growing ever higher.

Whilst the bloody war of attrition continued, the *landsknechts* taunted their enemies with the news that the French king, whom every man in the Black Band had sworn to defend with their life, was now a prisoner and would spend the rest of his days chained to the wall of a Spanish dungeon. With each fresh insult, three or four doomed men would charge at their tormentors, in a desperate attempt to take a few hated *landsknechts* with them to the grave, but a dozen imperial pikes skewered these men before they'd covered ten paces.

After thirty minutes of almost continuous carnage, only a dozen men remained alive out of the four thousand who'd left the *Porta Repentina* wagon fort barely three hours before. Brandishing their halberds, these paladins surrounded their standard bearer and dared the bravest of their enemies to try and wrest their sacred battle flag from them but the *landsknechts* did nothing. Every man in the imperial army knew that the Black Band's last moments had come and they'd fallen silent as if saying a wordless requiem for their oldest and most implacable foes.

When no one stepped forward to answer their challenge, the last members of the Black Band unbuckled their armour and let it fall to the ground whilst their standard bearer anointed his red and black banner with the contents of a flask hanging from his belt. When his comrades produced flint and steel, the *landsknechts* suddenly realised their enemies meant to burn their standard to prevent the dishonour of its capture and they surged forward but it was too late. The flask must have contained aquavit or some other flammable spirit for the first spark turned the cloth into an inferno.

"All is lost save honour!" yelled the standard bearer and, waving his flaming banner, he led his comrades in a final, futile charge at the front line of Frundsberg's *igel*. In reply the *landsknechts'* steel tipped pikes smashed their attackers' ribs and ripped through their lungs, leaving the twelve dying paladins transfixed like the impaled prisoners of Wallachian princes. The standard bearer managed a last defiant wave of his burning banner before the life drained from his body and the blazing cloth fell to earth.

Despite their devotion to duty, there'd be no honour in death for the men of the Black Band. The moment the standard bearer dropped his flag, the victorious imperials gave a great cheer and swarmed forward to loot the piles of dead that now covered the battlefield. Daggers flashed as the looters deftly sliced off fingers to retrieve rings or slit open bellies to search for swallowed gems, yet for all the *landsknechts'* savagery the plundering of the Black Band's dead was over quickly.

The seasoned veterans of the imperial *igels* knew that even greater riches lay in the undefended French tents so, as soon as everything of value had been stripped from the Black Band's corpses, a tide of greed-crazed *landsknechts* streamed towards their defeated enemy's camp. Thomas knew better than to keep his men from their plunder but he and Bos were reluctant to join the rest of The Devil's Band in the search for booty. The two men hadn't forgotten that they'd yet to settle with Nagel but they also knew that Prometheus and Quintana were waiting for them by the wood.

"We should follow our comrades, de la Pole may be dead but his treacherous trumpet player could be hiding in the French camp. Have you forgotten that Nagel tried to kill us when he blew up your infernal boat?" Bos said grimly.

"Actually I don't think it was Nagel that sank *The Hippocamp*," said Thomas thoughtfully.

"Well if it wasn't him then who was it?" Bos spluttered and he was even more surprised when Thomas named the Duke of Albany. The evidence, though circumstantial, was indeed damning. Albany had already quarrelled with de la Pole over their invasion and destroying Thomas' underwater boat would wreck his rival's plan to capture London before Edinburgh once and for all.

"Albany had plenty of opportunity to swap my saltpetre for gunpowder and besides, since when did a Scot ever need an excuse to kill an Englishman?" Thomas said wryly.

"Unfortunately the noble Scottish Duke is still besieging Naples, so you can't bring him to account, but it doesn't matter who destroyed the boat. Nagel tricked and betrayed us, so are we going to let him get away with that?" Bos insisted.

"If I know Nagel, he'll have fled the French camp the moment he realised the day was lost. He'll be half way to Flanders by now but Quintana and Prometheus are still here and most likely they're beset by looters and plunderers," said Thomas and Bos had to agree that the human vultures picking over the dead wouldn't hesitate to slit the throat of any wounded man, friend or foe, who resisted.

"Very well we'll leave Nagel to the judgement of God, at least for the time being, but if I ever see him again I shall do unto him what God did unto the Midianites," said Bos but Thomas had already set off back the way they'd come.

The receding tide of war had left the battlefield of Pavia strewn with wreckage. Broken banners, pikes and lances sprouted from the ground like the shattered stumps of a forest destroyed by a violent storm and everywhere swarms of scrawny women pushed handcarts piled high with looted clothing and armour between the piles of bloated, bloody corpses. In their wake, flocks of grubby children searched for spent shot that could be sold back to the gunners for a few *kreuzers* each. Occasionally an urchin would hold up a severed head, and pretend to mistake his gruesome trophy for a cannon ball, which delighted his fellow ghouls.

To complete this vision of Hell, the trees at the edge of the wood bore fresh fruit in the form of hanged men. Whether the dead were French prisoners or imperial deserters no one could tell but their torn hose, ripped doublets and hands pinioned behind their backs bore witness to their last pathetic struggle for life on a day dedicated to death. Thomas looked at the dangling bodies and touched his scarred throat. The skin had healed but he'd never forget the feel of a noose around his own neck.

They found Quintana, still lying insensible in the mud, a few paces from de la Pole's body and next to him was Prometheus. The Nubian stared at the sky with sightless eyes whilst a few yards away a coven of squalid Valkyrie fought over his clothing. So intent were they on their argument they failed to notice Bos and Thomas' approach.

"Bitches, foul daughters of Lilith!" Bos cried and he drew his sword. The women scurried away and the Frisian was about to give chase but Thomas stopped him.

"I think our friends live, but they need our help urgently," he said and drawing his sword he knelt beside the Nubian. Carefully, he held the flat of falchion's blade close to Prometheus' lips whilst Bos did the same with Quintana. Instantly, the cold metal of each sword became clouded and both men breathed a sigh of relief.

"Praise be to Christ, they're alive but who'd dare attack this Nubian buffalo?" said Bos.

"My guess is he was busy tending to Quintana when one of those hags hit him from behind," said Thomas, examining the lump on the back of the Nubian's skull.

"If only he'd kept his wits he could've healed himself and the Portugee," said Bos.

"Perhaps he still can," replied Thomas and he began to search for the pouch that he knew the Nubian always kept hidden beneath his shirt. Fortunately, the little calf-skin bag he was looking for had escaped the notice of the looters and Thomas soon found the phial of white crystals he wanted. He removed the cork and the air became filled with a pungent smell of a tannery but wafting the little bottle under each man's nose produced instant results. First the Nubian then the Portugee was dragged back into the realm of the living by the noxious vapours.

"By the stinking turds floating down the nine rivers of hell what's that odour!" Quintana spluttered.

"It's nothing but *sal ammoniac*, an elixir that would fetch Eurydice herself from Hades," said Thomas with delight. The crystals had also worked their magic on Prometheus and as soon as he'd recovered his senses Thomas asked him what had happened. As he rubbed his bruised head, the Nubian admitted that before he could revive Quintana an old crone had offered him a florin for the Portugee's sword but that was the last thing he could remember.

"So whilst you took her money her confederate hit you from behind, it's the oldest trick in the book and you fell for it," Bos chided but Thomas was more forgiving and he told Prometheus and Quintana that the imperial army had won a great victory. The White Rose and the Black Band were no more, the Swiss scattered and the French king was a prisoner. Moreover, the last of the enemy camps had been captured and was in the process of being looted by their comrades. Prometheus was delighted with the news but Quintana was horrified.

"What are we waiting for? We must hurry and see if there's anything left worth stealing," he said as he struggled to his feet but Thomas insisted there was no need to go back to the *Porta Repentina*.

"The camp will have been emptied of everything but lice and fleas by the time we get there but it doesn't matter. The only thing we need to make us rich is proof that the we've sent the last Yorkist prince to Hell," he said triumphantly.

The others refused to believe they could still profit directly from the death of the White Rose but Thomas ignored them and turned his attention to de la Pole's mutilated carcase. The signet ring the Yorkist pretender had used to seal the box of heron feathers would suit his purpose admirably but de la Pole's fingers had already been reduced to bloody stumps by the looters they'd chased away earlier. Cursing his own tardiness, Thomas drew his falchion whereupon Bos cried out in alarm.

"If you're going to hack off de la Pole's head and carry it back to Henry, remember what happened to the assassins of Pompey," said the Frisian uneasily but Thomas had no intention of committing such sacrilege. Apart from knowing that the men who'd presented Julius Caesar with the head of his greatest enemy were themselves executed for desecrating the famous general's corpse, Thomas knew that Bos' arquebus ball had shattered the White Rose's face beyond recognition.

However, there was one item on de la Pole's body that might convince King Henry that the last threat to his throne was truly dead and that was the White Rose's surcoat. The tattered cloth was covered in mud and gore but the golden sun of York was still clearly visible so Thomas began to cut the garment free of its late owner's armour.

"If you think that rag will prove we killed the White Rose you're a fool because any mountebank can take a piece of cloth, soak it in pig's blood and claim he killed the Shah of Persia to get it," said Quintana when he realised what the Englishman was doing.

"The Portugee's right, if you take that cloth to Henry you'll fare no better than Joseph's brothers who were cursed with famine after they tried to deceive Jacob with the bloodstained coat of many colours," said Bos.

"Think about it Thomas, take that coat to England and you'll have become worse than the Roman soldiers who diced for Christ's robe as he hung on the cross," added Prometheus.

Though Thomas now wore his religion as lightly as a summer shirt, the Nubian's words did make him stop and think. He stared at the filthy surcoat in his hands and had to admit that it looked more like the used bandages in a barber-surgeon's laundry than a piece of a noble knight's clothing. King Henry would never offer a pardon for any of their crimes, real or imagined, in exchange for a piece of soiled cloth of uncertain provenance so he tossed the surcoat back into the mud.

"So it's all been for nothing," he said ruefully.

"Not exactly, have you forgotten we still have the gold buried in the earth at Mirabello? There's enough for us all to enjoy at least a year or two of doing nothing so I suggest we dig it up before some other thieving bastard finds it!" Quintana replied.

EPILOGUE

MIRABELLO

I t didn't take much for the Portugee to convince the others that their last chance of making a profit lay beneath their temple to Venus so without further debate they set off for the French camp at Mirabello. They all knew that the hunting lodge would've been thoroughly ransacked by the Neapolitans who'd captured it but de Vasto's men would not have had the time to make a systematic search of every abandoned cart and tent in the baggage park. With luck, their treasure would still be where'd they'd left it but to reach heaven they would have to walk through hell.

Though they'd just fought a terrible battle, nothing could've prepared Thomas and the others for the horrific scenes of murder and pillage waiting for them at Mirabello. Every tent in the baggage park had been razed to the ground and the bodies of massacred men, women and children, all stained red with gore, lay scattered over the ground like fallen maple leaves. Already the air was foul with the stench of death and as the four men picked their way through this charnel house they found the remains of Mistress Kleber, she was half naked and the back of her skull had been crushed.

"Poor bitch, she cheated her customers and never made an honest bargain but she deserved a better end than this," said Quintana. The others nodded their agreement but, pausing only to cover their late benefactress with a tattered cloak, they continued their search.

They found their tent, or what was left of it, in the centre of the camp and it wasn't difficult to work out what had happened. No one would've questioned the sudden disappearance of four foreign bawds and after a week their abandoned property would've been seized and auctioned off by the provost in charge of the baggage train. Although their tent's new owners had failed to stop de Vasto's men from stealing what they could carry, and burning everything else to ashes, the ground beneath the charred remains of their seraglio had not been disturbed.

The former whoremasters quickly identified the spot where they'd hidden their gold and began to scratch at the blackened soil with their swords. After a few minutes, their blades struck something hard and with mounting excitement they prised the buried chest from its grave. As soon as the strongbox was free of the half-frozen mud, Quintana smashed off the padlock with the hilt of his sword and opened the lid but the only thing inside was a scrap of paper. Puzzled, Thomas picked it up and began to read the crude, spidery handwriting.

Dear Master Thomas and the rest
of you idle pig shaggers,
as we earned this gold lying on our backs,
and you did sod all,
we reckon it all be ours so we've taken it.
If you want any more, go fuck yourselves,
love Magda and Ulla

"The thieving bitches, I thought they hated each other!" Quintana cried.

"It seems they hated us more, truly a love of money is the root of all evil," said Bos shaking his head.

"So what do we do now? The emperor's won his war so the *landsknechts* will be paid off and sent home," groaned Prometheus but Quintana reminded them that none of them could return to their homes as they were all under sentence of death. Bos gloomily remarked that they must now starve or become brigands, which was the fate of all soldiers in time of peace, but Thomas was smiling.

"We still have one treasure left … The Devil's Band and I'm still its captain. Any peace between the Spanish and the French won't last long and even if it does, there's bound to be at least one king in Christendom who has need of the hanged man and his brave warriors who won the great battle of Pavia," he said and after a moment's thought the others nodded in agreement.

"Some say there's a peasants' rebellion brewing in Germany," said Bos thoughtfully.

"And the Turks are always threatening to invade the Christian kingdoms along the Danube," added Prometheus.

"So shall we earn our bread slaughtering peasants for the noble lords of Germany or infidel Turks for the Hungarian king?" said Quintana.

"That's an easy matter to decide," said Thomas, "if money is the root of all evil, The Devil's Band must serve whoever pays the most!"

THE END

Thomas' adventures continue in
The Devil's Lance
find out more at
www.thedevilstonechronicles.com

Made in the USA
Charleston, SC
11 May 2016